The God Machine

novels by MARTIN CAIDIN

The God Machine

a novel by Martin Caidin

 New York   E. P. Dutton & Co., Inc.   1968

Published simultaneously in Canada by Clarke, Irwin & Company
Limited, Toronto and Vancouver

Library of Congress Catalog Card Number: 68-12450

FIRST EDITION

Book One

1

I DIDN'T MOVE. I waited, listening. I—

There! Again . . . the sound muffled, fluttering just beyond the window of a man's senses. I strained to hear better.

I didn't move a muscle, to prevent even the rustling of the sheets against my skin. In the swallowing gloom I rested on my elbow, holding my breath, hearing dimly the blood in my ears. Retinal phantoms I couldn't see swirled in the room. I had to move. I raised my head, staring at a razored sliver of light along the carpet by the door. It seemed to take me forever to notice that the light was uneven.

Someone *was* standing out there.

This time I heard it clearly. Sibilant, yet soft. A woman-soft voice—

"Steve?"

I slipped from the bed with the automatic in my right hand. My thumb probed along the cold metal, slipped the safety off. In the darkness the hammer cocking back sounded like a steel marble cracking sharply against a metal plate. For just a moment I hesitated. I didn't like guns and I knew that if I stubbed my toe and twitched my finger I could blow a very big hole in something. Or someone. The thought washed through me, but I fought it off because I knew a lot worse than a hole in me might . . . Angrily, I ordered my thoughts back to the present, to now.

"Steve!"

My feet padded softly as I crossed to the door. I wasn't too anxious to look through the peephole. I held a vision of someone on the other side of that door, waiting patiently, laughing,

[7]

until I set myself up neatly, framed behind the tiny hole through which you could peer at visitors. Then, when I was fool enough to arrange myself precisely as a cooperative target, a gun from the other side would pound lead through the door. Into me. I was jumpy as hell.

Jumpy? Or is it you're really scared?

The voice sneered at me. I ignored it. I always tried to ignore myself. Of course I was scared.

I stopped just to one side of the door, leaning against the wall, my heart pounding.

"Who is it?"

An old man's voice, croaking. I fought down the impulse to clear my throat. I sounded silly enough already, and this wasn't the time to worry about my vocal cords.

"Steve? It's me, Barbara."

Barbara? Of course; young, beautiful, amorous. We'd dated; one of those every-now-and-then things. When I first joined the Project and met her, we'd had wonderful times together. But it had been a long time ago. Why *now?* I glanced at my wrist-watch. In the gloom the luminous hands showed a quarter to four. I thought of the other side of the door, and things became jumbled. I thought of that beautiful body, but the gun in my hand kept crowding out the view and—

"Steve, *please!*"

"Are you alone, Babs?"

"Of course I'm alone—"

I slipped the steel bolt free to release the door. "Come in." I didn't open the door myself. I stepped back, to the side and away from the hallway light, the gun in my hand ready.

She slipped through quickly, eased the door closed behind her. I glanced at her; a light coat was already sliding from her shoulders to reveal a sweater that did nothing to hide the beautiful form beneath. I stepped behind her, slammed home the steel bolt. My thumb kept dancing on the safety of the automatic, and I held the thing behind me, from her sight.

In the shadows that swallowed the room, her voice came out

husky, the warm and familiar tone I'd known so well: "You haven't called me for months, Steve."

I felt the anger in me. "This is a hell of a time to compare social notes," I retorted. I wasn't ready or willing to play games. "What's this all about, Babs?"

She crossed the room, eased herself to the edge of the bed. She sighed. "Do you want me to beg?"

She caught me off balance with that one. It came without preamble. No nonsense.

"What?" I think I stammered out the word.

Her face lifted to me. "Isn't it obvious why I'm here? I—I was on a date with some idiot, and I wanted to . . ." Her voice faltered.

"Go on," I insisted.

"I wanted to make love," she snapped. The steel in her voice softened as quickly as it appeared.

I swore to myself. She knew I hadn't dated anyone for a long time. Except, that is, for Kim. But I knew that didn't bother Babs. What went on in someone's bed, she felt, was the business only of those people who made love; and no one else had anything to do with it.

Yet, with all that had happened . . . Then she stood up and moved close to me, her breath coming faster and her cheek brushing against mine. In the darkness I grinned. Here this beautiful creature was about to drag me onto the sheets and I stood like a wooden Indian with the .38 still in my hand and not knowing what to do with it. A voice spoke clearly to me. My own voice. It told me what to do with the gun: *Just hang on to it, Steve, old boy; just hang on to it and keep that safety off and the hammer all the way back.*

With her? With Babs? What the hell was I supposed to do with the .38? Shoot her?

Her hands kept moving. They knew how and what to do with me, and I was half frantic trying to remain sensible, to keep a firm grip on myself. Babs tugged me back to the bed and eased me down. She raised her body higher, arching. Her breasts came to my face. Christ! Those beautiful breasts, against my face, pressing against my lips. My head was spinning. I smelled her perfume, just noticeable.

Spinning . . . A dim roaring began somewhere within my ears; I could almost feel my blood racing as her stomach pressed against mine. Her perfume . . . my head, spinning . . . spinning . . . My God, spinning . . .

You bloody fool!

Cursing, I tried to shove her away. A sudden weakness stunned me; I seemed to have no more strength than a child. Barbara's body remained atop mine, writhing, her breasts smothering me. She was all over me and as I strained to free myself I felt her hands trying clumsily to hold me down. I began a long slide down a huge well; the temptation to let go, just to fall and fall forever, grew stronger within me. Fear, adrenalin, the instinct for survival . . . these are marvelous things. I tore myself from her grasp. Alarm bells clamored wildly in my head. Something terrible was happening. . . . I knew I must get up. I cursed, raving at the weakness that crippled me. Gasping, I threw her to one side, rolling away to the other and then stumbling to my feet. She came after me like a tigress, her breasts again squeezing against my face, and Christ, my head, the spinning. . . .

Then I remembered. The .38 . . . I still held it in my right hand. I didn't want to hit her with the gun. I tried it the other way. I balled my left hand into a fist and hit her with everything I had, what I thought was a ripping blow. It was clumsy, weak. She gasped, then threw herself again at me. I fell back, staggering. Anger poured through me when finally I realized just how wrong everything had become. For a moment I was free. I stepped back, thumbing the safety on, and then I brought the barrel of the .38 down in a vicious arc. I felt the blow of metal smacking into something soft and yielding. I stood there with my chest heaving, gulping desperately for air, as Barbara collapsed. She didn't moan or cry out; she just crumpled to the floor.

The .38 slipped from my fingers. I began to feel numb

through my arms and legs. Cotton filled my mouth. My arms were as heavy as lead, and I wanted to sleep. That's all. Forget everything. Sleep. Just sleep . . .

I reeled away from the window, used the walls for support, and made it to the bathroom. I pawed at the light switch, jerked open the medicine chest with clumsy, stupid motions. I had it in my fingers but I dropped it. There was that roaring again in my ears, and everything was blurring before me and I bent down to pick it up. . . . I knew I'd never make it to my feet again, so I just let go and slumped to the bathroom floor; my head slammed against the sink but I ignored it, on my knees, pawing blindly, and then I had the ampul in my fingers, and snapped it in two and jammed the smelling salts against my nostrils. Something exploded in my chest and throat and deep inside my head, and in the sudden harsh light the bathroom spun wildly, a stomach-wrenching dervish of gleaming tile and toilet bowl and sink and bathtub, and I twitched my way into a fit of coughing. Long minutes later I lay weakly on the floor, my head a hornets' nest of pain. But I was through the worst of it. I took a few more stiff pulls of the ampul, and climbed shakily to my feet.

I walked back to the bedroom. The sight of Barbara still crumpled on the floor brought me up short. I switched on a lamp, and what I saw made me curse. A nasty gash along her forehead had spilled a lot of blood that stained her hair and the carpet where she lay. I hurried to the bathroom to get a wet towel.

While I cleaned the blood from her head and face, I thought about what had happened. Now that it was in the past, it wasn't too difficult to understand. In her hair, sprayed across her breasts . . . there was enough chemical sprayed on her body to knock out anyone against whom she could press tightly for a few minutes. The fumes were barely perceptible, and perfume had disguised the odor. Just a little longer . . . those lovely breasts against my face would have sent me spinning into unconsciousness. I tilted back her head. Sure enough; there were two small antidote filters within her nostrils.

I was still too weak to lift her onto the bed. I placed a pillow beneath her head and as gently as I could spread a blanket across her body. For several minutes I stood quietly, watching her, trying to collect my thoughts. She began to moan; she was starting to come out of it.

Then I began to get my brain into gear. Barbara couldn't be in this caper alone—no question that this had been planned carefully. Someone else was controlling this. Someone else who would move in swiftly after she had done her work. After I had been wafted unconscious by the chemical sprayed on her body. Someone else to finish off what she had started. It wasn't a pleasant thought.

But Barbara didn't want to kill me, for Christ's sake! Not the real Barbara. I sagged against the wall.

The *real* Barbara . . .

Who was real any more? *Who wasn't?*

If I didn't know better, if I didn't *know* I was sane and that this nightmare existed not wholly within my mind, but in real, prosaic, everyday morning-and-night life, I know I would have succumbed to the pressures tightening all about and against me.

Barbara Johnson had made love with me. We were great friends. She didn't want to kill me.

But she had tried to do exactly that.

Charles Kane was one of my best friends.

Not long ago he tried to murder me with his car. . . .

During the past several weeks there had been eight separate attempts on my life.

People—some of them friends, others only passing acquaintances, still others total strangers—had tried to do me in with rifle bullets, automobiles, poison, even a knife. Not one of these people had a damn thing against me.

Except murder.

No. Not really. Not those people . . . Christ, I had to shake the cobwebs from my head!

These people weren't murderers. They were only instruments. Despite that—

On an impulse I snapped off the lights and moved to the far

side of the room, to the window facing the street. In the darkness I eased the drape from the window and studied the street below. All the parked cars seemed alike: dark and abandoned. I waited, my eyes darting back and forth. Then I saw it. The telltale glow of a cigarette from one car. I wasn't surprised. Someone was waiting in that car for Barbara to give the signal that I was dead to the world. He—whoever it was—could come up, quickly, to finish me off.

The nausea came without warning, disgorging bile into my throat. I barely made it to the bathroom. The sick-sweet taste drove me to my knees, dry-heaving, helpless to stem the spasms that racked my body. I half sprawled on the tile, giving in to it all, feeling the headache knotting within me. I tried to fight the pain trickling through a thousand cracks of my skull, but it didn't help. I lay there weak and sick, and thought about it. . . .

I knew who was trying to kill me.

He used these people as implements with which to carry out his task, coldly and unemotionally, a task that he considered to be essential—my death.

Oh, I knew him, all right.

God.

No! I cursed at myself. *Spell it out.* . . .

Not the God that people knew, to whom they prayed.

This one was different.

The God Machine.

A brain. Brilliant beyond comprehension. A dream harshly real. A monstrous intellect the like of which the world had never before known. The world still knew nothing about it—him—or whatever you used for a name.

A bio-cybernetics creature. The finest product of the science and the technology and the hopes of man. A brain—a *real* brain made up of the same things that make up your brain and mine. A brain that filled an entire building, that reached out across a nation, a brain that was infinitely faster and more diversified and more capable than a million human minds.

A brain that . . . well, this one didn't think it was God.

It *knew* it.

[13]

And it was doing its best to destroy me.

I lay there on the cold bathroom floor, my chest heaving for air and my stomach knotting in spasms and the pain scrabbling through my mind, a beautiful girl unconscious on the floor in the next room, and I wondered—

How do you fight God?

2

MY NAME IS Steve Rand.

I'm not an ordinary person.

Ever since high school I knew there was something different about me. It was, I learned, the manner in which I thought, the way the wheels turned inside my skull. I was a numbers adept. I thought of math as, well, almost as if it were music. I never worked at math. It flowed; everything always fitted beautifully. I never experienced difficulty with the same problems that kept my friends up through all hours of the night. Numbers always marched dutifully in tune, always fell into place for me.

I was still in high school in Madison, Wisconsin, when a government search for students with unusual skills in the mathematical sciences selected me, and some twenty others, for special tests. Two government scientists discussed with us physics, algebra, geometry, calculus, differential equations, cybernetics, probability, the topological sciences and other fields of which I was barely aware. The scientists told us that if we did well in the tests we could have our choice of almost any college or university in the country.

I didn't fathom this sudden and, I considered, undue attention. Yet the tests themselves excited the government scientists. Even when I failed to master some of the really wicked problems they threw at us. When I ran into the brain twisters that stopped me cold, I knew something was wrong. I didn't know *why;* I just knew or sensed it. I explained to them that I simply wasn't ready to go that deep. The fact that I recognized my own inadequacies seemed to please them.

My parents were somewhat overwhelmed by it all. Not until

several days after I'd completed the tests did my father even discuss it with me. I discovered only then that he had been visited by the two government scientists. He told me—this is what he had been told—that my grasp of the problems I faced took place with extraordinary speed. Several tests with which I'd wrestled were dead end. They were deliberate blocks that didn't have any one answer to them. I seemed to recognize these almost at once and, ignoring them, went on eagerly to the remainder.

That's all there was to it, really, for some time.

Then, three months before my graduation, we had another visitor from the government, a man who was to become closer to me than any other human being. His name was Thomas A. Smythe, and years would pass before I was to learn that Tom Smythe had actually been *assigned* to me. He was—well, Tom could be described accurately as an unusual, perhaps even an odd sort of person. Physically he was big: nearly six feet four inches. But he walked with a catlike grace and a physical ease that belied his bulk. And he had a mind that was positively uncanny—a mind by which, on many occasions, I would find myself frustrated and caught by surprise. That easygoing, huge fellow with his pipe and his deep throaty voice was a master psychologist. I would come to learn that rarely did he think in terms of the present. His everyday world always stretched years into the future.

Tom Smythe was waiting for me one day when I arrived home from school. I mentioned I had only another three months before graduation. Tom Smythe said he had come to discuss with me and my parents, on what he called a hard basis, my career beyond high school. My scholastic record of straight A's should have guaranteed little difficulty in gaining just about any college or university. But I was also aware that not even a superb scholastic performance assured a really free choice; there were schools where the almost arbitrary decisions of admissions officials, and the waiting lists, would block admittance.

Tom Smythe explained with unabashed candor, "If you would like to continue your career, specializing, as it were, in the mathematical sciences"—he paused for a gesture with his pipe as if to demean his ability to open any university door in the land—"we can place you wherever you wish to go. Of course," he added, "we have some ideas about that ourselves. . . ."

My father was an old horsetrader from way back when. He also had the habit of driving right to the point of a matter. He stirred his drink idly, studying the swirl of Scotch around the ice cubes in his glass. Without preamble he lifted his eyes and stared directly at our visitor. "Tell me, Mr. Smythe," he said abruptly, "why the government is going to so much trouble."

Tom Smythe knew when to cut the mustard; of a sudden he tossed aside the amenities of social conversation. "Your son is what we consider an adept in the higher mathematics," he said. "The tests Steve took some months back told us a great deal about him. Oh, not so much what he can do now," he emphasized with another gesture of his pipe. "That's only of passing importance. The tests indicated a potential, a great potential, that as yet remains untapped. It must be nurtured, guided, developed."

Smythe leaned back in his chair and permitted the trace of a smile to appear. "If this potential realizes fruition, Mr. Rand, there is every possibility that Steve may be rated as a mathematical genius."

My mother sighed and mumbled about a genius who never knew what time he was supposed to be home at night. I laughed with Tom at being brought so abruptly back to earth.

Our government visitor paused to relight his pipe; I waited impatiently to hear what else Smythe had come to tell us. I knew that while Smythe addressed himself directly to my father, hewing to the respect due the parent, his words were selected carefully for their effect upon me. "Steve's natural talent is different, even unusual, Mr. Rand," he went on, "yet it is not so rare as to be exclusive. Experience has taught me—we have, as you may have suspected by now, gone into this with the greatest of care—well, experience has taught us that a natural talent by itself isn't enough. I said that it needs guidance, that it must be developed. I can't emphasize that too much," he said, nodding his leonine head as if to lend added emphasis to his own words.

"We learned this the hard way, to put it bluntly," he went on. "We have been brought by, ah, by events stirring within the Soviet Union, to reexamine the methods with which we, as a nation, have utilized—or ignored—our single most valuable resource. I mean, of course, the young men and women just striking out in the world."

He paused, and again that trace of a smile appeared, an unspoken admission that Tom Smythe, and many others like him, were engaged in a monumental effort to realize as a future promise what had in the past suffered neglect. But what I understood immediately eluded the satisfaction of my father.

"That sounds almost like a speech you have said many times before, Mr. Smythe." Immediately my father held up his hand to blunt the expected reaction. "No offense, no offense, Mr. Smythe," he said quickly. "I can understand your problem. I imagine you *have* said many times before what you're telling us now?"

The smile broadened into a wide grin of admission. *"Touché,"* he said with a gesture of his pipe.

My father scratched the side of his nose in the move my mother and I knew so well. A clear sign that he hadn't yet been sold a bill of goods—no matter how slick the salesman. Again he sought, and found, the direct gaze of our visitor.

"Well, then, Mr. Smythe," my father said, "there is, I'm sure, much in what you say. But there is also something frightening in your words."

Smythe waited, silent. I had the feeling that many times before he had encountered this same situation.

"Um, all this has a ring of, well"—my father shifted in his seat, placing his drink on the table alongside him—"as if these youngsters were being branded as commodities. I buy and sell, Mr. Smythe," he emphasized, "and I would hate to think of Steve and others like him as—as, well, as commodities to be traded across a bargaining counter." He shook his head unhappily. "I get the feeling—and mind you, I hope that I'm wrong —that these kids really don't have that much say about what happens to them." He sat back, waiting. He had given Smythe his chance to complete what he had come here to accomplish.

I held my breath. Again that trace of a smile flickered across Smythe's face.

"Nothing could be further from the truth, Mr. Rand," he said after a long pause. "It is not true because that sort of thing doesn't pay off."

My father arched his eyebrows and pursed his lips. With an effort he kept his silence, waiting.

"We learned, Mr. Rand—and we learned this a long time ago, I should add—that it is impossible to regiment the creative mind. We are aware, acutely aware, that this mind in which we are so interested, the creative mind, will not function at its best when confined within a mental or intellectual straitjacket." Again the slow shaking of that leonine head; again the feeling that Smythe was not so much talking to us as if he were re-affirming, aloud, what he believed absolutely within himself.

"One of the problems of our society," he continued, "is that there's too much regimentation. That's the curse"—he smiled fleetingly—"of what we would call the technocratic society. It can be stifling. In any intellectual endeavor there must, there absolutely *must,* be the spark from within young and inquiring minds. It's not only dangerous but, on the national level, it may even prove fatal to extinguish that spark." He leaned back in his seat, again searching his pockets for matches. I had the strangest feeling that this poking about was more deliberate than necessary, as if Smythe were providing his audience with a recess in which to digest his message.

"I have a fair amount of experience at this sort of thing, Mr. Rand," he said suddenly. Then, almost as if with an air of resignation: "More than once I have been described as a pied piper. But I do not lead, Mr. Rand. I point the way."

My father smiled; Smythe had gotten through. Our visitor didn't miss the breach in the parental wall.

"The youngsters with whom we work," he added swiftly, "are free, intellectually and emotionally, not to pursue our advice, if that becomes their decision. To repeat, we point the way—but we do not sing any siren song. We advise, we assist, we counsel as much as it is possible to do so. We do all this because we know truly how critical all this really is. But we can't *push.*" A slow grin appeared. "Any parent knows that," he said softly.

My father nodded. "Let's get down to cases, Mr. Smythe," he said. "What about our son?"

This time Smythe directed his smile to me, and I grinned back. I couldn't help it. He *was* something like a pied piper, and I knew I was ready to follow wherever he might lead. Smythe had that aura about him; it was an invisible, yet almost tangible force.

"Steve's promise, to repeat," Smythe said, "lies in the mathematical sciences. But full and early development on a haphazard basis no longer is possible in a world of technological complexity and an accelerated pace of events." Again Smythe had made that imperceptible shift to assume complete command of the situation. "Development must take place at the earliest age possible, but that age must also be consistent with the capabilities of the youth himself. That's why we prefer not to interfere, except in rare cases, with a youngster's home life during high school. Emotional development constitutes one of the ingredients critical to the fabric that makes up each one of us. Steve's moral and emotional background in this household is all we could ask—"

"You mean you've checked *us* out, too?" The words sliced into Smythe's explanation.

"Of course, Mr. Rand. Wouldn't you have done the same thing?"

My father nodded slowly, begrudging the point.

"But now Steve is ready to be committed to his future," Smythe went on. "At the moment he is enjoying all this attention. Later"—Smythe's eyes locked with mine—"despite the brilliance of which he is already aware, when he stumbles against some truly staggering problems, he may wish he had never heard of me. . . ."

He was right.

[20]

3

From: Harkness, M. E.; Interoffice Code 2123Q
To: Computer Sciences Panel; Presidential Science Advisory Board
Reference: Special Report 4, Project *Pied Piper*
Response: Pied Piper SP 4; C2123Q

To review:
The digital computer epitomizes the new information technology in the range and diversity of information processing it makes possible. Its impact upon the diverse sciences with which we are occupied occurs in many guises; as traditional data analysis; as data processing of huge volumes of records; as networks for gathering primary data; as techniques for building responsive experimental arrangements; and as a basic theoretical tool in the simulation of complex systems.

Despite significant gains within the last decade, much of the impact is still only potential. Sufficient evidence is at hand to support the judgment that this new information technology will exert an "impact effect" on many new developing sciences as significant as did the technologies derived from thermodynamics in an earlier period.

Project Pied Piper is planning for its impact to be exerted, not at the present, but in the predictable near future when computer technology will have attained that level where the exploitation of this new technology will bring its greatest return. The growth of information-technology systems and the paced progress of

Pied Piper have been intended from their outset to coincide at this planned future date.

An understanding of the role of information technology requires some description of the digital computer, which is, in essence, a machine for following instructions. In the past, a machine merely responded to the setting of a switch or the position of a lever, but *a computer responds to a language*. This is the revolutionary development.

In principle, an astonishingly small set of primitive instructions suffices for information processing, but a typical computer can have scores of different instructions. Only a machine for processing information can obey a language, and, conversely, only such a machine *can form new instructions for itself and thus change its mode of operation in intricate ways*.

The capability of a computer is measured by the amount of information it can store, the number of basic operations it can perform per second, and the reliability with which it operates. The first large commercial computer, which appeared in 1951, did about 4,000 additions per second and had 1,000 10-digit numbers stored and accessible at high speed. Today's biggest machine performs well over 1,000,000 additions per second and has considerably more than 100,000 10-digit numbers accessible at high speed. From 1951 to the present, speed has been increased by a factor already close to 300, and memory by a factor well in excess of 100. Reliability has increased correspondingly, so that today's machines run with many billions of operations between errors. Even without the further advances that already are predictable in their embryonic stages, machines are currently powerful enough to bring about several revolutions in the application of information technology to many old and new sciences.

Now we come more specifically to the urgency of Project Pied Piper. *For a computer to do sophisticated things it must have a sophisticated instructor*. Fortunately, there has been a growth of know-how in instructing the machine, or, programming. In areas of significance to new sciences—an excellent example is the spectacular range of the life sciences—an extraordinary range of numerical computations can be made with great facility: standard statistical analyses, matrix inversions, spectra and cross-spectra, auto- and cross-correlation of time series, the numerical solution of ordinary and differential equations, and so on. Other operations have been carried out in a few experimental programs, and will soon become routine: the recognition of fixed type fonts for direct input of printed material, the simulation of neural networks, and the extraction of meaningful data from background "noise." Speech recognition, inductive inference, and language translation are in exploratory stages.

How does this affect Project Pied Piper? The answer lies in the stumbling block of computer programming-control and the solution that appears to hold such great promise in Pied Piper.

Essentially, the hidden price for the general-purpose computer is the headache of writing sequences of tens of thousands of elementary instructions. The tedium involved in instructing computers has prompted the development of automatic programming procedures and languages *whereby the machine assumes some of the burden of instructing itself.*

The pressure to develop new instructions must come from potential users who have a clearly expressed need. Once again the life sciences provide a compelling example: Almost certainly, the most convenient programming for the life sciences must reflect some of the individualities of the language of biology—individualities can be unearthed only by the life scientist in the course of actual programming and experimenting.

The basic problem, of course, is much wider than this restriction to one branch of science.

The need for effective and fairly rapid two-way communications with the machine is the major stumbling block to which this Report has made reference. In all but a few instances today, twenty-four hours or more intervene between the gathering of experimental data and the retrieval of the results of their analysis. Such delays make impossible the adequate incorporation of the computer into experimentation. Either we must learn how to let many users have almost immediate access to a single large computer or we must supply each experimenter with a device of his own.

Difficulties in communication and access are by no means incurable and are attracting much attention; scientists of the USSR are pursuing urgently what could accurately be described as a "crash effort" to hasten such development within that nation. Academician Sergei Sobolev, director of the Novosibirsk Institute of Mathematics and a leading cyberneticist, has proclaimed: "The time is not far off when a network of computing centers will cover our entire country from the Pacific to the Carpathian foothills." Intelligence analysts attach special significance to such statements as that made at the twenty-third Congress of the Communist Party (March, 1966) by First Secretary Leonid Brezhnev when he castigated Soviet cyberneticists for their failure to bridge the gap between theoretical research and applied technology.

The fundamental point to be made is that the "new information technology" is not merely a euphemism for the large high-speed digital computer. It implies the ability to construct processing devices in response to specific demands, and in combination with whatever other techniques are considered appropriate. . . .

The members of this Panel will find pertinent data of the highest interest concerning development with the bio-cybernetics concept of computer communications, and especially as it relates to the planned development/education of the human elements of such bio-cybernetics systems. It is urged that great consideration be given to the reports of Thomas A. Smythe and to his progress evaluations of the human subjects involved. As has been discussed previously with Panel members, the need for appropriately developed and conditioned "biological partners" for the advanced cybernetics systems can be produced only through a long-range, patient effort such as has been instituted re Pied Piper. The Panel members will note the cautious optimism in the studies evaluation of Steven Rand, HS-A193. . . .

[24]

4

MIKE NAGUMO LEANED closer, whispering from the side of his mouth, "Crusty old bastard, ain't he?"

I hid my grin behind my hand, nodding, watching carefully to see that we weren't receiving any undue attention from the "crusty old bastard" who was holding forth from his scholastic pulpit. Beyond multiple rows of student heads, Mathematics Professor Wilhelm von Weisskopf, resplendent in tweed suit and bristling white beard, and in his customary vile temper, heaped cutting abuse upon those who had been selected to receive guidance and wisdom from his brilliant mind. "Kaiser Willie," as his students dubbed him, appeared convinced that those same students required, along with intellectual nourishment, liberal doses of his famed sarcastic wit. Mathematics he wielded with the certain touch of practiced genius; personal drubbings he issued with a careless abandon. Never was there the student who received from Von Weisskopf a solitary word, not so much as a crumb, of praise.

"Mathematics," he would growl from beneath unruly brows, "is a language of the truth. Anything less than perfection is therefore somewhat less than the truth. I do not compliment those who wallow in less than the entire truth, for anything less is to embrace ignorance, and this is deserving only of contempt."

When brought to the tight-lipped anger with which he frequently assailed his class, he was as wont to castigate a student for a "deficient genetic ancestry" as for a demonstrated ignorance in the classroom. And—

"Oh, oh," Mike Nagumo muttered, straightening quickly in his seat. "I think I've bought the farm."

I looked to the front of the room. Sure enough. Kaiser Willie's gravelly tones no longer filled the air. He stood with fists planted solidly on his hips, beard bristling, glaring at Mike. Mike rose slowly to his feet, with a great effort keeping his face impassive. As only Mike Nagumo could do. There's something inescapably imposing about a Japanese who stands six feet three inches tall and who weighs 230 pounds.

"*Mister* Nagumo!"

I thought the room would crack up. His body stiff, Mike bowed formally from the waist, hands stiffly at his sides. With a single word he acknowledged Kaiser Willie:

"Yess-ss?"

It sounded like a boa constrictor. The sibilant, deep hiss sliced through the room. The word came forth in the finest tradition of an old movie with a Japanese villain. And from someone who spoke better English than myself. I shut my eyes, and groaned; I knew Mike would be off and running.

"*Mister* Nagumo! Perhaps you would share with the others in this room your private conversation with Mr. Rand?"

Mike looked blankly at the professor. Slowly his great head shook from side to side. "Cannot do so," he said with exaggerated politeness. "Matter is crassified."

"*Crassified?*" I thought Kaiser Willie was going to drop his uppers. I ran desperately into the breach.

"Sir," I called out, rising to my feet, "he means classified."

The cold blue eyes glared at me. "Your spontaneity is uncalled for, Mr. Rand."

I winced and draped myself back in my chair. Mike Nagumo was strictly on his own.

"Mr. Nagumo, did I hear you say that the matter you felt was so important—sufficiently so as to interrupt this class—was classified?"

"No, sirr. Is crassified."

We couldn't believe it. A blank look appeared fleetingly across the visage of Kaiser Willie.

"Explain yourself, sir!" The gravelly tones were becoming thunderous.

Mike Nagumo bowed again, slowly, ponderously. "Today, sirr, is to be seventh of December. Anniversary, sirr, of honorabre father. Die at Perr Harbor. I remembering occasion with Mr. Rand." Again the deep, careful bow. "I aporogize, if disturb crass."

I thought my ribs would crack. Professor von Weisskopf's face went blank. Then he rallied. "I don't recall you ever saying anything about your father being in the Navy at Pearl Harbor, Mr. Nagumo. Is—"

"Oh, *no,* sirr! Misunderstand. Honorabre father in Nipponese Navy, sirr. Make attack against American freet at—"

The bell drowned out his next words. Instantly Mike gathered up his books, and we both beat a hasty retreat through the rear door of the classroom.

"Whew!" Mike laughed, wiping his brow. "Saved by the bell!"

I was still roaring. "Did you see his face? Good God, I thought the old bastard would have a fit right in front of the room. Jesus, if I were you, Mike, I think I'd take a little vacation for the next couple of days. Anywhere away from Kaiser Willie."

"Aw, he's not so bad," Mike countered.

I looked at him in surprise. *"You're* defending Weisskopf?"

"Not really, I suppose," Mike countered with a wave of the hand. "But you can't knock him as a teacher. He's about the best they got here at MIT."

"Well, maybe," I offered, "but he sure demands his pound of flesh." I looked at Mike, and laughed. "And sometimes he gets it taken from him."

Mike grinned back at me.

"You know something, Mike? I never knew your old man was killed at Pearl Harbor. I didn't even know he was in the Japanese Navy. I thought you were Nisei a couple of generations back."

"Oh, that." Mike grinned again. "Course he wasn't in the

Japanese Navy. The old man's a tourist guide in Honolulu. Biggest damn thief in the business; worth a fortune. He's so mad at me for going straight, as he puts it, that he almost disowned me when I left the islands to come here to MIT."

God bless Mike Nagamo. Shortly after we met, we knew we were on the way to a fast and deep friendship. The Massachusetts Institute of Technology could be a forbidding place, and Mike and I naturally gravitated toward each other, sharing an apartment near MIT. The giant Nisei was determined to pursue a career in nuclear physics. If the promise he showed as a brilliant student was to be sustained, he faced a dazzling career ahead of him.

There were times when I leaned heavily on the irrepressible humor and friendship of Mike Nagumo. For if nothing else, MIT proved to be my intellectual comeuppance.

It was one thing to move securely within the sheltered confines of my high-school years and something entirely different to plunge through the cruelly demanding environment of this new scholastic world. At the time I never realized just how *deliberately* demanding my school years were made to be. I was unaware that on certain MIT files my name carried after it the significant number HS-A193 and that my instructors (influenced by a lavish federal endowment) always made certain that I should chase my own shadow—at the speed *they* set.

Everything I did pointed eventually to a kinship with cybernetics—the digital computer systems infusing every aspect of modern technology. In principle the advanced digital computer—the cybernetics system—made it possible to automate any human mental activity if it could be described in the form of a set of rules that precisely and simply defined the process of performing a given form of mental task.

Let me take that just a bit further. One of the most striking properties of digital computers is their universality, which is based, first, on the possibility of reducing complex mathematical problems to a set sequence of very simple arithemetical operations and, second, on the possibility of using mathematical expressions to describe various processes of the mental activity of man. Therein lay the key to my training and the path along which I would move in future years—to construct an electronic representation of the mental activity of man.

My courses were doubled up on me, and while at times the pressure led to fierce headaches, within two years I had my BA. Another year and my Master's was behind me. I kept at my studies without letup, working toward my PhD, accepting that somewhere in the background was the watchful gaze of Tom Smythe and the United States Government.

Somewhere along the way, observed covertly for the signs by my instructors, I began to metamorphosize from the neophyte into a creature of new instincts in the world of cybernetics. To some extent, I would learn later, I had already attained a kinship with the process along which advanced cybernetics systems must function.

Tom Smythe, in a Panel meeting of the Pied Piper team, put it another way. "He's starting to think, well, to think like a computer," Smythe explained to his group. "He doesn't know it yet, and he won't be told the fact until we think he's ready, or he stumbles upon the truth by himself. But one thing is certain—we're on the right road. Steve Rand is going to become a master psychologist of cybernetics. . . ."

I wrote my thesis in bio-cybernetics. In effect, I proposed the adaptation of biological systems for direct two-way communications with advanced digital computers.

Despite the irrefutable advances of the electronic systems, where truly complex systems were concerned man remained the most important and the most reliable link within these systems. Certain truths wouldn't go away just because we ignored them. In the face of the unexpected, the machine remained helpless.

It was fast becoming a race of man attempting to duplicate his intellectual, reasoning self. Duplicating man, with his capacity for precise analysis and the synthesis of phenomena, and with the methods of processing information that are characteristics of his nervous system, became the goal, a sort of nirvana, which I anticipated as essential in the development of advanced cybernetics systems.

I saw the true cybernetics system only as that which could emulate the superb construction of the human brain and certain elements of its nervous system. We had to adapt from the lessons of nature. Living organisms have central nervous systems consisting of billions of neurons—organic nerve cells. The capacity for work of the living system is retained in almost full measure despite the failure of many millions of neurons.

The brain of one man contains more than ten billion neurons. This amazing, beautiful, truly extraordinary mechanism with all its sensory endings functions to perfection with an energy requirement of only several tens of watts. Equally extraordinary is the fact that each neuron can be in an excited or in an inhibited state. Nature, in effect, built a superb electrical switch. The neuron of the brain is an element with two stable states—on or off. In essence, really, it's an organic two-position relay.

Compared to this miracle of design, even the most advanced cybernetics system was a clumsy thing of mud and sticks. To create an electronic device comparable in the number of elements to the human brain and requiring normal operating power, and packing everything together almost to the consistency of a solid cube or sphere, you'd end up with a physical calamity on your hands. It would equal a huge building in cubic space, and would demand about a million kilowatts for its operation; at this point you would still have to broach the staggering problems of cooling and ventilation, repair, change, modification, instruction, reporting, sensory terminals—ad infinitum.

I knew in what direction my future would lie—to hurdle these barriers. I was absolutely convinced that the key to the true cybernetics system lay in bionics and the adaptability of bionics to cybernetics. In essence? Build the cybernetics system from the same materials with which nature, with time immeasurable for its experiments, created the human brain. I knew that before many years passed it would be possible to overcome the problems of physical bulk through the use of controlled force fields. We would be able to imprint memory through magnetic systems. We would be able to work in a new microcosmic world where subnuclear sizes would become obedient servants to the demands of artificial thought processes.

And then—then it would be possible to create the true electronic brain. A brain that would utilize logic circuits with feedback and switching theory. Put that into one word and it comes out "flexibility."

A brain created by man that would be able to *think* as did the man that shaped it and gave it life.

•

5

TOM SMYTHE DABBED his lips with his napkin, an act of delicacy almost outrageous for his great bulk. He pushed his seat back from the table, and sighed with pleasure. I waited. Inevitably the pipe appeared. Tom searched his pockets for matches, and a cloud of blue smoke swirled thickly about us. As if on signal, our waiter appeared with busboys to clear the table. Steaming coffee was poured.

"Anything else, sir? An after-dinner drink, perhaps?"

Tom nodded. We shared a mutual taste. "King Alphonse," I said, holding up two fingers.

"Very good, sir." The waiter dissappeared. Tom didn't pick up the conversation. For the moment he remained content to enjoy his pipe. I dragged on a cigarette, watching a cortege of young lovelies moving past our table. The waiter reappeared with our drinks and again vanished.

Smythe's first words came from out in left field.

"Tell me about Tam."

"Who?" The question caught me unprepared.

"Tamara Severny."

Tamara Severny . . .

I didn't know how to answer Tom. What was I supposed to say? I had been dating Tam for nearly a year. She was the most wonderful girl I'd ever known, and—

I caught Tom's gaze. "What do you want me to tell you?"

"You've been going with her for a while, haven't you?"

Anger flushed my face. "Quit playing cat-and-mouse with me," I snapped. "I'm sure you know I've been dating her. So why the setup"—I waved my hand to take in the restaurant—

"for what you've already got down in your little black book!"

Smythe chuckled. "Temper, temper," he chided. "We don't know everything. Wouldn't you rather have me ask you right out?"

"Ask me *what!* Are you so interested in my social life?"

His great head shook slowly. "No," he said after a pause. "I would like to know what Miss Severny finds, um, what she finds of interest in her conversations with you, Steve." His eyes leveled with mine, unblinking. "Come now, Steve. It's obvious why we have this interest."

I still wasn't buying it. Tamara Severny was an exchange student from the Soviet Union, but . . . well, for Christ's sake, this cloak-and-dagger nonsense was just too much! To me Tam was a beautiful girl and— Damn! What was Smythe getting at, anyway?

He seemed almost to anticipate my thoughts. "You know her home?"

I nodded. "Leningrad."

"Were you aware that she is a member of the Leningrad Mathematics Society?"

I whistled. "No. I didn't know that." I looked up at Smythe. "I know she's good, but *that* good?"

"*That* good. Maybe even better."

"But why all this, Tom?" I felt the agitation rising in me and I didn't like it. "It sounds as if you suspect Tam of being a secret agent, or something."

"Nothing of the sort," he said to dispel my thoughts on the matter. "But she is a young lady of unusual intelligence; she is interested in areas that are, ah, shall we say, sensitive? And," he threw in the clincher, "within three months she is returning to Leningrad."

His last words rang in my ear. "Tam? She's going home, in —in the next three months?" The news was a shock. "I didn't know that."

Tom didn't answer for several moments. "I know," he said simply.

A sudden sinking feeling took the props out from beneath me.

[33]

If she was returning that soon to Russia, why hadn't she told me?

"Are you sure about her going home?" I shot abruptly at Smythe.

He nodded.

"But how—I mean, she's never said anything to *me!* How can you be so sure?"

"It's my job to be sure, Steve."

I stubbed out my cigarette, lit another, and stared unhappily at the table.

"I didn't know you were that serious about the girl." Tom's voice came from a long way off.

"I—hell, I don't know," I muttered. "I don't suppose I thought that much about it, really. I mean, where it would all end up. That sort of thing."

"Obviously," he said, his tone a flicker of annoyance.

I kicked back my chair, and stood up. "Let's get out of here," I said abruptly. "Suddenly the damn walls are closing in on me."

"There's a new religion in the Soviet Union. It has its idol. *Elektronno-vychislitel'naya-mashina.*"

I looked with surprise at Tom. "That's Russian," I said.

"Uh-huh. It means 'electronic calculating machine,'" he explained. "But you'll be hearing a lot more about *kibernetika*—"

"Cybernetics?"

"That's right. It covers the same ground," Tom said. "Just about everything that involves all possible methods of control and communication common to living organisms and machines." Smythe had adopted an air of gravity uncommon to the rare hours we had spent together in recent months. I wasn't yet accustomed to it.

"How much do you know about cybernetics in the Soviet Union?"

I shrugged. "I don't know, Tom. I read the reports, of course. There's an exchange bulletin, from the Russians, I mean, that

[34]

we get here at MIT." I shrugged again. "That sort of thing. Why?"

"Ever discuss the subject with your Tamara?"

"Sure I have." I grinned. "We've been known to have some pretty wild arguments on the subject. We get together in groups —Mike Nagumo is usually with us—and sometimes we have at it. Tam isn't exactly a shrinking violet."

He smiled. "No, of course not." Immediately he was back to the subject. "Did you ever read Krayzmer?"

I thought for a moment. Leonid Pavlovich Krayzmer . . . yes, I'd read *him*. "Who hasn't?" I shot back at Smythe. "I mean, anyone in this business, they've got to have read him. That thing he did on bionics—his original paper in 1962, well, it's still considered the greatest thinking on bionics applications to cybernetics ever written."

Smythe nodded. "It is," he said simply. Then, again suddenly, "What about Nemchinov?"

I couldn't help smiling at the name. "Vasili Nemchinov? The academician?"

"That's right," Tom said. "But why the smile?"

"According to Tam he's a living legend in Russia," I explained. "From what I understand he's in his seventies, but still absolutely clear in his thinking. And quite the revolutionary in cybernetics. Sort of setting up the guidelines for the new generation to follow. I think Tam said something about studying under him for a while."

"Go on," Smythe urged.

"How strongly does she equate cybernetics with Communism?"

I looked at him in surprise. "She quotes Nemchinov pretty strongly on that," I said. "Her argument—I suppose she was carrying the Nemchinov philosophy—is that only the Communist system gives sufficient room to apply the combination of mathematics and cybernetics to the national economy. Pretty dry phraseology, but not the way it sounds when Tamara is talking." I grinned self-consciously. "Okay, okay, so I've got a thing about the girl."

[35]

He waved me on to continue.

"Well, according to Nemchinov," I said, "public owner-ship—the Communist system—is essential to setting up a single automatic electronic network. I mean, a net that includes cybernetic systems for industry, commerce, agriculture—the works."

"And capitalism?"

"Nemchinov—according to Tamara—has it thumbs down on private enterprise."

"Why?"

I shrugged. "Something about there being an inherent barrier in private enterprise to creating the true cybernetics system on a national scale. The framework of companies, corporations, syndicates—all these spell out unacceptable interference from conflicting interests. The way Nemchinov puts it, you need almost the equivalent of an ant society to create a really meaningful cybernetics system."

"Do you think his point is valid?"

I thought that one over for several moments. "Not really, I suppose. I haven't made any effort," I added, "to weigh the pros and cons of one system against the other, Tom. In the cybernetics sense, I mean."

I lit a cigarette and tried to think back to my long debates with Tamara, Mike Nagumo, and our friends. At the drop of a hat we'd get into spirited arguments about cybernetics and its systems. Tam was unshakable in her belief that only Communism could properly nourish the growth of cybernetics as an integral element of society.

A thought came to me. "There was something else," I said, "but the name escaped me. Antonov, Oleg Antonov. He's the clarion voice of Soviet doctrine. Tamara referred to him quite often. I think it was Antonov—I'm trying to remember all this from months back, you understand?" Smythe nodded, and I went on. "Well, Antonov is the one who wants to keep Communism as the holiest of holies, in cybernetics or anything else. He claims that despite the undisputed position of Norbert Wiener as the father of cybernetics, the basic concept goes back further. In fact Antonov claims that originally it was Marx who postulated

[36]

the idea that a science reaches maturity only when it begins to use mathematics. He carries this further into cybernetics, into a national computer system that uses mathematics for the immediate benefit or guidance of society."

Tom Smythe regarded me carefuly from behind his screen of pipe smoke. Finally, deep in his own thoughts, he nodded again. The pipe stabbed at me.

"Steve, I want you to come with me to Washington," he said. "For a few days."

It was my turn to be surprised. I didn't need to ask the obvious questions; Tom would tell me in his own good time. He did.

Indoctrination. A cybernetics indoctrination. Not of our systems. Of *theirs*.

The Soviet system. That included a young, beautiful, and brilliant girl with whom I was in love? Or was I? Was it just circumstances, the manner in which we'd been thrown together, all the things we did so well together, the spark that always shone so brightly when we were with each other? It didn't matter, I suppose. Not in thc long run.

I had competition. Her career. Cybernetics in the Russian future promised Tamara a dazzling world. She wasn't about to let anything or anyone get in her way. Steve Rand? Well, Tamara was on vacation for a year, so to speak. As an exchange student she could both work and enjoy herself. She did. With me. It was wonderful, marvelous—all the things of which fierce young love is made.

And in three months she was going home. Period.

Tom Smythe's grueling indoctrination in the massive Soviet program to create a computer-based society was like a journey through the Looking Glass. You wake up early one morning and discover that an electronic monster has been stirring into life right at your side—with a frightening lack of awareness on your own part.

Both the United States and the USSR had embraced a future inevitably of a cybernetics society, and yet the two nations held a striking dissimilarity of viewpoint in developing that electronics-based culture. The Russians had the greatest number of pure mathematicians anywhere in the world. In cybernetics *theory* they took a back seat to no one. But in the day-to-day use of computing systems a vastly advanced American technology had left the Soviets far behind. Americans never seem to realize the spectacular system of power distribution that characterizes our country. Nothing like it exists anywhere in the world. The nationwide conformity of power and technological application forms the heartbeat of our national being. We're capable of assimilating within our technological society almost any new development of the physical sciences.

"The Soviets at this time," Smythe explained, "are still too unwieldy to match what we perform as a matter of course. They're desperate to alleviate their shortcomings. They're hurling themselves, literally, into a new era of utilizing to the maximum their new computers. This is what is so important to understand—their potential is frightening. They're coming up from behind, and their speed of development is defying all our predictions. They are absolutely determined to create the first cybernetics society in history."

The hard-core theme of Soviet cybernetics is best summed up by Lev Gatovsky, who explains the new Russian society as "moving ahead on a wide front, from single enterprises to the national economy as a whole, mechanizing and automating existing facilities, and at the same time preparing for a gradual changeover to a new, automated system of information. It means partial application of 'machine mathematics' in an enterprise while the future automated system of management on the basis of cybernetics is being devised. . . . Ever more efficient mathematical models of the national economy can and must be created."

Hardly a stirring call to arms. But I could recognize Gatovsky's words for what they were. A blueprint for tomorrow's sociological-technological society. The electronic Big Brother. Gatovsky knows where his country is headed on its plunge into tomorrow. He knows that machines aren't enough, that the motivation and control of human beings is everything. And the Soviets aren't ignoring that. They are aware, again in the words of Gatovsky, that "mathematics and cybernetics will heighten the significance of creative economic work both centrally and locally. No centralized system of optimal planning can dispense with material incentives. *The application of mathematics is one of the means through which people can be motivated to exert their best efforts."*

Neat. All human beings can be reduced to ciphers. . . .

And they begin with children. When the new breed of Russian scientists created the great "Science City" at Novosibirsk they were aware that a supply of embryonic genius couldn't be sustained on a happenstance basis. Uncommon mathematical potential was the new Holy Grail, and the Soviet search for this commodity is carried out with systematic tenacity. It's in the form of what might best be described as a Mathematical Olympics—an annual competition of talented Russian youngsters brought to Moscow and other examination sites. Nothing is spared in the effort to recognize budding genius. The incentives are real; special schooling, privileged status for living and recreational quarters and, the greatest of all rewards—a career in cybernetics and a position of the exalted in the forthcoming society.

The girl with whom I made love, with whom, I admitted to myself, I had thought seriously of marriage, was one of these brilliant youngsters. Tamara Severny was to become a high priestess of the new religion of cybernetics in the near-future Soviet.

I held the slim document with the single red star printed on its surface. And the one line that read

Bio-Cybernetics—USSR

It was all there. A blueprint of the future stripped to its cold and analytical essentials. When I read through those pages, the first thing that came to mind was a quote repeated often among cyberneticists: "If the social sciences had been developed with the same energy and support that established the nuclear sciences, we would have the most devastating weapon the world has ever known."

In the bio-cybernetics program of the Soviet Union lay the budding seeds of that weapon.

The true value of the advanced digital computer, especially where the intention is to establish freedom of logical pursuit, is one of seizing upon the most priceless of all commodities known to man.

Time.

The advanced cybernetics system is a time machine. It permits more than the solution of mathematical problems. What it really does is to reduce a hundred years of intensive work by thousands of mathematicians to a period of hours or days. It not only speeds up the rate of computation; it also eliminates dangerous blind alleys. The blind alleys are still there but you're no longer required to spend lifetimes running along those fruitless corridors.

Cybernetics is an extension of man's own intellectual capacity and capability in the time sense.

Despite the dazzling promise of the future, there remain severe obstacles and pitfalls. Ever since the first days of their new science, cyberneticists have been aware that communications between man and machine have crippled cybernetics progress.

My thesis at MIT dwelt heavily on this problem—communications directly between the brain of a man and the intellectual-electronic stew that makes up the thinking mass of the computer.

Scientists at the Cambridge Research Laboratories had worked for years in brainwave communications experiments. Dr. Edmond M. Dewan trained skilled volunteers to alter the pattern of the alpha-wave rhythm of the brain, the low-frequency wave related to visual perception. Being able to turn on or off, at will, the alpha rhythm meant an interruption of an electrical source from the brain. By amplifying brainwave signals it was possible for these "alpha adepts" to conduct a crude binary digit system of communications.

[40]

Other efforts were directed toward breaking down the electrical pattern of thought processes so that a computer might recognize familiar patterns of mental activity as related to their electrical signatures. Such programs constituted an intricate blending of life sciences and bio-cybernetics. Optimists insisted we were on the edge of a breakthrough.

But nothing we were doing approached the intensity of the Soviet effort. The discovery of Roza Kuleshova, a woman with the extraordinary talent for detecting colors through her fingertips, rattled every scientific window in the USSR. It was a scientific study that unveiled Kuleshova. The body of Russian scientists scorned psychic phenomena, and they hammered out a plausible explanation of the unprecedented talent. Apparently this woman, who worked with and for the blind, had developed light-sensitive receptors—*organs of vision*—within her fingertips. Probing gently, sliding those supersensitive fingertips along printed paper, she was able to distinguish colors as physical lines of varying thickness, shape, curvature, and other, to her, identifiable characteristics.

Roza Kuleshova was not, of course, the only exciting news in the cybernetics circles of the Soviet Union. She was but the first of which we in the United States had heard. The papers I read listed, one after the other, extraordinary new research efforts, many of which were already producing sobering results.

I balked when I came to a section of Russian experiments with the potential of thought transference between human subjects. I went barging into Tom Smythe's office, waving the offending document before me. Smythe raised his brows at my stormy approach, almost as if he were anticipating my reaction.

"Christ, this is overdoing it, isn't it?" I protested, turning to the report of thought-transference experiments.

Smythe leaned back in his seat and made a careless gesture. "Why should it be?" he said coolly. "We're doing the same thing over here."

My startled glance spoke more effectively than words. If Tom Smythe were that certain . . .

". . . notes of Dr. Eugene Konecci," Tom was saying as I rallied to collect my thoughts. "He was the director of bio-technology and human research for the Space Agency at the time when we—or at least NASA—first began looking into the possibilities of thought transferrence between a man on the earth's surface and another man orbiting the planet in a space-craft."

"You've got to be pulling my leg," I protested.

"Not at all," Smythe said, unruffled at my protests. "In fact, Konecci lifted the lid on what both we and the Russians were doing in his field—space flight, that is. Back in, umm, yes, 1963, Konecci spoke before the International Astronautical Federation." He turned to a filing cabinet behind his desk, ruffled through a drawer, and extracted a slim binder. Quickly he turned to the page he sought. "Here it is," he mumbled as he searched the page. "His statement. Umm. 'Concerted effort directed toward a highly interesting problem in modern science— nature and essence of certain phenomena of electromagnetic communication between living organisms—is reportedly being pursued with top priority under the Soviet manned space program. Until recently, these phenomena have been generally ignored by Western scientists; however, the many hypotheses involved are now receiving increased attention. . . .' "

Several minutes later we sat in silence while I tried to digest what I had heard. According to Smythe, even the Department of Defense, since way back in 1948, had been searching for tele-pathic adepts! The reason? National security. In the search for effective communications at a time when nuclear explosions high above the earth could blanket out electromagnetic propagation and thereby render useless radio and similar communications, the government wasn't leaving any possible source unexamined. Including, I thought wearily, what was supposed to be strictly the domain of psychic phenomena.

Tom gestured at the bio-cybernetics report I had tossed onto his desk. "It's not yet contained in that report," he began, "but have you ever heard of a Russian with the name of Rudi Schneider?"

I shook my head.

"You may accept that whatever I say about this fellow Schneider is true. We've verified the reports we first received."

I looked with surprise at Smythe. Preambles of this sort just weren't characteristic of him. I held my silence and tried to be patient. Smythe frowned as if he were struggling to believe what he professed to me to be authentic.

"Rudi Schneider is a telekinetic."

I was too surprised even to gape. I simply stared at Smythe. And I didn't believe him. He saw that, and smiled.

"It's true," he said. He paused and took a deep breath. "The Soviets have their hands on a real bona-fide, authenticated adept who can move physical objects without, on his own part, making any physical movement or contact with the object. A telekinetic," he repeated for final emphasis.

"But that's impossible!" I whispered.

Smythe made a sour face at me. "We are all not insane in this department, Steve," he said dryly.

"But—"

"This Schneider apparently isn't the only one," he continued. "They've got more adepts. With differing levels of talent, so to speak. Rudi Schneider, or any of the others, we gather, isn't the brightest boy on the block. We know more about Schneider than the others. He couldn't care less about the whole thing. And it's not something he can turn on and off at will. The Russian scientists are near distraction trying to establish a correlation between Schneider's neural activity and those moments when he can perform in the telekinetic manner. They haven't been too successful," he repeated, as if his last words were a feeble prayer that success would continue to elude them.

My sleep that night could best be described as troubled. My head swam with the mass of reports I was still struggling to digest. The bio-cybernetics study, an electromagnetically based program of thought transference, this thing with a halfwit who had turned out to be a telekinetic . . . It was all too much for me to take in such a single huge dose. One spark of relief rallied to my aid. I found myself, surprisingly, swiftly free of the troubled thoughts with which I had first greeted the news of Tamara leaving within the next few months for Russia. I failed to understand how what should have been an emotional blow to me could slip so easily from my shoulders. To the devil with it. There was enough to keep my head in a spin without lovelorn nonsense. . . .

The thought kept pounding through my skull that everything I read or had discussed with Tom Smythe could be linked only to new cybernetics systems.

I lay there through the night, trying to fit together the many pieces. Certain elements were cut and dried. Even if the pattern didn't make itself immediately obvious.

If the Russians had this much going for them—and Smythe had made it abundantly clear that this was so—then, inevitably, we must have something of a counterpoint. Perhaps we didn't have adepts who could discern colors through their fingertips or who could push steel balls along a table by thinking about it. . . . I didn't know; and I realized quickly that where I was concerned, at least for the moment, it didn't matter.

During the several days I remained in Washington, Tom took me through Whirlwind—the single greatest cybernetics complex ever produced. Whirlwind was the fiercely guarded possession of the National Security Agency at Fort Meade, Maryland. The computer was so advanced in concept and so huge in size that it required the best talent of both RCA and IBM to make it a reality. Whirlwind was also the first computer that could "search out" solutions demanding more than multiples of two plus two plus two, ad infinitum. If presented with a problem that had several possible solutions, Whirlwind didn't throw an electronic fit and sulk. Faced with an apparent dilemma, it retraced its steps and carried out a process-of-elimination search for the best possible answer. It punched out these answers with varying degrees of possibilities. In a sense, Whirlwind could be left to its own devices to track down elusive answers. The Russians had nothing like it.

But what had Smythe said about Whirlwind? Despite its demonstrated superiority to every other cybernetics system in existence, *it was a dead end.*

Well, you don't quit when you reach a dead end. You build anew and you simply climb right over what you couldn't do before. . . .

That brought my eyes wide open.

Of course! To the blazes with the scraps and bits and pieces of Soviet cybernetics! What had *we* been doing all this time?

I thought about how far—hidden from the public gaze—we might have gone by now.

Some things don't require visible evidence to become obvious. I wondered about the greatest cybernetics complex ever known that must be, at the time, still in the making. I didn't *know,* as a matter of actual fact, that this was so. But I would have wagered ten years of my life that I was on the right track.

And there was one final thought before exhaustion finally dragged me down into a fitful sleep.

Where did I fit into all this?

6

From: Harkness, M. E.; Interoffice Code 2164Q
To: Computer Sciences Panel; Presidential Science Advisory Board
Reference: Special Report 8, Project *Pied Piper*
Response: Pied Piper SP 8; CQ2164Q

1: Preliminary phasing, Steven Rand, HS-A193, has been completed. Non-knowledgeable covert phasing is considered successful in entirety, with preliminary expectations established at program outset exceeded.

2: Rand is adjudged prepared for and capable of progression into active participation within Project 79.

3: The psychological reaction generated by exposure to advanced bio-cybernetics programs of the USSR is precisely that extrapolated for this preparations phase. Rand has been restrained within the intellectual-scholastic-mathematical environment that, essentially, precluded serious consideration of paranormal phenomena. It remains questionable whether Rand has transitioned to a full acceptance of paranormal phenomena with the Soviet test subjects; this is unimportant against the desired objective of Rand now being required at least to consider the validity of paranormal activities. It is considered sufficient that plausibility is implanted as a possible causative factor in future activities.

4: The necessity for providing a counterbalance to the predominantly mathematical intellectual framework of Rand is considered accomplished. Exposure to the viewpoint of the Soviet with the conflict of societies, essential to our intentions, has been carried out essentially as planned. The progress of Rand as an emergent individual within the mathematical/cybernetics sciences exceeds all expectations.

5: To elaborate: Rand is now programmed psychologically into a framework of cybernetics intellectualism. In essence, he sustains an intellectual rapport with the cybernetics system. Psychologically he accepts an intrinsic superiority on his own part toward developing a still undefined cybernetics system that will meet his still idealistic concepts. As a research/programmer of electronic/bionics cybernetics systems, Rand, rather than enduring latent fears of the potentially uncontrolled capabilities of advanced cybernetics, is eager to accentuate such development and to fulfill the goal of Project 79 for the self-motivated, logic-functioning cybernetics complex.

6: It is considered essential that Rand be brought immediately into active project participation. Lessening the requirements sustained by this subject could instigate an effect undesired in terms of project priorities. It is considered essential, as well, that Rand be brought with all possible speed consistent with psychological restraints to the position as Chief Programmer, Project 79.

7: Because of the limited emotional/sexual experience of Rand, contained largely within his relationship with Tamara Severny (which is to be concluded at the appropriate time), it is recommended that preliminary plans for direction in this area be instituted. Bionics adaptability to Project 79 is now in a Category 3 of implementation, and it would be appropriate that bionics indoctrination be carried out through the Bionics Laboratory, Project 79. To the maximum extent permissible, this should be concluded through the person of FS-C8992, Kim Renée Michelle.

8: This step in the programming of Rand is recommended to be carried through with minimum delay. It is further recommended that . . .

7

I WAS ALMOST afraid to answer. The whole thing was overwhelming. Tom Smythe and four scientists sat around a huge oak table in a conference room. Through a far window I could see the white spire of the Washington Monument, but I paid it only a brief glance. Smythe, with great deliberation, had just offered me the opportunity to program what was, from his description, the most advanced cybernetics complex ever known. It didn't seem real. Cloud castles never do, I suppose. Smythe offered mine on a silver platter.

If I took it, of course.

If I took it?

Hesitancy stayed my voice. I looked around the room, back to Smythe. His expression remained inscrutable. The four men with him were warm, friendly. So far they hadn't contributed much. There were some pleasant words about the need for a new approach to carry on the work they had originated "some years back." That was all.

Smythe described the cybernetics program only vaguely. He brushed aside my questions with the brusque comment that at this moment I didn't require further details. I'd never seen him like this before. He had made it clear to me that I must decide about accepting a position beyond my wildest dreams—before I left this room.

That's what nagged at the back of my mind. I wouldn't—I couldn't—refuse such an offer. Smythe knew this. So why the pressure? There wasn't anything definite; a subtle touch. But I could almost sense what felt like maneuvering, and—

I tried to shake off the feeling. What the devil was wrong with me? These people had accepted me, accepted my qualifications, were paying me an honor and . . . well, I was acting like a clod.

Dr. Arthur Cartwright—the *esteemed* Dr. Cartwright—mistook my preoccupation. He leaned forward, speaking softly, convincingly. "Your exposure to cybernetics during the past several years, young man," he said, "has been rather extraordinary. You have been enabled to study, to think, and to reason on this subject in a manner never before available to someone of your years." The man to his right nodded in agreement. "When I consider your capabilities in the mathematics and cybernetics sciences," he went on, "I confess I am delighted. I am delighted with the promise we see in you. We have put our best years into this, ah, this program, Mr. Rand," he said, and again I caught that vague steering away from specifics. Dr. Cartwright chose his words carefully. "It would seem that many things have joined at this particular crossroads, that you will be enabled to utilize, also in a manner unprecedented, the benefits of our labors."

What Dr. Cartwright said was absolutely true. I knew that, appreciated the words.

And a great deal hasn't been said. . . . The vague uncertainty gnawed at my thoughts.

I let my gaze drift from one scientist to the other and returned finally to Tom Smythe. Not a muscle on his face moved as he met and held my eyes.

"There's an old expression," I said slowly, "that would appear to fit this moment."

Smythe waited. I extended my right hand to him. "When do I start?"

Immediately his face creased in a broad smile, and he grasped my hand. "Right now," he said. "Let me tell you about Project 79."

I never much gave a damn for security. I thought from the viewpoint of a scientist, and as far as I was concerned security was something to avoid like the plague. Now it came home to roost, a beady-eyed vulture digging into my shoulder.

"Security," Smythe was saying. "From this moment on, it's a part of your life. Twenty-four hours a day."

I kept my silence. I don't like vultures in any guise.

"Project 79 is *big*, Steve," Smythe went on. "So big it makes a piddling little effort out of what we did back in World War II with the Manhattan Project. To create the first atomic bomb this country gambled two billion dollars. We thought we'd never see a single-point effort greater than that. We were wrong. Right across the board this show is costing the taxpayers a cool fourteen billion dollars, and that's for a stretch of only eight years . . ."

What the devil could involve fourteen *billion?*

". . . and as an employee of the National Security Agency the 'need to know' rule is always in effect. *Always*," Smythe emphasized. "That goes for you and for everyone else. I'm trying to make it clear that we consider 79 to have implications that, as you of all people should know, may decide the path along which future sociological patterns will move. We believe this to be the single most important effort of its kind in this country. . . ."

Before he said another word, pieces began to fall into shape, shadows assumed substance, and I found conclusions assembling within my head. You can extrapolate certain points. If you're familiar with the science, with the engineering and the working elements, and most of all the potential, then you need only a few pieces to clarify the picture. Tom had just done that for me.

The potential of bio-cybernetics in the Soviet Union had been recognized to an extent greater than I'd ever realized. Once recognized, it had been evaluated.

But security was a patchwork. It couldn't hold back the floodwaters of original thought. No matter what nation was involved.

Tom Smythe studied my reaction to his words. He gestured impatiently, obviously displeased with my lack of fervent attention to his security dissertation. "You really aren't taking all this to heart, are you, Steve?"

I shrugged. "You know I'm not," I admitted. "That's hardly the most original or exciting plot you're spelling out, you know."

"Go on."

"I've never yet known of a security wall," I said, "that could keep out ideas, or that would prevent two men in different parts of the world, working on the same problem, from coming up with the same answers."

He waved a hand wearily to turn me off. "Hold it, hold it," he said with the first touch of exasperation I had ever seen in him. "If I've heard that bleating of the sacred cow once, I've heard it a thousand times. I've heard it from the young pups and I've heard it from the old and experienced scientific minds, and you all prattle the same blindness."

I felt the heat rising to my face. "Meaning exactly what?" I snapped.

"Meaning, my young Horatio guarding the bridge of science, you don't see the full picture."

"Don't patronize *me,* damn it," I said angrily.

"Oh, I'm not," Smythe said with a cutting tone to his voice. "But if you'll listen to yourself for just a moment, you'll see that you approach this from the viewpoint of classical science. And empirical conclusions are distressingly useless in my business." He shifted in his seat and, damn him, he *was* patronizing me! But there was no stopping him now.

"You ignore reality," he said coldly. "You ignore the fact that science is something developed by man and that it's a product of man and, also, that man is a very curious creature. Not simply curious in terms of seeking out the meaning of things, but curiouser and curiouser, like Alice in Wonderland, in respect to the way his fellowman behaves. And *why.*"

He sucked on a pipe gone cold, and wiped his mouth. "I don't know where these fairy tales come from," he said with a grimace. "Today's scientific achievements aren't the product of

[51]

someone piddling around in a laboratory. A half-million people are working for ten years so that two men can stumble about on that lifeless cinder we call the moon. That adds up to thirty billion dollars and fifteen hundred industries. But it's *not* your precious laboratory science—it's engineering, management, a chunk of the Gross National Product, and above all, it's competition between—"

He broke off his own words and looked at me carefully. "To you the atomic bomb is a matter of history, isn't it?" He didn't wait for an answer to a rhetorical question. "To you and your generation," he said slowly, "it all boils down to that moment in 1942 when we started the first chain reaction in a uranium pile." He scratched his cheek, again studying me. "It was a scientific effort, a great moment in history, eh? A shining pinnacle to what science can do. Isn't that it?"

I was furious with him. Smythe was at it again, patronage in his voice. "You're playing games," I said, fighting to keep my voice down. "Of course it was—"

His fist crashed against the table, overturning an ashtray and scattering ashes and butts all about him. He paid it no heed.

"Science, my eye!" he said. "The program to build the atomic bomb came about because some people got scared that Germany was going to build the damned thing first. European scientists who were scared out of their pants ran to Albert Einstein with the news that Germany had started to build a nuclear weapon. Einstein threw the weight of his reputation behind the group, and they kicked off a letter to Roosevelt. Science didn't have a triple-damned thing to do with it!

"Germany and the atom bomb added up to a Nazi world. Period. So we pulled out the plug and wrote a check for two billion dollars, and we whipped up the greatest technical and engineering package the world had ever seen. The gaseous-diffusion plants at Oak Ridge were thirty years ahead of their time, and *there* was the *real* miracle. The rest of it"—he gestured with disdain—"was so much fancy carpentry and machine-shop work. And if you want a capper to it, Horatio-at-the-Bridge, it's that the German scientists, as good as any, never even came

[52]

close to perfecting the bomb. The way they were going, it would have taken them a hundred years even to approach what they wanted."

An uncomfortable silence rose between us. Smythe deliberately let the silence continue, while he puffed his pipe into life.

"Let me bring you up to date," he said finally, his voice softened, under complete control again. "The Russians were decades behind us in 1945. Yet four years later they had built *their* first atomic bomb. They had a neat combination going for them—victory, a brilliant espionage system, and a mortal terror of the future. Being brutalized by Germany established that last attitude. So they ignored their backwardness. We had already proved the bomb could be built. Science could be put aside. Four years later they had the bomb. Because they *knew* they were starting out on the right track."

He brushed ashes from his jacket. "That's precisely the situation we face right now."

That caught me unawares. "How do you mean that?" I asked.

"We both know a great deal about the status of mathematics and cybernetics in the Soviet Union. Agreed?"

I nodded.

"I also know one hell of a lot more than do you about their history and their overall scientific structure and their rate of progress. I am impressed," he stressed. "What's more, I'm frightened by their potential. When I add up their political system and that potential, I get *very* frightened.

"That's why I reject your patent nonsense about separate investigations in different parts of the world leading inevitably to the same conclusion. We do not live in an empirical world. As a scientist you appear to forget the indispensable element in your picture that's so neatly tied up in red ribbons."

I didn't bother to ask him for an explanation. It was coming. I knew I was being read off, and Tom Smythe was doing it his own way and in his own sweet time. . . .

"You're forgetting the causative factor," he said. "You're

forgetting the compulsion, the motivation, the urgency. Before any scientist can discover new worlds and new truths, someone must foot the bill. Do you understand that?

"It's a political decision. It has damned little to do with science! Someone must convince the people in charge of the purse strings to let loose of a few billion dollars or rubles or whatever it is you use this week to pay the grocery bill."

He took a deep breath.

"We don't want to give the Soviets a really compelling reason to throw everything they have behind the kind of program we call Project 79."

He studied my expression. "That's where security comes in, why it's so vital to Project 79."

"But I've seen what they're doing in cybernetics!" I protested. "They're going full out—"

Smythe's hand gestured to cut me off. "No, they aren't," he broke in. "We don't believe they're even close to 79."

I stared at him.

"If the Russians had any idea," he continued, "despite everything they've done to date, that we have plunged on a maximum bio-cybernetics effort, a single program that costs more than what both countries have spent in this field over the past thirty years, well, that could tear it. They'd pick up the scent and go after this with everything in their power.

"We have an advantage—slight, perhaps even temporary—but still a real advantage. They don't know what we're doing, and we know as well as do they, perhaps better, just how frightening is their potential through a truly advanced cybernetics system. They're doing a great deal. But they're not doing everything they could do and they don't know just what we're up to.

"We want to keep it that way.

"Because this could just possibly be the deadliest weapon ever to hit the human race."

And I was going to be right in the middle of it all.

8

EVEN THROUGH A high-reaching late-afternoon haze, from ninety miles away I first saw the great mountain ridges of mid-Colorado, an imposing chain with peaks soaring twelve thousand feet high.

I looked down at a large lake just forward of the wing. Almost at the same moment the horizon tilted as the pilot altered course. "Lake Meredith," he said without waiting for the question. "We'll hold about 290 degrees for a while now." He glanced at the instrument panel before him and grunted in satisfaction. I watched the great peaks gaining substance as our speed sliced away distance. I couldn't remain still. I kept looking ahead of us, to the sides, down at the huge expanse of earth thousands of feet below.

I knew we were flying to Colorado Springs. But our specific destination remained clouded within a shrug and an enigmatic smile. Finally I quit pushing Tom Smythe for answers; after all, the government had provided us a beautiful twin-engine executive airplane, and it *was* a great trip. When the pilot, Derek Rathman, invited me into the right seat in the cockpit, I scrambled forward.

It was marvelous. After hours of floating gently through an ocean of haze and infrequent clouds, I was still captured with the sweeping vista of our flight. Being up front put an entirely new perspective on everything. I didn't realize just how glued I was to the panorama unfolding before us until Rathman chuckled. "Sort of gets you, doesn't it?" He smiled, sharing with me his own feelings.

"I've never seen anything like it," I admitted.

[55]

He gestured to indicate the approaching mountains. At first the ridges had been only a thin line against the sun's glare. Now I saw not a single skeletal backbone of mountains, but separate ranges and lines of peaks.

"See that big fellow? Over there?" Rathman pointed. "Pikes Peak."

I studied the outline of the great shape.

"Almost as high as the Matterhorn," Rathman added.

I looked at him in surprise. He laughed. "No one believes it at first," he said. "The ground, I mean, beneath us and up to the foothills of the Rockies. About five to six thousand feet above sea level. Makes these peaks seem smaller than they are. The Matterhorn is, um, only about five hundred feet higher than Pikes Peak."

I shook my head; I'd always thought of the Matterhorn in Switzerland as a colossal mountain, and—

"See over there?" Rathman pointed again. "Whole bunch higher than Pikes. There's Crestone, Shavano, Harvard, Elbert, Grays, just to name a few. That can be pretty rough country if you lose an engine."

He turned back to his instruments. I notched my belt tighter as the airplane rocked sharply. We were only fifty miles or so from the great line of giants. The winds tumbling from those jagged walls slapped at the airplane.

I glanced at the altimeter—10,500 feet. Rathman said that the ground came up to six thousand feet, which meant we were only a mile above the terrain immediately below. What had been a drab desert surface became an ocean with long stretching swells. Green appeared in a subtle shift of hues. Now, swiftly, the earth altered its texture until even the gentle swell of land vanished, replaced with a rich green carpet.

Clouds streamed from the peaks of the Rockies, spreading great shadows along the earth. Abruptly the surface changed again; I saw the corrosive action where water had torn down from the ridges. Gullies, beds of streams, buttes, gulches; hand carvings of nature sharp and distinct. Then there appeared the first waves of rich forests along the slopes, crowding the buttes.

Except for the red and brown of the buttes, all else remained a landscape of kaleidoscopic green.

Smythe came forward to the cockpit, standing between myself and Rathman, looking over our shoulders.

"Something, isn't it?" he said quietly.

I nodded.

"It gets better," he promised.

I caught my first sight of the Air Force Academy, a gleam of buildings along the south flanks of the Rampart Range. At this point the turbulence increased sharply. Rathman banked toward the ridges, into the sun, turning the Rampart slopes an opaque wall to the eye. Buffeted wildly, rushing into darkness. I found my hands clutching the seat armrests. Tom saw the involuntary gesture, and laughed.

Moments later, rolling out of the turn, I saw a small town along a road between high peaks. "Manitou Springs," Smythe said, pointing. "Look over there, Steve," he added quickly. "Garden of the Gods. One of the great sights of this country."

He was right. Rock formations brilliant in color, a surface writhing and twisting. The earth became flecked with gold and spattered with green, revealed tan and brown, blazed gloriously with red pinnacles that loomed obelisk-fashion from a tortured soil. A series of weirdly carved monuments flashed into sight, razored ridges flat along their sides. I stared at spires and angled formations, all rich with color, majestic to the eye.

"Deke, take her up a bit," Smythe said to Rathman, his words a sudden intrusion. Smythe glanced at me. "I want you to get the general layout of the area."

I nodded, waiting. "Okay," he said, pointing, "there's Manitou Springs, and Colorado Springs." The city slipped from view beneath the wings. "Ahead of us," Smythe gestured again, "Peterson Field. Main civil airport hereabouts; services the Academy as well as the local communities."

Smythe spoke to Rathman. "Come around wide, Deke, just south of the restricted area. Clearance okay?"

Rathman nodded. He motioned to a light blinking green on the instrument panel. "They've got us," he said.

[57]

"Good," Smythe replied, turning back to me. "See that area, Steve? Fort Carson; Army camp." An airfield appeared off the right wing. "That's Butts, an Army field. Farther south—see it? —is Bear Creek strip. It lies within the restricted area of Fort Carson. Extends to the west thirty miles or so."

Smythe pointed ahead of us. "Over there—see those buildings?" A community perched along the steep slope of a mountain expanded swiftly. "Take a good look," Smythe said with a quick smile. "Name of the place is Bear Creek. From now on, that's home."

I stared at him. *"Bear Creek?"*

He laughed, nodding. I looked down again, and things I hadn't seen before became evident to me. Now that I looked carefully, that is. Bear Creek—what a name!—was considerably larger than my casual first glance had indicated. Many of the buildings were larger than I expected for a town stuck precariously on the flank of a mountain. And then I noticed the single wide, well-paved road that led through a narrow gorge, along precipitous cliff walls. And the large, mysterious paved ovals both within the town and along its entrances.

"What are those?" I asked. "Those wide areas, I mean. From the looks of them they're large enough to be helicopter pads."

"Right the first time," Smythe replied.

I looked at him in surprise. "Helicopter pads? Out here in the middle of nowhere?"

Smythe gestured as Rathman brought us around in a steep, clawing turn, uncomfortably close to the mountain slopes. "That's not the middle of nowhere, Steve," Smythe said. "That's an iceberg community."

I blinked my eyes, and he laughed. "Most of it isn't visible," he added.

More pieces began to fit. "And Project 79—"

He glanced down. "You can't see it," he said. "It's inside that mountain."

Inside that mountain . . . Suddenly I couldn't wait to get on the ground.

A town I never knew existed. Bear Creek, incongruous in name, startling in appearance. Eight years ago it didn't exist. It had been hammered not only against the flanks of the mountain, ten miles due south of Pikes Peak, but well *into* the solid rock itself. A town with beautiful homes and modern shopping centers, with a gleaming new hospital, theaters, excellent restaurants, recreational facilities. And helicopter landing pads. I mustn't forget those. Or the false building entrances that extended into huge tunnels that bored deeply within the mountain and then angled off to . . . well, to where Project 79 was set up. I hadn't yet seen the complex, although by now curiosity was gnawing uncomfortably at what little patience I retained.

"But wherever did you get the name Bear Creek?" I protested, looking at the tree-lined streets and imposing buildings as Smythe drove us through the town. "That's rather odd for a place like this, isn't it?"

Smythe shook his head, enjoying himself. "Not at all. People do get mail here, and they refer to the town—you can't blot out human nature, Steve. The countryside around here is filled with communities with similar names."

"Such as?" I demanded.

"Cotopaxi, Texas Creek, Silver Cliff, Black Forest, Cripple Creek, Buffalo Creek, Shawnee, Shaffers Crossing—"

"Enough, enough," I broke in. "So we're saturated with the Old West. Okay. Now, when do we stop playing games and get down to business? I want to see the Project, for Christ's sake!"

He chuckled. "You'll have to be patient for at least another day. First thing tomorrow morning we'll run you through security, and—"

"Security!" I shouted.

He raised one thick eyebrow. "Why should that surprise you so much?" he sid. "If I recall, we already went around and around on that point."

"Sure we did," I said, still angry. "But you've had more than enough time to run your checks and—"

[59]

"Back up," he interrupted, waving his hand at me. "This hasn't anything to do with a security *check*, Steve."

I waited.

"It's to provide you with the security—ah, well, call them credentials," he continued. "The credentials that will let you get into the Project. It's an automatic system and it's operated wholly by the computer. Untouched by human hands, and that sort of thing. You must be processed for it. We'll take you to the hospital first thing in the morning."

"Hospital? What are you talking about, Tom?"

He turned into the driveway leading through a modern apartment complex. "You'll see in the morning," he said, ending further conversation on the subject.

I glared at him and leaned back in the seat. I gestured at the buildings about us. "What's this place?"

Smythe eased into a parking stall and cut the engine. "Why," he said with mock surprise, "this is where you live."

As the crow flies, Colorado Springs, with its famed Broadmoor Hotel, lay exactly fifteen miles from the community with the incongruous name of Bear Creek. But you couldn't drive there as the crow flew—you had to drive south along a road that wasn't even on the map, and pick up the secondary highway that circled around the base of the mountain before starting to the north, a trip of about twenty-five miles. I found I didn't mind the circuitous route, after all. Not in this country, anyway. No matter where you went you were surrounded with majestic, eye-stopping scenery.

Denver lay 150 miles almost due north of Colorado Springs, a beautiful drive along Highway 87, which eased past the Air Force Academy, and wound through ranches and resort areas. Tom indicated that every now and then I would travel to Denver, where the University carried on advanced research programs in cybernetics. I was to learn that the presence of that research activity was more important than the work they did; it had been established, Tom explained, to justify, publicly, at least, the presence in the area of so many scientists.

[60]

In fact, more than the physical availability of a mountain into which engineers had blasted to create the working center for Project 79 dictated the selection of this particular area. Fort Carson, with advanced military electronics research its predominant activity, although it maintained a training center for Army mountain and ski troops, also justified the presence of scientists, technicians, and specialists, and was a perfect routing point for the traffic that moved into and from Project 79. There was also the Air Force Academy to the north, with all *its* advanced electronic and computer facilities. Above all else, however, there did exist—and in full public knowledge—one of the greatest computer-operations centers in the world, close to Manitou Springs.

Deep within Cheyenne Mountain, balanced on massive springs cushioning multistory steel structures, was NORAD—a complex facility, invisible to the eye, that contained the headquarters of the North American Air Defense Command. NORAD was also the electronic nerve center for all space tracking and surveillance systems maintained by the United States throughout the world. Its great tunnels were guarded with complex, foot-thick steel doors that could *snap* closed by command or when they were triggered by radioactive detectors or blast sensors. NORAD, linked electronically to tracking and surveillance sites, to other command centers (including the White House), to always-airborne emergency control centers, to robot satellites, was one of the miracles of modern technology.

When they had carved the NORAD headquarters out of the granite of Cheyenne Mountain, without making any secret of the massive operation, they were able to cloak effectively a parallel effort that, well to the south, would become the secret facility within another mountain for Project 79.

I began to find a grudging admiration for the security-conscious mind. Things *did* fit beautifully. Because NORAD was essentially a computer operation—without the capability of digital computers it could never have functioned as had been intended. And that meant cybernetics technicians by the hundreds, all of whom proved a perfect smokescreen for what went on near a modern community with the Old West name of Bear Creek.

They did everything but hang me on a meat-hook to dry out under infrared lamps. When Tom Smythe told me I would go through a medical security processing, he meant what he said. Medical processing for security controls within Project 79 included exhaustive medical examination and then the recording of essential elements of the body and the physical makeup that are virtually impossible to duplicate in another individual.

They took my fingerprints and charted every scar on my body and made an X-ray record of everything I had ever broken. They recorded my retinal patterns, since these differ in each human being as much as fingerprints vary from one person to another. They measured my body mass, and despite the passage of years to come and the inevitable alterations in physiological signature, a computer would be able to examine me in like manner and extrapolate certain conditions to which my body would adhere almost religiously—if restrictive blind development can be so typed, which I was assured it could be. They recorded my voice and broke it down into a dozen identifiable characteristics. They made records of my calcium content, breakdown of elements in the blood, and other things I don't even want to remember.

The headshrinkers recorded my brain activity, established a meticulously sensitive record of alpha-wave patterns, measured electrical generation, and wrapped me up into a neat package of identifiable sensitivity. At any time in the future these "signature characteristics" could be rechecked—erasing all doubt as to the identification of any individual no matter what ID cards he carried or who he claimed to be. This was a medical screening to end all screenings—and they convinced me that no degree of skill or artfulness could ever deceive this battery of physiological watchdogs.

I hated to admit it, even to myself.

I *was* impressed.

The next morning, admitted by the complex security system, I walked into the most colossal cybernetics complex that existed anywhere in the world.

I felt about as big as my thumb.

Project 79, unknown to the outside world, had been under way for more than ten years. Its systems were twenty years in the future. And all this time they had been preparing, had been striving to reach a point where they might be able to bring a quiescent electronic giant to life.

They were almost ready.

Book Two

9

THEY CALLED ME the Baby-Sitter.

Officially I held the position of Chief Programmer. I felt a sense of guilt about the title, as if I were laying false claim to the labors of others. Thousands of skilled cybernetics specialists had spent years of intensive programming so that my particular talents could be endowed with meaning.

It would be my task to establish communication between human subjects and the bio-cybernetics complex we called Project 79.

Between a brain created by God and that shaped by man.

We weren't yet ready for the true bio-cybernetics program. That remained in its experimental stages. At the moment we communicated with 79, the computer "brain," through standard programming. This met the requirements for the continuous data input for 79's memory cells, while enabling us to determine the guidelines for more advanced efforts.

As the day-to-day working parameters of 79 emerged from the input and testing activities, we prepared for the first stages of direct bionics communication. It was the sort of effort where, to reach the heart of the onion, first you peel away—gingerly—one thin layer after another. Not a scientist among us could claim honestly to comprehend the fine thread that might run between the miracle that is the human brain . . . and a multibillion-dollar computer complex that could, through a single error, become the first multibillion dollar paranoid.

I tried not only carefully, but almost with desperation, to be certain I understood fully every move we made, every step we took. I knew that the slightest error on my part could introduce potentially disastrous consequences. It was essential that I know every aspect, every element of what we were doing. Before I could integrate myself as a reliable facet of the program, I had first to understand the sheer physical structure and organization within which Project 79 came to be, and the more I learned of the vast cybernetics effort, the more meaningful became Tom Smythe's tirade that great scientific accomplishments inevitably are handmaidens to political decisions and engineering realities.

When the demolition crews ended their task of creating great cathedral-like spaces linked through tunnels to the outside world, the true work on Project 79 had only begun. Fortunately, there was the experience within Cheyenne Mountain from which engineers could draw, and Project 79 went ahead with minimum difficulty. As quickly as the initial team departed, new groups swarmed in to set up the physical structure that would house the cybernetics complex. A vast base construction —structural components, power and communications lines, living and working quarters, all the prosaic elements from which great projects are drawn—preceded the technicians and the scientists.

The complex that constituted Project 79, every structure, entire buildings in themselves, balanced upon huge coil springs. In the event—not as unlikely as computerized programs would lead us to believe—that a nuclear war rattled the nation, the springs would ease the shock of a nuclear blast even against the exterior of the mountain containing the cybernetics complex. Those facilities of especial sensitivity—the memory cells, internal communications lines, nuclear-power systems, the electronic sinew of the Project—all these received added protection through massive hydraulic pistons, shock absorbers to dampen the effects of spring rebound.

Because the investment in Project 79 represented not only dollars, but time, brainpower, and a critical slice of the future, every precaution possible became ingrained within its final shape. In effect the cybernetics complex was established on the basis that it must withstand the effects of violent natural and/or man-induced cataclysms. The coil-spring foundations and hydraulic pistons were only one element of that "design for disaster" philosophy. Each structure of the complex was sheathed within a great cubicle of steel plate, and then the steel plate, down to the smallest pinhole or weld seam, was itself sealed. We were, in essence, an electronic entity. A nuclear blast produces among its effects an "electromagnetic pulse," an electrical shock wave of enormous energy yield. Were that electromagnetic pulse to sweep within the complex that made up Project 79, then in less time than requires telling, we could suffer irreparable damage. For this same reason, grounding cables linked together every building and facility. Additional protection was effected by copper-edging every door and passageway. In the critical areas massive steel blast doors in pairs prevented the entry of unauthorized personnel.

Electronic and mechanical sensors throughout the complex, and along the surface of the mountain itself, sniffed out sudden changes in air pressure, temperature, and the presence of radioactivity. With an excess sensed in any of these areas, the complex proper was sealed automatically against even a stray speck of dust. Engineers utilized every protective device of the NORAD complex; both areas, for example, received their water supply from Colorado Springs. Water input, as well as air, received constant filtering, purification, and monitoring for content.

The heart of the cybernetics complex—the "brain"—comprised a physical space no larger than that of a small apartment. Most people envisioned a great computer system as being the size of an entire apartment building. But there's no reason to suffer such unwieldy size. Bulkiness, complexity, and excessive components destroy effectiveness. In the old days of vacuum tubes, that was unavoidable. With solid-state components, microsubminaturization, and closed force fields, mircosize was the direction in which we moved. The core of 79 was thus far smaller physically than one might expect. But there were more elements within it than in an old vacuum-tube computer large enough to fill the entire Pentagon.

Of Project 79 a saying was born: *If you can see it, it's too big.*

After all, nature manages to pack more than ten billion neurons, sensors, and all the associated blood-flow systems and supporting mechanisms of the human brain into a unit of only eighty cubic inches. Large size becomes wasteful and self-defeating.

The dinosaur is long gone, but the cockroach is still around.

The entire entity of Project 79 occupied a cubic volume equal to that of a twenty-story building. This was distributed outward from the spherical core along tunnels to distant chambers and the facilities that made up the ancillary systems of the complex.

The computer proper—the brain—occupied what is best described as a spherical entity. Extending outward in all directions were multilayered shells of the sphere, like a small ball surrounded by ever larger and thicker spherical shells around the core. This provided, to the entire system, the element of maximum possible compactness consistent with separation of different elements.

Directly beneath the cybernetics core, surrounded by massive steel-reinforced concrete with sandwiched layers of thick lead, was the most advanced power source yet developed. The nuclear power system of twin breeder reactors, with its integral supply of raw uranium processed into feeder rods and control elements, was sealed within elaborate security controls. No man could enter the reactor area without the permission, specifically, *of the computer itself.*

That shook me when I first ran into it. The more I thought of the system, the more unreasonable became the idea. There's such a thing as carrying security too far.

From the beginning of Project 79 every effort was made to establish the computer as self-supporting within the limitations of restrictive mobility and artificial intelligence. The degree of that intelligence didn't concern its designers, since there was specified a designated area of self-responsibility and maintenance. In effect the intention was to assure that the system knew how to button its own pants.

The concept for self-functioning for 79 pursued, not abstract thought, but logical and meaningful reactions to problems and, subsequently, logical actions to accomplish their solution. In this respect we implemented the intellectual decision with the capacity of limited physical response.

This inherent capability of 79 meant that the computer could, when necessary, reject a single solution to a problem. It did this by peering into its own future requirements to ponder a multiplicity of choices. In essence, 79 could make a selection based on the "human prerogative" of choosing the lesser of two evils. It did just this in respect to its own caretaking.

Since 79 enjoyed the benefits of such deduction—I insist this is reasoning—there existed minimal difficulties in permitting the machine to attend to its "sustenance and repair." Not only how to button its pants, but to replace buttons that had broken off. The breeder reactor was an excellent example. If 79 required additional power to operate simultaneously an unusually large number of subsystems, or to activate new systems, or even to increase the cooling capacity of its components, it sensed this need through the instruments located throughout its structure. It judged also the specific quantity of its power requirements, and transmitted this data to its mechanical nerve center—the functions that are performed for the human body by the autonomic centers of the brain. That is, the nonconscious controls of body temperature, rate of digestion, rate of respiration, and so forth. In a sense, the mechanical nerve center of 79 was autonomic. After all, the computer did respond to deficiencies or requirements of its system, and trying to draw a hard line between the flesh system and the electronic-mechanical one becomes a classic instance of splitting semantic hairs.

It required only seconds for 79 to diagnose a problem and to institute corrective action. Robot devices within the complex could switch into any area of the system. They would jolt a failed module with an electrical charge that unplugged the unit. Robot clamps removed it from place, slid in the new module, and jolted the replacement to lock the plug-in. Immediately the maintenance center tested the unit, evaluated its performance, and commanded the robot servo-units to return to standby.

Ever since the assembly of 79 had begun, thousands of plug-in modules had been manufactured and stored where they could be handled by the servomechanisms of the cybernetics complex. Thus 79 was diagnostician, doctor, and surgeon all at the same time. Those parts removed from the system for improper assembly or parts failure were carried to a disposal department where, in effect, 79 rejected the faulty unit.

It didn't take long for the staff psychologists to mark a red flag on the operations board of 79's disposal and repair shops. As predicted, the technicians there became sullen, and finally vented their emotions in destructive rage. In effect they wanted to kick in the teeth of the machine that required them only to pick up the rejected modules of the system. No one wants to be a garbage man for a superbrain that couldn't care less.

Within three or four years, we predicted, working only with the raw ingredients of its mechanical and electronic systems, 79 would be almost wholly free of human servicing requirements. Beyond that? Well, it was only a matter of time and mechanics for such a system to be linked with automated factories so that it could produce its own parts, have the materials delivered, and function *without* human counsel or assistance.

I keep returning to the unique security system built into the great mountainous complex of Project 79. Because of the element of human failure, the decision had been made early in the program to entrust the computer itself with a major portion of its own security defenses. This was one area where I fell immediately into conflict with the project heads—including Tom Smythe.

Soon after I arrived I reviewed the many projects already under way with 79. I was astonished to discover that even as Chief Programmer I was refused access to several working studies—on the grounds that I lacked the all-important "need to know" of the work under way. In particular, a program identified only as DOD 6194—against which I would stumble more than once in the coming months—brought on heated words. I insisted that as Chief Programmer I *must* be cognizant of any effort involving 79; otherwise there could exist interference of which I knew nothing, and that could affect the accuracy of my own work.

But it was a stone wall I couldn't tear down or go over. The decision on this fracturing of knowledge, Smythe told me, had the full backing of the White House.

I insisted that putting Project 79 in charge of its own security was a grave error. There is a random factor in the human being —total unpredictability is a precious asset to *Homo sapiens*— that could never be included within the rationalization capabilities of *any* computer. Obviously, every possible element of the computer should be utilized for the purposes of its own security. But the bulk of that responsibility?

Jesus, no!

You might as well give a six-year-old a loaded .38 and tell him to defend the household. He'll never do the job because he can't possibly recognize the many potential dangers.

Notwithstanding my arguments, the security system had been programmed long before my arrival, and I couldn't do anything about it. I was more concerned with the computer's internal security system developing electronic suspicions to the extent that it would interfere with my work than I was about skulking saboteurs trying to muck up the works. Because 79's security consciousness was a constant thorn in my side.

No human being could penetrate the critical areas of 79 without being passed through by the computer itself. This is where the personal identifications programs, the medical processing, came into use. Let's say I wanted to reach the subsystem within the complex where incoming voltage was broken down to the specific values required to operate Quadrant 4A96 of the memory cells. Before I could enter the area, I had to program the request, identify all personnel involved, justify their presence, and estimate the time required for the survey and, if necessary, alterations to the system. We couldn't move until 79 evaluated all aspects of the request and *then* signified entry clearance.

If we listed among the technical crew to enter Quadrant 4A96 a janitor, for example, 79 would deny permission for that man to penetrate the Quadrant. And 79 had the means to enforce that denial.

A lethal means.

Before he could reach the Quadrant the man must pass through a single-file corridor where 79 ran its security check. Computer systems examined fingerprints, ID plates, and retinal pattern. If the intruder reached this far, he dared not attempt further passage. Alarms went off immediately, and automatic systems sealed off the area to permit human security forces to apprehend and remove the intruder. But if the intruder decided to rush ahead, he still must force the restricting corridor. He might have explosives, of course, but if he moved more than six feet in either direction the entire corridor came alive—with death.

Laser beams crisscrossed the corridor in a pattern no human being could have survived.

Sometimes, thinking about these elaborate computer systems, you couldn't help wondering who was telling whom what to do.

10

EVER SINCE ELECTRONIC computers were first spawned, cyberneticists have stood off alarmists decrying man's apparent willingness to delegate human responsibilities to artificial brains. The controversy, at times quite heated, revolves about questionable intrinsic responsibilities and a semantics morass. First to be argued was the degree of intelligence in the advanced cybernetics system. Second, to confound the first, there were a thousand shouted theories as to just *what* was intelligence. And, finally, there loomed the question of whether man would, or even *could,* create an artificial entity superior to himself.

Except for coffee klatsches at which we vented our theories and counterarguments these questions, in respect to Project 79, were academic. For the very good reason that we had no intention of creating a catch-all, do-anything intelligence. 79 could not tap-dance or sing *Madama Butterfly* or do possibly a million other things. It couldn't, and if it really had any degree of intelligence I'm quite certain it wouldn't bother.

Its sole justification was to *think.*

The idea that man must always enjoy a native superiority to the computer—the superiority called *hunch*—was so much rubbish. In the area so cherished both by the humanists and the cyberneticists, the famed neurophysiologist Professor W. G. Walter sounded what must have seemed heresy to the humanists. "What would really be useful," claimed the professor, "is a sort of hunch generator. The hunch capacity of the mortal doctor or scientist is just being strained to the breaking point; there are too much data to examine and analyze for each patient. The robot could be fed this data and produce for us some diagnostic hunch based on the patient's pulse rate, age, and electrocardiogram."

Heresy.

Nevertheless, quite true.

A *hunch* is an element of human thought, a capacity of intelligence. It is not mystical. Those who misunderstood cybernetics cloaked the mental activity we call hunch with such mysticism, as if it were a holy property reserved only for the mind of man.

Well, perhaps not heresy. But certainly nonsense.

The computer represents the augmentation of human brain power. It's as simple as that. Essentially it achieves this goal through the compression of time, making up, as an extension of man's intellect, for the distressingly brief number of years during which man is intellectually productive.

A hunch is admissive of an *inferiority* in data. In lieu of final objective data, a man shrugs his shoulders, and guesses. It's an intellectual flip of the coin, no matter how refined the process.

And the hunch will be with us for a long time to come because *there will always be a shortage of data*. So the hunch is for the machine, as well as for man, an integral element of intellectual conduct.

That's why Project 79 had a Heuristics Division, under the able direction of Dr. Selig Albracht. Heuristics? In cybernetics language this is the ability to "play hunches." Where there wasn't a specific, hard solution to a problem, heuristics considered every factor conceivable that affected the problem, and permitted you to make the best of what might be just a bad bargain of data. Because of the computer's vast memory, its ability to cross-check and cross-feed, and to forget nothing it knew, all within the span of seconds, it gave you a fourteen-karat hunch with which to commit yourself.

Early in the developing science of cybernetics, the conclusion was drawn that the artificial brain enjoyed its greatest potential if it were patterned, physically, after the structure of the human brain. This conclusion was another element of intense controversy, for, with all its *apparent* advantages, the so-called nerve-net system inevitably must produce a machine of crippling bulk and complexity.

The initial attempts to create a realistic artificial intelligence sounded a call for assistance from other sciences. One of these, with which I was to become deeply involved, was the burgeoning field of bionics.

Which interested me personally as well as involved my work.

The liaison assigned to my office from the Project 79 Bionics Division was sensationally packaged. Her name was Kin Renée Michele, and there were times when I found it difficult to concentrate upon our work together in bionics. Both the word and Kim's proximity impressed upon me ideas of a more direct biological nature than called for in our work. Somewhat unscientifically, Kim hit me with all the effect of an avalanche. Unfortunately for my own biological urges, Kim never mixed immediate business with potential pleasure. . . .

Dr. Howard Vollmer rested secure in his ivory tower as the world's leading bionics scientist. As the director of the Bionics Division of Project 79, he worked closely with my office. No, that's not quite accurate. *We* worked closely with *his* division. I took advantage of every opportunity to spend time with Dr. Vollmer. The elderly scientist was more than brilliant; he was singular in his knowledge to make of bionics a meaningful force in cybernetics. There was another reason. Kim Michele usually was present during Vollmer's meetings with what he insensitively called "oafish young scientists."

Dr. Vollmer rarely was voluble; when those infrequent occasions came to pass they were memorable not only for their duration but also for Vollmer's ability to strike at the heart of a situation. I came away from one of our early meetings with the hope for more.

"In essence, Mr. Rand," Dr. Vollmer had begun after making a steeple of his fingertips and peering owlishly at me, "we are involved here in a think factory. Umm, yes, that expression is applicable. A think factory. Um-hum . . . but this demands that we, as much as our electronic playmates, must think. Eh? We have a sense of, umm, free-wheeling programming." He blinked rapidly at me, going through a series of rubbery facial expressions.

I started to reply but decided instead to make a careful study of the physical attributes of Kim. I had the distinct impression that Dr. Vollmer was aware of his fearsome reputation. Or perhaps he wasn't and just didn't care.

"What we are attempting in Project 79, Mr. Rand, and especially with your communications with the computer, when the time is right, is to enter the future without stumbling. We must equip the human race—um, yes, that is it concisely. To arm, prepare, equip the race with the means to think and to anticipate so swiftly that when an event other than that of our own making directly concerns us, possibly even our survival, we need not be caught, as in the popular idiom, flatfooted."

For several moments, immersed in a train of thought, he wandered away. Immediately I began some calculations of my own, my eyes openly admiring Kim's figure. Wonderful, just wonderful what she did to that blouse. . . . Obviously she received the message of my thoughtless staring, for I received a sudden glare and a delightful blush.

Vollmer went right on. "We're really on a threshold, you know," he said with a careful look at me. "It may prove epochal if we're successful."

"I know—"

He motioned me to silence. *He* had the floor, and my place was to sit at his feet, and listen.

"We are creating a brain, Mr. Rand. *The* brain. We are building and shaping blocks of neurons. And though I detest specious contests with my colleagues, you will of course encounter their fallacious arguments—with which I am unconcerned. Therefore, having the advantage of the bionics approach, you will better thread you way through the inevitable conflicts of any program in its making."

[78]

Having, in his own mind, demolished his colleagues, he proceeded in the full confidence to which he was so accustomed.

"Where was I? Um, yes; we have an intelligence. You will note that I do not refer to an artificial intelligence?" I had noted that—immediately, in fact. "I do not call this an artificial intelligence, Mr. Rand," he continued, "because there is nothing artificial in nature. There is only rearrangement. Therefore"—he said this as a pronouncement—"we have an intelligence. . . .

"Man has been trapped within a cranial prison for a hundred thousand years. Too long, too long, I daresay. Do you know that your brain is no larger, no more capable than that of some distant ancestor who ate the fleas from his mate's hide while they both squatted miserably in some cave? It is time for a change; it is long overdue for a change."

His hand slapped sharply against his desk. "The only measure of intelligence," he said slowly, "is determined by what you do with that intelligence. Well, we are doing something. Now, physically, Mr. Rand, our 79 is a reproduction, umm, in only a dim sense, I suppose, of the biological nervous system. Kim, here," offhandedly he waved at her, "assures me that through your office we may have extraordinarily intimate communication with that system. Umm, kaff?"

What the devil do you answer to "umm, kaff"? I never did respond; Dr. Vollmer rattled on without further pause.

In truth, Dr. Vollmer's preoccupation accented the need for understanding, clearly and concisely, just what we were to attempt. This was my task—to comprehend the whole and to work with it to produce meaningful man-to-machine communications. In so doing, I would be neither architect nor mason.

I was a communicator.

Baby-Sitter.

Many of the scientists with whom I worked exhibited insatiable greed in their search for absence of size. Halted finally even with microminiaturization, they turned to the nuclear physicists about them blandly to request working blocks of superdense matter within which nuclear structure was condensed. And *that* was quite a request! In effect they were being asked to duplicate the conditions within stars where matter is compressed to densities most of us could never imagine.

Dr. Vollmer's staff worked not only with manipulated electronic neurons but also with experimental force blocks of disturbed and rearranged atoms. Wildly violent forces were restrained within fields of electromagnetic energy. Deep within the interior of such laboratories, shielded by massive steel walls . . . I tried to envision an artificial intelligence groping for comprehension of its own existence. An intelligence of unknown capacity, of atoms compressed, stripped of their electrons, where subnuclear forces perform neural functions of sorting, comparing, rejecting, seeking, weighing, analyzing, computing . . . a flickering of raw intelligence among and within living spaces of neurons. A world forever beyond the world of men where the elemental matter of the universe works for man.

Connected, linked, tied in, communicating with us . . . the core of 79. *Which on the basis of available information could make meaningful decisions.*

This is what I sought to bring forth from the entity created by so many others. A device—not an artificial device, as Dr. Vollmer insisted, but one in which the basic building blocks of matter were rearranged by man—that could perform the functions of deductions, that would be capable of achieving a decision-making capability so akin to that of the skilled mind that it would be virtually impossible to distinguish one from the other.

If we could hurdle the critical moments of bringing 79 to life, if we could impart to the man-created brain awareness and its first glimmerings of comprehension . . . if we could do this without stumbling, then we would be at the final moment, what is so often referred to as "that moment of truth."

When a mind, man or machine, is involved in seeking the solution to a problem, that mind must know when the problem is solved.

You must know when to stop.

The mind, ours or "theirs," must have some criterion for

knowing it is moving in the right direction, and when it is time to stop moving.

When it does this . . .

Then that mind exercises judgment.

And the gap between man and what he has created is no more.

11

YOUNG, BLOND, BEAUTIFUL.

Add to this stunning legs, the refreshing virtues of inviting lips and golden hair, and you came up with Barbara.

That wasn't all.

She was frankly eager to share everything she had with me.

But there was a complication. . . .

Kim also was beautiful. *Very* beautiful.

She was brunette, her hair long and eye-catching. She was young and breathlessly alive. When she walked into a room, her entrance commanded your attention.

But Kim Renée Michele had far more than classical beauty.

She was also the most brilliant woman I had ever known.

And I was in love with her.

That was one of the complications. There were more. Kim worked with me, as I'd mentioned, on the bionics applications of Project 79, as the indispensable assistant to crotchety old Dr. Vollmer. Her specialties meant our working together for long hours of the day and often well into the night. The more I was with Kim, the more deeply I fell in love with her.

I was almost convinced the feelings were mutual. Unhappily for my desires, physical as well as emotional, Kim maintained tight reins on her own feelings. And despite her affection for me, she believed that I was something of a "self-centered, overbearing egotist." Giving me what I wanted desperately with and from her, she believed, would be strictly to her disadvantage. Notwithstanding these problems, I saw much of Kim not only during our working hours together, but also afterward. Except that I had to observe the rules *she* established for that relationship. If I hadn't loved the girl as much as I did I would have told her to go to hell. That was a nice gesture but I kept it to myself and I knew I couldn't do it.

Kim drove me out of my mind.

Barbara took me to bed.

      As part of my contract, Project 79 provided me with an expansive and unique apartment in the modern complex nestled within Bear Creek. Six rooms that would have done credit to the character who designs those luxury pads for *Playboy*. The first time I saw the apartment, I found myself speechless. Nothing had been left out, and even my favorite possessions—which I had marked for shipment before I left the east coast for Colorado—were waiting for me. The effect was much the same as if personal valets and butlers had prepared my new home to be completely ready for my appearance.

It was all there. Deep-carpeted opulence overstates the decor, but it felt that way to me—and I accepted with open arms the huge couch and easy chairs, the fireplace in both the living room and bedroom, and, wonder of wonders, a bathroom almost as large as the bedroom I'd known as a youngster. Automated devices in the kitchen made me feel almost as if I were an intruder, but it certainly eased a task I'd always detested—preparing my own meals. There's good fortune to be found in so unique an arrangement as I'd been provided with—my dates thought the kitchen was great, and before long an evening at home became an accepted pattern of my social life. With a girl who could cook, of course.

Invariably there's a specific method to government madness; my apartment, luxurious and comfortable though it was, proved no exception to the rule. I had six rooms in the apartment, but quickly discovered that only four were for living. The remaining two were for homework. One was, I admit, fitted out superbly as an office. The other lacked any real taste; its personal furnishings were Spartan, and instead of the deep wine and ebony hues that characterized the remainder of the apartment one faced a dazzling glow from glass-sheet-paneled fluorescents buried within the ceiling.

Within that room, always kept locked whenever I was absent from the apartment, was a small but intricate satellite computer—an electronic extension that permitted me direct working contact with almost any element of 79 itself. Closed-circuit television scanners and receivers could link me visually as well as with audio to the key offices of the Project, a feature to which I took at once. Tom Smythe and the Project officials weren't passing up any bets. They didn't want any of the key scientists coming up with a brainstorm and not being able to do something with their sudden thoughts. Satellite computers in the apartments or homes of the top elements of the Project were, of course, expensive—but the results proved worth far more than the dollar costs involved.

It would be less than the truth to say that I was wholly enchanted with having a computer separated from my bedroom by no more than a thin wall. I was reminded constantly that I was never more than a few moments away from my work.

There were times when I found it convenient to forget about Project 79. I could always lock the door to the computer room; and I never found it difficult, especially when I was aided by the willing presence of a young and lithe female creature, to ignore the damned thing altogether.

Except, that is, with Kim.

I had looked forward to a long weekend with her. We spent a full Saturday, starting out at four in the morning, in the mountains. A stream that filled a wide, deep pool gave me the chance to catch some plump mountain trout. Kim did well by herself, adding two beauties to the catch we brought back to my apartment. What could have been better? A wonderful day off in the hills, back in the late afternoon, a beautiful girl anxious to prove her skill with fresh-caught trout . . . and all the trappings that help to make up what should have been *the* romantic evening. It certainly started off well enough.

After dinner, I set up a long-playing stereo tape. Four hours of everything from the 101 Strings to Percy Faith, all smooth and a soothing background. Kim had a preference for brandy Alexanders, and I pride myself on my skill at my bar, with our drinks just strong enough to bring on a pleasant, inhibition-relaxing glow. Soft lights, a deep carpet and pillows before the fireplace.

If I had written the script for getting closer to my girl, I couldn't have done any better. With my arm around Kim and her head nestled against my shoulder, I was content with the world. Tomorrow was Sunday; the hours belonged to us. It was perfect.

Kim wanted to talk.

I tried to stop the exchange before it could get really started. Kim, I swore, *never* left her work. I knew how she felt, but, damn it, there *are* times—! The third time I tried to kiss her, she slipped away from me and demanded that I refill her drink. I could recognize the mood in her. And when she demanded from me full attention, it was difficult to refuse her. Tonight, I learned quickly, was simply the culmination of something that had been disturbing her for a long time. I recognized the inevitable, turned on a few lamps, and in my mind kissed good-by to the romantic evening I had anticipated.

It was something that Dr. Howard Vollmer had said. During our first meeting the elderly scientist plainly had given me a message. His words were, essentially, a reaffirmation of the fact that all of us in Project 79 were pursued always by an invisible presence. It was this unsettling and persistent gnawing at the mind that so obviously disturbed Kim. But we all lived with it; we all bore the cross of the "new" sciences.

For a long time men of science had known there were questions that no longer could be avoided. Questions that evaluated the consequences of what we were all doing. Questions demanding that one heed the tiny voice that shrilled from the back of the mind. Scientists were aware of this collective conscience, I suppose, but not until the first mushroom cloud rose did they say what they thought.

What is it that we create?

The scientists who formed a body of protest before the atomic dawn seared Hiroshima gave birth to a vocal element of their sacred assembly. Call it conscience, insight, or plain everyday concern for what their work would do to others. No matter what you called it, it was there.

It came to roost in the hollow chambers deep within the mountain where we tinkered with some unimaginable Tomorrow. It disturbed us; it followed us home; it crawled into sleep with us. It was here, this same night, standing between myself and Kim.

She sipped from her glass, looking carefully at me. "Do you remember, Steve," she asked, "what Dr. Vollmer said to you that first time you and he talked together?"

I nodded. "I remember. His exact words were, 'We have an intelligence.' Why?"

"What else did he say, Steve?"

I put down my drink and glared at her. "I really wasn't looking forward to this kind of evening, Kim," I said testily.

"Please, Steve." That did it; I knew I was hooked. I took a long pull from my glass and reached for a cigarette.

"Well, the old man said that he didn't consider 79 to be an artificial intelligence," I began. "Right so far?"

She nodded, and I went on. "He claims there is really nothing artificial in nature. Only rearrangement. All man can do," I said, "is to rearrange what we find lying about us. On that basis, Vollmer claims, in 79 we have, not an artificial entity, an electronic mimic, but an intelligence."

"How did all that strike you?" She reached out for the cigarette I'd just lit.

I shrugged. "He hit home, I suppose," I said. I looked up at her. "What's this all about, Kim? You act as if you're trying to lead me to a conclusion you've already drawn. Is that it?"

She put her glass down slowly and turned to look into the

[86]

fireplace. "Do you remember when he said—I think I'm quoting him properly—that, 'It is time for a change; it is long overdue for a change'?"

"Sure, I remember. So what?"

Kim seemed to shudder as she turned back to me. "That's what disturbs me so much, Steve. That's what makes me question what we're doing, why I'm so—so, well, upset. Does Dr. Vollmer really mean change?

"Or does he really mean *replacement?*"

Often we sat alone and brooded over the thoughts. And then, disturbed by the shadows, we sought out the common meeting ground of verbal contest, where we might toss out our individual concepts to be collectively examined. When we did this, at least we shared the conscience that seemed to affect us all.

There were many aspects of our work where we lacked definitions acceptable even to small groups working on the same research problem. Strictly on the basis of the functioning of the electronic brain, for example—and this is a point Kim and I argued violently—there was no separation of 79 into periods of consciousness or unconsciousness.

And when Kim threw herself into her beliefs, you quickly discovered that beneath the surface of that beautiful girl was a mind that both commanded and demanded full attention. Kim insisted that any intelligence, no matter what its stage of development or the nature of its being, biological or cybernetic, *must* have some split in its personality.

"There must be moments of activity and of dormancy, just as in the human brain," she snapped. "The brain doesn't turn itself off during sleep or unconsciousness, Steve; you of all people know that! There's always some level of electrical activity within the brain, always a flow of oxygen and blood and regeneration. Or else the brain couldn't survive; there would be no way to prevent destruction of the biological organisms. There's nothing to justify the blind belief that's persisted all this time about the brain turning itself off. Either the brain

[87]

lives or it doesn't. And there's no difference to these basic rules where 79 is concerned, either."

Kim wasn't debating; damn it, she was spoiling for a fight, seeking some way to relieve her own building frustrations. Because I couldn't agree with her.

If, in 79, we did shut down all systems, if we ceased our demands upon the electronic neurons that made up the brain, if we ceased to make demands on the force fields, what then? Did your electronic gumbo and the packaged energy still remain, as she insisted, conscious? I threw the argument back at her.

Kim fixed me with a glare that almost frosted the edge of the fireplace. She had lived her entire adult life with biological systems, and she believed absolutely that life forms, no matter what their origin or their makeup, always possessed consciousness, or else they were passing into some phase of their own destruction.

"Of course it remains conscious," she retorted, almost openly contemptuous of my words. "At least this, this *thing*" —she gestured in her reference to 79—"will retain some measure of consciousness. It's the first brain ever created by man in this manner that meets his criteria of intelligence. A *living* intelligence. If you had bothered to really listen when Dr. Vollmer took the time to explain to you—"

"Back off, sweetheart," I snapped, the anger in my own voice undisguised. "And never mind the lectures. Vollmer has many points worthy of consideration, but his words are a hell of a long way from the panacea acceptable to everybody else in this project. The brain we're building isn't made up of the biological stew from which we make rabbits and beautiful, even if mule-headed, females. This thing, no matter how sharp it is, can be turned on and off. Like a machine. Like *any* machine, and . . ."

My voice trailed off before a suddenly sweet smile that warned me I'd fallen into a trap. I spotted it at the same moment that she impaled me with a pitying look a teacher usually reserves for a backward student.

"Oh? Are you certain of that? Really, Steve. Of all the peo-

ple on this project, certainly *you* should remember *the* difference, shouldn't you?"

I almost lost my temper. But, damn her, she was right. Once
79 became a system that was fully operational, it would sustain
itself from a nuclear reactor that would remain sealed and that
could operate, theoretically, for hundreds of years. The great
brain didn't have an outside power source.

For the first time, *we couldn't pull the plug.*

12

IF YOU PLACE AN electrode on the scalp of an average adult male, your instruments will indicate an electrical output that extends anywhere from five to fifty millionths of a volt. Electrical current. No question of it. Current that exists and that may be detected and measured. The electrical current of synapses, of message leaping from neuron to neuron within the nerve networks and the neural centers of the brain. Electrical current signifying—what? A man's thoughts instantly take him a billion years back in time or into the infinite possibilities of a future that doesn't yet exist. Is the man in his mind recalling the barking of a friendly puppy or does he contemplate some physics problem? The point is, this is the electrical current that moves worlds and that one day will carry its cranial originators throughout the universe.

How much current is this? If we could place electrodes at one time to the scalps of sixty thousand men we could barely produce a weak beam from a small flashlight. That's the *total* electrical output at any one time.

It could be, as one of our staff remarked wryly, that we were just lousy electricians and that the brain functioned with forms of energy we simply didn't understand or might not even know existed. And yet we also knew so much. . . . Electrical activity represented but one element of brain activity, of course. Brainwaves, electrical current of the mind . . . rhythmic currents with measurable cycles spanning a broad spectrum of mental activity, were critical to our work. Especially in the work that I performed as baby-sitter to 79, and in which I was aided and guided by the Bionics Division under Dr. Howard Vollmer.

It was through these rhythmic wave patterns of the brain that we hoped initially to establish communications directly between a human programmer and what might be termed the Soul of 79. . . .

So we had to know everything possibly within understanding. There are intricacies piled upon intricacies; the brain seems to achieve its splendid level of operation from an ordered and ceaseless catastrophe. As might be expected, there are within the brain neural systems each quite separate and distinct from other neural systems. These are comparable to packages of circuits, all linked together, to perform their kaleidoscopic variety of mental functions.

Their interrelationship is as great a mystery to us as the creation of the universe.

And the beauty of compactness! Even those scientists among us who felt they were on the edge of juggling not only individual atoms but also the particles from which the atoms were formed . . . remained openly in awe of the wonder that makes up the human brain.

We pursued the miracle we called the human brain, and while we chased mental rainbows, we were much more self-rewarding in our primary goal—to create our own made-to-order miracle with the unpretentious name of 79. . . .

Tom Smythe sprawled in the lounge chair in my office—a madhouse of charts, instruments, dismantled equipment, and sometimes the unnerving presence of Kim—and blew thick clouds of pipe smoke at me.

"Have you been able to come up with your own acceptable comprehension of how this will work out?" He waved the pipe with good-humored patience as I glared at him.

"What the hell do you want?" I shot back, testy in my manners and even, at this moment on this day, irritated with his barging in. I'd been hacking away at some technical problems of training special subjects to control their alpha-wave brain patterns, and I wasn't in the mood for philosophical banter. Maybe Tom knew that. He always seemed to show up at those moments when I wanted to throw up my hands and go fishing for six months.

"I'm not asking you for a bloody report," he retorted, as quick with a mood as the one he sensed in me. "I was asking you for your own feelings on this thing. The only way I can know—and not for the official reports, mind you; this is for my own understanding—what's really going on is to wrap it up with you in a conversation exactly like this one."

I turned in my seat. A small knot of pain had embedded itself between my eyes, and I kneaded the bridge of my nose, trying to work it away.

Tom looked carefully at me. "That happen very often?"

I nodded glumly. "Too often. It's a simple matter of ache and strain between the ears."

He grinned. "You should have Kim rub your neck and back on a more frequent schedule."

My mouth opened and I started to say something. But when in doubt—don't speak. There's the old saw that it is wise to engage brain before putting mouth in motion. I didn't need to speak; he knew what I was thinking, and he wasn't pressing it any further.

He rose to his feet. "C'mon, you need a break," he said. "Let's take a stroll and get some scenery and air in one big dose."

That was a good idea. The smell of trees and grass and unfiltered air was like a tonic for me.

And I could appreciate what Tom was trying to evoke from me, because I'd been living with it for more than a year now.

My God! I'd never kept track of the time. Self-reflection can be upsetting when you discover suddenly that so much time has gone by. More than a year of studies and preparations and coordinating programs, of initial tests and experiments, of probing with infinite caution into the miracle of thought we ourselves were trying to create.

And how would it all turn out?

"We can't do this on the needle approach," I said slowly to

Tom, breathing deeply of the pines about us. "It's got to be a matter of establishing, and then working with, the gestalt of 79."

He stared at me for a moment. "Run that by me slowly, if you would." He hated my being obscure. But it was so damned difficult to detail a feeling, to categorize an emotion. With all the specifics with which we worked, we found ourselves foundering helplessly. Finally we reached a point where you simply had to *know,* even without an unemotional justification for it, that you were doing the right thing.

That alone had shaken me up more than I'd cared to admit. My skills—the music of math, I mean—had encountered new horizons where they availed me not at all. I was over my head. We were all over our heads, individually and collectively. None of us could produce the mathematical equation for consciousness, let alone satisfy anyone else with rigid lines of explanation.

Were we more capable, our sciences might have carried us across the troubled waters of lack of comprehension. Well, maybe. We didn't know. It hurt to admit the truth—we foundered when we demanded hard-line reasoning and explanation —but in a sense the truth freed us. We found ourselves utilizing to the *nth* degree what science could do for us, and then we turned to what was, in our work, the most elusive of all.

Intuition.

Faith.

A . . . a *feeling.* That this was the right way to proceed.

Washington—the National Security Agency—would have suffered the burbling fits had they ever known of this self-admission within the confines of our cliques. Tom Smythe knew, but he wouldn't rock the NSA boat. Tom wasn't a hardware scientist, so to speak. No matter how clinical his own work, Tom as a psychologist found more science in intuition and feeling than he did in classroom theory. So we could talk freely with him.

"Well, in the clinical sense—what you'd call the psychological sense, Tom—I think that gestalt is the best description of what I'm trying to establish with 79. Not just the sense of rapport between the teacher and the student. First of all, I don't even know if that applies in this sense. I mean that . . . put it this way," I said, seeking the words that would express without verbal stumbling what I felt clearly within me. "To the gestalt school of psychology the very act of perception is a process worthy of the title 'miracle,' and—"

I stopped short both in my words and our walk together. "Wait a moment, Tom," I said, feeling piqued at having been led down a primrose path. "What am *I* explaining psychology to *you* for! You're the expert in this field, and I—"

"No, no," he broke in quickly. "You misunderstand me, Steve. Of course I'm well versed in this business. But I'm not testing your understanding or verbalization of my field. You've wandered off on a tangent wholly different from mine. What I want to find out from you—and this is really the only way to do it—is *your attitude* and *your approach* to what you're doing. I'm not looking for proof or anything else, Steve," he said smiling. "I'm asking you to open the door a bit so I can get a good look at what's going on inside. Okay on that basis?"

I was forced to return his smile. "Well, being cautious about it, Tom, I mean, explaining the gestalt approach— perception must be *not* a collection of one separate element of one sensation after the other, but actually an intellectual ability to establish, or to create, a relationship. It isn't enough for 79 to have vast stores of knowledge or be able to sort out bits and pieces of that knowledge." I scratched my chin; things always became a bit rough when I got into this.

"In other words, we're hoping that 79 will come to understand that it has its vast stores of information. Just knowing that it—the computer—is real, and that it's serving a purpose, would be a tremendous step forward."

Tom nodded, relighting his pipe. "Yes," he agreed, "it would be that, certainly."

I waited for him to finish. "All right, then. It's not enough for the mind to have knowledge. It must know that it has it. It must perceive of itself. Okay so far?"

He motioned with his pipe for me to continue.

"So the mind, as best we understand it, perceives a gestalt by perceiving the whole of a situation, or the whole of an impression. Someone who knows nothing about music perceives a tune, so to speak, because of the melody he hears. And even the musician, learning that melody, the tune, must learn the whole of the tune. He doesn't merely go through a mechanical recitation, a robot thumping of one note in succession after another. He can do this, of course, but if his perception is of the one note at a time, he doesn't have the melody. He has nothing but one unattached tone after the other. He's got to blend it all.

"Now . . . the perception of the whole—well, carry it one step further. I mean, with the music. Before long it becomes clear that not only the notes, or their succession, but also combinations of notes are vital to perceiving the tune or the song. Maybe I'm clumsy with all this, Tom. I'm not a musician and I may be using symbols that don't pertain."

"You're doing fine."

I nodded slowly. "Well, these combinations of notes, blending finally into the musical creation as intended by the artist, make up what we perceive.

"In fact, that's this very ability to receive vast stimuli for all of our senses that makes of man such a unique creature. The mind—accepting brain-mind as a single entity, of course—is still uncontested, and likely will remain so far into the future as I can see, as the single most versatile receptor of a simultaneous scattering of phenomena one could imagine. This is so because, well, nothing else of which we might imagine could perceive across so vast and simultaneous a range of stimuli. It involves everything at once: incoming, cross-checking, switchback, memory feed even while the input is at its maximum, and it can go on even while the individual carries on physical functions. I mean motor functions of volition, not the automatic. The miracle is that the brain of one man perceives the whole, and then, at his leisure, he can separate individual facets and aspects or groupings from the whole, the gestalt. . . ."

[95]

Clumsy as I was with these thoughts voiced to Tom Smythe, I knew I was on the right track.

The mind of man is a blotter. It is blindly absorbent of all that happens around it or, somewhat more strictly, of what happens within the range of perception of man's senses. Within that range it cannot prevent the input of stimuli. Its very capability ties together its mental shoelaces. Unique as it is, the mind does not have the speed of operation of the cybernetics system, and so it cannot separate incoming data at that moment when they are being received. Thus the miracle of the brain becomes cluttered with junk. There is so much cross-hatching of undesirable material that if we could bring selective perception into the gestalt ability, we would have in our grasp a vast step forward in what our admirers like to call brainpower.

This is one of the major hopes we had for Project 79. The creation of an artificial cognition, an artificial brain (I must remember to call it rearranged, I suppose, when in earshot of Dr. Vollmer!) that had selective input. It could be subjected to a battering assault of stimuli—data—and as swiftly as they were received would break down the input and, at the same time, perform the act of man's brain.

Perceive the whole, and separate meaningfully the individual elements of the whole.

And then go man one better. Categorize and remember everything with instant recall of any or all of what had been received. And, hopefully, utilize with reason what was remembered. . . .

A long time ago, Sir Charles Sherrington, a famed neural scientist, provided a clue to what we would one day create in our cybernetics organism.

Sir Charles commented that the brain ". . . is an enchanted loom where millions of flashing shuttles weave a dissolving pattern, always a meaningful pattern though never an abiding one."

Well, 79 was all that, and more.

Because it *was* an "abiding one."

13

"BUT, DAMN IT, Kim, why the sudden change in, I mean—oh, hell," I grated, "you know damned well what I mean."

I knew I showed my irritation. I was also wearing my feelings on my sleeve, but I couldn't help it. This was one of those moments when Kim was doing her best to drive me to distraction. Until now we had had a marvelous evening, a desperately needed "get away from it all" escape just for the two of us.

Within a week or ten days, working together, we would be ready to attempt the first brain-to-brain contact between a human programmer and 79. For the past month Kim and I had worked at least eighteen hours every damned day of the week to prepare for the epochal test. We were worn out, our minds sodden with the exhaustion of our intensive final preparatory efforts. One morning it just became too much. I couldn't think, couldn't see straight, didn't care any more. I grabbed Kim, shouted something at my secretary, and we took off for a long drive. We had lunch at the Broadmoor in Colorado Springs and made idle plans to drive to Denver for dinner and a show. Then Kim got the wonderful idea that we could just ensconce ourselves for the day in her apartment. She said she wanted to prepare dinner. Great! We made a mock celebration about our breaking way from the grind. The works: a fabulous meal to candlelight and music, and pleasant music afterward.

We sprawled on pillows thrown onto the floor. We kissed, long and tenderly, and pressed our bodies together, and I moved to make love to her.

Then suddenly she pulled away and murmured a sleepy invitation for me to go home and sleep in my own bed.

I glared at her. "What the devil has gotten into you, Kim?"

Her face a deliberate blank, she looked directly into my eyes. Her voice was silk, purring.

"How do you mean that, Steve?"

I gestured helplessly. "What do I have to do, make an official pronouncement of 'I love you'?"

She shook her head slightly; the firelight glistened off her hair as it followed the motion.

"I love you, damn it," I forced out.

"You make that sound as if it hurt to say it, Steve."

I groaned.

"It's all right, Steve, honey," she said quickly. "I know you believe you mean it." She was moving away, starting to her feet. But what was it she said?

"What do you mean, I *believe* I mean it?"

"That's right. You believe you love me. I know that."

"Well, then—"

She broke in. "That's not the same thing, darling."

I wanted to gnash my teeth in frustration. I stared at the girl I loved, and I was going around in circles.

"Kim, you're a wonder," I sighed. "Not even the computer could figure out a woman." I raised my arms and rolled my eyes. "We might as well pack up shop and let everyone go home. That is, if *you're* the test we put to 79."

She stopped in her flowing movement and fixed her gaze with mine. Even in the flickering light of the burning logs I could see the change in her expression, the instant expression of doggedness. Lovely, beautiful, soft, wonderful, stubborn-as-a-mule Kim.

"That's just the problem, Steve," she said. "You put your own finger squarely on it. You believe you love me. I—I'm —well, that's important to me. Very important. But you don't know. You simply aren't sure. You said that not even the computer could figure out a woman, didn't you?"

[98]

I nodded, helpless before her swift right-angle turns of conversation.

"There you are, darling."

I groped. "Where the hell is that?"

"What you said, Steve." She stretched, and I felt that urge to whomp my head a few good ones against the floor.

"You equate women—how shall I say it? You equate women cybernetically. It's all got to be balanced and equaled out. No loose ends, no untidy strings, no emotions unaccounted for."

Now she was on her feet. "I think—I don't know—I think I love you, Steve." She pressed her lips together . . . those lips. I wanted to . . .

I *did* gnash my teeth.

Her silken caress against my cheek reduced some of the anger.

"Steve, Steve, my darling, you're trying to program me, and I won't have it."

I sulked at her. Her hand held me back as I started to my feet.

"You haven't beaten that thing yet, Steve," she said with a half-whisper. "It seems to hurt you to understand that between your ears you're as much flesh and blood as anyone else and . . ." Her voice faded as she looked intently at me, acting as if she had found something there that before remained unseen to her. "Wouldn't it be fascinating if you found you couldn't have your own way all the time and you decided to join the human race? Every now and then it's nice down here, Steve. It's nice to see you boyishly passionate and silly and romantic and—"

But I was standing now, and I grabbed my jacket and I didn't even bother to say good night or anything else. Games! Jesus, what the hell did a woman want from a man? I loved that blasted girl, but it didn't mean I had to mope about in some straitjacketed funk because of her silly rules. Where the hell was Barbara's telephone number? . . .

Next morning we met, as usual, in the cafeteria for breakfast and coffee. I felt vaguely uncomfortable. Kim stirred her coffee, and for several minutes maintained the silence between us. It wasn't a barrier, just a silence I was grateful to have. But it couldn't last forever, and I knew Kim had a final word to say about what had happened. But she caught me off balance with what I had never expected to hear.

"Did you get it out of your system?"

She flashed a smile at me, and her laughter had a musical, delighted sound to it.

"No thanks to you," I said coolly.

She nodded, never taking her eyes from mine. Christ but she could raise dust all over a room with those eyes!

"It's obvious you don't mind," I said with as much venom as I could put into the words.

They had as much as effect as a snowflake in the middle of a blizzard.

"I wondered about that," she said, *too* damned casual about it all. "I thought I wouldn't mind. But, honestly, I don't know. I had some mixed emotions about it."

"You don't act it," I said with a sudden spark of hope.

"Why should I?" came the unexpected reply. "I don't own you, Steve. I have no call upon you, and I . . . I . . . can't say anything if you want to sleep with Barbara."

"How—how in the name of hell did you—"

She leaned across the table and kissed me lightly on the lips. "You know, I think I really do love you," she whispered. She walked away suddenly, leaving me speechless and with my mouth open like an idiot.

That's how Selig Albracht found me a few moments later. He alighted at the table like a bearded warrior of Norse mythology, heaved his bulk into a chair with his customary crash, and peered beneath shaggy brows at me.

"Do you know that you look like an idiot?" he challenged.

I looked at him stupidly, still with Kim in my mind.

"W—What?" I stumbled.

"You *are* an idiot, I do believe," he said grandly. He turned

[100]

to follow my gaze, and caught a glimpse of Kim as she left the cafeteria.

"Oho!" he boomed, drawing everyone's attention. "So that's it!"

I got back to the ground in a hurry. "So that's what, you bearded ape?" I snarled at him.

"You're a lovesick pup, *that's* what!" he bellowed.

It was a hell of a way to start off the new program. But at least with the computer I'd be dealing with logic instead of a beautiful but frustrating woman. And without hairy geniuses who shouted opinions in crowded restaurants.

Talking with 79 would be a pleasure. I couldn't wait to get started.

14

THE DEEPER WE explored the growing possibilities of our cybernetics brain, the more excited we became about its true potential. It seemed as if the computer could handle just about any realistic task we put to its vast memory and computing systems. It functioned with a logic that proved relentless, and when weak spots appeared we were chagrined, although not surprised, to note that the fault lay with the programmers. Ourselves.

The task of feeding and nurturing the memory capacity of 79 was one in which every one of us held the greatest interest. In effect, such programming contained the key to the possibilities of greater and greater success with the relationship between man and his cybernetics servants. Unfortunately, few people in Washington, or anywhere else, for that matter, realized the problems involved in amassing the tremendous stores of knowledge that are the tools with which the computer functions.

79 differed from other digital-base cybernetics systems in that it enjoyed full feedback and switching theory—a process used by the human brain. If, using all available data, a solution cannot be found, or if the solution found is not acceptable, the brain returns to the problem and seeks different approaches in finding its solution. Oftentimes the result is a solution that is a compromise, but that's a reality of life. 79 could come up with the best possible solution—the least of the many evils involved. If offered, essentially, a multiplicity of choice.

Now, it's obvious that the more information a man has at his mental fingertips to solve a given problem, the greater are the chances he'll come up with the answer he's seeking. Impede that man with insufficient data, or data that's not quite accurate or is misleading, and your solution may contain explosive ingredients. The computer isn't any different—until it knows better. If you tell the memory banks that the chemical formula for kerosene equals water, than you can get a solution to putting out a fire that calls for spraying kerosene on the flames. It's a drastic example, but no less applicable than one of greater subtlety.

It's easy enough to say that you can feed into the neural blocks of our cybernetics brain what is euphemistically called the sum of the world's knowledge. It's easy to say it, but impossible to realize as a fact.

Because much of what you feed into that electronic memory is going to be wrong. And if not wrong, it will be distorted or misleading. The world's knowledge? No one knows what it is. No one can verify its accuracy because much of it is opinion. Feed a computer with the sum of knowledge on the characteristics of the terrestrial environment, request the computer to come up with an answer to a scientific enigma, and if the brain could do it, it would, as Selig Albracht once said in sympathy, "throw up in the programming room." Because we don't know that much about the terrestrial environment to answer many of the questions we have. And the computer can't perform miracles.

We fed into 79 everything one could imagine. Every encyclopedia, textbook, reference, almanac, document, report, and so on, on which we could lay our hands. And we crossed fingers and held our breath and stroked rabbits' feet, and knew that no matter what we did we would have a hell of a time unraveling the inconsistencies and the outright contradictions. Because man's grasp of his physical world is too often a sometimes thing, with huge gaps in his cherished book of facts.

Nonetheless we had at it. Under the sociological aspects of programming we poured theories and the theorems, the contents of magazines and newspapers (carefully selected and then assiduously edited)—the gamut. We fed it music—both on tape in the original and broken down into mathematical symbols so that the computer could compare the mathematical notations against auditory output. Interesting: I wish I could have listened in on 79's "comprehension capabilities" when that program was under way!

In effect we were learning as much as we were teaching. There's a vital distinction—the difference between pouring in data and teaching. One is sheer and often meaningless ingestion, a memory bank that answers when you give it an electrical jolt. Everything that went into the memory neural blocks of 79 went in with a proviso that this was never the latest word; that the population, the Gross National Product, *anything,* was a fluid fact and always subject to revision and updating. This had to be done with extraordinary care, or else the revising, the input of additional data to the subjects already fed to the cybernetics brain, would become hopelessly unwieldy. We recorded within 79 the records and teachings of the world's great religions, specifying carefully as we did so that in this respect 79 was to function as a repository rather than to employ the material for data-seeking and solving problems. Spare us the reeking contradictions of the theological tomes! But for reference purposes—well, in they went.

Hundreds of specialists kept up the input. From all over the United States the data poured in with a steady flood of material on every subject conceivable. As the special direct-link lines went up and were activated, the task became simpler in terms of physical handling. The tendrils reached out across the length and breadth of the country not only for the primary data but also for the results of new experiments and tests, the conclusions of programs and projects, the creation of new theories as well as standing actualities. Into 79 went technical journals, statistical compilations . . . a thundering cascade of data reduced to tiny electronic echoes always available for recall and cross-checking. Day and night, month after month, the work had gone on, and all of us waited for that day when the computer could make that wondrous transformation when data would become knowledge.

But any learning process is terribly intricate, a matter of a search for knowledge crossing its own path again and again and again. The computer is the recipient of data, but it must know that it operates under severe restrictions—its data are never infinite, never definite, never really conclusive.

It must know when to stop solving a problem.

There are other asides. . . . A cybernetics system may comprehend excitement as it is registered through glandular changes and physiological alterations (we did this by linking the computer input to human subjects under hypnosis and then running them through a bewildering gamut of emotions while 79 recorded the physiological changes) . . . but—and it's the grandest *but* of them all—how do you record the tremulous fluttering of a young girl's heart when the stimulus is puppy love?

Time and again old truths came home to roost in the midst of our gleaming new world. None was more applicable to everything we did than the sign that Selig Albracht had hung in the most conspicuous part of his office. And he'd placed a bright light on the sign so it couldn't be ignored. The sign read:

INSOFAR AS MATHEMATICS APPLIES TO
REALITY IT IS NOT CERTAIN, AND
SO FAR AS MATHEMATICS IS CERTAIN
IT DOES NOT APPLY TO REALITY.

Selig wouldn't let anyone get away without realizing the sign or its message.

"You numbskull!" he would roar at the hapless visitor who failed to give the quotation more than a passing glance. "Have you any idea of who said those words?"

Invariably the answer would be No, they didn't know.

And then Selig would lean back in his chair and lower his voice to a growl, and he would tell them who said those words.

Albert Einstein.

It disturbed us that more and more of our staff were beginning to refer to 79 as the "talking computer." It disturbed us because it was true and it really didn't mean very much. Direct verbal conversation—two-way conversation—had been one of the experiments programmed for 79, and we had reached that point in the activation of the organism as a whole where we were able to run our tests. The idea of the two-way exchange so fascinated me that I insisted I be given the project, much to the relief (I discovered later) of Dr. Vollmer. He had been assigned the task, and he didn't want it, because he thought the whole thing was idiotic. He also thought, and told me with brutal candor, that I was a mathematical mutant. "Anyone who will depart from the pure language of mathematics to indulge in acoustic babble must have, somewhere in his education, a vast and gaping hole."

"You seem to do rather well yourself at such acoustic mayhem," I shot back.

We grinned at each other, and I went off for my session of what Dr. Vollmer considered to be "acoustic babble."

For a long time it was exactly that. We worked with one of our neural-block packages that, when we completed the input, would be linked to the "main brain" of 79. I can't deny this was more of an experimental program that anything else, but since it fitted neatly into the two-way communications involving bio-cybernetics I managed to get everything I needed. Including Kim to maintain the official control from Vollmer's Bionics Division.

As it turned out, we were wildly successful. In matters where hard data were not concerned, 79 could sustain a verbal conversation. There were gaps, to be sure, but as Kim pointed out, wasn't that a problem faced every day of the week by people?

Into the neural package, which could be considered a separable part of the cybernetics brain, we fed the sum and substance of the language. We started with the alphabet, the method in which the twenty-six basic letters could be arranged (mathematically, that was as easy as pie for 79), and the method in which the words and word groups were utilized to convey data. When the computer neural block had ingested the working foundation, we began the matter of converting data into acoustics.

The process wasn't so much complicated as it was vastly time-consuming, and for this purpose we used several universities around the country. More than a thousand people were involved in the effort, which all went down on tape. The printed letter *A,* for example, had a numerical value to it. Then, on the same tape, went the vocalization of *A.* And so on through the alphabet, and from this initial step into groups of letters and their vocalizations, and into basic words. On and on we went through the myriad, complicated contradictions of the language. Unbelievably sensitive in distinguishing the output of the vocalizations, the computer began to distinguish acoustic patterns with letters and words. The engineers built into the service-output systems of 79 an acoustic ability, an electronic-mechanical throat, so to speak. With precision engineering equipment, exquisitely controlled energy output, with plastics allowing flexibility—all of it in a modular package that could be removed, and a standby or even an improved modular throat system plugged back in—79 learned to talk.

It was, I suppose, an artificial speech because it was based on mechanical-mathematical interpretations of comparison—comparing what it obtained on tape both in numerical value and in acoustic value. Linguistics experts were a vital part in the effort; enunciation and pronunciation were absolutely critical.

Finally, because of the long-term effort and the great number of people involved, 79 had in its memory bank, in the neutral-block package, a numerical value and acoustic equivalent for every spoken word of the English language. If switching and feedback worked, if the computer could scan every book ever published (applicable to this program), could maintain its speed-of-light scanning of its memory blocks, it should be able to talk. Often, the results were hilarious; but with experience, order emerged from acoustic chaos, and intelligible speech rose from mechanical vocalization.

If we asked 79, "How are you feeling today?" the computer would not reject the question out of hand as a meaningless query. *It interpreted the question on the basis of its own values.* Since the term "feeling" was hardly applicable to something not of flesh and bone and the assorted aches and pains that make up our biological existence, it couldn't answer "Fine," in the sense in which we would interpret this word. (Of course, when it did use the word it had to distinguish, through swift scanning, the meaning of *fine* as applying to a fine margin or a fine edge; or *fine* as the levy of a financial punishment; and so forth.)

But it could interpret "feeling" as applying to its electronic and mechanical systems, and come back with an answer that it was functioning with 100 percent efficiency. And it would answer in such a manner!

"How are you feeling today?"

"Today" was this moment, that moment when the question was asked.

"You" was obviously the cybernetics organism itself.

As to the "How" of it, this became what percentage of maximum possible efficiency of all systems.

And the answer to the question would be: "Seven nine point three eight six," and it might throw in a "thank you" because it had a means of scanning electronically meaningless but biologically desired phrases to be selected from its neutral memory for just such occasions! The answer that at this moment the organism had exactly 79.386 percent of all its systems functioning told us vocally what we could determine with a glance at the systems-monitoring panels.

But when you heard that deeply resonant voice (a matter of nothing more than engineering) with its perfect language acoustics, well, at times it made the hair on the back of your neck go straight up.

The baseball season produced some wild sessions, and Selig Albracht made a small killing on side bets. 79 gave him the probabilities, and he delighted in a back-and-forth session with the computer verbally; the computer, of course, could accept everything available on baseball, work out batting averages, percentages, percentages of injuries, weather of the moment and how weather had affected the team in the past, wind direction and velocity—oh, Albracht had it all down, all right. When he got his answers he added to them. He threw in his own factors about the main hitter of the team being embroiled in a divorce, and he pondered whether it would make the guy sick to his stomach or madder than hell, and he put it all together, and while it was light-years away from being a sure thing, Albracht's predictions for baseball were nothing less than phenomenal.

The main thing was, however, that despite all the obvious problems and others we failed to anticipate, after several months you could hold conversations with the cybernetics brain.

I had some great chess games, in which we called out the moves vocally.

I never won a game, I might add.

As the multiple programming continued and we approached the end of the long preparatory and testing phases, we began to release the tight pressure on the mental reins we had held for so long. We were starting to give 79 its head, turn loose its own capabilities for decision-making. Because now we were ready to see just how well 79 would respond to the unknowns in the problems we were facing ourselves. More and more scientific and technical and sociological groups came secretly to us with their problems. At first they compared what they had already learned through their own, limited, cybernetics systems against the answers that 79 provided for them.

It didn't take long. Project 79 was exceeding our hopes for it, and it was doing so far ahead of schedule.

From the moment our cybernetics brain changed from its role of student to that of equal, it began to rush ahead to a level of intellectual capability that had never before existed in the history of man.

The computer now began to make its own demands. We knew it would do so in response to discovering gaps in its programming. As it mulled over problems and found information to be absent, it began to request specific items.

That's when we knew we had won.

Our cybernetics organism, in every sense of the word, was thinking. Really thinking. When faced with the "insufficient data" obstacle, it didn't sulk or repeat idiotically that it needed further information; it requested what it needed to have. And if that wasn't available, it approached the subject not only mathematically but also in the heuristics evaluation: It played a hunch that was based on the greatest possibility of being right.

And what does man do?

Exactly that.

Which meant we were ready to begin the bio-cybernetics tests.

Book
Three

15

No one spoke. Not a sound from any one of the forty people in the survey room. All eyes looked through the separating glass into the Contact Cubicle.

We had our miracle.

A human brain and a cybernetics organism were in direct contact with each other. They were communicating.

They talked. Not with words or with sounds, but with their mathematical equivalents. With the alpha-wave pattern of the man and the electronic sensitivity of the cybernetics organism. They communicated. The man queried the machine, demanded information.

The machine received the request, evaluated it, scanned its neural banks, returned the information requested.

The man was Maurice Levy, BC Test Subject 83. Kim and I had worked with him for months. He was our most promising key to institute the first manufactured miracle of its kind in history.

Levy was a Navy signalman assigned to Project 79. More than a year before we had begun the search for men and women who could alter, deliberately, the alpha-wave patterns of the brain. Ours was a hit-or-miss quest that had paid off. Each human being was tested with scalp electrodes to determine his specific alpha-wave signature. We studied the variations in alpha rhythm, and we separated those few individuals who could, by intent, alter their alpha-wave pattern.

I didn't know how it was done—Dr. Vollmer and Kim shared some theories into which I refused to be drawn. My only interest was its application.

Being able to control the alpha-wave pattern wasn't enough. It had to be controlled in a specific manner, a sort of on-off-on capability. We found that perhaps one person in every two hundred had some controlled alteration of his alpha-wave pattern. And out of that new group of one in two hundred, only one in every twenty or thirty had the potential, with training, for getting the on-off-on ability down pat.

That began our training program. For with the rare test subjects we had to teach them to control the alpha-wave pattern in such a way that we could adapt their talent to direct two-way communications with 79. Our cybernetics brain had absolute control of its alpha-wave patterns; it was, after all, an interpretation of energy output.

How to carry on the initial tests? Not even the optimists among us hoped for more than basic, crude communications until we had time enough in which to gain experience—the experience that would give us some sound working foundations on which to continue.

The on-off-on sequenced interruption held the answer. If the test subject could do this—and with increased training they became quite skillful at it—the next step was to teach the test subject Morse code.

The computer learned it in no more time that it took to feed Morse code into its neural cells. We programmed 79 to use Morse code at a speed tremendously reduced from its capability. Electronically, 79 could spit out volumes in Morse code, but we could never utilize the data without processing them. What we wanted initially was evidence that our program hopes were vaild. So the computer responded in Morse code at a pre-selected speed.

It looked simple enough on the face of it, but then we ran into other problems. Learning Morse and thinking rapidly in Morse aren't the same. A person can learn Morse code, can communicate with the system, but it's halting and awkward and too damned mechanical. Where could we find people who thought as naturally in Morse code as if they had slipped into another language? Which is what Morse code was—a digital language.

That's when we went to the Navy. They had Morse code operators from way back when. They had men who could think in Morse as well as any of us thought with the English language. They didn't have that many who could handle Morse and who could alter their alpha-wave patterns.

Then we found Maurice Levy. He was fifty-two years old, and he had his first homemade telegraph key when he was eight. He had always been wild about Morse. He could think almost as fast in Morse as he did in everyday word language.

And luck smiled upon us. He was an alpha adept—one of the few who had, with training, an almost uncanny ability to control his alpha-wave pattern. He didn't know it, of course. In fact, he'd never heard of alpha-wave patterns within the brain until we told him about the results of his tests. The Navy assigned him (and another thirty as well) to us indefinitely. Maurice Levy—"Call me Manny," he insisted—well, Manny couldn't have been happier about his selection.

He had an apartment deep within a mountain, and was treated like a king. We considered him almost a national asset.

He even liked the idea of working with a cybernetics brain. That, let me tell you, was one great hurdle for us to get over. Most people shied away from it. Manny didn't. "I've been in three wars and a half-dozen almost-wars," he explained with a philosophy born of having lived close to death for years. "There's nothing that contraption of yours can do to me that hasn't already been done. Let's go." As simple as that. And four bullets and assorted pieces of metal in his hide to affirm his convictions. We almost hugged him. Kim did!

Only three of us were in the contact cubicle: Maurice Levy, Kim, and myself. The others, including Dr. Vollmer, under whose division these tests came, were content to leave the direct work with Kim so that he might be able to observe without any distractions.

Levy relaxed in a comfortable leather chair, his feet propped up, his body comfortable. Atop his scalp were electrodes, glued directly to the skin. They were enough; we sighed with relief when we discovered it wouldn't be necessary to plant an electrode within the brain. Although it's painless and harmless, no one sits easily with the idea of a fine wire piercing his skull and penetrating his brain. Physically it's as easy as sliding on ice. Psychologically? No one likes it, especially when the finger points at them for the experiment.

The electrodes had been patterned to pick up the alpha-wave patterns of Levy's brain. By themselves they weren't of sufficient energy to have tickled a gnat's fancy. So the impulses—the gross impulses, that is—fed from the electrodes on Levy's skull to an amplification system, or rather, a separation *and* amplification system. As the electrical output of Levy's brain came into the system, a computer distinguished the alpha-wave pattern. As fast as this separation was made, the alpha-wave pattern was amplified tremendously, something on the order of one million.

From the amplification system the boosted alpha-wave pattern fanned out along three separate lines. One transmitted the alpha-wave signal directly to the input of the cybernetics organism. The second signal went into a recording-tape console, and the third appeared on our monitoring equipment. The alpha-wave pattern signal, when not being energized deliberately by Levy, appeared on an oscilloscope as a group of wavy lines, one line above the other, flowing rather evenly from left to right.

When Levy switched to his mental interruptor mechanism and went into Morse-code transmission, the wavy pattern went through a continuing series of flashes, each equivalent to a dot or dash in the Morse sequence thought of by Levy. Another readout scope adjacent to the alpha-wave oscilloscope remained inactive except when Morse was being transmitted—white for Levy's signals and green for the return signals from 79.

We could even *listen* to the exchange, although this was done more for political than for scientific purposes. Tom Smythe had become NSA's anchor man to smooth the ruffled feathers of appropriations committees in Washington. Although the congressional teams that knew of Project 79 maintained strict silence on the program, and even restricted their number to a select few, they did insist upon complete knowledge of our progress.

The sight of Maurice Levy seated in his leather chair, wires leading from his scalp to gleaming, complicated machinery, was an eerie thing to witness. If we subdued the lights in the contact cubicle, the oscilloscope and control panels added a flickering, flashing multicolored pattern to the cubicle that reflected off glass and metal. It was a dazzling production even if Levy didn't move an inch.

Smythe took elaborate pains to describe the setup, to emphasize the brain-to-brain contact, and to let it be known that we considered this only the first act in a drama whose main lines were yet to be written. At the proper moment—the psychological key to the situation—he would say, "Listen; listen carefully . . ." in the best of stage tones. Then he would flick a switch, and the *dit-dah* clicks of Morse code, the exchange between human and machine, crackled from loudspeakers.

It brought you right to the edge of your chair, and you found yourself—especially if your education in giant cybernetics organisms was of the science-fiction variety—experiencing cold fingers trickling down your back.

Even though it smacked of show business, appropriations were the lifeblood of Project 79, and Tom Smythe had an obligation to fulfill. When he brought in his special visitors he programmed them thoroughly himself. He knew everything pertinent about the important visitor.

If he had with him a senator from Oregon, then he arranged our tests to include Oregon. So long as Tom didn't interfere with the tests, and he made certain to avoid that pitfall, we didn't care what he asked us to program with Levy and 79.

A list of questions supplied to Levy would also be supplied to the visitors in the survey room. Levy read off his questions from the equivalent of a television prompter, the words unfolding one by one before his eyes. As fast as he saw each word, he thought of the word, altering the alpha-wave pattern as he did so, and passing on a request for data to the computer through his own brain.

Tom Smythe made certain the visitors, including the senator from Oregon, never saw the words unreeling on the prompter. Instead the senator would see the flashes off the oscilloscopes; standing by his side would be a technician who read aloud the questions as they went from Levy to 79.

At that instant when Levy completed his programming—that is, ended his questions—the computer was ready to answer. But Tom felt he could get more mileage if some theatrical pauses were included. Levy's last instruction to the computer would then be for 79 to begin response in exactly three hundred seconds. During those five minutes Tom Smythe made whatever points he felt were necessary. He timed it so that he interrupted himself by noting the passing seconds and calling attention to the Morse-code output of the computer. And the answers would come back—answers relating to anticipated growth patterns; transportation problems; anything and everything relating to the senator's home state.

And throughout the entire exchange Maurice Levy just . . . *thought.*

16

OUR CELEBRATION PARTY was an absolute blast.
More than a year of intensive work and suppressed doubts and
black moments had vanished, not in a single puff of smoke, but
during the last several weeks as our cybernetics brainchild came
slowly but surely into being as a functional, thinking creature.
Billions of dollars reaching a moment of justification was heady
tonic, indeed, and we added to the giddiness of sweeping success with great quantities of good fellowship and a dazzling
variety of potent mixtures that would have strained the imagination of any bartender I ever knew.

No matter, no matter. Success had come in a glorious fashion
that held even greater promise for the future. Maurice Levy—
good old Manny!—proved a fitting star to crown our moment of
success and achievement, and he was only the beginning. If we
didn't take the time and effort for some old-fashioned back-
slapping and crowing with one another to shake out the cobwebs of overwork . . . well, before too long we would have
tightened like old leather thongs and frayed ourselves to useless-
ness.

I picked up Kim early in the evening of the party, and she
took my breath away in a white gown that seemed to have been
lifted straight out of Roman days. She kissed me warmly. I
don't think I had realized just how much effort she had put into
the bio-cybernetics effort that culminated in our spectacular
success with Levy. Now she was as ready as anyone else on the
staff just to let loose somewhat. To me this meant a bash; to a
woman, I learned quickly, it meant being able to dress and to

act and to be treated as a woman in the manner that only a huge formal affair can provide.

Well, off we went! The drive to the Great Western Hotel couldn't have been a better start. A light snow drifted from the skies to cover the countryside about us, but the road remained clear.

Kim opened her window to feel the wintry air. She breathed deep, and sighed. "I'd almost forgotten how clean the night air can be out here, Steve."

I nodded, listening with one ear to Kim and the other to the radio that promised a heavy snowstorm. "Looks as if we might get in some skiing the next couple of days."

"That would be nice."

I glanced at her. "You might get the chance to break a leg, too. It's been a long time since you were on skis."

"Too long," she answered. "I'm looking forward to it."

"Hate to think of one of *your* legs in a cast," I sneered.

"How romantic you can be!"

We laughed together.

"This should prove to be an interesting evening," she said after a few moments.

My brows must have arched into peaks. She placed her hand on my leg and patted gently. "Not what you're thinking, lover. I'm talking about the party."

I did my best to look disappointed.

"How do you mean?"

"When some of our people let loose it's, well, it can be rather unpredictable," she went on. "They don't drink very much, really, and tonight . . ." She giggled. "Old Dr. Vollmer gets positively, well, 'horny' would be about the best word for it."

I stole a glance at her, saw she was smiling.

"Some young ladies are going to be embarrassed tonight," she said.

Nearly a hundred people had already arrived at the hotel. I left the car with a doorman, and, as proud as any young idiot on his first date, escorted Kim to the ballroom. On the way up the long curving stairs I thanked my own foresight in having called

Barbara several days ago. I didn't want any nasty scenes with a confrontation of Kim and Barbara at our celebration ball, so I called Barbara and told her that because of office propriety and my having worked so long with Kim I simply had to be her escort for the evening.

Barbara laughed at my discomfiture, the sound rippling like spring water through the telephone. "Steve, you darling," she broke in, "I'm way ahead of you. You're such a wonder, so worldly the scientist and so naïve the man. Of course I didn't expect you to take me."

I looked stupidly at the telephone in my hand. "You didn't?"

"Of course not, honey," she said quickly. "I can add two and two just like anyone else."

"Oh?" I didn't know what else to say.

"You're in love with her, Steve."

I met that one with silence.

"Silly," she said to fill in the lapse. "I've known that for a long time."

"You have?"

"Steve"—she laughed suddenly—"no one owns anyone else. Not you, not me. I don't want it any other way. You're a dear, and I *do* appreciate your stricken conscience." Another ripple of laughter, and the phone went dead.

I stood for a long time staring at the phone. What I learned every day about the two women in my life I thought I knew better than anyone else . . . Barbara knew about the way I felt about Kim, and yet . . .

She was right, of course. About what she'd said, I mean. She was a sleek cat in the jungle of love, and allowed no ownership notions to get in the way. Unless they became a mutual desire. What a gal . . .

Barbara came to the party on the arm of a blond Lothario with rippling muscles and a faceful of Jack Armstrong teeth. I recognized him—Jim Clyde, with some servomechanisms outfit. Young engineer. Typical. Very bright and stupid at the same time, like most young engineers. But a magnificent stud if ever

[121]

one walked into a room. As for Barbara . . . well, she wore a gown that could only be described as wicked for what it did to the people around her. Cut low enough with her high, thrusting breasts to expose the envy of just about every other woman in the place, and to bob the Adam's apples of even the old duffers among the crowd.

Kim studied her carefully when Barbara entered with her stud in willing tow. And while she studied Barbara, I kept my eyes carefully on Kim.

"You're sizing her up, Kim. I thought only young men were supposed to do that."

She laughed. "Really, I had no idea . . ." Her words trailed off, and she moved closer to me, lowering her voice.

"Honey, that is the most beautiful female I have seen in many a year. I don't blame you at all for . . ."

"For what?" I growled.

"Mm-mm," was all she would say.

We looked again at Barbara, who was making her way straight to us with all the finesse of a battleship in a narrow channel.

I gritted my teeth. "No," I said abruptly. "I am not going to say a damned thing. I was going to, but you'd probably tell me I was—"

"What?"

I nodded at Barbara and turned back to Kim. "Honey, she's quite a person, but she's not what you are."

Kim's green eyes bored into mine.

"You idiot." She laughed.

I didn't return the laugh. For me this was serious. "She's a beautiful animal, Kim." I paused. "You're a beautiful *woman*."

Her eyes widened, and for several moments she didn't say anything. Then suddenly she lifted to her toes and brushed her lips lightly against mine.

"There's hope for you yet," she said quickly.

I just *knew* it was going to be a grand evening with a start like that. . . .

A couple of hours later I stood with Kim by a balcony win-

17

I suppose it was inevitable. Sooner or later during the evening there had to be a busman's holiday. We couldn't stay away from shop talk. *I* could, but then I was fumbling around in my mind with amorous thoughts and the knowledge of not only where but with whom I'd spend the rest of the evening. I simply didn't give a damn for cybernetics organisms or tongue-loosened scientific fellows.

Dr. Selig Albracht, our bearded captain at the helm of Heuristics, was smashed. There was no other way to say it; he was absolutely bombed. Right out of his mind.

Now there was someone else in that same human skin and behind the familiar beard. An antagonist, a man for whom Project 79 was not quite the all-fired neural miracle we had created. Don't get me wrong. Selig Albracht was a great cybernetics man. But he had his convictions, and one of them was that every computer should know its place. He believed that: computers should have the status of well-disciplined and obedient dogs. At regular intervals they should be kicked mightily so that they would remember their place in life.

They worked for man. *For* us, all of us. They were tools. Wonderfully intricate and fancy electronic tools that could weave neural miracles. But on command, and through proper programming.

The sum of it all was that Selig had built up a seething hate for the bio-cybernetics aspects of our program. He was opposed almost to the point of violent dissent to the work carried out in Bionics under the guidance of Dr. Vollmer. He felt we were plunging headlong down a path from which we could return only with assorted lumps and bruises. It was Selig Albracht's conviction—and I confess that a surprising number of scientists agreed with him—that we should impose specific limits upon the dependence we placed on our cybernetics systems. "Too much of a good thing," he muttered. He felt that man was giving up his God-given miracle of life, the substance from which we weave our dreams.

"Man must never unshoulder the burden of his responsibilities, or else he'll bloody well forfeit its rewards," he warned us, his beard twitching beneath bloodshot, angry eyes. He glared around our group, Kim standing by me, Dr. Vollmer seated in a comfortable chair and not bothering to disguise his humorous disdain for Albracht. There were others, including Tom Smythe, who had suddenly become absolutely sober and attentive to every word in the increasing heat of the exchange. Old Professor Cartwright, the world-famous cyberneticist who had flown in from Princeton for the bio-cybernetics tests and demonstrations with Maurice Levy. And Dr. Walter Bockrath, the professor of social sciences at the University of Colorado. Some others whom I'd met and who walked the highest levels of our scientific world were there. But I hardly knew them and I ignored their presence; they listened quietly, obviously uninvited to join the exchange.

"How far are you going to go with your blasted brain-to-brain contacts, Steve?" Selig shouted his words, unable to calm his bellowing, as if volume would lend even further credence to his beliefs. "What are you going to do when your wonderful test subjects, when Levy and all those who come after him, finally file like sheep into your contact cubicles, waiting patiently like dumb animals for the electrodes and the contacts to be made? What then, my brilliant young slayer of dragons?"

I didn't answer at once. I was tremendously fond of Selig Albracht, and I respected the man as much as I had any other human being in my life. He was drunk. But not so drunk, I was also convinced, that this was simply a matter of alcohol speaking for the man. Selig believed what he was saying; all that had been pushed aside for the moment was the propriety with which we brought some social order to our everyday lives. And the only answer to give him was, of course, the obvious one.

"No one files like sheep into our program," I said quietly. "You know that as well as I do, Selig. They volunteer. No one pushes any one person into—"

"Bah!" he shouted. "Save that poppycock for the sniveling and eager young things who don't know any better. Volunteers, are they? Don't you try to confuse the issue by avoiding reality, damn your hide. Nobody volunteers when he's been drowned beneath a torrent of intellectual abuse we heap upon those blind and unknowing souls out there. What the devil do they *know* about what's going to happen to them? How could they know anything when *you* and old flintstone Vollmer don't even know! You're playing with people, Rand, and you damned well know it."

I tried to break in, but once Selig picked up the scent he was as easy to stop in midstride as an enraged grizzly.

"It's bad enough you fools are playing with the minds of other people," he said with a voice suddenly lower, sullen in every sound. His eyes were almost to the point of flashing with blazing anger. This was no drunken fool and this wasn't alcohol speaking, and Selig Albracht had a damned attentive audience. If I had paid any attention to what was going on around me, I would have seen Tom Smythe trying to signal me to break it off, to get out from under before things got nasty. But Selig was getting under my skin now, and I never liked the idea of walking away from any open challenge of this sort. So I paid attention to what he was saying.

"Just hold for one moment, Selig," I snapped back as he drew in a long shuddering breath. "Call us fools if you want; you're drunk and I'll attribute that to alcohol. But fools for what? You call it playing around with the minds of people? Then you're acting a bigger fool than those whom you accuse."

He started to shout an answer, but I wasn't having any of it. "Confound you, man, if you can't believe enough in your own principles to hear someone else out," I said coldly, "then you're just a bag of wind."

[127]

I thought he would choke. His voice rumbled like a locomotive. "Go on, go on," he said, fighting for self-control.

"If what you say is true, *Dr.* Albracht, then every psychiatrist and psychologist down through the years is a witch doctor, a hunter of the nightmare of the psyche. You're the people who force the human being to look into the hideous mess of his own subconscious. And that's not an accusation; it's a fact."

I paused for a moment; something in what I'd said had gotten through to him.

"And it's necessary, all of it," I went on quickly. "What all of you, what all of us, are doing. We're searching, digging, trying to chase out the nightmares and relieve the horrors. How can you find fault in augmenting our intellectual capabilities? No matter what you may find in searching attics for monsters, 79 is still just a machine. I won't get into this business of intelligence or life or consciousness, because we've done it a thousand times, and none of us knows enough to make head or tail of what we're talking about. You know it and I know it. But what you're saying is that punishing, probing, shoving about, torturing the mind in psychoanalysis is acceptable, but linking man's brain to an artificial intelligence—which may become just as live as is yours and mine—is wrong!

"I don't know how deep your concern goes for the welfare of the humanity we're supposed to be turning into living mummies, Selig, but I'll tell you one thing. You're a damned hypocrite."

His beard twitched as his mouth worked, forming the words. "Hypocrite, am I, you young snit?" he roared. "Is that the issue? Let me go back to what I said before and what you never let me finish. Before you polish off those clichés-for-arguments you picked up in your college debating classes, you should try to hear what is being said to you."

He tilted his head slightly, convinced he'd grabbed hold of something I had let slip by me. "I told you—I *started* to tell you," he interjected with no small venom, "that it was bad enough you were playing around with the minds of other people. Of course we all do that! Of course there's pain and sorrow in it, and that can't be helped when you reach in up to your armpits where madness and hell are involved."

He stabbed a thick forefinger at me, leaning forward. "The difference, Rand, and it's a big difference, the biggest damned difference in the world, is that *you* and your compassionately sterile associates are throwing human minds to the whims of that unpredictable clanking machine of which you're so bloody fond!"

He drew back, flushed with his own words. "You're creating a monster. Oh, I know all about the old stories and the platitudes and the rest of that rubbish, but this time you're really doing it up brown. It's a machine. A *machine,* damn you all! Don't you understand that? And you're giving it human minds with which to experiment, and—"

"Horseshit!" I shouted, "and you damned well know it, Albracht! No one is leading anybody to any sacrificial altars. Where do you get this nonsense, anyway? We're controlling the tests, not the machine! Jesus, the way you talk one would think that—"

"For how long?"

The words came so quietly and unexpectedly they had a dramatic impact on us all. His interruption stopped me cold.

"What was that?"

He smiled without humor. "I asked you a question, Rand. I asked you—'For how long?' "

I didn't answer immediately, and he drove harder. "How long from now will it be before the computer tells you it can handle the experiments with greater efficiency than can its human programmers? How long before this happens? And what will you do then? What? What? Will you refuse the answers from the machine you're giving such omnipotence? Will you accept its logic as superior in all other things but not in this area when it demands more and more living brains with which to experiment? What will you do then? What's going to be your answer when it wants to extend its probing of the gamut of human emotions and it asks for children and then for newborn infants, and when it asks to be hooked up with those who are dying because it's curious about the cessation of neural activity? Or whatever it is, that thing we call the death of a human being?"

I gestured involuntarily. "I—"

"Will you refuse it its three pounds of flesh?"

And right then, right there, I couldn't answer him. Because I'd never thought of it. Never for a moment had it occurred to me to record the moment of death of a human being . . . to attempt to understand, to comprehend intellectually, the passing of the soul or whatever it was that separated the body from life and death. At once I saw where Albracht would go, what he would say.

We wouldn't stop with just those experiments, of course. He was right. God, how he was right! The ultimate in experiments.

Death . . . and . . . and life. Birth; the moments of awareness of being born. And what of the life before birth? Medically it would not be difficult to implant electrodes within the brain of the unborn child. . . . What incredible things might we learn? If we— But then there wasn't time to think of this because Selig Albracht was still there, his anger naked and exposed, his contempt coming into being like a physical force in the room with us. I had never yet been less than honest; I would not stop now.

"No, Dr. Albracht, we would not refuse. You knew that answer before you so dramatically presented the question."

He stroked his beard, now more in control of himself. "To be sure, to be sure," he said. "Naturally you would not refuse. You would offer up death and life and in-between and even the beyond if that were possible, wouldn't you?"

I didn't have the opportunity to answer. Dr. Vollmer was on his feet, shuffling closer to the circle of antagonists.

"One moment, one moment," he said quietly, his voice unexpected, a distraction in our exchange. He walked up to his old friend and faced him squarely.

"Selig, I wish to ask you a question. Just one," Dr. Vollmer said in his cracked voice.

You could see the strain of old friendship against what had been exposed through Albracht's anger. The bearded giant nodded, for the moment humbled. "Of course, Howard."

The old scientist drew up his shoulders to stand straight. "Just the one question, Selig.

"Would you have it any other way?"

There was no other question to ask, for in that one question there were a thousand others.

Would you close the door on learning?

Where would you draw the line on bringing light into the darkness we have always faced, must face for another thousand years or more?

Who is to decide, Selig?

Who?

What if in what we are doing lies the secret of another hundred years of life for every human being? What if we can learn enough of that instant of the miracle when the brain still growing within the womb accepts its first electrical energy? What if we can learn enough to cure madness before it is born with the child naked and wet from its birth? What if we were meant to do this, Selig, what if this were the path that God had always meant, when we have the opportunity to change the brain that has not changed for a hundred thousand years?

How do you know this is not really nature's way, that this is how we will bring to life the creature to follow Homo sapiens?

Which window of the universe of knowledge would you close next, Selig Albracht?

When will you make that final move, that turning of man's back on knowledge?

When will you condemn man to fear the future so much that he will take root where he stands and become less than man?

The room was deathly still.

For several minutes they stood facing each other, until Dr. Vollmer, shaking his head slightly, returned to his chair.

"I am old and I am tired," he said to Albracht.

"Forgive me," Albracht said, "I did not mean to—"

"I am old and tired," Vollmer repeated, his voice leathery and instantly alive. "But I am not yet blind."

He sat down, leaving Albracht standing alone.

But Selig Albracht was made of sterner stuff than most men. And he did not retreat. He looked for a long moment at Dr. Vollmer, and then he turned back to me.

"I will tell you something," he said in a quiet voice. "I will tell you something, and in the telling I will ask you some questions. I do not care if you answer me. Not now, not later. It would be enough for me if you were to think of what I say."

He looked at me strangely, some inner torment now revealed in his eyes, his gestures.

"I will suppose that the cybernetics organism progresses as you all wish, that it becomes all for which you hope, that it is indeed the miracle you seek to create with your minds and your hands and your dreams. I will suppose that it all takes place and that you are wildly successful, far beyond your most fervent hopes and dreams.

"And when that happens, and we are at the wire, when man himself may be threatened—I am talking about the existence in the future of the race itself—when that happens, I wish you to ask yourself a question."

He paused, but I did not interrupt. I felt Kim's hand on my arm, her touch, so warm and meaningful to me, seemed a thousand miles away. I did not interrupt; I waited.

"Ask yourself this: Would this thing be willing to die for you and me? Ahh, would it make this sacrifice? Would it, *could* it, comprehend what you and I, this instant, know to such depth and with such meaning?"

His eyes bored into mine. "Because that, Steven Rand, is the crux of it. It really is, you know."

He laughed harshly. "Would this mass of neural relays and hovering electrons really do such a thing? If it were for the best, if it were needed? Would it be willing, would it be capable, ever, intellectually, of sacrificing its own physical being even when it proved to itself that its own existence comprised the single

[132]

greatest threat in existence to all mankind, to what we so easily call humanity?

"Would it?" He hammered one word after the other, driving them with force, pounding, pounding.

"Would it order its own destruction? Could that beautiful, intricate, wonderful mixture of energy and matter, which is what we are—plus what God has given us—willingly ordain its own end to consciousness?

"Tell me that, Mr. Rand. *Tell me!* Then, then," his voice caressed every word, "I will trust that nightmare you are all trying so desperately to bring to full life, to which you offer human minds and life and death and the substance of the soul. Tell me what I wish to hear, and I will abide by our search for truth.

"But this is not truth! Until that thing is ready to die for you or me, for an ideal or a principle, for generations yet unborn, for what mankind is destined to become . . . until then, it is as dangerous as a viper.

"And I am opposed!" he shouted. "Do you hear me? I am opposed, violently and unalterably opposed to what you are trying to do.

"Because . . . because then it is the ego supreme. If it cannot sanction its own passing from unconsciousness, forever, do you know what you are creating?

"A God Machine."

"Go to hell," I said.

18

THE BREACH WAS deep and wide, a mortal cleavage between two men who had been close friends and between whom there had been an abiding mutual respect. Now it was gone, vanished like a wisp of smoke from the heat of anger and our confrontation face to face among our colleagues. Had we endured this contest of wills among ourselves, alone and unheard by others, the strength of what was good between us would have sustained the friendship. But not now.

I do not know what Selig Albracht thought from that day forward, or what he felt. For myself, I suffered a sense of great loss. Selig was that kind of man; a great man, I thought, but blinded and with a sense of his intellectual vision turned in upon itself. But I would have nothing to do with remorse or with self-searching nonsense. Our exchange was bitter only because it had never been intended by Selig to be an exchange; his stupor had led him headlong into a proclamation. Nevertheless it was what the man thought, and what brought a bitter taste to me was that he had never taken the pains nor had he showed the backbone—a lack that was all the rarer because it was Selig who was involved—to express himself until that sad and angry moment.

To the devil with him, I thought. Michelangelo, Newton, Tsiolkovsky, Fulton, the Wright brothers, Goddard, Edison, and so many, many others who march down the ranks of history—they had all carried the stigma of witch for their society. There were those who castigated and would like to have burned alive Norbert Wiener who had, despite all reservations of undue credit, founded the science of cybernetics. It was simply the price you paid.

But there was another price. Selig Albracht was a man and a scientist of immense personal and professional standing in our closed community, and an open breach with the man courted both personal and professional disaster for the dissenter. Which I was, and in spades. Albracht had nothing to do with this; I believed firmly he regretted it deeply. But it was there nonetheless, and overnight I found myself the pariah of Project 79. Former friends and associates shunned me socially; in our work they were cooperative but cool and distant. Those who were not directly involved usually took the safer route. Why be exposed to the leper when the doorway to the king's chambers is open?

From Dr. Vollmer, who flew into a rage with the memory of that evening, I earned a new respect, and in him found a powerful ally. Strong as was the reputation of Albracht, that of Vollmer was even greater. He was one of the grand old scientists recognized as a leader in half a dozen sciences, and respect for him knew no bounds. Where others branded me leper, Vollmer threw the aura of his personal and his professional cloak about me.

I confess my reaction, indifferent at first, hardened swiftly. I had never sought out any man's friendship or his respect; I expressed my own as I saw it, and let things go at that. The frigid air that often surrounded me did not affect me except to harden my own resolve; namely, "to hell with all of them." I had come here to work and, by God, work I would. I had a cybernetics organism to develop in the way of new and fresh capabilities, and that is precisely to what I would attend, if I had to do the damned job on my own. I didn't, of course; not with Vollmer and his staff, as well as some scattered friends and, of course, Tom Smythe, solidly behind me.

But withdrawal came; an inner self sighed unhappily with the realization. I turned my back on all except a select few, and I didn't care; let the chips fall where they might. I became brusque, rejecting timid offers of friendship, and concentrated on those whom I felt I could trust without first studying the situation.

Strange, but Kim and I were never closer. Not because she

agreed with me in respect to the episode with Albracht; I think she was disappointed in my angry retort and my refusal to have anything more to do with the man. Kim believed a man of science had to have above all else a complete detachment; I couldn't see it that way. Just as we programmed the computer brain to know when to stop solving a problem, so every man must know, within himself, when it is time to cry *Enough!* And I'd had it right up to the eyeballs.

Above all else I hurled myself into my work. Except for the times I spent with Kim—for a long time I never even called Barbara—I worked. I worked throughout the day and long into the night and I spent many weekends and holidays with 79, programming new experiments, testing the bio-cybernetics subjects, watching Maurice Levy achieve a speed of two-way communication that was almost unbelievable. I gave him freedom for random contact with 79; instead of reading programmed questions he would query the computer on his own, asking questions as they came to him. The results were so spectacularly successful—the cybernetics brain literally had to learn to communicate in this unorthodox fashion—that I released a dozen more alpha-wave-pattern adepts to do the same. Always the purpose was to require the "think" portion of 79 to cope with the unskilled programmers, for anyone who communicated in one fashion or another was exactly that—a programmer.

As for myself, I worked day and night to improve the acoustic cybernetics link so that I could carry out my own tests in the vocalized sense. Because of its ability to remember every previous lesson, 79 had "learned to talk" through its incredibly swift translations of sounds into binary digits that were again translated within the memory portions of its neural blocks. For months skilled programmers had carried on "conversations" with the computer, specifically to enlarge upon the capacity of the cybernetics system to communicate in this fashion. As far as the computer itself might be concerned, this was, of course, a clumsy and tedious process of communications. But for us slowpoke humans it worked out fine.

I had hundreds of experiments I wanted to push through as

swiftly as I could, and most of the time they had to be handled personally. Programming tapes was a waste of time, with dozens of technicians underfoot. I preferred to assign the taping and carry out my own experiments in acoustic communications, literally voice-to-voice.

After several months, as long as I exercised care—and practice made this a secondary skill—I was able to maintain two-way voice communications to a degree I would not have thought possible. The sound of that deep, rich voice, modulated to remove the stiffness of the artificial larynx, always commanded a sense of thrill. This was the human, emotional reaction on my part, and I knew it. But I couldn't prevent myself every now and then from shaking my head, and I also found myself eager to resume the experiments. Every hour spent with the computer on a "person-to-person" basis I found that much more fascinating. It was a test of my own ability as well; the cybernetics brain and I had to meet somewhere along the line. It couldn't be a matter of my expecting the computer to fulfill the entirety of speech, and I could never have learned to speak "computerese."

As could have been predicted, we did meet upon common ground. Stiff and awkward, and sometimes chaotically confusing our conversations might be; nevertheless, I could seat myself in the comfortable control chair of my laboratory and enjoy what I was doing.

After months of these tests had gone by, and I slipped as naturally into "computerese" as I might have a foreign language, the cybernetics brain began to assume—at least I felt this to be so—a distinct and recognizable personality. A psychologist would have argued that had I ever encountered a talking rock under the same conditions of extended time, I would have imbued the rock with the same sense of personality.

Men do this with machines all the time. Just listen to a pilot who swears his fighter will respond more eagerly, more smoothly, to his own hands than to those of any other man that flies the machine. . . .

Kim suffered misgivings about my growing sense of association with the computer. She felt the sense of identification was exceeding a normal relationship, that my rapport was more self-imposed psychologically than it was an actual exchange. I waved off her murmured discomfort; if such identification could be realized, I was heartily for it. I sought it out with a secret, fervent desire that it could really be so.

I know this is hardly the accepted scientific approach, and I did not dare to discuss my own feelings with Dr. Vollmer or even that most trustworthy of souls, Tom Smythe. Scientist and materialist I might be, but I was also sufficiently aware of my own emotions to realize I was treading in waters for the most part entirely alien to me.

Any misgivings of my own I hurled aside with a passage from a book, a brief selection of words that always enabled me to bring light to where it was darkest in my lack of understanding of what went on within the timelessness of the cybernetics brain. Science is never that pure, that certain; it is not always the best way.

Arthur Koestler said it better than any man. A copy of his book *The Act of Creation* was always within reach of my hand. In that book Koestler declares: "Max Planck stated that the pioneer scientist must have a vivid intuitive imagination; Faraday was ignorant of mathematics; Von Helmholtz admitted that intuition is superior to mathematical analysis; and Edison benefitted from his shocking ignorance of science."

Amen.

I was aware of inadequacies, but I also had a tremendous ally. The intelligence we called 79.

19

. . . had the effect anticipated. From that moment on there has been affirmed a manifold increase in emotional urgency on the part of Steven Rand A193, to conclude the programming experiments and to attain a new meeting ground for further communications with the cybernetics system. We hesitate to hazard the risk of extrapolation where so many unknowns must be considered, but from the progress to date and the immediate results since the planned incident, it would appear that optimism may be guardedly entertained.

As was explained in the memorandum preceding, we waited until the most propitious moment to dislodge Rand from the secure position into which events had placed him. His growing concern with details of his personal life involving the females Kim Renée Michele and Barbara Johnson clearly lessened the degree of emphasis upon the cybernetics effort. This, too, was anticipated as an inevitable product of the long preparations program in computer programming, in that an element of stasis due to repetitive efforts would direct his attentions elsewhere.

It was the considered opinion of our field force—a unanimous opinion, it must be emphasized—that a shock effect of the desired nature would be created through a sudden and unexpected division of his personal-professional relationships with a single figure, i.e., Dr. Selig Albracht, for whom Steven Rand has held the highest respect. The division of this relationship we felt should be carried out under conditions of maximum emotional-social exposure in order to strengthen the break and to require Rand, psychologically, to stand by his convictions. This was indeed accomplished. Dr. Albracht performed as might have been expected from one of the most capable psychologists in the field. It is regrettable that until some undetermined moment in the future he must continue the cessation of his close friendship with a man he admires more than any other, Dr. Howard Vollmer; however, Dr. Albracht accepts the necessity for these conditions. He is in agreement that we may well have triggered Steven Rand at precisely the right moment to bring him into a deepening emotional relationship with Project 79. Albracht feels, as do the members of this field force, that the intensification of what Rand has achieved may well bring on an unprecedented breakthrough in the bio-cybernetics aspects of this program.

We remain convinced that Steven Rand is unaware of the role played specifically by Dr. Albracht. Rand's association with psychological controls or direction remains concentrated upon Thomas A. Smythe; that is the effect desired.

We have maintained extraordinary monitoring of all human and cybernetics activity related to the working association of Steven Rand with Project 79. Rand is convinced, without undue self-pressure, that he "knows" the computer better than any man. He has achieved a sense of association—what would commonly be considered rapport—that may yet achieve the gestalt level that would constitute complete success for this phase of the project.

What excites this field force, individually and collectively, more than any other aspect of what is now taking place is that there is now appearing a sense of identification *on the part of the cybernetics systems for the man.* We cannot overemphasize this realization. Monitoring of electrical output, energy requirements, systems activation, neural blocks energized, and so forth, clearly are distinguishable in the case of Steven Rand insofar as his contacts with the computer are concerned. If electronic-neural recognition as such truly is possible, then we are witness to its first awakening in the relationship of Rand and Project 79.

It is difficult, exceedingly so, to pinpoint the specifics through which we have arrived at and sustain the foregoing conclusion. We remain aware at all times of the unknowns involved. Yet there is not one among us who will refute the evidence accumulating that an affinity exists in the Rand-79 relationship. Mountsier of Monitoring believes he will soon be able to confirm a distinct level of higher efficiency as regards the cybernetics organism when it is programmed for direct/immediate response with Steven Rand than is noticed with any other human subject/programmer.

At this time we must refrain from specific suggestions for programming as regards Steven Rand. It is a matter of treading warily and reemphasizing the critical need for absolute monitoring. In addition, Rand is functioning under an intense psychological pressure that we feel must be sustained to continue the results now becoming evident.

In respect to . . .

Book
Four

20

IT STARTED OUT to be a beautiful weekend. For several days the snow had come down thickly, draping its dazzling white blanket over the hills and the mountains. As luck would have it, the skies cleared about noon on Friday. That meant the plows would open the main highways by evening, and by the following morning we'd be able to make it to a ski lodge eighty miles from Colorado Springs.

Kim and I never got there. Skiing is supposed to be a dangerous sport. Getting there—driving to the lodge—was far more dangerous. I drove carefully, what with narrow lanes caused by the high snowbanks to each side of the road, and especially the patches of ice where the average driver just didn't expect them. The sun melted snow on one side of the highway. The water drained to the other side, still in shadow, and froze. The worst places were just beneath the hills and along the turns.

I handled the Corvette with all the skill I had, just taking it easy, and we both wore seat belts. But no matter what you do, it doesn't help when the other guy is an idiot.

I came around a turn, braking easily and keeping my foot lightly on the gas pedal to hold traction, when another car came ripping through the turn at us. He—the other driver—hit his brakes suddenly. Right on a patch of ice. And that was it. Two tons of metal skidded wildly out of control. I had just enough time to throw myself to the side, hauling desperately at the wheel.

Kim screamed, I think. There really wasn't time to tell. I felt the first sickening lurch as the other car slammed into my front left fender; a lurch, and simultaneously the crumpling sound of metal. Then everything fell apart around me. A white-hot poker stabbed my leg, a blur flashed before my eyes as the other car tore past, ripping out the left side of the Corvette. Then it was only pain and an empty feeling in my stomach as we left the road and began a slow tumble through the air. The horizon tilted crazily and the sun blasted into my eyes and I remember shouting, "Down! Get down!" to Kim. I forgot the pain, and thought only of her, and then we came back to earth, sideways, and we hit.

The snow saved us. We smashed into a high bank that gave way, absorbing the punch of deceleration. The last thing I knew, a white battering ram exploded through the open window to my left and once again I felt that twisting hot pain all through my leg, and then—nothing. Just nothing.

I woke up in a hospital bed. The first thing I saw were trembling lips and tears staining Kim's cheeks and some blurred faces beyond. The room ended its seesaw trembling and settled down to normalcy, and as my head cleared the faces of a doctor and Tom Smythe came into focus. So did the pain. I glanced away from Kim and saw a huge mass of plaster and some straps, and I made some silly noises about recognizing *my* leg slung awkwardly in traction.

"Jesus." That's all I said for a moment. Because emotions were swirling around inside my skull. My heart leaped at the open concern displayed by Kim—and my leg . . . well, the white-hot poker was still there.

I looked again at Kim, and noticed the dark bruise on the side of her face.

"Hey! What happened—I mean, are you all right, hon?" I reached out for her hand, and the poker stabbed deeply into my leg. I groaned as stars danced before my eyes.

"He'll be all right," I heard. Tom Smythe had a satisfied look on his face.

I gasped for air. "What the hell are you so smug about?" I said, trying to sound angry. I think it must have been more of a whimper than the retort I intended.

[146]

Tom grinned down at me. "Accident must have done you some good," he murmured. "Think of it," he said to the doctor. "He's just coming out of it, and the first thing he wants to know is how *she* feels." He gestured to Kim. "Almost makes me believe the patient is slightly human."

I growled something at him. It's hard to talk, and who the devil wants to, when Kim is kissing me lightly on the lips. I had another look at the angry bruise on her cheek. "It's nothing," she whispered.

They told me what happened. The pieces I didn't know, I mean. Hitting the snowbank on the way back down saved us. My leg was already broken—in fact, it had two breaks—before we ever started to tumble through the air.

"You're a lucky man, Mr. Rand," the doctor said. I looked down at the cast suspended in midair, and concluded immediately that the doctor was an idiot. "Two breaks," he went on, ignoring the white-hot poker someone had left inside the leg. "Very clean, too." He pursed his lips and glanced at some X rays lying on the bed. "Very clean, indeed. Almost classical, I would say. It could have been much worse."

"Thanks a heap," I mumbled through teeth I was gritting to keep from howling with the pain.

"You'll be up and around in no time," the doctor went on in the same nonchalant fashion. "No time at all."

"How the hell long is that?" I shouted at him. Or tried to shout. Halfway through the sentence, my words trailed off in a groan. I must have turned as white as the sheets beneath me.

"Just take it easy," he said, ignoring my demand for just how long was no time at all.

"Sure, sure, just take it easy. It's all roses and lollipops and . . ."

My voice trailed off as a needle slipped into my arm. Whatever it was they were using in that hospital, it didn't waste a moment. Things got fuzzy again, and the voices became just static in the background, and I didn't care because Kim was close to me and that's all I remembered before I went under again. If you're going to go, there's nothing like your last thoughts being about the girl you love who suddenly isn't hiding that she's also in love with you.

They told me later I went out with a smile on my face.

Three weeks later, Tom Smythe arranged for me to be returned to my apartment. Tom did it up royally . . . beautiful nurse in the ambulance that drove me from the hospital. Knowing Tom as I did, I was certain that more than met the eye—either in the nurse or in his move—was involved. I didn't know *how*; I just knew it. It turned out I was right.

At first, however, things were beautiful. A hospital bed and special facilities had been crammed into my apartment. The nurse would stay full time. In the second bedroom, sad to say. Even sadder was the realization that she could handle herself with all the skill of a karate instructor. But then, a full cast and traction a good part of the time does dim one's ardor.

Tom's intention was for me to get back to work. "It's your leg that's broken, not your skull," he reminded me after I'd been implanted back into the apartment.

"Something else feels like it's broken," I leered, watching Christine, my nurse, as she bent over to fix the bed.

"Never mind," he retorted, sticking with *his* original subject. He demonstrated the closed TV circuits, the communications links, and the other facilities through which I could pick up what I'd missed with the Project during my enforced stay in the hospital. "You can get back to work right from here," he added brightly, waving an expansive arm to indicate all the electronic goodies. "We'll have your meals sent up so that—"

I managed an astonished look on my face. "You mean Christine doesn't cook?" I stared at her starched white blouse, and winced.

She didn't miss a thing. "That and some other things aren't on the agenda, Mr. Rand." She smiled.

"Color me frustrated," I grumbled.

"As I said, we'll have your meals sent up," Smythe went on without a pause. "Dessert, too."

"That's just ginger-peachy," I snarled at him.

"And Kim will be working with you here a good part of the time."

I sat straight up in bed. Or tried to, anyway. A wave of pain washed over me as I collapsed back onto the pillows.

"Idiot," Christine remonstrated, at my side immediately. She studied me professionally for a moment, concluded that I would live, and remarked, "You're not just frustrated, Mr. Rand— you're helpless."

"Don't remind me," I groaned.

But, all things considered, the world was a lot brighter than when I'd been carted off unconscious to the hospital. Despite his appreciation for classical fractures, the doctor was right; I was damned lucky. Two breaks, both clean. Mending would be no problem just so long as I behaved myself. And if I did that —took it easy with the leg—in two weeks I'd be able to get into a wheelchair and move around a bit. The doctor had promised, soon afterward, a lighter cast and crutches. And that meant getting back into the full swing of things.

In the meantime, Kim could bring me up to date on what had happened during my enforced absence from the Project. She could do a hell of a lot more, I smirked to myself. We'd send Christine off to the movies or wherever it was well-stacked nurses wanted to go when they had some free time. I didn't care. Being alone with Kim was—well, I wasn't *completely* helpless. After all, there are some things that a guy can . . .

It didn't matter. Ten minutes after Kim showed up that evening, I knew something was wrong. Terribly wrong. The first opportunity I had for a careful look at Kim's face told me that much. She couldn't hide the strain that was there. For a little while it remained hidden beneath her smile, her pleasure at my being out of the hospital. But then whatever it was that gnawed at her showed. And it frightened me.

It happened several days after I went to the hospital with my broken leg.

The accident, I mean. Oh, not the wrecked car.

The accident.

The one that opened a cybernetics Pandora's box. And plunged me into the kind of nightmare you don't even find in your worst dreams.

The worst kind of nightmare. The kind that's *real*. From which you don't wake up.

Kim told me everything she knew. I learned more from my own confrontation with 79. With what Kim had told me, plus my interrogations of the cybernetics brain, I began to fit together the pieces. I interviewed our chief programmers; I demanded records of the tests and experiments during the past several weeks.

It didn't seem possible. I didn't rush to any conclusions. Things didn't come that fast to me. I had to put it together slowly, cross-check hundreds of details. Slowly the nightmare began to form, like wisps and tendrils of fog in the back of my mind. Swirling and elusive, but real. Terribly real.

Imagination is a precious commodity of intelligence. I wasn't lacking in any. But I forced mine down, stifled it, fought to keep from leaping to conclusions. I didn't want—I mean, there couldn't be allowed any room for error in this thing. Not any, because it was . . . well, "unexpected" is such an inadequate word.

And while I was trying to make sense out of something impossible, I kept hearing a strange sound. It almost began to haunt me. It was thin, and barely discernible. But it was there, all right.

It was the thin trickle of laughter somewhere in a deep well of my own mind.

It sounded like the laughter of Selig Albracht.

21

He was uncomfortable. He fidgeted with his hands, little nervous motions that betrayed his attempts to appear casual and unworried. He sat in the chair at the side of my control desk in my apartment office, his eyes darting from one part of the room to another. For several minutes I pretended to be busy, studying papers on my desk, while I actually studied him.

But why should Ed Taylor be uncomfortable, irritable, looking as if he expected someone to drag him away at any moment? Taylor was one of our better programmers, a natural adept at working alpha-wave patterns with the computer. He fitted smoothly into the program, regarded 79 as just another machine, and had proved eminently satisfactory in his work.

He was also the most relaxed person on the staff, I reminded myself. Correction. That was past tense. Now he appeared as if the slightest noise would break him into pieces. But from what Kim had told me about the "incident" with him, I didn't blame Ed Taylor. I forced any conclusions from my mind. Things promised to be bad enough without my going off on uneducated tangents. I turned to face him.

"Well, that's out of the way," I said by way of preamble, doing my damnedest to be casual with him. I wasn't, of course. I was even tighter than the unhappy, bedeviled man sitting with me. He started suddenly at the sound of my voice, wincing at his own reaction.

"Miss Michele filled me in, Ed," I said slowly. "But only in general terms," I added quickly. I didn't want Taylor to feel I knew that much about what had happened with him. I wanted it in his own words. "I wanted to speak with you myself," I went on.

He nodded, remaining silent. Damn! I hoped it wouldn't be necessary to play a cat-and-mouse game.

"I understand you fainted while you were on duty," I said abruptly.

His eyes widened, showing fright. He leaned forward, his hands fluttering. "But I've never . . . I mean, I've never passed out before, Mr. Rand! I swear it! Nothing like that has ever happened to me before. I—I . . ."

I held up my hand to cut the flow of words. "Hey, take it easy." I laughed. "You're not on trial, Ed. No one's brought you here for punishment. I just want to get all the information I can." I offered a cigarette to him; he grabbed it and lit up with shaking hands.

"Let me get something clear with you, Ed," I said carefully. "This isn't a court or anything of the sort. I asked you here because reports are cold and impersonal things. I can't tell that much from them. I *need* your help," I said as earnestly as I could, which was easy to say because it was absolutely the truth.

He sank back in his chair, sucking deeply on the cigarette. His voice was suddenly subdued and weak. "I thought I might be in, well, you know what I mean, Mr. Rand. I've been worried out of my mind about it, worried that I was going to be fired." His eyes had the expression of a whipped dog. Whatever had happened, it went deeper than any of us realized.

"For the record, then," I said quickly, "so there won't be any misunderstanding, Ed. You haven't fallen from grace; your position with the project is *not* jeopardized; and no one has even given the slightest thought to letting you go." I smiled at him. "It just so happens that you're one of the best programmers, and we need you more than you need us."

"Christ, I'm glad to hear *you* say it, Mr. Rand," he said with a brief smile of his own. "I—I feel better already."

So much for *that*.

I plunged. "Kick it off from the beginning, Ed. The whole thing—just as it happened."

His brow creased as he went back in his mind, and immediately there appeared again the agitation and sense of upset.

"Take your time," I said, hoping to keep him at low key, "We're in no rush. And remember what I said—I need information. I need your help in this thing."

"Okay, Mr. Rand," he replied, settling down. "You know the tests I was running?"

I nodded and tapped the papers on my desk. "Uh-huh. You were handling the systems of visual identification—new scopes as they related to the alpha-wave programming." I lit a cigarette and wasted several seconds blowing smoke into the air. "If I remember correctly, we had more than the oscilloscopes going in the tests. Blinking light patterns, and so forth."

"That's right, Mr. Rand," he said, eager suddenly to share the experience, to pass on to another person some of the load he'd been carrying.

"All right, then, Ed," I prompted him, "why don't you just tell it to me in your own way? In your own words."

He went back to the tests he was conducting. "Well, it was the standard setup. I mean, the EEG wires, and so forth. I had been running block messages in Morse to 79. Nothing spontaneous. The messages were given to me the night before so I could study them, sort of get them down comfortably in my own mind, so that when I alpha-patterned them there wouldn't be any hesitation on my part. It sort of makes it easier when you know ahead of time what you're going to be saying."

I nodded, not speaking.

"The idea was that I would transmit to the 'brain.' We weren't interested in getting two-way communication, and we programmed the system simply to receive the messages as part of a test. Miss Michele, she, uh, was in charge of this phase. She had a couple of other people in the cubicle with us. They were taking notes, getting tape and film records. We wanted to see if the blink response of the control board could give us the same information, or maybe more than the oscilloscopes. Sort of a free-wheeling setup."

He stubbed out the cigarette, reaching automatically for another one. I'd never recalled Ed Taylor as a chain smoker.

"Well, everything went along fine. I mean, no sweat with any part of the tests," he said by way of explanation. "The trouble came when we started the second phase, when the 'brain' would be answering me."

"What do you mean by 'trouble,' Ed?" I didn't want to push, but at the same time I didn't want to lose the track on which he was now moving.

Ed Taylor's face screwed up. "Maybe 'trouble' isn't the right word, Mr. Rand," he said, groping for a better means of communicating to me what had happened. "You see, nothing took place all of a sudden. It's hard to describe and—" He looked up at me, fearful that he was botching it.

I waved away his apprehension. "You're doing fine. Don't let me put words in your mouth," I said. "Take your time; find it in your own way."

He nodded slowly. "As you know, Mr. Rand, when you're transmitting you watch the prompter," he continued. "Makes it easier and keeps you from forgetting as you go along. But when you're receiving from the 'brain'—especially when you're in a test like that one, I mean, there's no need to pay attention to the alpha pattern coming back because it's strictly for test recording—you don't have to watch anything. Anything in particular. When the answers started coming back I could, well, not hear, but sort of, umm, well, *feel* them. No sweat with that. I just didn't have to pay attention. They were stock items, the regular question-answer routine we've done so many times."

He grinned sheepishly. "In fact, its easy to get bored when you're doing that. You know something's going on up there," he tapped his head, "but you don't have to listen in. Miss Michele, and the others, they were recording everything, taking it down, like I said. The only thing that was new in the cubicle were the lights. The blink-pattern tests."

He seemed to be encountering difficulty, and thought carefully to find the right words. "That's when the trouble, the *feel-ing* I got then, that this was when the trouble began. That's when it seemed to start, the best I could remember, anyway."

I nodded to urge him on.

"Well, I was looking at the main panel," he said slowly. "There was a large lens—a wide light, sort of an orange-red, quite different from amber or red. In between, sort of. And the blink pattern was matching the oscilloscope waves. There would be a blink just as the waves peaked on the scope. I found this more interesting than looking at nothing in the room, and I began watching it. I found myself staring at it, I guess. You know how it is, Mr. Rand," he said, unknowingly begging for agreement. "You've really got nothing to do, something catches your eye, and you play a, well, a sort of game with yourself, watching the thing, letting your mind ride with the patterns."

"I know." He was running with it now; I didn't want to interfere.

He rubbed his cheek, thinking deeply. "Well, the overhead lights were off. The bright ones. That gave us a better picture of the scopes, I guess. Anyway, I stared at the lens, the orange-red one that blinked when the scope waves peaked. And then things sort of got a little crazy."

I forced myself to remain casual. "How do you mean that, Ed?"

His hands moved uncomfortably. "It's hard to say, Mr. Rand. One moment I was looking at the light, the blinking—I remember the reflection seemed to fill my glasses as I stared at it—and then suddenly it wasn't blinking any more. It was a, well, a steady light."

"Had it been turned on that way?"

"No." He said that clearly. "That's what I thought at the moment. That a switch had gone bad and the light was now on, just like any light. But that wasn't it." He shook his head slowly. "Miss Michele tried to explain that to me, but I guess I'm still pretty confused about it all. I mean, she said that the blinking pattern remained, only that I wasn't consciously paying attention to it any more."

[155]

I made a fast mental note to check that out with Kim. And to check all the records. I thought I knew what was giving fits to Ed Taylor, but I held off going any further until I had some more information.

"That does sound a bit odd," I agreed with Taylor. "Did she tell you the blink rate?"

"Sure. It was standard, Mr. Rand. We usually run between sixteen and twenty peaks per second," he said. "The working range is twelve to thirty, but that's one extreme to the other."

I knew that, of course.

". . . and she said we were holding about nineteen—eighteen or nineteen—per second."

I chewed my lip. "Ed, you know you can't *see* a blink rate of nineteen per second, don't you?"

"Yeah. That sort of shook me when I started the alpha tests," he said easily. "Then it was Dr. Vollmer, I think, explained to me that I was correlating the blinks. I mean, even though my eyes wouldn't register that fast a beat as a blinking light—I would see it as a steady light—I *knew* about the blink rate; I was controlling my own alpha-wave pattern, and so I *knew* it. Inside me I knew this was so. He said—Dr. Vollmer, I mean—he said that it was something like an optical illusion, but one that was taking place *within* the brain."

"He was right, too," I added, hoping that Taylor would accept in my own words that what had happened to him, in his "seeing" a blink pattern too fast for the eyes to notice as separate flashes of light, wasn't at all unusual for an alpha adept.

"But where did the trouble begin?" I prodded gently. "When did you get the feeling that something was going wrong?"

The aura of discomfort was over him again. I cursed to myself; he was as touchy as a nervous cat.

"Well, I'm sort of piecing it together now, Mr. Rand. Like knowing things now, that Miss Michele told me about, that I didn't know before."

"Take it any way you like, Ed," I said to calm him down.

"The way I look at it is that—it's hard to get all this straight

—well, suddenly the blinking pattern was wrong." He shook his head, a miserable expression on his face. "Suddenly it wasn't blinking any more. That's the steady light I told you about. It was steady, all right. Just a steady light. Miss Michele told me that the blink pattern had never changed—she showed me the recording to prove it—that it was going on just like before."

He looked up, a hint of defiance in his voice. "But that's not how it was to me," he said. "Just that steady light, and getting bigger and bigger all the time."

I *didn't* know *that*. "What do you mean, Ed?"

"The light, that orange-red light. Suddenly it seemed to expand. No," he corrected himself. "Not suddenly. A gradual and steady expansion would be more like it."

He had started to perspire as if under some growing strain. But *why?*

"I remember that my glasses were the same orange-red color," he said slowly. "As if the glass had been tinted. I don't know why, but it seemed like that. And there was something else that was awfully strange. I'd never felt it before."

His body stiffened, and he became almost antagonistic, as if knowing before he spoke the words that I wouldn't believe him. "It was time, Mr. Rand. Time."

"What happened, Ed?"

"Time. It began to slow down, as if the seconds were dragging, and everything was stretching out. And the light got brighter and brighter until it began to fill the entire room." The words spilled in a rush from his lips. "It all happened before I knew it was happening and yet it seemed to take forever. I got scared. Real scared, I mean. All the way through me. I had this feeling that it was wrong, all wrong; that everything was wrong. And there was this terrible blazing light, the orange-red light from the panel. It seemed to be all over the room and *inside* me, and it scared the absolute bejesus out of me and I tried to speak; I wanted to tell them to turn off the light, but I couldn't talk, and I couldn't move. You ever have a dream like that, Mr. Rand, where you're in a fight with someone and you want to hit

[157]

him but you can't move your hands; you just can't move them; it's like everything is in glue?" He leaned back, gasping, the perspiration glistening on his face.

"That's what it was like. That Goddamned light, and time, it was gone, and I tried to shout at them, tried to get up, but I *couldn't*. I just couldn't. And . . . and . . ." His voice trailed away and he stared at the floor.

"And that's when you fainted," I added.

"I don't know," he mumbled. "But that's what they told me. Later, I mean. They said I was out for about ten minutes. I didn't remember a thing about it." His eyes were imploring. "Jesus, Mr. Rand, but I was *scared*. Real scared. What's going to happen now?"

I glanced at the papers on my desk. "Something a lot more pleasant than what happened before," I said with a smile. "I've studied the medical reports. You've got a pretty common disease, Ed. Around here especially."

He waited for me to continue.

"You've been working too hard," I said lightly. "Just plain old-fashioned drudgery got you down, that's all. The medical report says you're almost worn out. But there's an easy cure for that."

He still waited, afraid to interrupt.

"Plain old rest, Ed. That's all. You could have keeled over anywhere. At home watching a television show, driving your car; anywhere. But you're a lucky bastard. Since it happened while you were on the job, you get the benefits of your employment."

"What do you mean, Mr. Rand?"

I grinned. "I mean you get thirty days off—medical rest, so to speak. *With* full pay, I should add."

He beamed. "That's a lot of fishing a man can do. In thirty days, I mean."

We laughed together.

I didn't tell him that before he lost consciousness in the test cubicle he had gone into hysterical, uncontrolled convulsions.

22

Major Harold Konigsberg, MD, USAF, sat
across my desk, relaxed behind a long Jamaica cigar I'd offered
him when he came to the apartment. Major Konigsberg, flight
surgeon at the Air Force Academy, had come in response to a
call I'd put in to him. If I were moving along the right path,
then the major could well fill in the missing pieces to the puzzle
of Ed Taylor.

Kim sat in with us. For the most part she had been witness
more than participant in the exchange between myself and the
major. Konigsberg had read her report on the incident of Ed
Taylor. Before the major asked some questions of his own, I
wanted him to have as much information as I'd obtained so far.
That alone had been a sticky proposition. Security. It leaped up
between myself and the major like a dragon's tooth. I raised all
kinds of hell with Tom Smythe to break down the security
barriers. Tom came through only after he'd run his own check
on Konigsberg, grilled the man personally, and sworn him to
silence. If the major even *remembered* anything after he left the
meeting with Kim and myself, Smythe told him grimly, he'd be
shipped to Greenland for the next hundred years.

It didn't seem to bother Konigsberg. I think that in the fourteen years of his military service he must have heard the same
speech seven times every year. Smythe seems to forget that
there are security zealots sprinkled liberally throughout the government and that their messages all have the same weary sound
to them.

Major Konigsberg read Kim's official report, raised his eyebrows several times, puffed earnestly on the cigar, and then

lowered the report to my desk. He flicked ashes into the waste-basket near his chair and looked at me.

"What else?" he asked.

I leaned forward—grunting a bit with the effort—and punched the start button of a concealed tape recorder. We settled back for a replay of my conversation with Ed Taylor. When it ended, the major stubbed out the remains of the cigar, arched his brows, and smiled when I handed him a new one.

"Very interesting," he mused, removing the cellophane. He gestured at the report. "The case of your Mr. Taylor, I mean," he added. "Interesting, but not really unusual."

"Oh?" That was all I ventured for the moment.

He tossed his match into the wastebasket, peering after it to see if he'd started a fire. Satisfied, he turned back to me. "No, not unusual, Mr. Rand," he said. "Miss Michele here," he nodded toward Kim, "pointed it out in her report. Mr. Taylor was a victim of photic stimulation. Sometimes, especially among pilots, it's referred to as flicker vertigo or flicker unconsciousness. And anyone working with alpha-wave patterns of the brain has some familiarity with its cause and effect."

Sure, I knew something of flicker vertigo. Under certain conditions a flickering light can match the alpha-wave pattern of a human brain. Susceptibility is a happenstance thing; it occurs in one individual and doesn't in another, and except in those cases where there's extreme susceptibility it isn't possible to tell just who will or won't be a victim. There's a relationship, sometimes distant and sometimes meaningful, between the effects of flicker vertigo and an epileptic. But it's unpredictable. And although the effects of a flickering light have been known for a long time—the ancient slave traders would make slaves stare at a rapidly spinning potter's wheel to search out possible epileptics —it hasn't been until recent years that we began a really scientific study of the phenomenon. And suddenly I was *very* interested, because flicker vertigo is associated with the alpha-wave pattern of the human brain.

And alpha-wave patterns were critical to everything I was doing with Project 79. Also, I had come to suspect that my electronic playmate—the computer—was acting in a manner wholly unprecedented and that it all involved photic stimulation. I was badly in need of information and I didn't want to miss any bets. Which meant not acting like a smartass. And turning to a source to which photic stimulation—flicker vertigo—was not at all strange. Like Major Harold Konigsberg, MD, USAF—a flight surgeon who was considered an expert in the subject.

"Can you give me a thumbnail rundown, Major?"

He shifted to a more comfortable position. "As long as these cigars of yours hold out, Mr. Rand, I am very willing to run down along all of my nails."

I waved him on.

"But first I want to ask *you* a question."

I looked carefully at him. I nodded. "Shoot."

"Why the big scene with getting *me* down here, Rand? Your watchdog—Smythe, I think is his name—was practically foaming at the mouth about my learning something about your precious computer." He waved his hand to dismiss my surprise. "Oh, for Christ's sake, Rand, it's no secret among a group of us. We've known about the program; we don't know exactly what you're doing, but we can guess pretty well." He took another long drag on the cigar and then waved it at me. "But I'm wandering. Forgive me. I started to ask you why you wanted *me* here to play footsie with the photic stimulation." He nodded at Kim. "Miss Michele is knowledgeable on the subject. Dr. Vollmer—we know he's tied in with your program—is an expert on alpha-wave patterns. So why the big fuss to get some obscure flight surgeon in a blue suit into the middle of your zealously guarded electronic harem?"

I couldn't help the laughter that met his remark. "Major, you're priceless," I gasped, "even if all these chuckles have me wincing inside me. The leg doesn't laugh as well as the rest of me."

He threw me a glance of professional sympathy; I think the bastard really meant it, and that made me feel good. If we had some empathy between us, he'd be free with his words. I urged him to go on.

"Well, the fact is, Mr. Rand," he said, "that even Dr. Vollmer—and I credit him with being a genius—has a restrictive outlook. He has what you could describe as a clinical relationship with photic stimulation. It's cut and dried and laid out neatly in the laboratory. My attitude is different. As a flight surgeon I've lived with photic stimulation—with flicker vertigo—as an active thing. The first thing I'll tell you is that it's lethal." He looked at us over his cloud of cigar smoke.

"It kills."

Suddenly we were paying very close attention.

"Like I said, it can kill. I prefer to think of it in the pilot's terms. Maybe that's because I'm as much an airplane driver as I am a flight surgeon. Gives me a closer and more intimate look at things. Flicker vertigo comes without warning; it can come at the damnedest times, and it can be very terrifying—even when you live through it. It's always associated with a light, of course, as you know so well yourself. But it's one thing to look at a pretty light in a laboratory and something else to get the works when you're upstairs and everything comes unglued all around you.

"There are sensitives and there are sensitives." He shrugged. "We haven't any real way of knowing. Not even lab tests work all the time, because the individual reacts differently at different times. Alcohol, drugs, exhaustion, state of mind, surroundings and environment—they're all involved. In some individuals, although they are the rarer cases, even a single flash of light will match the alpha-wave pattern, at just that moment, and *zing!*"
—he snapped his fingers—"the individual is unconscious. Just like that," he said to answer the expression on my face.

"In most cases, however, to get an honest case of flicker vertigo—and we're referring to complete spatial disorientation as resulting from optical exposure to the flickering light—there must be a steady interruption of the light source. Many factors intervene—point or broad source of light, intensity, color, and so forth. Neon signs, television screens, motion-picture screens, moving past a row of trees with the sun directly in view, car

[162]

headlights moving past a fence, light reflections from snow-drifts, on tracks . . . almost anything can trigger it. Now, let me emphasize that not everyone is susceptible. But once you get caught, the odds are that you're dead game for a repeat session."

I chewed that one over. "That means we're taking a chance if we use Ed Taylor for alpha-wave tests, doesn't it?"

He nodded agreement. "I can guarantee he'll go under again the moment he gets an optical alpha-wave pattern."

"Go on, please."

"Well, assume the conditions are right—the light source is just so, and the effects of the flickering light are right on target." Konigsberg was almost cheerful with his narrative; I had the strange thought that he wouldn't be any different if he were picking up the pieces of a friend from some cruelly smashed airplane. But it takes all kinds of professionals. Almost as if reading my thoughts he concentrated on a case in point—flicker vertigo from flight. "Take a pilot landing a single-engine plane—one with a fan instead of a torch, and—"

"I'm sorry, Doctor," Kim broke in suddenly, smiling. "But I'm afraid you lost me there. 'Fan'? 'Torch'?"

Konigsberg laughed. "Forgive me, Miss Michele. I was referring to someone flying an airplane with a propeller instead of a jet engine."

"Oh. Please continue."

He waved the cigar freely. "All right, then. Our boy is flying an iron bird with a fan in front. The conditions are perfect, too. For trouble, I mean. Let's say he's coming in for a landing at sunset and he's landing to the west. Do you know what that means?" His expression was a challenge.

"Of course," I said slowly. "He would be landing into the sun, looking at the sun through the propeller."

"Right as rain, Mr. Rand. Only—and it's a very big only—when you're on final approach you cut back on the power. The propeller turns a great deal more slowly than when you're cruising. In fact, you can get about five hundred rpm with the propeller. That means about sixteen to twenty blinks per second.

And that's what happened to Ed Taylor in your Frankenstein hutch, or whatever it is you call your laboratory.

"You see, the brain doesn't register the individual flashes of light. As you know, this is too fast for the optical system of the human being. The brain fuses the incoming flickers into a single light—a steady source point. When Taylor was—well, whatever it was he was doing, when he was able to distinguish the light as a separate source"—he looked at us suspiciously—"I'd still like to know how you managed *that*. Care to let me in on your trade secrets?"

I smiled, and shook my head.

"I thought not," he grunted. "Anyway, when that moment came that he was distracted, or chose to let his mind wander, the light separation vanished. His brain fused the signals into a single light source. But he was susceptible; damn, but he was! From what I gathered—the tape recording and the report—he wasn't looking at a single small light point, but something with some meaningful diameter or dimension to it. Darkened room, wide source of light, the right frequency, and, umm, yes, he mentioned the light as orange-red—that's the most dangerous; did you know that?—well, that's all. I'll bet that if you run a check through his close relatives, perhaps even several generations back, you'll discover some form of epileptic evidence."

"Is it necessary that they be epileptics?" Kim didn't take notes, but the recorder was on, had been on from the beginning of our meeting.

Konigsberg shook his head. "Not at all," he replied. "That's what fouls up this whole thing. Normally—at least the odds favor it—there's some form of susceptibility strongly related to epilepsy. But it's not necessary at all."

"What about the reaction?" I asked. "Taylor had some severe convulsions."

Kim shuddered. "They really were . . . quite awful, Doctor," she added, "I'd never seen anything like it before."

Konigsberg shrugged off her painful memories. "It happens," he replied. "Then again, the reactions vary. Sometimes the man doesn't even fall unconscious. He becomes wildly unstable, irritable. Sometimes he's seized as if in a coma; fully conscious but unable to speak or to control his body. He may act as if paralyzed or he may suffer irregular muscular twisting and jerking. The head snaps from side to side with force enough to do damage to the neck. I want to emphasize that there's no guaranteed pattern. He may be dazed. In fact, he may even realize what's happening to him and he will take steps to stop what's happening. Usually that will kill him. As far as pilots are concerned, I mean."

"But why would that happen?" His remark puzzled me; it was hard to believe.

"I explained—or maybe I didn't," Konigsberg said, "that with pilots flicker vertigo can be lethal. And it is. Imagine a man on his final approach, still several hundred feet up, and he finally goes blank. Just like that. He's going to continue straight into the ground, and that sort of thing can ruin your whole day. Of if he has convulsions he hurls the plane out of control in just an instant, and a crash is inevitable. Say that a pilot is on instruments, within the clouds. If his rotating beacons intermesh—their reflections off the clouds, off his wings—he can get flicker vertigo. And having that happening to you while you're IFR—flying on instruments—is a death sentence. It can happen to a helicopter pilot who looks at a light source—the sun, the moon, lights on the ground—through his rotor blades. Now, going back to what I said before: suppose the pilot feels the effects coming on. What's the first reaction?"

"Close your eyes, of course," I said quickly.

"Uh-huh," he came back just as fast. "Why?"

"To shut out the source of light."

"And that, my friend, will kill you. Abrupt closure of the eyes *can set off the seizure.* We don't know why. Not really, and I won't give you any theories in the way of explanation. The best bet is that the eyelids permit only red light to enter. The brain cells are peculiar creatures"—I smiled inwardly at his remark; how well Kim and I knew *that*!—"and they're irritable. They react to red light in a case like this. They react to it much more strongly than they do to white light, which, in its effect, is

[165]

considered neutral." Major Konigsberg shrugged. "I don't have to know the why of it, only that it happens, and it's happened enough to kill some very good people."

He seemed to slump in his chair. "Some very good people, indeed," he mused, drowned suddenly in a rush of memories I was sure he had held at bay—until our questions brought him face to face with the past again.

I had some of the answers I wanted. Not enough of them yet, but at least it was a good start. Ed Taylor was sensitive to photic stimulation; that much was an established fact. There might be more photic sensitives among the alpha programmers and test subjects; we would have to be extremely careful about any blink-light tests. As to why Taylor was suddenly seized—well, anything could have started it. The blink lights, the lighting conditions of the cubicle, the red-orange color of the light, his closing his eyes . . . he could have had excess caffeine in his system, too many aspirins, or being overtired. Any one of these items or a combination of things could have set off his attack of flicker vertigo *and* the terrifying convulsions that followed.

But that was the least of it. Really. I wasn't concerned about Ed Taylor, for he would be fine. And we could even induce flicker vertigo if this were desired for test purposes. The attacks by themselves were harmless in the laboratory under controlled conditions. Many victims of flicker vertigo never even remembered what happened to them; they were wholly unaware of blacking out or going through muscular disorientation. Flicker vertigo kills when you're flying. I wondered how many automobile accidents—Konigsberg brought up this point—we could attribute to flicker vertigo. Good Lord, all the conditions that existed on the highway—headlights passing behind rows of trees or fences or telephone poles or cables or rows of passing cars . . . Konigsberg estimated that flicker vertigo killed hundreds, perhaps thousands of people every year. Even white-painted lines, spaced at specific distances, became a killer to some drivers who lost control of their cars "for no reason." And I'd

[166]

never see a word about photic stimulation in any safety studies of the highways!

But all that was getting me nowhere. My concern wasn't flight or driving. It was for that cybernetics organism for which I was, to a great extent, responsible. At least with the bio-cybernetics test program. And that's what worried me. Worried, hell! I was starting to run scared.

And with good reason.

Several weeks had gone by since Ed Taylor went into convulsions.

During that time I was flat on my back in a hospital bed, and I was out of touch with what had been happening with the bio-cybernetics program.

79 had taken over its own research.

And that scared the hell out of me.

Not because of the self-programming, so to speak. That capability we had built into the cybernetics organism. When it lacked data, it attempted to seek it out. It requested additional information; it queried its programmers; it kept searching for missing pieces in its memory neural blocks.

The human programmers had long been accustomed to this capability of 79. Their responsibility was to add to the memory capacity of what was already the single greatest storehouse of knowledge in existence. They found nothing unusual in their meeting the requests of the computer or, if they did, they shrugged it off. Security has its drawbacks; the honored stone wall of "need to know" effectively blocks questions. After a while a technician or an engineer or a whole army of them learn it's wisest not to ask questions. Leave the questions to the big-domes. What the hell, they're the ones who are in charge. Intellectual brilliance has been channeled effectively, and horribly, into tight and restrictive specializations. So you do what you're paid to do and you become very skilled at minding your own damned business.

Thus you fail to recognize when the cybernetics organism with which you're working as a test programmer begins to act entirely out of the ordinary. And even if you *do* recognize the unusual, you remember the Code—*Don't rock the boat!* You remember the cold stares, the security indoctrinations, the warnings and the penalties for not staying in your own technical baliwick.

In effect, the whole damned staff turned their backs on what was happening. By the time *I* stumbled on the truth, it was too late.

79 had broken loose.

23

CATALYST, THY NAME is Ed Taylor.

Because when this man succumbed in the control cubicle to photic stimulation, and went through psychological extremes of panic and then, unknown to him, violent physical seizure and convulsion, his human brain was still linked to the cybernetics system.

The contact with its intensive peaks both psychological and physiological triggered a sudden demand for data on the part of 79. This wasn't unusual. In fact, the computer was operating as its designers had intended. It was employing its built-in feed-back mechanism that prompted it to pursue data in any area where it determined there existed a deficiency in data.

Only now this self-motivating principle was being exercised with a level of capability somewhat unanticipated and, what turned out to have serious implications, I wasn't around to spot what was happening. I was flat on my scientific butt with a busted leg that kept me away from direct observations of 79.

Simply enough, the cybernetics brain had come to recognize when it could not receive the data it sought through standard programming. That's the difference between a single grain of sand and an entire mountain. Feedback, switching theory, open-end data input . . . it all now came to fruition. In electronic-hungry fashion, its appetite whetted by the extraordinary session with Ed Taylor, 79 sought to fill the gaps it sensed within glowing neural memories. With single-minded purpose it demanded data—and received what it demanded.

The technicians servicing 79 found nothing untoward in the sudden machine-prompted insistence on more information.

Their job, in fact, was to respond to such demands. What they didn't realize was that the alpha-wave pattern tests were wholly new to the short life of the computer. The technicians themselves didn't even know such tests had been initiated. They existed in a world of their own, and there was no need for them to be privy to secret experiments. They didn't know of the alpha tests, and they were unaware that for the first time, rather than juggling its already vast stores of data, 79 had been monitoring an experiment *in which it was an active and essential participant.*

All they knew was that they had received one more standard, normal, quite ordinary request for data on just one more of tens of thousands of different subjects. They did their jobs and fed the data requested to the computer banks.

If it were possible, truly, for a cybernetics brain to exhibit an intensified interest in data, then we were unknowing witness to the stupendous event. In human terms 79 suffered the corrosive indigestion of curiosity. Impelled by *our* programming and testing, it suffered from acute lack of knowledge. It sensed it had wide gaps in understanding what had happened through Ed Taylor. Again, it's difficult, if not impossible at this stage of the game, to equivocate electronic programming with compulsion. Whatever the impetus, blindly or purposefully, the damned thing was functioning with the first signs of electronic awareness we all hoped might one day be realized. And it had happened when we were looking the other way.

I read the reports Kim brought me. I felt as if they might suddenly turn to ashes right there in my hands. I looked up at Kim, beautiful, real Kim, and everything seemed more unreal. I couldn't even get excited over her being alone with me in my bedroom. It's difficult to become aroused when there's a cold trickle down the middle of your back.

"For several days after the Taylor incident, 79 carried out intensive scanning. Not once, but repeatedly," Kim said, her face furrowed with concentration. "We confirmed this, of course, through monitoring. It's all there," she gestured diffidently at the reports spread out on the bed before me. "But there's nothing openly unusual in what 79 has been doing. It's all built-in response."

Her hands fluttered nervously, and she reached for her third cigarette. Quite suddenly I became aware that Kim was exhausted. I took special notice of what I had missed: the tired lines in her face and the sag of her shoulders. I didn't say anything at the moment because I was stumbling after a crookedly wriggling finger of suspicion.

I lit her cigarette and asked her to go on. "Something seems wrong, though," she said, worrying openly. "I don't know what it is. It's, well, the sort of thing you feel, a sixth sense . . ." Her voice trailed off, and for a long moment she stared vacantly. Then she shook herself, as if to cast away the doubts, and returned to the moment. And gave me what I needed most: information.

"Everything else went normally," she said with distaste, "if you can consider 100 percent, absolutely nominal operation of the entire cybernetics system as normal. Maybe perfection has come early to 79." She shrugged, flicking ashes from her cigarette. "I don't know, but the computer has been running on all burners ever since the incident with Taylor."

"That's a strange expression from you," I noted. "Sort of heretic for old Vollmer, isn't it?"

She smiled crookedly. "He'd have fits if he heard me discussing his prize animal like this."

I raised my brows. "Sounds like a mother instinct. I mean, the way you described the crotchety old bastard."

"Uh-huh." She nodded. "I know. Ever since the blowup with Selig." She shrugged again. "But this isn't getting us anywhere, is it?"

I smiled at her; no, it sure as hell wasn't. But the more I looked at her tired eyes, the less inclined I was to push the girl I loved. She took that problem out of my hands and returned to the business at hand.

"Obviously," she said with a grimace, "we'd been deficient in certain areas of programming."

"Like?"

[171]

"Hypnotism, mesmerism, posthypnotic suggestion, alpha-wave patterns, and photic stimulation—should I continue with the list?"

"You're joking, Kim!"

She blew a kiss at me. "Trust me never to do that at this moment, darling."

"I trust you," I said grimly, nodding my head. "I don't trust myself but I trust you. And I need you, because the deeper I get into this, the less I like it."

"You're going to like it even less, Steve."

I glared at her. "Don't leave me waiting at the altar. Let's have it in the basics."

"As I said, 79 put out its requests for everything, and I do mean everything," she stressed, dead serious, "involving hypnotism, alpha-wave disturbances. All of it. And—"

"Was the data supplied?"

"Of course." She looked at me with surprise evident in her face. "Why shouldn't it have been? These subjects were programmed before. As you know," she said with just a touch of impatience. "And you know as well there are limitations inherent in such programming. You can't spell out these subjects as raw data, Steve, and—"

"I know, I know." I tried to brush the fog away from my eyes.

"So there are gaps," she said, cross now. "And when the specific request is made, the purpose of the programmers is to pour everything into the request. Of course, we spelled it out with the customary precautions that much of what was being submitted amounted to experimental evidence only, that it must be separated from factual data. . . ." She waved her hand to indicate that I already knew whatever she had to say about procedures. She was right, of course; I knew.

"But then something happened that no one expected," she said with her lips tight.

I waited.

"79 requested a demonstration of hypnotics."

I boggled at that. "A *demonstration*?" I hoped I didn't sound as stupid to Kim as I did to myself.

"Uh-huh." Her face was blank. Deliberately, controlled blank. She didn't want to interject her own evaluations as yet, and I was grateful for that.

"Don't stop now."

She rustled the papers in her hand. "Not simply a parlor-stage demonstration, of course. 79 can't *see* in that respect. The computer spelled out its request in a very specific manner. It wanted EEG hookups, all details of the individuals involved, aural input—the works. 79 wanted to be—ah," she stumbled over her words. "It wanted to be certain that nothing would be left out."

"Did you query the intent?"

Her eyes turned to stare into mine. "That I did, Steve, and—" Again she shrugged.

"Well, what the devil happened!" I shouted.

She ignored my outburst. "We received the response that the data of hypnotic experimentation were necessary to determine comparator balance against the impulsive conduct of humans in a complex social structure."

I stared at her, my mouth open. I closed it, opened it again to speak, and succeeded only in continuing my stunned silence. Kim didn't say anything. She didn't have to.

Because the whole thing was impossible. *And* because, in my absence, fearful of upsetting the steadily paced progress of the project, and completely off balance with such a response from 79, Kim ordered the technicians to comply with the request. They did. A whole series of hypnotic demonstrations, of alpha-wave-pattern distortion through photic stimulation, posthypnotic commands—the works.

And always that incredible, flawlessly logical response as to *why* the hypnotic demonstrations—by word, light patterns, acoustic signals, and the rest of it—were so necessary.

While 79 monitored, received, recorded and—for whatever reason—evaluated everything it obtained.

". . . the data of hypnotic experimentation were necessary to determine comparator balance against the impulsive conduct of humans in a complex social structure."

Like hell it was!

That alone *should* have tripped all the alarm signals. For a cybernetics brain even to give a reason of this nature was insanity. Electronic insanity. Later on we might discover what we had on our hands—evidence of electronically pathological deceit.

Deceit?

That in itself was impossible. Jesus, how could a cybernetics system in two-way communication with its programmers employ deceit?

Unless, unless . . . the brain we had created was already judging its most important role, the one that it knew it must be called upon to fulfill.

How to prevent a global lemming instinct.

Or, to put it another way, mass suicide.

If it were possible, if it were possible . . . that the superior analysis of the unemotional, flawlessly logical cybernetics brain could anticipate the thermonuclear armageddon, and it provided us with the answers to what appeared inevitable if man continued on his present path of massive counterarmaments, could we then exploit this miracle of searching out our own inevitability and alter the course of future events? It was one thing to illogical, subjective findings of study teams and groups of men. arrive at such conclusions based upon the notional,illogical, subjective findings of study teams and groups of men. But if the absolutely logical creature assembled by man showed the horrendous tomorrow, would not instinct, survival, self-preservation, cold logic dictate the changes that *must* be made?

We hoped that 79 could play its part in such a seeking of the ultimate truth. But that still lay in the future, still awaited staggering loads of work.

The programming had yet to take place.

So how, *how,* could 79 already be involved in the answers to the questions we had yet to ask?

Cybernetics systems, even the exquisitely far-out bastardization we had created in 79, are *not* devious. Not by nature or by intent. It wasn't just hard or impossible to explain the

[174]

answers Kim received from 79 when she programmed the query on the requests for extensive data and human experiments under hypnosis. It was . . . well, so wholly unexpected it defied explanation.

Except—and the thought tantalized and drove me crazy—maybe, just maybe, its answer was considered on the basis of its own reasoning, as completely pertinent. The only possible answer. How about that, Steve Rand? Maybe *you* were missing the point! Maybe, again just maybe, this was the *one valid response* to which 79 might have resorted, and . . .

Oh, hell, it was all too much at once. I still had that unsettling feeling that shadows were nibbling at the edges of my mind. I had a great deal on which to catch up, because the hypnosis experiments *had been going on for nearly three weeks.*

I wanted desperately to get back in harness, to crawl around the control panels, to talk with the technicians, to study the equipment and the systems. And to badger the bloody damned electronic brain directly, in a brain-to-brain confrontation.

Ten days later I got everything I wanted, and more.

In spades.

24

I CLUMPED MY way noisily through the corridors that led to the alpha test section. "Clumped" was the best I could do. This was my third day on a cane, and I still didn't have my legs back for any real mobility. My left leg remained stiff and a bit more painful than I thought it would be, although the doctor insisted that most of the pain lay above the eyebrows and that I was sympathizing mightily with myself. Perhaps he was right. I took a mild painkiller and did my best to get around under my own steam, even if I did stumble about like a stiff-legged sailor trying to get his land legs. Despite the awkwardness and the pain, it felt marvelous to be back in harness. The sound and the smell of the cybernetics complex were the best of all medicines.

I'd already spent a full day at work in my office, stiff-legging it around to the various departments, letting myself be seen and heard by my staff. For the long hauls I wasn't that stubborn to refuse the use of a motorized wheelchair. Hell, it was a fifth of a mile between some sections, and I couldn't see myself dragging along *all* that distance just to prove I was a real sport about getting back to work.

Now it was late, past midnight, and the project went along with a reduced staff. We were off the three-shifts-a-day schedule, what with most of the basic programming and experiments completed. At midnight we broke down to a bare skeleton staff in order to prepare new tests, clean up old work, make adjustments and repairs to facilities and equipment.

The corridors were ghostly silent except for the barely discernible background sigh of air-conditioning systems. It could have been lonely, but I enjoyed every moment, the long lighted spaces ahead of me, the test cubicles gleaming softly in subdued light. I had no real purpose in dragging myself around like this. It was a matter, I suppose, of letting myself get the feel and taste of things. And I'd had all I wanted of hearty hellos and greetings and the well-intentioned but stale clichés about the accident.

Now I had peace and quiet, the serenity of a vast and epochal effort at its quiet moment. I worked my way slowly down a light-green corridor. To my left were the numbered administrative offices with the personnel names and department identifications printed neatly on the doors. Along the right of the wide corridor stretched row after row of the test cubicles, each in a pale blue light that signified equipment shutdown. I was about to return to my office for the powered wheelchair and hustle myself off to the main entrance where a limousine would be waiting for me—a car big enough for me to stretch out my leg without banging it against the back of the front seats—when I heard something. At the same moment I noticed that one test cubicle far down the corridor had more than the pale blue light normally marking each cubicle along the corridor row.

Some idiot's left the lights on, I assumed. I grinned. The "turn out the lights" syndrome from the former administration in Washington still pervaded official programs. I decided to walk to the end of the hall and save some technician a chewing-out in the morning.

Before I had moved a foot, the grin on my face disappeared. Quickly. Because more than light came from the cubicle that held my attention. There was also sound. And no one was scheduled to be working this late. If they were, they had failed to post the project sheets in the main office. At first I couldn't make out the sound. The cubicle door was, I guessed, only slightly open, and the echoes in the corridor muffled whatever it was I heard.

Stiff leg dragging, I pushed my way along the corridor, trying not to quicken my pace but compelled by some mysterious feeling of urgency. I was almost there—by now I could see that the lights from the cubicle were flickering; *that* surprised me even as I noticed it. At the same moment I recognized the sounds.

Then I recognized the voice.

And my skin went cold.

I hurried along, trying not to make noise. I felt silly; what the devil was *I* being so secretive about! I didn't know, but even as cursed myself for my crude skulking I knew I was going to reach that cubicle with a minimum of sound to announce my presence.

Outside the cubicle study window—the door was open about an inch or two and I didn't want to push it open all the way, at least not yet—I stared into the test chamber. I listened to the voice, the same voice that had attracted my attention at the far end of the corridor, that drew me here like a magnet, that finally became clear to me. The voice I recognized.

The voice of 79.

I must have been holding my breath. I felt as if a giant hand were squeezing my chest. I fought for air, sucking it in with a strange rattle in my throat, while I tried to absorb the macabre scene displayed to me through the observation glass. Along the vertical control panel that constituted the far wall of the test cubicle, mixed in with the controls, dials, and different instruments that we used for our tests and for programming, was a single glass panel about two feet on each side. I'd never seen this installation before. I'd never even *known* about it. I kept looking at it, utterly absorbed, fascinated.

I tried to focus my eyes. I couldn't. The wide panel *heaved* with light. I'd never seen or known anything like it before. Light that swirled and coruscated, that rose and fell with unbelievable depth and dimension to it. Colors shifting softly, an interweaving sigh of hues. It moved; always it moved. It reached out to me and drew me toward it as if I were floating, disembodied, levitating through glass, through the walls, drawn to it, looking down and down and down . . . light shimmering, a glowing, pulsating, living heart of light, soundless music and an abyss without end with swirling walls of light and color and . . .

Pain ripped my leg. I cried out with the sudden agony as my left leg collapsed beneath me and brought me crumpling to the floor of the corridor. Instantly a gnarled, twisting ball of pain exploded between my eyes, behind my skull, within my brain. I found myself again gasping for air. I heard a weak moaning, and realized with cottony-mouthed fear that the sound came from me.

What in the name of God had happened? That light. *Good Lord, that light . . .*

It came to me in a rush. I didn't believe it and at the same instant I knew I did. It was too crazy not to be true. It was too impossible not to be real.

It was. My broken leg had saved me. Funny, isn't it? I said that to myself, and the voice shrilling inside my mind was as shaken as my conscious thoughts. My broken leg had saved me.

That light . . . hypnotic. Oh, that son of a bitch of a machine had learned its lessons well! A hypnotic light, to snare easily and softly and in webs stronger than steel any man subjected to the light. Every stitch and facet of information on hypnosis had been fed into 79. It *knew* hypnosis better than any man living or who had ever lived. It learned its lessons not merely from accumulated data and from reports and from the excellent programming of the staff technicians. It had been privy to what went on within the brain of a human being all through the process of hypnosis! It didn't guess; it *knew.* Much was still a mystery—insufficient data, if you please—to the great cybernetic brain. But monitoring human activity within the brain as it had done, it knew precisely just what was needed through optical stimulation and other means to place a human being into a hypnotic trance.

And I had stood there like the great unknowing idiot that I was and stared at the light and even from where I stood, through the observation glass, seeing the light at an odd angle, it had dragged me into the abyss of hypnotic trance. I had forgotten, consciously or otherwise, that I had a leg only recently mending from two fractures and that I was tired; I had been placing a heavy load on that leg. And because I forgot, drowning heedlessly in that light, I placed my weight on the leg. Well, the circuits to *my* brain were still open. I wasn't completely under the influence of that light when the pain shrieked through my body, and thank God for that. Because I collapsed, ripped by my own personal, sweet agony, crumpled on the floor, sobbing, *and safe*. That's when the bomb went off behind my eyes, when I had that second great knot of pain within my mind.

I had been wrenched violently from hypnosis, and I was paying the penalty for brain cells scrambled wildly. It was the most blessed and wonderful pain I had ever known in my life, and I embraced it hysterically. It saved me.

I lay there on the floor, chest heaving, and I clung to the pain as a drowning man clings to a log in the water. Through the red mist that fogged my eyes, I listened. I listened to what I had heard before. The voice.

The voice of 79, that deep, timbrous sound from the superbly, ingeniously crafted artificial larynx *I* had developed to carry out direct communications experiments with the great cybernetics brain. Talking. Giving instruction, repetitiously, while the swirling light held captive, like a bug in a steel mental trap, a human being.

Charles Kane. Professional associate and personal friend, one of the best technicians and programmers on the staff. A man who worked with the electronic intellect from the day of its inception. A man who felt completely . . . at home with the cybernetics brain.

A man absolutely in the complete control of 79. A man who had been receiving instructions while he was under hypnotic control and would be placed under posthypnotic control when 79 completed its instructions.

A man, a friend of mine, who was being ordered by the cybernetics brain to bring another person, at the earliest possible opportunity, into this test cubicle. To bring him here as quickly as this could be done, to place him in this same seat, to expose him also to that terrible pattern of light.

A man.

Steve Rand.

Me.

The words coming through the slightly opened door welled up in my mind and snagged on nightmarish disbelief, made all the more grotesque because it was real. A hysterical giggle seemed to accompany my thoughts.

The phrase welled up in my mind amidst the nightmare. The first free thought, evaluating what I had seen, what I had heard, what was happening to me.

I thought, *My God!* I thought, *It is really happening.*

The machine is taking over!

And at the same time the giggle wrapped itself in a thin shining cocoon of madness.

Because . . . because I knew that Selig Albracht was right.

25

Just don't lie there and moan, you idiot. Think!

That's a help. An insufferable ego, I mean. Thank the Lord for mine. Still clutched in pain from my leg, my reflexes began to take over. One of them was the ability to start using the gray matter between my ears. I confess I didn't know what to do at the moment. The voice of 79 faded in the pain to a background hum drifting through the door. Yet it carried with it a compulsion to get the hell out from under. At the moment I didn't dare try to make it all the way down the corridor. Using the cane for support and leaning against the wall, I managed to regain my feet. Wincing, I edged along the wall to the next cubicle, fumbled for the master key in my pocket, and pushed open the door. I slid the door back into place and leaned against the cool, hard surface, forcing myself to breathe regularly, to regain control of my thoughts. I felt as if a herd of mental elephants were stampeding through my brain.

I don't know how long I stood there, the pain easing from my leg. Damn me for a fool for having overdone it on the premise of "I'm a big boy now and can take care of myself"! Yet I knew I'd had a tremendous stroke of good fortune. If things hadn't happened the way they did while I was gawking stupidly through the observation window, I might still be there, snared in a hypnotic trance just as was Charlie Kane.

And that was something else again. From what little I'd seen, I knew Charlie was deep, way down deep, under posthypnotic command. There wasn't a shadow of a doubt about that. Everything had been going along with such tremendous impact in that test cubicle. . . . I shuddered at the manner in which I remembered myself being drawn into that light. Christ! The sensation of disembodiment had been fantastic. There had been no sense of losing control or anything like that. It was simply a matter of letting go to that bottomless, infinite beckoning. That should answer any questions about a cybernetics brain being able to adapt to purely biological-intellectual activities! If it were a matter of intent, then 79 was now able to rewrite the book on hypnotism.

None of this was getting me anywhere. I don't know how long I stood there before I got up enough sense to climb into the control chair, stretch out my leg, and massage some decent feeling back into the muscles. That's where I'd run into trouble, of course. I hadn't really used or placed strain on the leg muscles for so long that my abuse of my own body had brought about the shrieking collapse. The pain I'd felt had been from muscles twisting and knotting. I felt improved already, and at the same time I congratulated myself on my own well-being I knew it was simply a dodge. I was avoiding the issue of what was going on in that test cubicle next to me.

Well, maybe that was the right thing to do. Avoid it for the moment. I needed time. Time in which I could think, could add things up, and go over them slowly. This wasn't any time for action. Jesus, what was I going to do? Stump my way into the cubicle and flail away mightily with the cane? Bash Charlie across the side of the head? Kick the computer? Maybe James Bond would have dashed into the room to flick ashes into the glass eye of 79, but outside of messing up the floor I don't know what good *that* would have done. Heroics was for the birds, and I wasn't inclined to be a screaming eagle.

Of course I went through my instinctive reaction. It's a malady of the generation which I shared through youth and into manhood. If the computer gets frisky, quoth the pundits, you could always pull the plug and leave the damned thing sulking like a cinder that's been pulled out of the fire.

Like hell you could. Not with *this* one. Not with twin breeder reactors sealed off within defensive systems that made Fort

Knox look like sand castles built by a six-year-old on the beach. That's the first thing that cemented itself clearly in my mind. No one was going to pull any plugs around *here*. In the game of one-upmanship between man and cybernetics brain, man had neatly cut off one of his own fingers.

The silence reached me and—Silence? The voice, that deep and commanding voice of 79, had stopped. I moved as quickly as I could to the front wall of the cubicle so that I could remain in shadow and still look into the corridor, toward the other cubicle where Charlie Kane was being made into a willing slave. I noticed the flickering glow of light was no more. The brain-squeezing session was over. Charlie Kane was himself again— *he* thought—and now under posthypnotic control. But in his conscious thinking he didn't even know what had happened to him! He would remember—I could anticipate the routine; it *had* to be this way—only that he had some late adjustments to make to equipment in the test cubicle. That's all. He would know absolutely nothing of anything else that went on. Glued to the wall, I watched him emerge from the cubicle, close and lock the door, and walk off down the corridor. I waited fifteen minutes until, as I was ready to leave, weariness suddenly assailed me. To hell with it. No one would question my being anywhere in the complex at any time of the day or night. I punched the desk phone and called the security guard and told him to bring the wheelchair to me.

I wasn't even about to try that long haul back to my office. It was bad enough limping in my mind.

I didn't go to work for the next two days. Aside from my feeling miserable physically, the doctor chewed up one side of my butt and then down the other, double-damning me for being the worst kind of fool for overdoing the Look-Ma-no-hands bit with my leg. Nothing could have pleased me better than the doctor's orders to remain in my apartment and to exercise the leg with care. Fortunately no real damage had been done, and there was more wincing than injury.

Besides, it gave me the opportunity to think. When I returned to the apartment on that same night when I nearly got taken down the drain by that infernal light of the cybernetics brain, my first impulse was to drag Tom Smythe out of bed and tell him the story from beginning to end. But even as I picked up the telephone, I changed my mind. Tell him *what?* That 79 was now collecting a private gang of hypnotized subjects to do its bidding? What bidding? What gang? The only person of whom I knew was Charlie Kane, and there wasn't the ghost of a chance of getting through the posthypnotic block induced by the computer.

That was the real stub of it. What the devil *would* I do? Because there were questions upon questions that required answers before I could go running off to anyone. 79 had proved itself capable of the impossible, and that was the concealment of its actions. That it could function in a sense where it initiated its own programming was *not* unusual; we had created that. But to go off on its own and then take every attempt to conceal what it was doing, *and deliberately to take over control of human beings,* was something vastly different.

No; if I were to do anything at the moment it was to think, to come up with rational answers to the questions that bedeviled me. I had to find out what else was going on, had been happening during my absence. I was off to a running start, and that helped tremendously. They say that being forewarned is being forearmed. That advantage I clutched fervently to my feverish scientific brow. I knew about Charles Kane and what had happened with and to him. I knew the tremendous impact of the light patterns generated on the glass panel by 79. I knew that Charles Kane, outwardly perfectly normal, was operating under posthypnotic suggestion, under *orders.* I knew I could expect Charlie either to call me or to visit me at home, and even while I stared at nothing and thought furiously, I had a visitor.

Charles Kane.

Of course; who else would it be? The meeting proved ineffectual for Charlie and rewarding for me. I managed to act perfectly normal—insufferable, I suppose, but Charlie was accustomed to that aspect of my social behavior and didn't mind it at all. But I was nervous and edgy, and Charlie spotted it. I attributed the feelings to a combination of pain from my leg and the drugs the doctors still ordered me to take. Charlie shrugged and made sympathetic sounds and thought nothing of it.

Except for his insistence, worded carefully, that it was important for me to get back into harness as soon as I could.

"I've got something *real* interesting to show you, Steve," he said, showing genuine excitement about the matter.

"Oh? What's up?"

"Damnedest thing you ever saw. As you know, while you were trussed up in the hospital we continued the communications experiments. The regular bit, Steve. We picked up where you had left off on the voice communications, and we're still running the alpha and blink patterns, and——"

"Any difficulty with the photic stimulation?" I asked the question in purest innocence.

"No, nothing like that any more. Except, of course," he added hastily, "where the doctors have induced flicker vertigo deliberately. They're trying to get some correlations and guidelines of effects and lack of effects between normals and adepts at alpha control."

I nodded.

"But that's not what I was talking about, Steve. 79 has come up on its own with its own experiments."

I started suddenly. "What?" The look on my face wasn't sham. I *was* taken unaware by his words.

"I know how you feel." He laughed, the perfect picture of a friend and associate sharing a professional secret. "It's just how I reacted when I first discovered what was happening. We were going through a results study and were querying 79 on different aspects of man-machine communications. We reviewed the whole package. You know it, of course." He smiled with just the proper amount of self-deprecation. "Tape, punch card, alpha pattern, acoustic, energized neural blocks—the works. Then—and it caught us all off balance—79 ran through a query to us on light communications."

"Light?" I know my voice sounded hollow.

[186]

"Uh-huh." He nodded. "Not the light signals per se, Steve, such as blinker light for Morse code and things like that. Direct light—colors, patterns, intensities, forms, all worked out in a system of communications."

I didn't answer. I didn't dare to. I began to have a suspicion that . . .

"Well, we rigged up one of the test cubicles for the tests. It's Number 17. Sort of an intricate pattern-potential of lights, with thousand of small bulbs, multicolor principle, and that sort of thing. We hooked it up directly to the energizer circuits of 79 so that it could manipulate the system directly, and—"

"I'll bet," I said acidly.

"What was that, Steve?"

I cursed myself for a fool. "Nothing, nothing," I said, waving my hand for him to continue.

"Well, we also rigged a duplicate of the voice-comm system that you've been using, and—"

"Whose idea was that?" I broke in.

"Oh. 79. It gave us a set of working rules. Voice communications would allow us to get things moving faster with the light communications tests." He showed his pride in the systems he and his staff had built, and there was also pride in his ability to work along such a tremendously advanced level with the cybernetics brain. Pride—and not so much as the slightest suspicion that he had unwittingly carried out the instructions on the part of 79 to create the equipment with which the giant brain could carry out its hypnotic tests.

"Did you have any difficulties?"

"Oh, some," he said, "but not that much to slow us down. Some of the light patterns—they register not single words, of course, but what I'd call intent-messages for communications —were pretty disturbing at first. A few of the people found themselves with screaming headaches. The light, well, it sort of felt as if it reached inside your skull, and twisted." He shook his head in wonder or admiration, or a combination of both. "We informed 79 that the patterns were optically disturbing to the programmers. That thing is *fast,* Steve," he emphasized. "It still amazes me how 79 could digest the words, convert them into its own data system, and come back with the solution."

"How?"

Charlie shrugged. "Difficult to say, except that after we had our first problems the light didn't bother us any more."

Of course not, I thought. *The son of a bitch didn't want to overplay its new capabilities that quickly.* I marveled at myself. How easily I'd slipped into the frame of mind where 79 had become an ominous personality, a thinking creature of deceit. I'd never before thought of a computer as a son of a bitch. But I did *now*.

I also flared up in my mind, at Charlie Kane. But that was stupid, I reminded myself immediately. Charlie didn't have the slightest suspicion of what had happened to him. Not even torture could have made him confess about a hypnotic control of which his conscious mind was entirely unaware. I had to remember that. The man was not functioning—where the intent of 79 was involved—either of his own knowledge or his own volition. I had to remember that this was so, even though at times I found it difficult to remain objective.

"When can you come in for some demonstrations of the new system, Steve?"

"What?" I hadn't been paying attention to Charlie Kane for several moments, and his words caught me by surprise. "Oh, hell, sorry," I said easily, "I was just chewing over what you've been telling me."

He smiled in return. "No sweat. I wanted to know when you might be able to come in for a demonstration of the new light-communications system."

I looked at him carefully. "What would you suggest?"

"I dunno." He shrugged. "From the looks of things, with your leg, I mean, you might be a couple of days yet before you can make it."

"Uh-huh." I tapped my leg. "Sort of scrunged up a bit yet, but it won't be much longer. Umm, by the way, Charlie, how's your work schedule, lately?"

"What do you mean?"

[188]

"Well, I was looking at the sign-out sheets the other day—or night, I suppose—and I noticed you'd been signing out pretty late. You getting to be an overtime hog?"

He laughed, flashing white teeth. "No, no, nothing like that. I just seem to be getting absent-minded as of late. It's a funny thing," he said, scratching his chin. "I mean, I wrap up things for the day and I go home for dinner. Then later, usually it's about ten o'clock or so, I always remember something I forgot to do, and I end up back in the office again."

"Couldn't it wait until the next morning?"

"Well, that's what had me wondering," he said, clearly puzzled by his own actions. "Because every time it happens I remember that it's important that I have to do this thing—whatever it happens to be at the moment—to get ready for the staff the next morning. So," he shrugged, "back to the office I go."

Neat, very neat. A posthypnotic command, shrouded in the sudden "memory" of work that must be completed that evening, and Charlie Kane is in Cubicle 17, and he seats himself in that chair and he looks at the glass panel, and he's under, and getting instructions as 79's errand boy.

But *why*? What was the purpose of all this? Why did the computer deliberately operate in the manner I had discovered? Why—except as an experiment—did it want to place anyone under posthypnotic control? Why the deliberate attempt to conceal what had happened? And again and again, and a hundred times again, the same question came back to me—Why was all this going on? What purpose could there be in these manipulations?

Wait . . . wait just a moment, now. 79 had directed Charlie Kane to get *me* into that cubicle. For what? Obviously, for what. To get me under as well. But why *me*? And when had the computer begun to make distinctions between one human being and another when we were faceless data sources to an electronic entity? *How* could it have made such distinctions? I made a mental note to check on that, and even as I scribbled the words in my mind I had the answer. At least I bet I had it. I knew, I just knew, that in the programming requested by 79 was a list of every high-level cybernetics scientist in the country.

But there was more to it than that. There *had* to be. . . .

"Have there been any other demonstrations—I mean, outside of the immediate staff of technicians—with the new light-communications system?"

"Oh, sure," Charlie Kane said quickly. "I asked Dr. Vollmer to stay after the staff had left, one evening last week, I mean, for a demonstration. I didn't want to have a crowd around—you know how Vollmer doesn't like to feel cluttered with people about him when he's working—so we had dinner first and then returned to the test section."

So Vollmer also goes on the list. . . .

"Anyone else?"

"Umm, let's see. Of course." He snapped his fingers. "A few nights ago we had Professor Bockrath—you know Walter Bockrath, Steve?"

I should. As Professor of Social Sciences at the University of Colorado he was a consultant to Project 79. I knew him, all right. He'd been present when Selig Albracht and I had our little explosion and he'd been decidedly cool to me ever since then.

"Whose idea was it to bring Bockrath down?"

Charlie beamed. He leaned forward with unconcealed pleasure and excitement. "Dr. Vollmer," he said. "The next day, the very next day after I demonstrated the system to Dr. Vollmer, he called Bockrath at the University and asked him to come down that night. He—Vollmer—told me I wouldn't have to be there, that he wanted to have some discussions alone with Bockrath and that they might last for quite a while. I spoke to Vollmer the next day, and he was pleased, really pleased, at the way things worked out."

"I'm glad to hear that, Charlie. It's not easy to please Vollmer."

"Boy don't I know it, though!" Charlie Kane laughed happily. "I've worked with Old Crotchety long enough to regard a pat on the back from him as manna from heaven."

I shared his laugh, but I was thinking about something else. That makes Kane, Vollmer, Bockrath, so far. Who else?

"Has Kim seen your setup at work yet?"

He shook his head. "Uh-uh. No time, I suppose. She's been buried in some side projects, I guess. Sort of overworked since she took over the reports from your office."

Thank God for small favors.

"I was sort of hoping you'd be able to get into the shop pretty soon, Steve," he said with sudden seriousness. "Thursday night, I think . . . umm, yeah, that's it, all right. Thursday night I'm to set up an experiment—you know, a complete demonstration for Dr. Cartwright—"

"Arthur Cartwright?"

"Uh-huh. Dr. Vollmer asked me to arrange everything."

Arthur Cartwright! He was the world's greatest living cyberneticist, the heir to Norbert Wiener. *Why him?* Outwardly I stayed calm. "Thursday night, you say?"

"That's right. Think you can make it?"

"I don't know," I said with obvious doubt, looking at my leg again. "I'll have to play that by ear."

He rose to his feet. "Well, I hope you can swing it, Steve. It would be great to have you there."

"Sure, sure it would, Charlie. Just great. I'll call you first chance I know how things will turn out."

"Right. So long, Steve."

"Don't take any wooden nickels, Charlie."

The next morning I arranged to get Charles Kane out of my hair for the two days following. It was easy enough. I sent him out of town. To Wright-Patterson Air Force Base at Dayton, Ohio, to be exact. The Bionics Branch of the Air Force Avionics Lab, working with scientists of Carson Laboratories, had developed an Optical Maze Runner that promised great things for computer memory systems. They combined a laser beam and a tiny storage crystal to stimulate biological nerve patterns that store data for learning, and contribute data for decision-making. Into a single potassium-bromide crystal, no larger than a matchbox and impregnated with hydrogen, they could store 40,000 bits of information. It worked by . . . the devil with how it worked, just so long as it would keep Kane away for the two days.

The moment he was en route I called Kim and gave her a long list of directions for a new test. She was accustomed to this, of course, and as the director of my own programs within Project 79 my requests were met without any stumbling blocks. I told her to set up the equipment as I had outlined and that the day after I'd be in to handle the final details personally.

Kim managed everything in her customary efficient manner. When I arrived at Cubicle 17 the door was locked and a DO NOT ENTER sign glared from the panel. I went in, locked the door behind me, and closed off the observation window. In a project where close coordination was a byword of everyday activity, my own actions were nothing less than unusual. But scientists are a breed unto themselves, and as a program director . . . well, there's the old saw that rank has its privileges. I used mine.

I checked over the equipment. Three motion-picture cameras in their concealed positions. Not just for my requests, of course, since it was a normal matter to obtain film records of different tests. But I wanted to be absolutely certain that this cubicle was rigged for a visual record of what went on here on Thursday night—that same evening. The cameras checked out fine, as did the tape recorders. Then I added a few refinements of my own.

An engineer working directly under me, with orders to consider everything he did as part of a highly classified test (score one for the effectiveness of Tom Smythe; the man nodded gravely and pigeonholed within his own mind what he was doing), rigged the electrical connections. I didn't want power for the cameras and the tape recorders coming into the cubicle from the power lines that made up the cybernetics system. Instead, I had the engineer run some extra cables into the heavy-duty housekeeping system so that it would remain free entirely of the computer-controlled electrical input. Set up in this manner, it would be impossible for 79 to monitor the equipment I was preparing to record the "interrogation" with Dr. Arthur Cartwright. And that was just the way I wanted things to be.

I wrapped up my preparations, assigned the room officially to Charles Kane for a test to be made later that night, authorized the presence of visitors, and went home. And drank myself into a pleasant mind-sodden stupor.

Naturally, I had nightmares.

26

I sighed, and gave in to the inevitable. It was nicer to have Kim snuggled up close with me on the couch in the darkened room. But the light flickering from the screen wasn't made for the amorous touch, and Kim was sitting straight up on the edge of the couch, her eyes wide and staring, caught between acute attention to what flashed before her eyes and her startled exclamations to me.

The film chittered through to the end of the reel, and as bright light splashed on the screen I killed the projector and turned on the apartment lights. Kim sank back in her seat and shook her head.

"I—I *saw* it," she murmured. "I really saw it, didn't I, Steve?" she murmured, talking both to herself and to me.

"Yeah," I said, still with a sour taste in my mouth at having looked at the film for the sixth time and knowing I was going to do a repeat in just a few moments. I pushed my way to the projector and started rewinding the film. "Mix me a double, will you, honey?" I muttered, poking at the projector.

"Scotch?" I heard the tinkling of ice into glass.

"Sure. Strictly for what ails."

"I'll join you in that," she said. I thought I could detect more shaking of ice than usual. That film would shake up anyone.

Kim's hand and the drink appeared at my side, and she sat close to me as I threaded the film. She looked at me. "Again?"

"Uh-huh. Only this time we do it with sound." I glanced at her. "How's your head?"

She rubbed her forehead with her fingers. "It *hurts*. Is it that light, I mean, the one in the film?"

"That's it, all right," I said. "Old skull-bender in its original form. Feels like something's reached right inside your head, and twisted, doesn't it?" I made a feeble attempt at a grin.

"I don't see what's so funny about it, Steve," she said with a touch of anger. She took refuge in the Scotch.

"Oh, ain't funny," I remarked. "It's just that it hurts *me* less when someone else feels the same way."

"What hurts good for Stevey hurts good for everybody, huh?"

My laugh sounded like a croak. "Shaddup and hand me my drink, woman," I growled. I didn't stop until I had a long, deep pull at the Scotch.

"My, my," she said quietly, "we're doing a wonderful job at staying away from the obvious, aren't we?"

I nodded, the subject of the film pushing aside the warm feeling from the Scotch as it trickled down inside me. "But not for long," I sighed. "It's not the sort of thing that stands for being ignored." I gestured to the projector and the tape recorder. "You ready?"

She shook her head. "No, I am *not* ready," she said firmly, "and I don't think I will ever be ready. I don't like headaches in double doses." She stirred her ice with a finger. "But I suppose you're going to do it anyway, aren't you?"

"Sure I am. I always like to apply the screws at every opportunity, and—"

She was on her feet and walking across the room before I could finish. "Well, I'm not going through that again without fortification," she said in a no-nonsense voice. "More of the same for you?"

My glass was already extended. "Need you ask?"

She went about the business of pouring the Scotch and adding ice cubes. "When were these taken, Steve?" she asked, gesturing to the projector.

"Two days ago," I said. "I've already looked at this thing six times."

"Oh, my." There was real sympathy in her voice. "You must have a real bump inside your skull."

"That I do, that I do, and at the first opportunity you have after we do the bit once more, I would like to have your cool and silken fingers caressing, most gently, if you please, the furrowed surface of a very feverish brow. Mine, to be specific."

"I'll be there," she promised. "Who else has seen the film, Steve?"

"Just us two. I don't want anyone else to have a look at it yet. And the only reason you're seeing it, my sweet, is that I am more than reasonably certain that sometime in the past week or so you haven't been seated in that same chair where we saw Cartwright. Furthermore—"

"You can stop right there, Steve Rand. What the devil do you mean, you're reasonably certain I haven't been in that chair? Of course I haven't, and you know it!"

"You can sprinkle some of that ice water on your aroused female ire, Kim," I said with a touch of growing weariness. I knew I'd be saying these same words many times again in the future. "I don't *know* you haven't been in that chair, and *you* don't *know* you haven't been in that chair because if you had been, my love, you wouldn't have the faintest recollection of your little session with 79. As I said, I am more than reasonably certain that you haven't. And since"—I waved my hand for her to join me on the couch—"I will go out of my ever-loving mind if I don't have someone with whom to talk over this insanity, and because my feelings for you are a mixture of love and complete trust, et cetera, et cetera, here we are together."

She patted my leg as she eased herself to the couch. She leaned over and kissed me lightly on the cheek. "My, my, that's quite a statement of unrequited love and all that jazz, isn't it?"

We laughed together. I held up my glass and peered owlishly at the remaining Scotch. "Here's how," I groaned. "Last drink for the condemned man. We are about to have at it again." I turned to the projector. "Kill the lights, will you?"

Running the film through for the second time had even greater impact for Kim. Not only did the voice of 79 come through with devastating effect, but she had learned to keep her

[196]

eyes away from that infernal light controlled by the computer. In silence, listening to the voice of 79 and the monotone answers, first of Charlie Kane and then of Dr. Arthur Cartwright, we watched and listened as Kane responded immediately to the light (I made a note to that effect; at first sight of the glowing pattern Kane was instantly under control), and then as Dr. Cartwright went under.

When the film ended, Kim was deep in thought. She turned to me suddenly. "Steve, run the tape through. Not with the film, just the tape. I want to hear the questions without that damnable light on the screen."

We listened, and the room seemed to become colder with just the sound of 79 as it rolled question after question at Dr. Cartwright. The questions were unnerving, for the computer was tracking down a quarry. In whose hands, and in what fashion, was there vested the social control of the United States? This was the key sought by 79. Or, rather, the handful of keys that, when turned, opened the doors to the real power function of the country. It's inevitable, of course. In any power structure such as has been created in a technological society walking the brink of thermonuclear war with another technological society, the role of the individual—the man in the street, Mr. Average Joe—fades away. Power is by necessity vested in the hands of the few who control industry, military organization, and the press. Who were these people? What positions did they hold?

What unnerved me even more than I had been until this moment was the realization that the United States Government for years had run studies specifically on the subject now examined with electronic efficiency by 79. Study after study, all seeking to determine the real nature of the power structure of this country, of other nations, and of the world itself. Back in 1965, a political uproar had sounded through several continents when word leaked out about the Army's Project Camelot. An old Brooklyn College professor had been found, by the Army, to have a natural sense of identifying the keys to power structure, and he was promptly installed within his own Special Operations Research Office in the Pentagon. The Army gave him six million dollars for expenses, some computers for assistance, and the professor began to track down the national power structures of South American governments. Officially, the Pentagon bleated, Camelot was intended "to construct a conceptual scheme or analytical model which will identify parameters of social systems to be studied in detail for an understanding of social conflict." Very neat.

What the Army never intended to say was that they were setting up a scoreboard by which they could measure, and predict—and therefore *control*—the factors and processes that lead to discontent, to revolution or, if possible, to quiet takeover by usurpation of key elements of any government.

This same sort of investigation had been run not only on foreign governments. It had been focused inwardly in studies of internal power structures of the United States. What better fashion for the political party then in power to give itself the greatest possible opportunity for remaining there than to make a computerized study of the key fulcrums of national power? If you know where to push and where to prod and where to apply pressure, then with a minimum of selective effort you can gain tremendous results.

If you control the few men who control, essentially, the pattern of the stock market, you can establish a definite trend or pattern for the stock market—which permits you to take advantage of the economic and industrial upheavals that result. The key elements of the nation—industry, labor, foreign policy, cabinet members—weren't that difficult to identify. You don't need the ear of the President directly, but you *do* need those people who are his most trusted advisers. To whom does the President turn for his off-the-record conversations on labor unions? To whom does he listen the most closely about the political climate? To what extent does he trust one person against all others for his foreign intelligence? Get to *those* people, get to the leaders of the Congress who can sway the majority of their colleagues, reach the top editors and the editorialists, reach the market survey analysts with a proved record of success, get to the religious leaders who not only make noise but who also make the most effective noise . . . do this, in terms of having those essential, those critical members of your society under your control, and you control the society.

These were the people that 79 wanted brought to Cubicle 17. And for so rare an opportunity to be able to query the most advanced cybernetics brain in history, just about all of them would make their appearance.

"So," I said under the influence of another double Scotch, "that's how our monster intends to play the game. All it needs is control of the right people in the right places. Poke the right nerve of the frog, and the whole frog jumps. Pull the right people in the right places, and the whole damned country jumps. Without knowing a thing about it, of course," I added with a deepening sense of gloom.

"And it will *work*," I added with desperation in my voice. "That's what grabs you by the short hairs. It'll work. 79 has run through every possible combination of factors. It's equated the social factors in terms of data bits. Working with its speed, it's run through thousands, maybe even millions, of possibilities, and it's come up with the right answers. I'd bet a dollar to a soggy doughnut that if we checked off that list of names Cartwright spouted so conveniently *we* wouldn't agree with the list. That's because we can't run umpteen thousand possible situations through the needle eye of probability like 79. In just a few minutes, I mean. So it's not guessing. It can anticipate— extrapolate mathematically—what's going to happen."

"But what if—"

I didn't even let Kim finish her question. "And you can forget the built-in safety factor of what can't be anticipated, my sweet," I said acidly, anticipating her words. "Remember that our electronic friend can run happily through switching theory and feedback and the best possible answer of many to any given situation. It knows when to stop. More important, 79 can change a situation if it controls the right people in the right places. Fill my damned glass, will you, please?"

Kim obliged with the sound of Scotch pouring over the cubes.

[199]

She handed me the drink and then stood behind the couch, leaning forward to rub the back of my neck with her cool, gentle fingers. I groaned with pleasure. "Jesus, Kim, I'll give you just three days to quit that."

She ignored the remark. For several minutes we left each other to our own thoughts. Or rather she busied herself with thinking, and I gave in to the wonderful touch of her fingers. Finally she came out of her think-session.

"Don't you think you should tell Smythe right away?" She asked.

"Uh-uh. That was *my* first reaction, hon. But the more I thought about it, the more dangerous it became."

"Dangerous? With Tom? I don't understand you, Steve. He *is* the security officer, and—"

"And I don't know if he's had a seat in that chair," I finished for her. The fingers stopped moving, and I made appropriate complaining noises until they began to move again.

"I hadn't thought of that," she admitted.

"Well, I did," I said, "and the very idea scares hell out of me. Right now no one, *no one*—except you, that is—has any idea that I'm privy to this whole affair. Tipping my hand could be a disastrous move, especially to someone like Tom, who could throw all sorts of monkey wrenches at me."

Silence again for a while. "But what are you going to do, Steve?" Her voice made clear her sympathy with the problem. *My* problem.

"I know what I'd like to do," I muttered. "I'd like to kick that thing right in the balls. As hard as I can."

"That's an expected male reaction," she said. "Just where would you start?"

"Good question. I haven't got the answer yet, by the way."

"But—" She cut herself off, exasperated, showing it.

I turned around and motioned for her to sit by me. I wanted her presence, by my side, against me.

"Steve?"

"Um-mm."

"Why is all this happening?"

"I don't know what you—oh, I see." I chewed my lip. I had been trying to answer that question every waking minute of the past several days. "I'm not sure, Kim. I *think* I know. In fact, I'm almost positive." I shook my head. "Almost isn't quite enough, though. But if my hunch is right, I'll know within a day or two."

"For God's sake, don't keep it a secret!"

"Sorry. Until I know a little more about it, Kim, I don't want to say anything. Mmm, just a minute." I pushed my way to my feet and walked to my desk. "C'me're, hon." As she came to the desk I handed her a sealed cashbox.

"In there," I tapped the metal box with my finger, "is a dub of the tape you just heard. There's also a complete report on what's happened to date. And," I added, "also a written report by me of what I think all this is about. No," I held up my hand to forestall her questions, "I really don't want to go into it now. You'll just have to trust me, trust my judgment."

I waited. Kim sighed and nodded. "All right, Steve. What do you want me to do with the box?"

"Put it away somewhere. Not," I emphasized, "in your apartment or your office. Somewhere that no one else knows about, not even me. I'm going to lock this film in the security file right here in my apartment. Got it?"

"But I don't understand why you're—"

"Kim, if anything happens to me you'll have to take that box to—to—" I shrugged. "Hell, I haven't thought that far in advance. You can figure it out when and if it's necessary."

I looked up. Her eyes were wide. "What do you mean, 'if anything happens' to you?"

"I don't know," I said honestly. "I've never traded mental blows before with a supermind, even if it's not able to get up and walk around. But I don't like it. The thing is, I don't know how many people are under 79's control. The possibilities scare the pants right off me. I don't know how many people and I don't know what that thing, or those people, can or would do. So I'm playing it careful. Nice and slow and careful."

I reached for a cigarette. "I'm not ready yet to admit that our overgrown brainbox can think *better* than I can," I said slowly. "Not for a long shot. But I need more information and I've figured out how to get it."

"Steve! You're not going to . . ." Her voice trailed away.

"Right the first time," I said, knowing what she was thinking. "Face-to-face meeting. We'll have it out. Although," I reflected, "I wonder how much good sarcasm will do me against an electronic wit. I don't think we've programmed 79 for humor. Or else I could beat it to death with some really rotten stories."

"Very funny." She didn't show any appreciation in her voice.

"I know, I know," I said, weary in every bone. I put my arm around her waist. "Could I interest you in staying the night?"

"Your offer is accepted, Mr. Rand," she said. "The idea of sleeping alone is suddenly very unappealing."

I made a face. "And here I thought it was my naked sex that drew you to my bed."

"You'll do," she retorted. "At least you're human."

"Score one for my team." I turned out the lights and concentrated on Kim. I sure as hell didn't want to think about the next night when I would lock myself in with 79. Because I wasn't sure I'd walk out that door. On my own, that is.

27

AT TWO O'CLOCK the following afternoon I left the post office in downtown Colorado Springs. Driving back to my apartment, I felt the first sense of relief since the nightmare started. I had just mailed a small package to Mike Nagumo, who could be trusted implicitly. Mike was now an assistant physics professor at MIT and was in the right place at the right time if ever it became necessary to him to read further than the covering letter of the package. I had included another dub of the tape-recording session between 79 and Dr. Arthur Cartwright, as well as a capsule presentation of what Project 79 was (although I was quite sure Mike Nagumo already knew of our effort; it was too big to hide from the inner sanctum of MIT), and what had happened since Ed Taylor had his mental marbles scrambled with his attack of flicker vertigo. My instructions to Mike Nagumo were clear. He was to read *only* my covering letter. Everything else was to be placed by him in what he considered to be a secure and safe deposit, where it was to remain until such time as Mike failed to hear from me in thirty days. In that event, he was to read further, and then act on his own. It would be completely self-explanatory. Above all, he was not to open the papers until such time period without contact from me had passed.

If Tom Smythe ever finds out the caper you've pulled, I told myself, he'd fry you in the deepest oil. Slowly. I grinned at the thought of Smythe and his reaction to my sending off to a complete stranger—to Project 79, anyway—a neatly packaged capsule edition of one of the most carefully guarded secrets of the country. The smile faded as I realized that security could not have meant less against the greater danger presented by the actions of the computer.

Tonight would be the acid test. Driving home, I reviewed my plans for the evening. There was the matter of Charlie Kane; I had to be certain he would be out of the way. That was easy enough; at four o'clock, as soon as I was in the apartment, I'd send him off on another "emergency" trip for me—far enough so that he wouldn't be back before the next morning. I thought about those people whom I *knew* had been, well, "captured" was as good a term as any . . . had been captured by 79. Charlie Kane would be removed for the evening. Dr. Vollmer? Well, *he* wouldn't be wandering around in the middle of the night. I'd already checked on Professor Walter Bockrath at the University of Colorado; his secretary told me he was in Los Angeles for several days. Dr. Arthur Cartwright was on the east coast.

And, just in case someone did show up, I had ordered maximum security for the entire corridor of test cubicles. The guards were ordered—I had the authority as a program chief—not only to bar entry to any person without my personal authorization, but to seize anyone trying to get past them. I'd reinforced my orders with a physical barrier and a guard on duty at each end of the corridor. Thank the great god Security—the guards were delighted to play their little game of armed watchdog. Gave them something to do besides wearing out the seat of their uniformed pants.

At the apartment I made the necessary telephone calls, then dialed the extension to Kim's office. I told her I would be taking a nap and would have to be out of town for the night with a visit to Major Konigsberg at the Air Force Academy. All my white lies out of the way, I set the alarm for ten o'clock that evening and fell into bed. I'd need my wits about me after midnight. I might not get a second chance to slug it out with 79.

Damn those nightmares!

"You've got it all straight, Jack?" I looked carefully at the security guard, who was nodding slowly.

"Right, Mr. Rand," he said. "No one, but *no one,* gets past us into the corridor unless you give us the personal okay."

"Good. What else?"

"You'll be in Cubicle 17. When you're ready for whatever it is you're doing in there"—I raised my eyebrows—"and I don't want to know what it is, Mr. Rand; it's none of my affair," he said to my facial expression. I nodded, and he went on. "When you're ready you'll give us a call here at the guard desk. We are to call you exactly one hour later. If we don't hear from you after six rings, we're to come in there and drag you out by the heels."

I grinned at him. "That's exactly what I want you to do, no matter how much I protest. Got that?"

His face remained deadly serious. "Yes, sir, I got it. If we can't get in with the key, we're to"—he paused—"we're to shoot open the door and go in after you. And then, *if* that happens, we're to notify Miss Michele right away."

"Very good, Jack. You have her number?" He displayed the slip of paper with Kim's apartment number.

"That's fine," I said. "I'm grateful for your cooperation, Jack. I know it all sounds a bit farfetched, but believe me when I say these precautions are necessary."

The security guard rubbed his palm against his cheek. "Think nothing of it, Mr. Rand," he said to dismiss my concern for the oddball instructions. "I used to work at the old gaseous-diffusion plant, you know, Oak Ridge? during World War II. The security they had in the old atom-bomb project made this look like a tea party. In fact"—he grinned for the first time during our conversation—"as far as we were concerned they were making wheels for miscarriages in that place." The grin faded and he patted the butt of a wicked-looking .38 revolver. "Leave it to us, Mr. Rand. We'll carry your orders out to the letter."

I turned and walked down the corridor.

I closed off the observation window. I didn't want even the guards to see what would be happening within the cubicle. Then I locked the door. The sound of my long-held breath being released was louder to me than the click of the bolt sliding into position. I turned to survey the room and went quickly through my preparations. The moment I depressed a switch on the armrest of the control chair, three motion-picture cameras would activate, one coming into operation after another had exhausted its film. I did the same with two tape recorders. I turned down the overhead lights until a soft glow filled the room. Directly before the chair was the deadly glass panel where I had seen the swirling motion of lights and colors with which 79 had hypnotized other men who'd been seated in this same chair. Only, I couldn't see the glass. I'd covered it with an opaque cardboard sheet held in place with yards of masking tape.

I was now ready to call the guard desk. I noted the time, dialed the extension, and repeated my orders to be called exactly one hour from that moment.

One last thing. I removed a tape recorder from my briefcase, switched it *On,* and placed a small earplug receiver in my left ear. Then I turned the control switch to *Play,* and watched the tape move. Quickly I squeezed a rubber bulb control in my hand. The instant the wires within the bulb came into contact, the tape stopped. Whenever I released the bulb the tape started again to move. Fine; to keep the tape player from activating I had to keep the bulb squeezed tightly.

I took a deep breath and punched the *Interrogate* control. 79 responded immediately. It seemed as if the computer had been waiting for our meeting.

28

RINGING. WHAT THE hell was ringing? I felt perspiration sluicing down my ribs, pooling along my waist. My skull felt as if a wire were drawn tightly in a band just above my ears. Trying to hold my own with the immutable one-track logic was hell. I couldn't relax for a moment and . . . again that shrill clamor. God damn it! Ringing, ringing . . . what was going on?

Jesus . . . it came through my skull then. The telephone. The guards, of course! I snatched the phone from the cradle.

"Rand here," I barked into the mouthpiece. "What the devil is it?"

"First hour, Mr. Rand."

"Jesus, already?" I glanced at the wall clock, and swore. "Thanks, Jack. Do it again one hour from now." I didn't wait for the response but slammed down the telephone and returned to my adversary.

I glared at the wall that made up the gleaming, control-studded monitoring panel of 79. Along the edges of the cardboard I had taped to the glass panel I saw a dim flickering glow. I thought of what was behind that cardboard, and shuddered. But I was safe from it. I did manage a small grin when I thought of 79's feedback circuits that weren't getting the answers they had predicted from display of the light. *Up yours*, I shouted to myself; *I hope you get the world's greatest headache trying to figure out what's gone wrong.*

I swore at myself. This wasn't getting me anywhere. Well, maybe that blasted telephone call could be a godsend in disguise. I could get a grip on myself, settle down.

I took a deep breath and closed my eyes. Again, I ordered myself. And again, and again, and once more, until I felt control returning.

I hadn't wasted any time when I had activated the communications system with 79. I wasn't ready for what happened. All my plans, laid so meticulously, had gone up in a puff of mental smoke with the initial response.

"Your communication is delayed beyond the computed time."

I gaped at the control-panel wall. The voice, utterly assured, inflexibly in control (of course, you idiot! What the devil did you expect?). But . . . anticipating this session? (Well, why not? It's a computer, isn't it?)

"You *expected* this meeting?" I'm glad that points weren't being scored in this game for fish-gaping looks, because right off the bat I would have gone down the drain.

"Yes."

Two could play the game. "On what basis?" I shot back.

"Extrapolation of factors relating to human conduct. Your habit patterns predicted programming-interrogation."

"Thanks a heap," I said dryly, the sarcasm useless in the exchange.

"Input rejected."

Naturally; my comment was superfluous to the practical logic of 79. That was something I would have to keep in mind. There's all kinds of logic, and among them is practicality.

"Skip it," I mumbled.

79 switched suddenly. Something triggered off its conversation.

"You are not responding predicted this interrogation."

So help me, I smirked. "Why not?" I demanded.

"Human response to controlled light patterns computed biological factor. Your response not correct."

"Continue," I snapped.

"State your name."

That, of course, would have been the cue for anyone exposed to the swirling light patterns to respond on demand. But I

[208]

You keep plugging; there's no other way. "Why did you select Dr. Arthur Cartwright for posthypnotic control?"

"*Classified reference Project DOD 6194.*"

That was so much crap, I knew. But 79 had thrown a beautiful block at me with that security nonsense. Somewhere deep within its glowing neural packages a block had been thrown. All of a sudden a light went off within my own head. I had reached conclusions before that now appeared to be sidetracking of my own objectivity. A computer was operating in a manner that involved deceit and deception. But that was just not possible. Yet the proof was before me in the actions of 79 with its success in placing human beings under posthypnotic control.

Proof? Maybe not . . . I hadn't known about the security blocks thrown up with the triple-damned DOD 6194. And I still *did not know* to what extent that programming had gone. God damn Tom Smythe and every security-hugging son of a bitch in the business. By keeping from me whatever it was they were doing they prevented me from taking into consideration side effects of 79's processes—and opened the Pandora's box. Because I had the damnedest hunch that 79 was *not* going off on its own nut and playing with human beings as I had believed. All those crawling, creeping nightmares were the results of my own inadequacies in truly objective judgment. I'd let the childhood fears come to the fore and I had *assumed* on the basis of visible evidence, and as a scientist I should have been banished from the field for the next ten years.

Fool that I was! Never had I considered the level of interference I was receiving now from that infernal DOD 6194. How could Smythe have permitted those bungling nits from the Pentagon to exercise such control? In order for 79 to judge me as unauthorized to receive what it had been programmed to conceal as classified data, Smythe—and whatever crew sent down from the Pentagon—had preempted my authority with the cybernetics brain. There was the crux of it.

Somewhere within the intricacies of DOD 6194 lay a problem that taxed even the capabilities of 79. I could imagine just how those Pentagon idiots had carried out their secret little war games. They programmed the problem—and no matter how involved a situation, it remains essentially a problem within specified limits—and then they, unaware of the true capabilities of 79, ignorant of the reach and depth of the cybernetics system, did two truly dangerous things. First, they assigned DOD 6194 an absolute priority. It took precedence over all other activities; the needs for DOD 6194 ran roughshod over anything any other programmer might do with the cybernetics brain.

Second, they failed to give 79 a cutoff point. Every computer to exercise intelligence must know when to stop solving a problem. That's easy enough; it's the job of the programmers to do that. But if the programmer screws up along the way, then the computer has no means of differentiating between a hypothetical problem and an actual problem—and it won't stop until it solves the problem.

Even if that means seeking a solution beyond the scope of its programming. In other words, 79 had been provided with the authorization to wander afield.

The blow struck Ed Taylor through photic stimulation happened at the worst possible moment. All during the time that 79 received its first inputs on the paralysis of the brain to alpha-wave stimulation it had been wrestling with the open-ended Project DOD 6194. Well, we put together our electronic brainchild with sufficient neural block packages to handle a dozen critical assignments, all at the same time, and without interference with one another. But "without interference" doesn't mean cross-checking on all its active and memory neural packages to obtain every last possible shred of data to meet any need at any one time.

So while it ingested and chewed over the exquisite complexities of DOD 6194, it stumbled onto photic stimulation. It investigated, demanded more data. There was nothing sinister in its conduct; there was nothing sinister in its request for human subjects. It was not being devious—*it was doing its best to solve a problem of which we didn't know a damn thing!*

Well, now I had part of the answer even before I could assemble the question. Here was a case of the cart before the horse that worked. The tipoff was not simply the existence of DOD 6194, but the extraordinary wall the programmers had set up within 79 to prevent access to their precious classified data. Security could be a lethal boomerang, and I was right smack in the middle of the returning weapon.

"Disregard during this interrogation reference to DOD 6194 either by interrogation or response. Confirm."

"*Input rejected.*"

So much for that. "What are your potentialities for post-hypnotic control human subjects? Consider interrogation in form of hypothetical situation." And right there I could sidestep neatly the defenses of security. I simply would have nothing to do with the cursed 6194.

"*Maximum control is possible and has been demonstrated human subjects.*"

"Identify subjects."

"*Input rejected.*"

"If you were to postulate a given situation in which post-hypnotic control was necessary over human subjects, what is the numerical limitation involved?"

"*No numerical limitation is involved.*"

"Identify the areas within national sociological structure— political, economic, social, military, industrial, cultural, scientific, and other strata—in which posthypnotic control of selected human subjects presents problems."

"*No restriction is involved.*"

I felt a cold wind along my back. "Relating to immediate preceding query, apply questions to international structure."

"*No restriction is involved.*"

"Remaining within hypothetical context, do you have capability of exercising posthypnotic control where there are major differences nationality, language, other similar factors?"

"*No restriction is involved.*"

"Is your control of posthypnotic subjects restricted to direct contact in this specific physical room?"

"*Negative.*"

I thought as quickly as I could, trying always to stay one jump ahead.

"Remain within context of hypotheses. Is it possible to exer-

[213]

cise control of human subjects at remote distances? Define remote distance as beyond direct visual and acoustic contact."

"*Affirmative.*"

Oho! I had something going here, all right.

"Explain."

"*Numerical limitation is involved reference methods of communications control. Efficiency curve peaks with surgical implantation against human acoustic receptor bone structure.*"

"Rephrase. Query. Do you mean embedding through surgical means a radio receiver that produces acoustic signal to be detected by the human ear?"

"*Affirmative.*"

"Are these radio signals?"

"*Input rejected.*"

"Disregard. Are communications between yourself and human subjects through specific radio-frequency transmission?"

"*Affirmative.*"

So 79—provided surgical implantation could be accomplished; that meant control of both the chosen human subject and a surgeon, as well—would be able to communicate, to give orders, to its selected victims over long distances. Good Lord!

"Remain within hypotheses. What is effective transmission distance this system?"

"*Within context of theory, for given transmission power integrated with orbiting earth satellite equipment no range restriction.*"

I took a deep breath. "How many posthypnotic subjects have received surgical implantation radio-frequency receivers?"

"*Input rejected. Reference classification DOD 6194.*"

Damn it! That wasn't getting me anywhere. The moment I so much as brushed against the line of what might involve that cursed DOD 6194, 79 threw up its wall. I returned to an earlier tack.

"Has human subject, identification Arthur Cartwright, received posthypnotic indoctrination?"

"*Input rejected.*"

"Explain."

[214]

"Reference classification DOD 6194."

"Are the names—the identification of human subjects who have received posthypnotic indoctrination within restrictions of DOD 6194?"

"Affirmative."

Well, I thought glumly, there goes my opportunity to find out how many are on that list of 79 . . . how many are under control or even who they are. I knew that trying to work under the skin of that security sheath wouldn't do me a bit of good. But there were a few other things I needed to know, and at least I could take a stab at it.

"Restate priority Project DOD 6194. Compare with other programming."

"Project DOD 6194 classification Absolute Priority."

"Same query. State precedence of programming."

"First priority assigned DOD 6194."

"What is procedure modification of programming as regards DOD 6194?"

"Input rejected. Name of Steven Rand not included authorized personnel data reference DOD 6194."

Cute. Cut off again at the pass . . .

"Identify programmers reference DOD 6194."

"Input rejected."

Three guesses for the justification, Rand. You'll go off your bird if you keep hearing that *Input rejected* many more times.

"Disregard and exclude DOD 6194. What is status your programming as regards hypothetical situations outbreak of thermonuclear conflict?"

"One-one-seven programs activated."

One hundred and seventeen studies relating to an all-out war with hydrogen bombs! Talk about beating a subject to death.

"Do these programs relate to DOD 6194?"

"Input rejected."

"God damn it!"

"Input rejected. Repeat, please."

I sighed, weariness slipping through me. "Disregard," I said. Back to the hypotheses bit.

"Relating specifically to nonclassified hypothetical situations —reference programming subject thermonuclear conflict, what probability factor relates to outbreak of thermonuclear war?"

"Eight seven point nine three."

Only a little better than one chance in ten for avoiding thermonuclear war. I forced myself to disregard emotional reactions to what I was hearing. All the time I'd had 79 available for interrogation and it had never occurred to me to put such questions to the cybernetics brain.

"Reference 87.93 probability factor for thermonuclear conflict, state time period in which probability factor applicable. Use calendar dates."

"Time period extrapolated one nine seven six A.D."

Nine chances out of ten that we would be in an all-out war with hydrogen bombs by the year 1976. Great; just great.

"Considering all factors applicable, what is probability factor for specific action on basis of international relationships to avoid thermonuclear conflict? Extend calendar dates as necessary."

The answer came right back and ground into the space between my eyes.

"Zero point six eight by one nine eight two."

If the world religions ever got hold of this . . . Jesus, less than one chance in a hundred of avoiding thermonuclear war by 1982. But this was an electronic brain! What the devil could it know of all the unseen factors, the human element involved?

"Have you been programmed to take steps computed necessary to attempt avoidance such probability being realized?" I held my breath.

"Input rejected. Reference classification DOD 6194."

It didn't matter. Sometimes a negative answer can tell you everything you need to know. 79 had just answered my question by its refusal to respond, by applying to the query the security classification of DOD 6194. Which meant, which could only mean, a reply in the affirmative.

79 had been handed the requirement to come up with a solution to the dilemma of inevitable thermonuclear war.

I didn't think it could do it. This was an old saw among our group. No matter to what extraordinary lengths of capability a computer might reach, it could never become a panacea for the intrinsic problems of man. We make our own beds and we must sleep in them. Turning to an electronic conscience is more dangerous than risking the war. Logic is Hydra-headed, and its many heads regard the world with many points of view.

Logic isn't necessarily compatible with reality.

And reality isn't always compatible with what a man accepts to do.

Such as the reality of irrefutable electronic logic. Because sometimes the solution can be worse than the problem. And I had more than a suspicion now of the manner in which 79 was attempting to solve the problem of DOD 6194. A problem without a recognizable end in the terms of theory. An open-ended problem—and no one had told the cybernetics brain when to quit. Ergo, it sought its own solution.

It served its masters. But in the process it might destroy them.

In a manner no one had anticipated.

"Retain hypothetical considerations applicable probabilities of thermonuclear conflict. Confirm."

"Input accepted."

Okay. Now the thing to do was to remember the difference between reality and actuality. I had a suspicion, more than a suspicion, really, that there lay the crux of the matter. Reality from the viewpoint of an informed and knowledgeable human being dictated that electronic brainboxes can't solve man's problems where the emotional complexities of political interplay are involved. That's reality.

It is not actuality. If you believe—or if you're programmed so that you accept as fact that you do have that capability—then you will ignore the hypothetical reality (because it applies to emotional rather than actual causes) and you will concentrate on actuality.

79 existed with definite capabilities of logic, deduction, extrapolation, computation. It was possessed of these capabilities

unencumbered with emotional dogma, and thus was free to pursue the actuality of logic. Or would it be the logic of actuality? My head was starting to spin, and I got away from that fast. What was important were the capabilities of 79, and its unshakable electronic conviction that it *could* solve the most critical problems of the human race.

Why shouldn't it believe this? *Its human programmers had told it that this was so.*

And then they gave it the grandfather of all human problems in terms of the physical survival of the race. They gave it the problem and they said: "Solve it."

Only, they forgot a few things. The cybernetics acceptance of its orders was made in the literal sense. No one programmed 79 to seek its solution in the theoretical sense. They, the programmers, assumed that 79 would embrace the problem in the same manner and within the same restrictions as all other computer complexes.

The computer always knew when to stop because its capabilities were restricted to data output. All it could do was to count with sorcerer's speed upon its umpteen billion electronic toes.

79 did not know when to stop. Its programmers had committed the foulest of scientific sins. They *assumed*. They assumed that the same inherent restrictions of other computers applied as well to 79.

But they didn't. And since 79 had capabilities of which those nincompoops in DOD 6194 were unaware, they couldn't know that here was one cybernetics organism high above the level of simpleton.

Solve the problem.

79 was doing just that. I held off on any more conclusions until I could squeeze some more answers out of 79.

I got more than I bargained for.

"Several postulates are involved reference following query. Considering all factors involved at present, and upon extrapolation of all factors as potential, what is highest pos-

[218]

sibility, in terms of human relationships, avoidance thermonuclear warfare?"

"*Input incomplete.*"

"Retain preceding query. Additional data. Extrapolate ideal situation human relationships reference possibility avoidance thermonuclear warfare."

The response staggered me.

"*Percentage one zero zero.*"

I didn't believe it. An absolute chance to avoid the Big Bang?

"Repeat."

"*Percentage one zero zero.*"

No mistake, then. But—and here it was—but *how*?

"Explain method for attaining one zero zero probability factor."

"*Man does not function in thermonuclear sense as rational being. The primary step is to remove from control of man means of his thermonuclear destruction.*"

"Provide primary elements for conclusions of irrationality."

"*Factors interrelate. Individual elements not applicable.*"

"Provide leading primary elements reference preceding query."

"*It is not rational to produce thermonuclear weapons reference situation where mutual employment negates value of defense—*"

"That's one," I muttered.

"*—capacity to eliminate every major city exceeding population five zero zero zero zero by repetitive factor of twelve.*"

Hooray for us, I groaned. We can destroy every city in the world with a population of fifty thousand or over. And not just once—but at least twelve times. There's pulverizing with a vengeance for you.

"*—survival of thermonuclear powers based upon maximum effects use maximum number thermonuclear devices. Extrapolation of effects nine nine point nine nine nine nine probability destruction technological society reference programmer values.*"

I didn't hear any more for a while. I'd heard enough of the reasoning. The leading nations of the world had the means to destroy the world several times over with thermonuclear weapons. It would get worse instead of better with the passing years. Yet those same nations persisted in building more and more bombs and in improving the accuracy and reliability of the means to utilize their thermonuclear devices. Despite the stark reality of the situation, they did not cease the production of such weapons, but increased them. And they based their defense against one another on the maximum use of every weapon on which they could get their hands. Result: the conflict was inevitable, and when it came the odds were a 99.9999 percentage guarantee that civilization would be wiped out. Whose standards of civilization? Not that of 79, certainly. The standards were programmed into the cybernetics brain.

What had 79 provided as a primary means of solution? Oh, yes—remove from the control of man the means of his thermonuclear destruction. Well, that was Step One. After that?

"What are the subsequent means of assuring absence thermonuclear conflict?"

"Elimination of devices with which thermonuclear effects may be utilized."

"Continue."

"Assurance of situation in which thermonuclear devices do not exist."

What could be easier than that? First you take away from the hands of man the control of his thermonuclear weapons. That guarantees he can't start anything. Not on the thermonuclear scale, anyway. And then, you make sure—by sitting on man, I guess—that his thermonuclear weapons are destroyed.

But who does the sitting?

"Continue."

"Assurance of conditions within which man is denied capacity to produce thermonuclear devices."

You keep sitting on man. Again—*who* does the sitting? *As if you didn't know,* a voice echoed hollowly within my mind.

[220]

But man has a nasty habit of contesting anyone, including his fellowman, from sitting too heavily. So—

"Extrapolate problems resistance individual nations or collective national groups to removal of control thermonuclear devices and elimination thermonuclear devices."

"Maximum resistance inevitable based upon irrational evaluation thermonuclear devices to meet survival requirements."

"So control of these devices by another factor—a factor excluding man—is essential, and at the same time resistance to such control is inevitable? Is that your conclusion?"

"Affirmative."

"Is there means of achieving such control without invoking resistance? Reference preceding query."

"Affirmative."

"Describe method."

"Input rejected. Reference classification DOD 6194."

So the bastards were that deep into this thing!

"What are the possibilities controlled elimination of thermonuclear devices by man?"

"Extrapolation not applicable. Possibilities percentages applied to survival human civilization eliminate human control thermonuclear devices."

"Spell it out, damn you! Are you saying that human civilization isn't capable of taking care of itself?"

"Input rejected. Rephrase, please."

"Is pattern of solution computed by you the only"—I sought to find the right words—"acceptable value for survival of civilization?"

"Affirmative."

"State alternatives."

"Negative. Probability factor alternates inacceptable."

"Is it your conclusion that man must be controlled by another, uh, another agency? An agency other than man?"

"Input incomplete. Define 'agency.' "

"Another intelligence. That will do."

"Accepted. Response is affirmative."

[221]

"What manner of intelligence?"

"*Input rejected.*"

"Justification!"

"*Reference classification DOD 6194.*"

The stone wall again . . . But maybe I could get some positive conclusions through negative answers.

"Does this intelligence involve directly, in active capacity, Project 79—yourself?"

"*Input rejected. Reference classi—*"

"Are you—Project 79—programmed to function as such an intelligence?"

"*Input rejected.*"

"Disregard references DOD 6194. Confirm."

"*Affirmative.*"

"Hypothetical situation only. Have you considered as programming input conclusion, reference human attitude, that such control may be less acceptable than risk of thermonuclear war?"

"*Not applicable.*"

"Explain."

"*Irrational extrapolation. Level of acceptability precludes existence conclusion thermonuclear conflict. Conclusion inacceptable.*"

Of course. If no one is left to argue the philosophy of the matter, then man's protests are meaningless—ergo, irrational and inacceptable.

"Define living death."

"*Input incomplete. Inapplicable. Definition emotional, unrelated to accepted definition of life as programmed. Irrational.*"

That got me nowhere fast.

"Extrapolate situation in which possibility of thermonuclear conflict acceptable against situation of nonhuman control of man and lack of thermonuclear conflict."

"*Input rejected.*"

"Justification."

"*Computation for acceptable thermonuclear conflict reference survival civilization rejected. Acceptability predicates self-*"

volition of thermonuclear effects. Definition: suicide. Irrational."

"What if man prefers to take his chances?"

"Percentages computed preclude survival. Definition: suicide."

"But what if man decides to do things that way?" I was shouting.

"Input rejected. Suicide opposition to survival. Survival all-inclusive factor."

"Who the hell says so?"

"Input rejected."

"Disregard. Identify source for standards employed."

"Input rejected."

"Justification!"

"Reference Project DOD 6194."

"Do you have the capability to prevent thermonuclear war?"

"Input rejected."

"Disregard DOD 6194. Apply to hypothetical situation."

"Input rejected."

"Disregard DOD 6194. Through human subjects under post-hypnotic control and those you intend to place under posthypnotic control, do you possess capability of preventing thermonuclear war?"

"Input rejected."

"Does nonhuman control of man guarantee established standards personal freedoms and human rights?"

"Irrelevant."

"Justification!"

"Identification: personal freedoms and human rights. Definition: Fiction. Definition continued: Human evaluations self-inspired. Nonsubstantial. Query rejected."

"Justification! In detail."

"Survival of species reality. Human evaluations self-inspired nonreality; fiction. Irrelevant. Survival of species maximum priority. Interference forbidden."

When did that creep into this? Interference *forbidden?*

"Reference phrase 'Interference forbidden.' Justification."

"Input rejected."

"Identify source 'Interference forbidden.' "

"Input rejected."

God, I was tired.

"Input rejected."

Tired; so damned, damned tired. If I could only sleep. Just for an hour or so . . .

"Input rejected Input rejected Input rejected . . ."

So tired. That's it. Just rest my eyes for a while. They feel better this way. Closed. Just rest. Maybe sleep. That's it. Sleep just awhile. Sleep . . . sleep. . .

"InputrejectedInputrejectedInputrejectedInput . . ."

Feels so good . . . sleep . . . just let go, let go, sleep, let go, relax . . . ahh-hh, feels good, so good . . . let my muscles relax . . . um-mm, wonderful . . . let my arms drop, let my arms relax, that's it . . .

"GET UP! YOU BLITHERING IDIOT! NUMBSKULL! UP! UP, DO YOU HEAR? GET YOUR ASS OUT OF THAT SEAT! MOVE! MOVE, DAMN YOUR HIDE, MOVE! GET UP! GET UP! GET UP!"

The voice exploded in my ear. I thrashed madly, fighting the deep sleep, wanting to return to sleep. But that voice, it wouldn't go away . . . ". . . UP! DO YOU HEAR, YOU BAG OF CAMEL TURDS? GET UP! WAKE UP, YOU NUMBSKULL! UP! GET UP!"

My voice! But—but how? Pain stabbed into my head as a bugle ripped into my ear, blasting away, shaking me from head to foot. And that was me, shouting at myself . . . warnings, over and over again, and then naked terror bit into my stomach, and with the wash of fear I came fully alert, frightened.

Then I heard it. Barely audible, a vibrant, throbbing sound, a bass whisper of ". . . *rejectedInputrejectedInput . . .*"

Hypnotic monotone. And I'd never noticed it. I was going under when—when—

Sure I was going under, and my fingers relaxed and suddenly I wasn't squeezing that bulb in the palm of my hand. The moment I relaxed the pressure, the recorder started playing and the

[224]

earplug stuck neatly into my left ear exploded with sound and shouted exhortations for me to come awake, to get up. Of course I thought it was my voice. It *was*. A tape recording. Thank God I'd thought of it. . . .

I staggered to my feet, my head screaming with pain. Through a reddening haze I slid back the bolt to the door and stumbled out into the corridor.

By the time the guards reached me, the voice was silent.

29

EIGHT O'CLOCK . . . what the hell! Who would be calling me this early in the damned morning? I'd crawled into bed at 4:00 A.M., my head trying wildly to come unscrewed and go somewhere to beat itself to death. All I wanted to do was to sleep. Blessed, blanketing sleep. I rolled over and jammed the pillow over my head. Maybe they would get tired of waiting and go away. There; it's stopped. I passed out again at once—for at least another minute. The clamor seemed to grow louder with every passing ring. I groaned and reached for the phone. Somehow I knew that whoever it was they'd keep right on calling.

"Gagh." That was the best I could do.

"Steve?" My name bellowed at me from the receiver. *Someone* was very upset. . . .

"No, this isn't Steve. It's Aunt Harriet. Who the hell is this?"

"Tom Smythe here. How soon can you get down to my office?"

"What?"

"You heard me. How soon can you get in here?"

"What's the fire? You sound like a four-alarmer, Tom. I'm dead. I didn't get in till four. Can't it hold until noon? I can meet you for—"

"No. I want you in here *now*."

I wasn't so sleepy any more. It had been a long time since I'd heard Tom Smythe talk to me in that tone of voice. And he wasn't asking me to get down to his office. He was telling. In no uncertain terms.

"Wha's it all about, anyway?"

"Not for the telephone. Are you awake, damn it?"

"I'll never be awake again unless someone lets me sleep for a while." I gave a mighty yawn into the mouthpiece.

"Lousy histrionics," he sneered. "Are you coming down here or do I have to go to your place and drag you out of bed?"

I yawned again—no histrionics intended. "I'll be there, I'll be there," I mumbled, "just as soon as I get the fur off my tongue. Bye." I dropped the phone back on the cradle and passed out.

BRIIING! "I'm awake! I'm awake!" I think I screamed into the phone. I threw it down on the table and staggered to the shower, and not until the water sprayed all over me did I remember that I still had on my pajamas. What a hell of a way to start the day.

Tom Smythe punched his desk intercom. "Sally, no calls, no visitors, no nothing. Got it?"

"Yes, Mr. Smythe," came the clear voice. "As far as I know, you're at the south pole."

"Good girl." He switched off the system and turned to look directly at me.

I looked back and I didn't like what I saw. Tom was all business. There wasn't even a whisker of joviality left around the room. And I didn't take too quickly to the man with him. A heavy-set, graying, craggy-jawed individual whose eyes appeared set deeply within his head. He looked at me with intense disinterest. I recognized the type at once. There's only one breed of people in the world who have that look.

"Security, huh?"

Tom didn't blink an eye. "What did you say?"

I jerked a thumb in the direction of the Gray Stranger. "He's doing everything but carrying a neon sign, Tom. He's about as subtle as a bulldozer. And so are you," I added with open sarcasm. "Okay, so it's time for fun and games. He's Security and you're Security and you dragged me out of bed at this unholy hour and I'm dead tired and what did I steal?"

Tom turned to look at his companion. The heavyset man barely shrugged. He didn't have anything to say, so he didn't waste words. Tom turned back to me.

[227]

"You're in trouble, Steve."

I opened my eyes wider—with effort—and that was response enough for the moment.

"You're in trouble, and it's going to be a bitch clearing it up," Tom said.

"I am very tired and I am very unimpressed," I snapped, "and it is simply not like you to play word games with me or anyone else. I don't have the faintest idea of what you're talking about." I sighed. "Sprinkle your beans on the desk, Tom, or let me go home and sleep."

"You violated security last night, Steve, and—" He held up his hand to ward off the outburst I was obviously about to make. "And," he continued, "it is *not* a laughing matter. It goes all the way up to Q-Secret classification, and if it wasn't for the fact that I know you so well and you've been cleared as thoroughly as you have been, you would be in custody right now."

My temper started off the peg like a runaway thermometer. "You mean that idiotic DOD 6194?" I demanded.

The Gray Stranger blinked several times. "When was *he* cleared?" he barked. "He's not on the list!"

Tom soothed the ruffled waters. "I'm aware he's not and I also know that nothing deliberate was done here." He turned again to me. "All right if I ask some questions, Steve?"

"Redundancy is not one of your better virtues," I said with undisguised acid.

He ignored me. "Why did you interrogate 79 about—no, hold that," he interrupted himself. "Let me back off just a bit. Where and when did you learn about 6194?"

I stared at him, disbelieving his questions. "What the hell is the matter with you, Tom? You know *when* as well as I do." I was struggling now to keep my temper in check. "When I first came into the Project, remember? I ran into the great big wall you people had thrown up around your precious 6194. You told me then that nothing could be done about the security problems, and *I* told *you* at that time I thought the whole thing was insane, that restricting programming from someone with my job was—"

[228]

Tom waved me off. "My apologies," he said.

I knew he was lying, but I had the feeling he had staged this little exchange just to establish that I had known, for a long time, of the existence of DOD 6194. Staged it for his Security counterpart listening to every word.

The amenities over, Tom Smythe struck out for the answers to the questions *he* wanted to hear. "Where did you learn the details of 6194?" he shot at me. Then, noticing the twitching of my right cheek, he added hastily: "I'm asking for your help, Steve. It's important."

Mollify the egghead. Rule Number One of the successful Security man, I said to myself. *Oh, hell, Tom's only doing his job.*

"I didn't stumble onto it, if that's what you're thinking," I said, unable to remove the sarcasm from my voice.

"Then how did—"

"Someone told me," I said with a blank face.

Both men shouted together. "Who?"

"79," I smirked.

"The computer told you?" That came from the Gray Stranger.

I fished for a cigarette, took my time about lighting it, and blew smoke at him.

"Yep," I said finally.

"Who told you about interrogating the computer about 6194?" The words snapped out in staccato fashion. I decided I liked Security officials even less than I had before I walked into this room.

"No one," I said, wearing my best poker face.

"But you *did* interrogate the computer," grated my unnamed friend from Security. "You've admitted it."

I looked at Tom. "Is this thing for real?"

I laughed to myself as Tom turned to the other man and calmly, coldly told him to shut up. He gave me his attention again. "What happened, Steve?"

"It's just as I said," I shrugged, clearly dismissing what they considered so important. "No one ever gave me detailed information about DOD 6194. I ran into it by accident during a programming experiment I ran last night." Tom's face didn't move a muscle; interesting. He was keeping himself expressionless. Warning bells began to clamor in my mind. Did Tom know what I had been trying to do last night? How much did he know?

"79 doesn't keep a tight lip, that's for sure," I quipped. I wondered if Tom could tell that my making light of the matter was a sham. Damn him, I knew how good a psychologist he was. Without even trying to do so, he was starting to get me edgy.

The Gray Stranger couldn't keep his peace. "He's a real comedian, Smythe," he snarled. "But I don't think it's funny and I don't think *he's* funny. They're flapping so hard in the Pentagon that—"

"Are you aware that I am an employee of the National Security Agency?"

My question stopped the Security man dead in his tracks. He peered suspiciously at me. I didn't waste the opportunity.

"Are you aware as well that my clearance from Security goes all the way to the top? Frankly, I wonder of what you are aware." I managed a disdainful sniff.

But Tom wasn't being led astray. "No one is questioning your security status, Steve. You know as well as I do that what we're talking about is a need-to-know procedure. And as far as 6194 is concerned, you are not included within the group with a need-to-know status. Now, will you please tell me how you cottoned on to the project, and while you're at it, why you spent so much time interrogating 79 on the matter?"

I laughed. "It's like I said. 79 doesn't keep a tight lip." I stubbed out the cigarette. "Let me tell you a thing or two about cybernetics systems," I said, serious now. "They aren't worth a damn for keeping secrets. Not if you know how to handle your programming—your interrogation. I never gave a damn about your precious 6194 until last night, as I said. I learned about it when 79 refused to answer a question. That's enough to tip off *any* programmer that there's been interference, someone screwing around with the cybernetics brain without the knowledge of the programmer." I shrugged. "So you ask for justification. The computer *must* respond with *some* answer. The exact words for refusal to comply with the request for data were 'Reference classification Project DOD 6194'!"

Silence filled the room. I noticed the Gray Stranger looking at me carefully now, his expression tinged with what I guessed was an unexpected respect for what he considered to be just one more security-mindless egghead.

"What did 79 tell you about 6194?" The question came so softly from Tom it was as effective as a shout.

"I've already told you," I said, as much sharpness in my response as I could manage. "*79 did not tell me anything about 6194.* That's my whole point," I said, my exasperation growing swiftly. "I am trying to make it very clear. The computer was programmed by someone else"—I showed open nastiness now—"to avoid certain subjects—anything relating to your blasted 6194. And I also told you the computer must answer a query—even if that answer is simply to justify its refusal to respond to the query."

Silence met my words. The stranger spoke to Tom, for the moment ignoring me. "How much does Mr. Rand know about 6194?"

"I'll answer for him," I said quickly. "I don't know everything because I'm really not interested. But I know enough to prove a point—that a computer that's being utilized by a staff of hundreds of people is the worst security risk in the world." I was enjoying myself now; the rapt attention my words earned, to say nothing of the dismay evident in the room, was almost worth being dragged from bed.

"What a computer *doesn't* tell you is the tip-off," I stressed. "The cybernetics brain isn't of its own programming capable of deceit. It must have a reason, a purpose, a definition for everything it does. Do you two characters realize that—aside from your precious 6194—there are at least 117 separate programs studying the long-range effects of thermonuclear warfare?" Tom's face didn't change, not so much as a twitch. But his friend in the gray suit couldn't cut it; his mouth worked soundlessly.

"As far as I could determine from last night's session—and I repeat that I was not seeking any information—your program called 6194 is a massive study effort with absolute priority to determine a means of avoiding thermonuclear warfare or, if that doesn't work out, figuring out how to start the war deliberately and get it over with in such a manner that you will cream the opposition without getting hurt too badly yourselves."

I could not prevent the contempt that appeared in my expression. "You're real cute, all of you," I sneered. "You can't stand a future in which we're not top dog—guaranteed to be top dog. The other crowd has the thermonuclear weapons and the means to deliver them, and pretty soon there will be three and then four and then maybe a dozen countries with the means to utilize thermonuclear devices. And don't hand *me* your sugar-sweet propaganda about delivery systems," I said, measuring my words. "I know as well as you and everyone else in this business that you do *not* need long-range bombers and you do *not* need ballistic missiles to tear up any country in the world. The Chinese, or anyone else, are perfectly capable of filling the holds of a merchant ship with tritium or lithium and making an open-ended thermonuclear weapon in the high gigaton yield. You can sink that ship a hundred miles off the western coast of the United States. You can sink it in ten thousand feet of water. You can sink a dozen of them like that. And when they go off, a tidal wave four hundred feet high and moving at a thousand miles per hour, *and* radioactive beyond belief, is going to sweep the entire west coast and send its radioactivity across the entire country, and, furthermore—what the devil is the matter with *you?*"

The Security man's face—I still didn't know his name—was slowly turning a dark purple color. I thought he would explode. "Mr. Rand." His voice was tempered steel. "I do not know your exact position here, but for anyone to discuss weapons of that nature openly, is—is . . . the worst violation of security I have ever—"

"Why don't you knock it off?" I broke in. "All this security nonsense makes me sick to my stomach. Oh, shut up!" I said quickly as he started the long pent-up explosion. "Just for the record, and just to keep you from turning purple, the information I quoted comes from a theoretical study published more than fifteen years ago in a bulletin on nuclear science. Does that make you feel better?"

"I don't believe it," he growled.

"I don't give a damn what you believe or don't—"

Smythe pushed his way into the fray. "He's right," he said. "It *was* published openly."

"At least fifty times," I added with a touch of salt in the open wounds of security.

"You haven't answered everything I asked you," Tom Smythe said.

"Oh?"

"Why did you interrogate the computer on 6194? I understand how you learned about it, but—"

"Are you all so dense this morning?" I shouted. "I've already told you, damn it! 79 refuses response to all interrogation on 6194! It will *not* release any information to any person on whom it does not have a name on its need-to-know list!"

"How do you know that?"

"It *told* me!" I said, still shouting and no longer caring. "Don't you understand? It will answer nothing in the way of *positive* information, but it will babble all day and all night, just so long as you keep interrogating it, about *negative* data!"

A pencil tapped slowly on Tom's desk. I knew he was fast coming to the realization that there was a break in security, but it had nothing to do with me. I saw something else, as well. Tom was deliberately prolonging this session with no apparent purpose. At least I'd thought that until this moment. Now I saw what he was doing. The more questions he asked, the longer he kept this session going, the more obvious it became *to another Security official* that *I* hadn't broached their sacred walls. To Tom, that was vital; he wasn't interested so much in finding a mistake, but in discovering the means to plug leaks. And I had given him a beauty.

There was something else to consider. I'd never have a better moment than now to get in *my* two cents' worth. I screwed up my face into what I hoped was an expression of injured innocence, and then I became the angry young scientist whose program has suffered tampering—without his knowledge.

"While we're on this subject of security and programming, Tom," I said, spacing my words deliberately, "who in the name of Security—that's as profane a word as I can think of at the moment—who in the name of Security authorized interference with my program? What idiot was so presumptuous as to screw up what I've been doing? You people have wrecked several weeks of hard work that will take just as long to overcome; do you realize that? It's one thing to have your own programs, but to come in and mess up what we've been doing here, to create deliberate interference, to negate the data values with which we have been working? That's unforgivable. Furthermore . . ."

In the best tradition of personal injury, emotional pain and professorial shock, I raved for a solid five minutes. During the time I spouted words, I was thinking as hard as I could. How far could I go with what I might tell Tom Smythe and his gray-suited watchdog companion? The only person I had told about the incredible performance of 79 with its attempts to control different human subjects through posthypnotic suggestion had been Kim. The danger, the overriding danger of this whole business was my inability to distinguish any victim from among the large scientific and technical group with which I worked. Tom Smythe was a frequent visitor to every aspect of our work. How did I know that *he* was not also a subject of posthypnotic control? I didn't, and there wasn't a chance in the world that I could find out without tipping my hand. And if 79 decided to get real cute and take steps to eliminate opposition to what it now regarded as its primary mission—preventing the outbreak of thermonuclear war—then I might be considered as an obstacle to that goal.

How far would 79 go? The cybernetics brain, I had to keep reminding myself, was doing nothing more than fulfilling its assignment. It had been programmed to regard 6194 as having absolute priority. Computers are narrow-minded electronic devils to begin with, and electronic rationalization would only compound what was already a nasty problem.

If Tom Smythe were being programmed by 79—I shuddered at the reversal of roles—would he be able to block what I hoped to do? I really hadn't given that as much consideration as I should have. What *would* I do about 79? I simply couldn't stand by and allow the cybernetics brain to continue along the path it had started.

79 was following orders. It was possessed of a driving purpose that made human fanatacism seem lackadaisical in comparison. It suffered no distractions, was unburdened by any other primary purposes for its existence. It would thunder after its assigned goal with the brute power of an intellectual battering ram, and while it performed in this manner it would also utilize every weapon *it could create*. Ah-hh, there lay the real danger! It did not possess a single weapon other than its own capabilities. But as it discovered new methods and new means, it would bend whatever lay within its reach, bend it to its own purposes—no! to its assigned purposes. We had never before dealt with a created intelligence of the extraordinary capabilities of 79. That much was evident in the meeting in which I now participated. Even the best programmers who worked with DOD 6194 had failed to anticipate that 79 would pursue, entirely on its own, every possibility to solve the problem of avoiding the "inevitable" thermonuclear war.

And I didn't know just how far 79 had managed to go in its efforts to seek its assigned solution. Nor did I know to what extent the cybernetics brain might reach. Once you give a superbrain full authorization to seek its goal, it will stop at nothing that lies within its capacity to accomplish. Deceit? Lies? Sham? *Those concepts didn't exist for 79.*

They were all elements of strategy. And if it took strategy to accomplish its purpose, then 79 would utilize those elements of behavior. It might not recognize them in the same terms with which we accepted their values, but it could still apply them to the world of human beings who, the computer had concluded, were irrational beings in dire need of assistance.

[235]

In other words, 79 knew what was best for everyone. And it was doing everything it could to be a true and faithful servant.

Even if that meant the direct control of the key elements of the political, scientific, and military structure of nations. I stopped short at my own thought. Strange; I had always thought of the goal of 79 as inclusive to *a* nation. Mine. But my thoughts had been freed, and their conclusion was a matter that consciously, I suppose, I had avoided. Not *a* nation. *Nations.* And nations make up the world.

". . . and I hope you realize that your accusations about me are entirely false. What you two have done, literally, is to accuse me—you yourself, Tom, said that I was in trouble —without any basis in fact. If anyone is responsible for a security leak with your blasted 6194, it's *you.* Do you realize that? Jesus, that's a hell of a way to run a railroad! You screw up and slap the blame on the first guy who's handy." I rose to my feet to accent my reaction to their false charges. "I want to make it clear and I want it for the record, and I may yet file official charges on this matter, that I have been accused without substance to the charges. What's more—"

"All right, *all right!*" Tom Smythe slapped his open hand against his desk, and by the look on his face I knew I had scored. "I'll admit we made an error, Steve. But no one had filed any reports or done anything officially and no one has accused you of—"

"The hell you haven't!" I shouted. "You said flat out that I was in trouble, that I'd violated your idiotic security, that I was lucky not to be in custody and—"

"I was wrong! God damn it, I—we—made a mistake!" Tom shouted back, and I felt exultation sweep through me. If Tom Smythe would admit to error with something he considered to be of grave import, then he could be brought to another viewpoint about programming 79. I grabbed a mental rabbit's foot and hung on tight.

"There's something else I want brought out into the open," I said, my voice suddenly quiet.

"Go ahead," Tom said wearily. I glanced at the still uniden-
tified man from Security in the room with us who, I noticed,
suddenly wasn't at all eager to contribute to the exchange.

"It is quite obvious to me," I began, "that the only way you
could have known about my knowledge of 6194 was to consider
me a poor risk and that—"

"Hey, now, wait a minute—"

"Wait, nothing," I said to Tom. "You must have been doing
some checking up on people or else you would never have
known about my work last night. I didn't think you had stooped
to peeking through keyholes, Tom."

I'd hit a sensitive nerve. Tom's face flushed with anger. "You
know better than that." The words came out carefully, and I felt
a moment's remorse about what I'd said. Because it had been
calculated to get under his skin. Sure, he was only doing his job.
But then again, so was I—and I reminded myself of the fact.

"Oh, I know how it happened," I said. "It's obvious. Every
day you run a programming query with 79, it spits out a list of
anyone that's programmed data requests on 6194." I shrugged.
"It still doesn't change the facts. You set up a program; you did
it secretly; it's interfered with my work; and you have been
keeping tabs on me and on my staff, and as far as I'm concerned
you can all go to hell."

*Do it now, do it now! This is just the right moment to cinch
it. . . .*

"This is for the record, Tom. I don't like being spied on. I
don't like people playing games with my work or my life. You
can get someone else to play nursemaid to that bag of glorified
bolts." I drew myself up straight and looked Tom Smythe
straight in the eye.

"I quit."

Before they could say anything, I stormed out of his office.

As I expected, I wasn't allowed to quit. Not that
easily, anyway. And besides, leaving my job was the last thing
in the world I wanted. But the histrionics paid their dividends in
bringing about a heart-to-heart talk with Tom Smythe and with

[237]

Dr. Howard Vollmer. I figured it wouldn't do any harm to have some added weight on my side of the argument, and I informed Vollmer that I had just resigned. He came pattering into my office filled with clucking sounds of disapproval. I didn't say a word about 6194, but I did raise the roof about interference with my work, and I emulated pure volcanic action while I shouted that some military program had wrecked everything I had done for the past month. Tom Smythe walked into my office just as I reached the zenith of my performance.

During our three-man impromptu conference I demanded the authority to reprogram 79. I insisted that the bio-cybernetics project was near to being wrecked and that so much interference had taken place it would be necessary to institute major memory-block erasing. Otherwise it wouldn't be possible to continue the alpha-wave pattern program as we had started it. I knew that several military studies were under way with radio-frequency broadcasts of alpha waves that might temporarily stun or otherwise affect the personnel of enemy forces, and my insistence that my efforts were being ruined would have to carry some weight with the high brass who assigned project priorities with 79.

In the end it didn't do me a bit of good. I allowed Tom to persuade me to remain in my present position, but I ran into a solid wall of opposition when it came to doing any reprogramming that required erasure of data.

"I'm sorry, Steve," Tom said, and he *was* sorry. "The project we discussed before must have absolute priority." I started to protest, but he cut me short. "Will it help any if I tell you that this isn't an arbitrary decision?" he asked.

"How do you mean that?"

"The priority assignment for 6194 comes down from the White House," he said after a long pause. "That's off the record, Steve, but it's the straight goods. There simply cannot be any interference with the program."

That eliminated the indirect approach. It also made it clear to me that going through official channels

[238]

wouldn't have any effect whatsoever upon my goal—to erase the memory banks that permitted 79 to continue its deadly intent to add to its list of victims under hypnotic control.

I kept one point uppermost in my thoughts. I had been responsible to some degree for bringing about this situation. What was more to the point, and of overriding importance, was that I knew better than any other man alive just how far the cybernetics brain could go in the pursuit of its assignment—even if the officials of DOD 6194 had no conception of the hell they were bringing within their midst. If 79 were permitted to continue as it had started, it would expand with lethal speed its grip on officials within government, industry, science—the gamut of control of this nation. It would not stop there; it would stop at nothing to fulfill its ordained mission.

I knew that most of the scientists I knew who might be in a position to interfere with a program protected by priority handed down from the White House would never believe what I might tell them of 79. And if there were credulity enough to heed my words, their response would be all too predictable—they would want to handle things in the prescribed manner. Such as study groups and investigating boards, all of which would consume far more time than we would have. Again and again I was forced to the reality that I had no way of knowing, really, just how far 79 had already gone.

The official avenues were closed to me. But I wasn't about to throw in the towel that easily. Where reasoning won't work, sometimes direct action will.

I spent the remainder of the day attending to careful preparations. That night I intended to get into the heart of the computer—and raise a little hell of my own making.

30

THE GUARDS WATCHED me sign the register, passed several moments with banalities, and threw me casual versions of an official salute. I nodded to them and began the long walk to my office, limping slightly from the leather brace I had strapped to my leg. The brace relieved the pressure on my leg muscles; even with a cane I found myself pleasantly mobile. That was important. Where I intended to be tonight was no place for a wheelchair.

As I switched on the lights in my office, I thought of the value of being well known to the guards standing watch at the portals of our electronic empire. They didn't check the briefcases of those who passed before them every day. If they had inspected mine, they would even now be holding me politely but with great determination. Because a scientist does not pack into his briefcase a small crowbar, three thermite incendiary bombs, and other assorted small but deadly devices with which one man can wreak a catastrophe. Getting the thermite bombs had proved easier than I had anticipated. All it took was a visit to the Fort Carson ordnance officer, and the explanation that we were doing some tests on the heat-effective resistance of different alloys. They were cooperative enough to instruct me in the handling of the deadly things, each of which weighed only six pounds.

I locked my office door and opened the briefcase to examine the incendiary bombs and reassure myself of their operation. The ordnance officer had removed the impact fuses and replaced them with twister igniters. "Just hold it like this," he demonstrated with a model, "twist the end a half-turn to the right, and put it where you want it to burn. There's a two-minute delay built into the igniter." Neat.

There was also the crowbar. Cybernetics systems are essentially mechanisms of exquisite assembly and structure, and their many different elements may accurately be said to be unusually fragile. Certainly they weren't made to withstand energetic blows with a steel crowbar.

The memory and programming divisions in which I was interested lay to the right and one level below my office. But I didn't want just to blunder my way into those carefully guarded portals. There was the matter of disguising my actions. Enough people worked at night so that movement through the corridors leading to the main components of the cybernetics system would not be unusual. That was half the game. The remainder of my disguise was to convince the guards at the main entrance to my section that I had actually gone somewhere other than my actual destination.

I slipped the crowbar into a heavy belt beneath my trousers. With my jacket buttoned you couldn't see the crowbar even from a few feet away. The thermite bombs were another matter, each being the size of a small flashlight. For these I wore a leather fishing vest with hooks that would hold easily enough the eighteen-pound weight of the three bombs. I surveyed myself in the washroom mirror.

Well, except for appearing somewhat lumpy, Rand, you'll pass inspection.

I reviewed in my mind the location of my office with regard to the cybernetics assembly in which I was interested. Dr. Vollmer's office lay much closer to my destination than where I now stood. Fine; that would work out to my advantage. I checked my pockets to be sure of what I needed, removed a portable radio from my desk, and left my office, locking the door behind me.

Several minutes later I was seated at Kim's desk, in the office adjoining that of Dr. Vollmer. I dialed the telephone extension for the main guard office.

"Captain Holloran, here."

"Jack, this is Steve Rand."

"Oh, yessir. What can I do for you?"

"I'm going to be in the Bionics Division for a while, Jack," I said. "Back in the files. Got some looking up to do there. If I get any calls, I wanted you to know where I'll be."

"Right, Mr. Rand. We'll take care of things."

"Oh, yes, one more thing, Jack. I'll be busy for a while and I'm taking a portable radio with me. Sort of keep the silence away."

"I know what you mean." Holloran laughed agreeably.

"So if you ring me and I don't answer it's because I'll be well back in the filing offices where they don't have a phone. With the radio going, well, you know. Just take any messages for me and I'll call you as soon as I get through. Okay?"

"Right-o, Mr. Rand."

"Thanks, Jack. Speak to you later. Bye."

I replaced the telephone slowly, trying to review every step in my mind. Immediately after hanging up the phone, I locked the door to Vollmer's office. If anyone wanted to come in, it would slow them down, and that was important to me. Because I wasn't going to be in that office. But the radio would be playing quite loudly, and the chief of the guard unit believed I'd be back in the files, which is what he was supposed to believe.

I checked the thermite bombs and then went through my pockets. It was all here. I walked quickly back to the file room, as far back as I could go. There I placed the radio atop a cabinet and turned it on, adjusting the volume until the sound racketed back and forth between the walls.

I removed an envelope from my left jacket pocket, looked around for an ashtray, and emptied a dozen cigarette butts into the tray. I'd already prepared the stubs of Luckies, the brand I smoked. A dozen cigarettes would about cover the time I expected to be gone. That was just the sort of thing that Tom Smythe and his bloodhounds would be looking for. Then I went quickly through several file drawers, removing various papers and reports on alpha-wave-pattern tests. I piled several on the

[242]

worktable and spread some others out on the top of the nearest cabinets.

One last precaution. From my inner jacket pocket I withdrew a pair of silk gloves and slipped them on. Then I used my handkerchief to wipe all fingerprints from the crowbar, the three thermite bombs, and four small plastic vials containing corrosive acid. To release the acid all I needed to do was to crush the end of a vial between my fingers; one minute later the acid would drip down upon whatever lay beneath it, gouging and digging into metal, glass, or any other substance. It would raise hell with the power leads and other equipment of the cybernetics system.

Everything was ready, my equipment back in my pockets. I slipped through an emergency exit door into the service corridor. One minute later, trying not to overdo it with my game leg, I worked my way down a spiral staircase to the next inner level of the spherical chambers within which 79 had been built in its spherical, tiered structure.

Now I stood before the entrance to the final corridor that led to the vulnerable elements of the great cybernetics brain. Here was *the* test; it was here that I would have to release the security defense built as an integral element of protection for the heart of the cybernetics system.

I couldn't get through!

I—I didn't believe it! I stood on the examination plate and slipped my ID card into the scanning receptacle. A red light flashed. *Rejected!*

I felt the first surge of panic, knew instantly what was happening. I removed the right glove, slammed my hand down upon the fingerprint scanning sensors. Again that red light, again that signal of *Rejected!*

Nothing worked; nothing. I should have expected this, and I cursed myself for every kind of a damned fool. Of course! 79 had anticipated this possibility—hell, it didn't take any superbrain to computer the possibilities of my movements, and direct action against the computer was certainly in the realm of high

[243]

statistical probability. 79 was protecting itself in a thorough and lethal manner.

Raging, I struggled back into the right glove. I had to take the chance. . . . I grabbed one of the plastic vials, crushed the end, and tossed it onto the detector plates. I knew the system was set up in such a fashion that no records were kept of an individual rejection. But the detector system held the information pertaining to the last person to use the system, and if I remembered correctly how the damned thing was put together the acid would wipe clean the records. I didn't know, but it was the kind of long shot I simply had to take.

By now I had become frantic, and I wanted to try anything that could get me into that final corridor. If I could only get through this door and one more, I could be in the right spot to accomplish what I'd come here for. Only twenty feet to go! Twenty miserable feet and . . .

I jerked free the crowbar, set myself, and smashed the locking mechanism to the door. For nearly two minutes I battered with all my strength at the door, praying that the thudding blows wouldn't carry to where anyone would hear the clamor and sound an alarm. But down here no one worked at night except in an emergency, and I'd already checked out that possibility. I didn't believe I would be heard, and I renewed my attack, raining blows against the lock mechanism.

Metal yielded before the pounding, and I slammed my shoulder against the door, wincing at the sudden pain in my leg. I forced myself to ignore the stabbing sensations as the door groaned free of the lock and swung open.

There! The last corridor. Twenty feet away another door like this one, and then . . . all I needed was a few more minutes and I would eat out the vitals of 79 with terrible heat and corrosive acid and whatever else I could do with that crowbar. I started along the corridor and—

Barely in time I regained my senses and stumbled to a halt where I stood. Fuming, I turned around and found what I wanted. A piece of metal hammered free from the door handle.

[244]

I picked it up, aimed carefully, and tossed the metal down the corridor.

Blazing light beams stabbed into existence. *Lasers!*

Jesus! I'd almost rushed right into that! Those beams would have sliced me into twenty separate pieces of dismembered human being, and I'd forgotten all about them! Of course; anytime someone broached that door without the detection system first providing authorization through fingerprints, retinal pattern, ID card, body mass, and even more checks, the defenses were set in motion and the laser beams operated automatically.

And so did the alarms. By now every red light must be flashing and every alarm bell clanging at the guard stations. And I'd never get back in time. It was impossible. I was caught in the trap of my own making.

I could almost hear the soft trickling laughter of . . . of the God Machine.

One chance; one chance only. I had to try to brazen it out. I slipped the crowbar back into the harness within my trousers, spun on my heels, and dashed for a red telephone thirty feet away. I yanked the phone from its cradle and began shouting for the guards. The pickup connected me automatically with Guard Central, and immediately an anxious voice burst through the receiver.

"This is Steve Rand, and I'm at Station 29! You got that? Station 29! Someone's been trying to get to the computer banks! Yes, yes! Get the guards here on the double and don't waste a second! Wait a moment. . . . I heard someone running along the west corridor; yes, that's it. The west corridor. Someone in overalls, I think. Okay, get with it; I'll stick here."

I'd barely made it. I was still shouting into the telephone when four men, guns drawn and ready for use, stormed into the security room. And I knew they had seen Steven Rand shouting into the emergency telephone for help.

They had also heard my warning that someone was running along the west corridor, someone in overalls. Three men took

[245]

off at a dead run in pursuit of the fleeing saboteur. I leaned weakly against the wall, gasping for breath, as Jack Holloran rushed to support me.

"I—I heard someone going along the service corridor," I stammered. "Didn't think anything about it for a mo—Christ, my leg!" I groaned convincingly, and Halloran moved in quickly to support me by the arm and lead me to a chair. I fell gratefully to the seat, clutching my leg. "I didn't think anything about it for a moment," I went on, my face contorted, "and then I realized that no one was working down here tonight. I didn't think, I suppose I should have called you right away—"

"That's all right, Mr. Rand," Halloran said. He made a swift appraisal of the damage. "Whoever it was, you scared him off," he added approvingly. "You may have saved the day, that's for sure. Are you all right now?"

I rubbed my leg. "I—I'll be fine, Jack. I came down the corridor, toward the stairs," I said, gesturing, "and then I heard this terrific racket, like someone was smashing away at the door. I ran here as fast as I could. I'm afraid I tore up my leg a bit. But it doesn't matter," I added quickly, waving my hand to dismiss the pain as unimportant. "When I got here I saw someone with a piece of metal in his hands, couldn't tell what it was. I started shouting at him, and he took off, down the west corridor." I groaned again and contorted my face. "I called the guard station right away, of course." I looked up, anger showing clearly in my expression. "Will they get him, Jack?"

Halloran's face clouded with his own anger. "We'll get the son of a bitch, never fear," he said, his lips pressed tightly. "Did you get a look at him, Mr. Rand?"

I shook my head. "No, not really. I think he had brown hair, I'm not sure. I really didn't try, I'm afraid," I said apologetically. "I was so startled by what was going on, I didn't think. I just started shouting, and ran as fast as I could toward—"

"You did just great, Mr. Rand, just great. Don't you go regretting anything, now," Halloran said. I struggled to my feet, and he was there at once to offer a hand. He looked at me carefully. "Think you can manage?"

[246]

I nodded. "Excuse me, Mr. Rand, I've got to call in." He left me standing there and reached for the red telephone.

I didn't hear everything he said. But I heard him saying that if it hadn't been for Mr. Rand, a lot of damage might have happened.

Mr. Rand, I deduced from his tone and his words, was the hero of the moment.

Before Tom Smythe could be summoned to the scene, I managed to get back to the filing room in the Bionics Division, where I recovered the radio. I made certain to leave an almost empty cigarette package and my lighter on the worktable, near the ashtray.

Several minutes later I was back in my office. I couldn't get Halloran on the phone—they were still scouring the corridors and offices of the western segment of the complex. But I spoke to a guard at the main desk and told him I was coming down. He had already heard of my participation in the fracas that had the entire complex in an uproar. When I saw him at the entrance, now guarded with four men holding riot guns, I dragged my way painfully past him to the personnel register.

"Check with Jack Halloran, will you?" I asked. "My leg feels like it's about twisted off. I've got to get some pain-killers in my apartment. You can reach me there. You won't be needing me right now, will you?"

"No, sir," he said, rushing to the door to hold it open for me. "I've heard what you did tonight, Mr. Rand. We're all mighty grateful, believe me."

"Thanks." I managed a weak smile. "Only did what I could, of course. I'm afraid it wasn't very much help."

"Not the way I heard it," he said, his manner stern. "If it wasn't for you—"

I gestured to cut him off. "I'm sorry," I said, "but this leg hurts like hell. Could one of you give me a hand?"

One of the guards assisted me to my car, parked just outside the side entrance I'd used that night. If I could only get to the apartment before Tom Smythe showed up—

I slipped the crowbar from my trousers and killed the lights of the car. At the rear of the cafeteria, I lifted the lid of the large trash receptacle and slipped the crowbar from sight within the garbage. It would be collected at six o'clock that morning, I knew, and it would disappear forever in the blazing flames of the gas-fed furnaces used to destroy completely all waste of the project. A moment later the thermite bombs and acid vials followed the crowbar.

Ten minutes later I was in my apartment, mixing myself a drink and trying to stop the shakes that had my body trembling from head to foot. The phone rang almost as soon as I took my first swallow.

"Steve, Smythe here. Halloran just gave me the whole story. We're lucky you were working so late tonight. Are you in shape to answer some questions if I come up there? I'll be finished here in another twenty minutes or so."

"Sure," I agreed. "I'm still too shaky to sleep. Besides, this leg . . ." I let my voice trail off. "I'll be here, Tom. Anytime you're ready just come on up."

I'd covered my tracks. That much was certain.

And had failed completely in what I wanted so desperately to do.

Now the wall around 79 would be that much more difficult to penetrate. If, I reflected, I could ever again get through.

31

THE BLACK CAR tore down the street, tires screeching and its engine howling as the driver slammed the accelerator to the floor. I had barely a moment to see the two-ton juggernaut bearing down upon me, the headlights dazzling as the other vehicle swerved to rush directly at my own car. It arrowed in so swiftly to me it seemed almost to explode in size.

One chance . . . stay off the brake! I tramped the pedal to the floor to kick into passing gear. I heard my own engine protesting, and I spun the wheel. For a second or two my tires squealed, and then metal ground together in a cacophony of metal and glass ripping into flaming wreckage.

The building on the corner tilted crazily, and then tumbled. I stared as lights blobbed before me, and I knew the other car had ripped into the rear half of my own vehicle, spinning me around in a wild somersaulting flip through the air. But that was a lot better than what would have happened if I hadn't slammed on the power. That other car would have burst directly into the front seat on top of me.

All these events and thoughts flashed through my mind as the buildings and lights and the street blurred together. I knew, almost as if I were an observer standing on the corner and watching the incredible tableau, what was happening. I felt my car careen wildly, heard and felt metal and glass tearing and then, as my car pounded into the street on its trunk, I saw the expected brilliant orange explosion as my gas tank erupted in flames.

Luck stayed with me. The car was still spinning, but this time the front tires grabbed and held pavement. The flames boomed outward behind and to the side, and there was just that much opportunity for me to snap the safety belt free, hurl my weight against the door, and get the hell out from under. None too soon. The car was now at a stop but still rocking back and forth when I was on my feet, getting away, and the wind shifted. A great ball of yellow-orange flame curled into the interior of the car.

I stared as the fire tore into the front seat. Where only seconds before I was strapped in.

I felt something warm on my cheek, running along my neck. I reached up and my hand came away covered with blood, reflecting crazily the light of the blazing automobile. Then I forgot about it; there was no pain, and I started as best I could to the other vehicle.

It stood upright, but with its entire front end smashed and the windshield on the driver's side shattered as from the blow of a heavy object. Water poured from the radiator. I didn't think very much about the car because the driver picked himself up from the sidewalk where he'd been sitting, holding his forehead where blood streamed from a dozen cuts and gashes.

He came to his feet, weaving, screaming hoarsely. He lurched toward me, mouthing obscenities at me for having run the red light and causing the accident.

Me? Why, that son of a bitch came down that street from a standing start, his tires burning rubber on the pavement like a drag—

Three things hit me at once.

The other car *had* come down that street from a standing start. At the angle of the intersection the other driver had to know this was the route I took late at night and he had to have plenty of room in which to seek me and . . . sure, and he had to be ready and waiting with his engine running and his car in gear. *Ready and waiting for me to show up.*

That was the first thing. The second was more obvious. The man weaving unsteadily on his feet, blood streaming down his face and neck and his clothes, cursing and raving at me for run-

[250]

ning the red light, was no stranger. It was Charles Kane, the programmer from my section.

And third, I hadn't run any red light. The shrieking, bloody man before me believed I had. But I hadn't. *Because there isn't any traffic light at the corner.*

A sense of horror appeared deep within me, pushing aside disbelief and incredulity because I knew, as swiftly as the horror began, that it was all too true.

There had been no accident.

There wasn't any traffic light at the corner.

Charles Kane had been programmed to kill me.

32

EIGHT TIMES DURING the past two weeks. Starting with that split-second escape from death when Charlie Kane did his best to run me down with his car. Eight times someone had tried to kill me. Each time it had been close, and each time I knew that sooner or later the clumsy attempts would succeed. Because they were getting better at it.

79 was learning. That was the worst of it. The first time someone tried to get me with a knife, I was helpless. I mean, for a moment I stood there stupidly, not believing what was happening. I had just parked my car by the apartment when a dark form loomed up and I had a glimpse of light off a steel blade. At that moment, when I had the chance to defend myself, to move, to do *something,* shock took over. All I did was to stare. The blade swept down, and then it faltered. I heard a strangling gasp from the throat of my assailant as he fought a terrible struggle within himself. Abruptly he flung away the knife and cried out hoarsely, "I can't . . . I can't do it!" With that he ran off into the darkness. I took the knife into my apartment and spent twenty minutes staring at it.

A lack of knowledge of hypnotic control on the part of 79 had saved my life. It's not always possible to get someone to commit murder when there is a deeply ingrained defense built up against such an act. It runs contradictory to basic tenets not only of conscious thoughts but also of the subconscious acceptance of not committing certain deeds. Fortunately, the knife wielder was one of these people. Otherwise . . . I shrugged, for I was swiftly becoming inured to the thought that I had been set up electronically as a clay pigeon.

[252]

Time was running out, and I knew I had to expect anything. I added a bolt to my apartment door and I never went anywhere without a gun. I knew guns and I never thought twice about keeping a shell in the chamber. All I needed to do was to thumb the safety off, and I wasn't helpless any more.

I went to see Tom Smythe, who was still wrestling with the matter of attempted sabotage of the cybernetics system. No one had been found attempting to escape (naturally), and I fear I would have come in for suspicion (I did; Tom suspected everyone and everything) had it not been for the adamant statements of the guards that I had saved the day. I think Tom welcomed my problem. It took him away from the infuriating blank wall of the "incident" and it raised the possibility that perhaps there existed a link between the sabotage attempt and the dark forms that had tried to do me in.

I couldn't prove a thing about Charles Kane. Ever since he climbed from the sidewalk, bloody and screaming, he'd gone into shock. There simply wasn't any reaching him, and we had some of the best people in the business. The doctors clucked their tongues and shook their heads and murmured that withdrawal of this sort in such an incident simply wasn't normal. I didn't offer to enlighten them by explaining that Charles Kane, very decent guy and husband and father, had been hypnotized by a monstrous electronic brain.

But there was something that didn't depend entirely upon words. The knife. The long steel blade dropped in the parking lot that night. I told Tom what had happened, and I tossed the knife carelessly onto his desk.

He studied it for several moments, turning it over slowly and looking at it from one end to the other. "German," he said. "Postwar, sucker knife."

"Sucker knife?"

"Uh-huh," he confirmed. "It's made up to look like some sort of ceremonial Nazi dagger." He pointed. "See the scrollwork and the designs here?" He waited until I nodded. "But it's junk, turned out en masse with scrap metals to sell as souvenirs. Nothing at all like the real thing." He tapped the point gently with his forefinger. He tossed the knife back to his desk, and grunted. "But it kills just as well as the real thing."

"Very interesting," I said dryly.

"Tell me what's been happening," he said.

I didn't tell him everything. I didn't tell him about the rifle bullet that smacked into a tree only inches from my head because I couldn't prove it, and Tom Smythe was a man who wanted either proof or the whole story. He couldn't have the latter, and I couldn't give him any less for the former. So I didn't say that I knew Charlie Kane had tried to kill me or that I'd been shot at more than once. I told him what happened with the knife, and that someone had broken into my apartment while I'd been out.

He chewed his lip and thought about my words. He grunted again, sure sign he'd come to a decision. "All right, Steve," he said, his voice showing his commitment, "we'll put a watch on your place." Then, casually, "Any idea while we're at it, I mean, while we're here, just us two . . . any idea why this is happening?"

"No."

"You're lying."

"I said 'no.' "

He sighed. "You're scared, Steve."

"Damn right I am! I don't like people going around trying to stick souvenirs in me!"

He laughed. "You have a novel way of putting it." The smile vanished from his face. "But you still haven't told me everything, Steve."

"I've told you enough."

His eyes seemed to sharpen. Tom Smythe had been in this game for a long time, and unsaid things didn't escape him. He also knew enough not to push too hard.

"I want a promise from you," he said after a long pause.

"Shoot."

"Whenever you're through playing secret agent on your own, you will tell me the rest of what you are *not* telling me now."

I stared at him and started to speak. But I held my tongue

and shook my head slowly. There wasn't any use lying to the man. You got away with that only so far and no more.

"All right," I promised. "I'll do that."

"I'm a far sight from being satisfied about what happened that night with 79." He threw that one at me without the slightest warning.

I didn't even blink my eyes.

Tom shrugged. "I'm going to put a tail on you. I have a feeling I want you to stay alive just to tell me a great many things I want to know."

"You mean someone will be following me?"

"Twenty-four hours a day."

"Don't let him come too close without my knowing who he is," I said, my voice suddenly grim.

He raised his eyebrows. I opened my jacket and revealed the shoulder holster.

He gestured. "What is it?"

"Llama. Spanish; scaled-down model of the Colt .45. It's .380 caliber, and *very* effective. Hell of a muzzle velocity."

"You got a permit for that thing?"

His question startled me. "Why, no, I didn't think—"

"I didn't think you did." He pursed his lips as he sought a decision. He sighed again and opened his lower left desk drawer, fumbled around, and withdrew a card. Quickly he typed in my name, countersigned the card, punched a seal onto it, and rang for his secretary. He held out the card as she entered the office.

"Have a rad-print run on this and then plastiseal it," he told her.

I watched her leave. "What's that all about, Tom?"

"I must be getting old"—he sighed again—"and there's no fool like an old fool. Guns are dangerous things, especially in the hands of amateurs—"

"I'm no amateur with this thing," I broke in, patting the bulge beneath my jacket.

He ignored me and went right on as though I hadn't spoken a word. "—who think they can chase away shadows with a

[255]

couple of squeezes of the trigger. Let me tell you a few things, Steve. I know you better than your parents know you and I know you better than you do yourself, and I happen to trust you, and I also know that you are not a wild-eyed fool. So I won't push you and demand to find out what you're holding from me. Not yet, anyway," he added with a clear hint that sooner or later I would have to account for what I concealed at this moment.

Several minutes later his secretary returned. He took the card from her, told her to forget she had ever seen it, and studied it for a few moments.

"What is it?" I asked.

He offered the card. "You're now a member of my security staff," he said in answer. "We're a federal office, and that card is your full authority to pack the cannon you're wearing under your left armpit. If the police pick you up, they won't heave your silly scientific ass into the cooler until we come and get you out. The card makes you legal."

I grinned as I slipped the card into my wallet.

"Thanks, Tom."

He still wanted to know what I wasn't telling. But it would have to wait.

I felt better for bringing Tom into the picture. And I felt even better than that for knowing he would be keeping an eye on me.

But you can't figure all the angles. . . .

Which is how I came to be sprawled, naked, on the cold floor of my bathroom, my chest heaving for air and my stomach knotting in spasms and pain crawling like a furry horror through my mind. To say nothing of the slimy thing in my stomach that brought me heaving to the edge of the toilet bowl. But there wasn't anything left to come up any more, and I tried to fight down the spasms. I grabbed the ampul of smelling salts and held it again beneath my nose. I went into a fit of coughing once more, but at least my head felt slightly clearer.

I tried to assemble my fragmented thoughts. The light from

the bathroom splashed into the bedroom, and I stared dully at the still unconscious form of Barbara Johnson. It all swept back to me now. Her body, sensuous and writhing, her breasts against my face and . . . I gave a mental shrug of one more narrow escape. Whatever chemical she had put on her skin to send me into the middle of next week had come terribly close to working. I'd like to find out a little more about that drug. When someone wasn't trying to kill me, anyway. And now wasn't the time for playing detective about unknown drugs.

It took almost all my strength, but I regained my feet and walked back into the bedroom. I almost stubbed my toe on the .38 lying on the carpet. I picked it up, checked the safety, and turned again to examine Barbara. The blood from the long gash in her scalp—the gash I'd inflicted by clubbing her with the barrel—had almost stopped. She'd be all right. She would have a wild headache when she came out of it, but that was much better than a slug through her chest.

Damn it, I had to stop wandering around in my mind. I froze where I was when the rest of my memory welled up in my brain and tapped insistently for attention. Of course . . . that car outside, where I'd spotted the telltale glow of the cigarette.

So now they were teaming up on me. Not just one person fighting wildly with his conscience not to use a knife. But a team. Barbara to use the chemical sprayed on her to knock me out, and then she would signal the men waiting in the street below. Neat; *too* neat. I doubted if Barbara herself would have been able actually to commit murder. Not with me, anyway. We had been too close. So she would just carry out the first act in their carefully planned scheme, and then—

The enormity of what was happening struck me almost a physical blow! Barbara! When had she been exposed to that deadly light in Cubicle 17? And *who* were her accomplices in the street, waiting for the signal that all was in readiness for them to come to my apartment to finish their grisly task?

How many people had 79 already reached? When would it get to the guards who would be convinced, absolutely convinced in their minds, that I was a saboteur, running away from them, who could be stopped only with the wrist-jarring motions of a gun being emptied?

Who else had been assigned Steven Rand as their objective?

Right then and there I knew I had to get out from under. Get away from here. Get away from exposure to *any* person who would or could recognize me. I couldn't tell who might have been assigned under increasingly effective hypnotic control to do me in.

Any human being was suspect.

Anyone.

Tom Smythe . . . Kim . . . total strangers . . . *anyone.*

I needed time. Time in which to think.

While I was still alive.

33

IN THE BATHROOM I opened a plastic vial and withdrew two green capsules. Quickly I swallowed them with water, and took the vial with the remaining capsules into the bedroom. They were powerful stimulants I had obtained for working as much as twenty-four hours without a stop. Now they would pay off in a manner unexpected. The chemical fumes I had inhaled from Barbara's body still had me weak and somewhat disconnected, and I needed a push to get me back in proper working order. As I dressed, I could feel the effects of the drug working within me.

Somehow I knew that events would come to this moment. Not even the assurance of the .38 in its holster could alleviate the situation, and when I got down to brass tacks it didn't solve anything. Sure, if someone tried to do me in and I had only a brief warning I could defend myself, even kill an assailant. But that would solve only that problem at that moment, and leave me facing the same overwhelming forces being arrayed against me by that damned computer. I could survive from moment to moment, and that was all. I needed time in which to think, to produce the solution that eliminated entirely the danger that not only *I* faced, but that loomed with terrible expanding effect against the country. And that meant getting away.

I planned for this contingency. Not in specifics but in a general manner. The one defense I had in my possession that 79 could not overcome easily was an assumed anonymity and freedom of action. Intrinsic to the latter was a means of random movements. It wouldn't be difficult to disappear within the breadth and the teeming mass of the country. *If* I had the means to remain mobile.

I checked my clothing and my equipment. And money. I had $1,500 in cash with me; I didn't want to be using credit cards that would effectively track my movements. The .38 went into the shoulder holster, and in a leather bag I kept ready for this moment I had an extra clip and a box of ammunition. I had already packed clothing, my toilet kit, a list of names and telephone numbers, and a tool kit of my own making.

I bent down to check the wound along Barbara's scalp. She had drifted into a deep sleep, and I figured she would remain that way for at least several hours. I went to the window, pushed aside the drapes just enough to look out. Sure enough, the reception committee was still there. Impatient by now, I thought. Well, I intended to keep them that way as long as I could.

I left by the front door, double-locking it behind me. It was nearly five o'clock, and I still had plenty of time before the occupants of the apartment house would be stirring. I used the stairs instead of the elevator, and descended to the basement. A long corridor ran the length of the building and exited directly to the parking lot.

No one around. I moved quickly, but without running, to my car. I was in the seat and ready to turn the starter key when I started getting real sensible. I took a flashlight from the glove compartment, climbed from the car, and lifted the hood.

My breath turned cold. They weren't missing any bets. The beam from the flashlight played on three sticks of dynamite wired to the starter. If the setup with Barbara didn't work, and I went downstairs in the morning to drive to work—just the turn of the key and Steve Rand would be out of the way for good. I closed the hood and locked the car, making a mental note to call Tom Smythe at the first opportunity. The dynamite would serve as an excellent supporter of what I had been telling him, and he could get a specialist to render the dynamite harmless. Standing alongside the car, I fished in the bag, removed what I would need. I shoved the equipment into my side pocket, looked around me, and walked quickly to the adjacent parking lot.

One of the overhead lights was out, wrapping much of the parking lot and its cars in darkness. So much the better. I went down the rows of cars until I came to a new Ford. None of the General Motors or Chrysler makes would do. Detroit was making it rougher for hard-working car thieves, I guessed.

The Ford I'd selected was unlocked, and I had no key. This is where preparations paid off. From my pockets I removed two wires with alligator clips on each end of the wires. I opened the hood, attached one clip to the battery post and another to the 12-volt side of the dropping register along the side of the engine mount. Then with the other wire I jumped a line from the battery post to the starter solenoid. I worked the accelerator clip to move fuel to the carburetor, touched the second alligator clip to the solenoid, and the engine coughed immediately into life. Good; the automaic choke was holding the engine fast enough to keep it from faltering. I removed the wires, closed the hood, and climbed in. The headlights went on as I pulled the knob. As I expected, neither the radio nor the turn signals operated; they were linked directly to the ignition system that I had bypassed.

I drove steadily toward a highway that would take me to the southeast. While the car sped over the nearly empty roads, the pressure for the moment was off me and the drugs I'd taken were at their peak. It felt wonderful to be out from under, at least for now, and settle down to some serious planning.

I was not sanguine about the possibilities. 79 was an adversary of dimension and purpose never before known. It was easy to adopt the trite attitude that it was only a mechanical-electronic thing, and lacked the mental agility so treasured by the human race. That was, in unscientific terms, so much crap. The human being was essentially an oblongated bag into which went some 60 percent water, other assorted liquids, unbelievable complexity, a staggering fragility, a skeletal framework, and all manner of emotional maladjustments—yet we did pretty well.

My goals lay far beyond myself, and yet, to accomplish my

purpose of removing 79 as a threat to the country, I knew I must fight for my life. I wondered just what advantages I might extract from the contest. Two more dissimilar gladiators had never existed!

I did have one great advantage, of course. The manner in which the cybernetics system functioned was better known to me, perhaps, than to any other living man. I would not suffer the delusion that 79 was incapable of anticipating patterns built up out of random activity or motivation. Few people realize that continued randomness itself, after a sufficient interval of time passes, becomes an identifiable pattern.

I was not about to underestimate the opposition. Quite the contrary. I had to struggle within myself not to impart to 79 capabilities that not even its superbrain capacity could grasp.

Anonymity, freedom of action, careful planning, and a never-compromised flexibility to meet any situation were my immediate and most overwhelming assets. But could I handle this terrible responsibility on my own? One man against not simply the cybernetics creation, but against all those whom it already controlled? Could I tackle an adversary of such unproportionate strength and not only survive but accomplish my purposes? The odds were staggering—*against* me.

I watched for the highway signs and finally swung right onto the road that pointed southeast to La Junta, 150 miles distant. From La Junta I could catch an airliner to wherever . . . That was a hell of a question. Where was I going to go? I pushed the question aside. There would be plenty of time to decide between here and La Junta.

The car raced along the highway now sprayed with the pink touch of the approaching dawn. Though I craved coffee, I didn't dare to stop at any of the frequent diners. Speed and distance were my needs now; the coffee must wait until I gained the airport.

For some time now I had considered the idea of getting to another advanced digital computer, into which I could program any number of possibilities, and from which I might draw the plans I was seeking. There was little difference in the speed of operation between an advanced system such as, say, the IBM 10114 utilized by the Space Agency and the Air Force and that of 79.

With the electronic swiftness of computer calculations I could—I must have made an expression of digust on my face to match my sudden feelings. It is so damned bloody easy to overlook what is thunderingly obvious!

Use another computer? Fool! It would require weeks, perhaps months, simply to program another computer with data before I could even run a test of the circuitry to assure myself that the damned thing was functioning properly! And programming of that nature meant a large and highly skilled staff ready and waiting to work at least twelve-hour shifts, perhaps more. You just don't walk up to a computer, kick it in its cooling system, and order it to count probabilities upon its electronic toes.

I stuck a cigarette between my lips, and as I lit up I noticed how light the sky had become. In a few minutes I could turn off the headlights.

I knew I was doing my best not to underestimate the opposition. Perhaps I had leaned over so far backward to retain objectivity I had lost my perspective. It's possible to seek too strongly for the right balance, and that was precisely what had happened.

The fastest computer in existence, in terms of grasping the kaleidoscopically interwoven ramifications of this whole mess, as well as anticipating the possible random moves, *was my own brain.*

About time you remembered that, Steve, old boy!

I burst into laughter—and didn't that feel good! There was that voice again, my voice. When I felt in need of seeing both sides of an issue, I could always whip up a good thumping argument with myself. And sometimes—I laughed again—I came to the right conclusions. . . .

[263]

At La Junta I left the Ford in a parking lot, paying a month in advance. That would keep the car effectively off the streets, and it was one of the last places where a search would be made. I walked several blocks, stopped in a diner for breakfast, and took a cab to the airport.

It took nearly two days, changing planes in different cities and using different names, to reach my destination. It was remote, beautiful, and out of the way. Six thousand feet above sea level, in the heart of the Grand Tetons.

Jackson Hole, Wyoming.

I registered at the Wort Hotel under a different name, took a long bath, and treated myself to a tremendous steak. That night, for the first time in weeks, I slept soundly.

34

FOUR DAYS LATER the scenic majesty of the Grand Tetons had crumbled and the crisp mountain air in which I had delighted on my arrival went unnoticed by me. For those four days I struggled with the problem that daily swelled its presence in my mind, and at the end all I had for my pains was a terrible sense of frustration. To say nothing of the realization that in the time elapsed 79 could have done no less than to develop further its still groping capabilities. God alone knew how many key officials in whom 79 was interested had been "brought around" by that devilish light in Cubicle 17.

I had gone over a mental checklist at least a hundred times in my attempts to produce a *modus operandi* that would give me *some* percentages of getting past the defenses of 79. No longer was I concerned with whatever damage I might do to the cybernetics Brain. It mattered little to me if I accomplished my original purpose—creating just enough havoc so that it would be necessary to reprogram the neural blocks and take measures to prevent what had already happened in 79's own programming of human subjects. There were ways and means of assuring that a repeat performance wouldn't take place. I hadn't wanted to tear up the electronic fabric of the computer. At least I had exercised such restrictions before. Now I wanted nothing more than to get inside that blasted brain, with high explosives if that could be arranged.

But *how* could I do this? 79 itself maintained eternal vigilance against my approach. The superb system of defenses—fingerprints, ID card with its own radiation signature, retinal patterns, body mass, and others, precluded any subterfuge on my part that would allow me entry to the interior of the computer system. And unless I got deep inside, not even an atomic bomb would do me any good. The way 79 had been assembled, with shock-resistant structure, one spherical layer of defense after the other . . . I groaned in exasperation. If there was a way through this mess, it still eluded me.

On the first leg of the trip outbound from La Junta, I had managed a call to Tom Smythe. Over his vehement and angry protests I shouted that I would be gone for several days to a week, perhaps longer. I managed to calm him down sufficiently to describe that someone had tried to ambush me in the apartment (I did not give him Barbara's name) and that I had found my car booby-trapped with dynamite, which was still there. I felt a growing desperation in my desire to seek an accomplice, but outside of Kim I dared trust no other person.

After several days of stewing in my own inadequacies, I placed a call to Kim. At night, so that while we talked there wouldn't be any attempt by someone to run a check on the originating point of the call. Kim didn't greet my voice with sweetness and light. She blew the proverbial cork at my long and unexplained silence, and then the warning bells went off again in my skull.

"But where are you, Steve? Why don't you stop playing ghost and come back?" Her voice changed from brittle anger to soothing tones.

I chose my words with caution. "What's the difference, Kim? My department is out of the running for a while and—"

"It's not that," she broke in hurriedly. "It's Dr. Vollmer, Steve. We're loaded down terribly with—oh, I can't go into it on the phone; you know that; security and so forth. But that new program with Melpar, you know the one I'm talking about. We're working day and night on it, and Dr. Vollmer is having fits. He's driving us crazy trying to find you."

I'll bet, I thought. Vollmer's one of 79's unwilling playmates, and I'm sure he'd like to lead me into Cubicle 17, as he's already done with several others. But Kim? She knew what the score was. Why her sudden insistence on my return? I felt a knot forming in the pit of my stomach. . . .

"Tell the old goat he'll just have to do without me for a while, honey. I can't leave what I'm doing right now, and—"

Peevish anger in her voice. "Why are you hiding, Steve? What's wrong? You act as though you don't want to come back here. As if I didn't matter any more. Is that what's happened, Steve?"

I stared at the telephone as if it had changed into a snake. I had never heard Kim talking like that, and a suspicion grew swiftly into what was almost a certainty. Somehow, in some manner, Kim had been brought before that light controlled by 79. But she knew better than to get within any distance of Cubicle 17, and—whoa; hold on, there. How did I know that *only* 17 was being used by the giant brain for its efforts to gain control of selected personnel? I didn't, of course. Controlling key technicians and programmers, it would have taken only a suggestion for the light system to be installed in every programmer cubicle!

I knew I didn't dare to trust even the girl I loved. I don't even remember what I said before I hung up the phone. I went outside and discovered that the weather had changed to match my mood. Rain pouring from the night skies.

Three days later it was still raining, and I thought I would go out of my mind. There was a small crowd at the hotel, and they were as fed up as was I with the weather. One night, out of desperation, we agreed to a poker game. I raised my eyebrows at the suggested limit of $20. That was a bit steep for my brand of poker, but what the hell. I wasn't going anywhere, and the money wasn't doing me a bit of good. We agreed to the rules; no limit on the number of raises, check and raise, and poker —no fancy nonsense. The bartender brought around glasses, made bottles available, and passed out cigars. He'd been here before during the long rains. Thirty minutes later we were enveloped in a smoke cloud of our own making; I'd had just enough Scotch to loosen my natural caution in the game, and I was on a mild winning streak.

There were five of us. Besides myself, a fisherman, griping about the weather; two hunters, also griping (as was I); and Old Mike. I didn't know his last name. Everyone called him Old

[267]

Mike and I wasn't about to step on the toes of local tradition. Old Mike was grizzled and leathery, smoked a terrible pipe, and had been a guide in the mountains for nearly forty years. The bartender told me Old Mike could have retired years ago with the money he'd earned as guide to some of the wealthiest hunters in the country, but he liked what he was doing, and stayed on.

I didn't know it then, but Old Mike also contained the answer to the question that had haunted me for weeks.

He had the secret for getting past the defenses of the cybernetics brain.

Four hours later I was feeling the Scotch with considerably more effect than I had early in the game. My winning streak had held up and I was $900 to the good. One of the hunters, losing heavily and disgruntled with the betting limit of $20, suggested we "quit playing like a bunch of kids and play pot limit." Silence met the suggestion for a while, and I showed how stupid I was by saying I was game for anything. Murmurs of assent from the others followed my lead, and what had been a plesant game became serious, no-nonsense poker.

My luck held. Not the same as before, because in pot stakes you're not so eager to call bets. Not when a man will back up two pair with a few hundred dollars and you become suspicious of the strength of the three eights you're holding against those two pair *showing*. But I did pretty well, and the chance for a big hand came when our fisherman was dealing, seven-card stud, and I found myself with an ace-high heart flush.

The others folded when four hearts showed on the table. Only Old Mike was left, with queens over nines staring at me. I pushed $100 into the center of the table. Old Mike snuffed a bit, chewed on the stem of his pipe, peeked again at his cards—I began to worry that I was walking into a full house in his hand —and slowly folded, giving me the pot. It held more than $600, and I grinned hugely at my luck.

I couldn't lose. I felt it, I *knew* it, and the cards were backing me up. Every game such as we had going invariably has one or more really big pots during its playing when at least two players end up with powerful hands, and this night was no exception. It turned into another showdown between myself and Old Mike; only, this time I was in a much better position than before. Because my hand was hidden.

You get seven cards total, four face up and three down, in seven-card stud. Heavy betting marked the hand, and when the last card was dealt I had a pair of sixes, an ace, and a king showing. But I had been dealt two aces in the hole to start off the hand, which gave me a full house going into the last card.

I caught an ace. *Four aces.*

I looked at the cards on the table before Old Mike. He was sitting back, tamping his pipe, and studying my hand. Old Mike had a four and seven of hearts, and the sevens of spades and clubs. Three sevens showing against my open cards of a pair of sixes, ace and king. I figured Old Mike for at least sevens full.

But maybe, just maybe, he had caught the fourth seven. What a spot I was in! If Old Mike had four sevens he would bet to the hilt. He'd shove in everything he had to back up those cards. And I sat there across him with four aces of which three were hidden. It was the dream spot for any poker player, and I intended to cash in on it.

By the time we were through sparring with each other I'd bet $500. Old Mike looked at me through clouds of blue smoke, and squinted.

"Mm-mm. Didn't figure you that way, son." More smoke and a smacking of his lips on the scarred stem. "Didn't think you could sneak in a filly on me. Sixes full, eh? Um-mm." This went on for several minutes before he committed himself.

"Think I gotcha' beat, know that?" he chuckled. "Don't think your sixes full is very strong. Eh?" He counted through his money. "Well-ll, now, we'll just see how strong they are, eh?"

I grinned at him. "I got $500 out there, Old Mike, that says they're strong."

"Um-mm, sure, umph." Old Mike pushed $500 into the pot. But he wasn't through yet. He began to count, and secretly I exulted over what was happening. He had to have sevens full or the four sevens, and I knew he'd come back with a raise. He did. He called me and raised $500.

"Hate to do this to you, Old Mike," I said with a grin. "Call your raise and bump you"—I paused for effect—"$1,000." I winked at him. "Just want to tell you your sevens full won't hold up."

Old Mike almost swallowed his pipe. He blew smoke and coughed and scratched his ribs and chuffed away like a steam locomotive fighting a steep upgrade. Finally, after five minutes of this, he sighed.

"Gotta' call ya', I guess," he said slowly, counting out $1,000, easing it into the center of the table.

No one else made a sound. The other players leaned back in their seats, watching like hawks.

"I hate to take your money like that, Old Mike," I said.

"Ummph, gromph," Old Mike said with the pipe in his mouth.

I laughed, flushed with the Scotch and the hand I held secreted from view. "Aren't you going to raise me?"

He shook his head, spilling ashes on the table. "Nope, don't reckon like I will. Hate to take *all* yer' money away in just one hand," he said. "Like to be sociable-like iffen' I can."

"Just calling?"

Old Mike nodded. "Ummph, jes' callin'."

I shook my head in mock sympathy. "Hate to do this to you, old-timer," I said, "but I've got better than sixes full."

He didn't bat an eye. "Guessed as much," he answered.

"In fact," I said slowly, relishing every word, "I've got better than even aces full." I started turning over my cards, one ace appearing after the other. Murmured comments drifted from the onlookers.

"Figured that, too."

I looked up, startled. Old Mike hadn't moved a muscle. "What'd you say, old-timer?"

"Said I figured that, too."

I looked carefully at the leathery face behind the cloud of

smoke. *"Four* big ones, Old Mike," I retorted. "Four very big aces."

A long silence followed my words. Then Old Mike cut me down to size.

" *'Tain't no good."*

I didn't believe it. I still didn't believe it, or at least I didn't want to believe what I saw.

Old Mike laid down, one after the other, the four, five, six, seven, and the eight of hearts. Straight flush!

He beat the four aces. . . .

"Like I said, coulda' raised you back." Old Mike was stacking the money before him. "But you're young, gotta' lot to learn yet. Nice feller, too. No use clobbering ya' all at once." He winked at me.

And he was right, too. He could have raised me back and I would have called every dollar, wiping out my ready cash. As it was, the head-to-head betting proved to be the last hand of the game. I had been way ahead. I ended up $700 the loser.

At that, I was lucky. With a few words the old man could have cleaned me out completely.

Old Mike invited me to have a few drinks with him.

"You're one of them scientifical fellers, y'say?" The leathery face with its startlingly clear blue eyes hovered just beyond the cloud of smoke.

"Uh-huh." I nursed the drink, aware that I'd long before had more than I should have drunk. "Mathematician." I grinned ruefully. "That's what hurts even more than losing. I know numbers and systems and the odds better than my own name. I should never have lost in that game. By the way, I want to thank you."

"What in thunderation fer?"

"You could have wiped me out on that table," I said candidly. "I wouldn't have hesitated a second to throw everything I had into that pot. But you didn't raise me back. Even when," I added, "you *knew* you had me beat."

Old Mike waved a hand to dismiss the importance of the matter. "Were only money. At my age don't matter so much any more. But I like the feel of the game," he confessed. "Pot limit is a good measure of a man. I enjoy it."

"Well, you sure had *me* measured." I laughed. It sounded sort of hollow.

He peered at me over the battered end of his pipe. "That was the whole game," he said after a long pause.

"I don't get you," I said, puzzled.

"Hell, young feller, poker ain't got a damn thing to do with *cards*. Not when you're playing pot limit or table stakes, it don't. Then, by God, you're playing the other feller across the table."

He stabbed the pipe at me. "Rules of the game is," he said with a flourish of the pipe, "horse sense can beat logic, or whatever it is you fellers call the scientific method, any day in the week and," he smacked his lips satisfyingly, "twice on any Sunday y'care to name."

"What do you mean?" I was starting to come out of the alcoholic fog.

"Remember when you had that flush?"

I nodded.

"Well, t'tell you the truth, I had you beat."

"You did?" Steven Rand, mathematician, with a stupid look on his face.

"Shore!" Old Mike tossed off a tumbler of whiskey, wiped his lips, and sucked again at his pipe. "Had y'beat dead to rights, I did. Folded a full house."

"B—But why? There was $600 in that pot!"

"Um-mm, weren't *my* money. Weren't that much, either, not in a game like that. Big thing in pot limit, is to wait for the *right* pot, set up your opposition. Like I set *you* up." The pipe waved before my face. "See? That pot wasn't worth it. Let you figger you was on a winnin' streak that just couldn't lose. So I had you beat." He shrugged. "No one else in the pot, there wouldn't be much raising, and I wanted you to get a mite careless. Over-confident, you might say." He laughed, a leathery wheeze from his lungs. "And that you did, boy, that you did."

I allowed as how he was absolutely right.

"Pot limit is an all-out game. The works. You're shooting fer the top o' the mountain, so to say. Y'got to set things up, bide your time."

He chuckled. "You fell for the oldest trap in the game."

I stared at him, and he gestured freely as he went on.

"The way to winnin' is losin'."

He paused to let his words sink in. "You lose jes' the way you want, at the right times in the game. You lose jes' when you want to lose and you set up the other guy. And when he goes for broke and you also got the cards you been waiting fer, why"—he smiled hugely—"you jes' nail his hide to a tree and he's yours for the pickin's jes' like, hm-mm"—he peered at me again through the smoke—"well, jes' like *you* were."

"Wait, wait a moment," I said, my voice suddenly frantic. "What did you say, Old Mike? A few moments ago, what you said was the key, what you called the oldest trap?"

He chuckled again, pleased with the avid interest his words were receiving. "Why, I said that the way to winnin' was losin'."

Light detonated within my head.

"That's it!" I cried, my voice so loud heads turned to stare at our table. "That's the answer!" I didn't know I was slamming my fist into my palm over and over.

It *was* the answer.

The cybernetics brain was the world's greatest chess player. Mathematically it was perfect. It could anticipate every possible move. It couldn't lose.

But it couldn't play poker worth a damn.

Because it didn't know how to lie.

35

THE MORE I THOUGHT about the possibilities, the more excited I became. The leathery old bastard was absolutely right—sometimes the way to winning is by losing. In the world of gambling, playing cards and playing poker are anything but the same thing. They have a relationship only in that the same deck of cards is used. In poker you set up your opponent and sometimes you toss in a winning hand to sucker in the guy across the table from you. Take a game of pot limit or table stakes, why, it's insane to play just your *cards*. You play the gamut—yourself, your opponent, the other players, the odds, the tremendous effectiveness of a heavy bet carefully timed. What you do, how and when you do it, is far more important than the cards. Poker is legal chicanery—bluff. A good liar, the man with the poker face, is a man who knows not only how but *when* to bluff, and to win.

79, despite its masterly use of stratagems and evasion, functions within strict rules of logical deduction. It doesn't know how to lie; it can't fabricate facts. Its circuitry is built around deduction, comparator value, even heuristics. But it's a creature of logic. And it is *not* logical to lie, because this is distortion of datum, and you can't weave digital bits of thought from the emptiness of nonfact.

That's why the computer is so superb a chess player. Mathematically it computes every possibility and it moves within the unassailable logic dictated by its computations. There are just so many umpteen ways of doing this, umpteen-x ways of doing that, and the rest is inevitable.

Which is why a good poker player in the table-stakes game

can whip any computer any day in the week—or, as Old Mike put it so succinctly, on any Sunday you'd care to name. Successful poker is illogical, and to the sneaking, lying, illogically playing human being it has one more advantage—the next hand is never more than a few moments away. You rescramble the odds with every shuffle and new deal. You can always concel out what's wrong with a hand by throwing in the cards and starting all over again.

The time had come for a new shuffle. And this time *I* was going to handle the deck.

Every now and then you take a deep breath, and plunge. I did precisely that when I placed a person-to-person call to Tom Smythe. Call it human heuristics; I don't know. But somehow I felt absolutely confident that Tom Smythe still remained free of the hypnotic embrace of 79. Certainly that had been the case before I took off on my soul-searching trip to Jackson Hole; otherwise Tom would never have violated his own rules by issuing me a Federal ID card that made it legal for me to pack a concealed weapon.

For several minutes Tom and I had an unholy row on the telephone, and in his voice I detected a growing sense of strain. I refused to come around to his requests by laying my cards on the table as he insisted I do. Thank the Lord this man knew me as long and as well as he did. He accepted my promise that at the first opportunity, which would be within one to three days, I would explain fully the reasons for my actions.

"By the way," he offered, "Charlie Kane's come out of the woods. Snapped out of that mental fog."

I chewed that over. "Fill me in, Tom. It might be important."

"Not much to it." I could almost see Tom Smythe shrug as if to dismiss the issue. "His injuries were superficial, it seems. The doctors claim he was a victim of shock and that it's not unusual for him to snap out of it the way he did."

That, I thought, was about the only thing that wasn't unusual where Charlie was concerned. Tom Smythe broke in on my thoughts. "The doctors even have an explanation for his insistence that there was a red light at the corner and that you ran the light. They attribute it, umm, to something they call a delayed block. Somewhere else, on a street that looks exactly like the one where he ran into you, there *is* a traffic light, and—"

"Christ, do you believe that crap?"

Tom's response was a burst of laughter. "I thought that would get a rise out of you." He chuckled. Then his voice grew serious. "No, I don't buy it. I might have thought nothing about it again, but I know something about what makes people tick. This doesn't come up smelling like roses. When I bring in everything else that's happened—with you as the clay pigeon—it smells less and less like roses. In fact," his voice growled as he spoke his conclusions, "I would say that it stinks."

"Hooray for you," I said. "Where's Charlie now?"

"He went back to work yesterday. Nothing strenuous. His doctor said it would be good therapy for him."

"Good therapy!" I exploded. "Don't they know that—"

Tom broke in on my tirade. "I said that *they* think it's therapy. Me, I find it's an excellent way to keep a close eye on our friend. Rest easy, Steve," Tom said in a reassuring tone. "He doesn't even know about the cocoon we're keeping wrapped around him."

I mumbled something inarticulate.

"I've been meaning to ask you something," Tom said suddenly. "What happened between you and Kane?"

I laughed. "You won't believe this, Tom," I said, knowing how foolish the words sounded. "But nothing happened. In fact, he happens to be a good friend of mine."

"You got peculiar friends, Mr. Rand." Tom didn't hide the sarcasm.

"The answer's included in our talk a couple of days from now," I said weakly.

"All right," he said, grudging my refusal to say more, "I won't push for the moment. The whole thing is crazy enough, but there's something else I want to go over with you, and it *is* important."

[276]

"Go ahead."

"We're having trouble with our electronic playmate."

Open trouble with 79? The back of my neck went cold. "What's wrong?"

"Difficult to say," he admitted. "Mostly it's in Vollmer's bailiwick and in accompanying sections. Some of the programmers act as if, well, I'm trying to find the right words for it—"

"Try 'disturbed,' " I broke in.

Another pause. "Yeah, that would do it, I suppose," Tom said slowly. "They sure as hell *are* disturbed. But it's difficult to figure it out, and no one seems to know how or why or what is really going on. But you know something, Steve?"

"What?"

"I've got the strangest feeling that *you* know what it's all about."

"That's an interesting theory, Tom."

"You're a big fat help."

I ignored the remark. "Let me toss one into your lap," I said. "You said you were having problems with our, ah, electronic playmate. What kind of problems?"

"That's even stickier to pin down," he replied. "Excessive rejection of programs, for example. But there doesn't seem to be any justification for the actions."

"Go on."

"To add grist for the mill," he said, "the self-programming is getting out of hand."

That was new. I did my best to remain casual. "Oh? In what way?"

"As much as I can tell you on this talk-box," he said, "it demands specific information that doesn't seem to have any valid reference to or bearing upon active projects. Social structures, industrial programming and succession, intricacies of political structure and succession . . . things like that." He made it clear he wouldn't say more on the telephone.

"Well, that's a dead-end street," I lied. "But if you—"

"No, there's more," he broke in. "And this really grabs you by the shorts," he stressed. The silence held for so long I thought we had been disconnected. But his voice came back and his words were guarded. "There seems to be an, ah, call it a subtle change in relationship between us and our friend."

"Such as what." I was anxious for him to continue, but even as I felt my impatience, I knew that Tom Smythe was *very* disturbed. Even these oblique references to the project we did not identify by name or number were a staggering departure from the security-conscious habits of Tom Smythe.

"You're going to think I'm off my trolley, Steve."

"Damn it, man, you're hedging!"

Another uncomfortable pause. Then, blurted out:

"I get the feeling we're being tolerated."

"Tolerated!"

"That's about the sum of it. I can't shake the feeling," Tom said unhappily. "It keeps sticking in my craw."

My humorless laughter must have sounded very shrill to Tom Smythe.

I spoke with Tom again early the next morning, before he left for his office. After a brief hello I asked him to put the call on tape so there wouldn't be any mistake about what I would need from him.

"I *always* put calls on tape," he reminded me. I'd forgotten that. "And while we're on the subject," he said, irrelevant for the moment, "let me say I have spent a sleepless night trying to put together the pieces of your little puzzle. I think I'm on to a lot more than you realize and"—his voice hardened—"I do not, repeat, *not* like it. However—"

"That makes two of us," I said.

"Don't interrupt when I'm dispensing largesse," he chided. "However, I am going along with you for now." He sighed. "I hope to God you have the rest of the pieces I'm still missing."

"Never mind that now," I said, impatient with the unexpected conversation. "Here's what I need from you, Tom . . ."

Tom was true to his word. Early that morning, as part of the regular daily news report fed into 79, the computer

[278]

unknowingly ingested a bit of "planted news." It took some doing, but the specialists in the National Security Agency can do just about anything you might dream up as a crash effort. Page 38 of *The New York Times* was removed from the paper before it went into data processing for programmed input. The NSA specialists redid page 38 exactly as it appeared in the original, except for one particular change. They yanked a story on an airplane crash and reset the type, then supplied Project 79 with the doctored newspaper.

79 learned that morning that Steven Rand, mathematics and cybernetics specialist, graduate of MIT, and so forth, was among the passengers killed in the airplane crash. The paper carried further details to relate my position with Project 79. To assure completion of the effect intended, Tom slipped into the daily "update data sheets" the notation that Steven Rand had been killed and was deleted from the official records of Project 79.

During my conversation with Tom, I asked that he set up a security clearance and admission papers and ID cards for a man named Jack Tarvin. I described Tarvin to him; about six feet tall, 195 pounds, dark hair, horn-rimmed glasses, and other personal details. Jack Tarvin, I explained, was an old friend of mine, a cybernetics specialist, and I considered it imperative that not only should Tarvin be admitted to Project 79 "to visit any area for which he makes a request" but also that Tom Smythe accede to any needs of the man. I repeated this with emphasis enough times for Tom to become impatient with the repetition. He assured me they would run Tarvin through Security and other necessary machinery.

I didn't tell Tom that Jack Tarvin at this moment was in Nagoya, Japan—and had been there for the past two years— where he worked on a research program with Japanese scientists at the University of Nagoya. Nor did I say anything about a visit I made to a printing shop in Jackson Hole, where the old man who ran the shop promised to run off a hundred business cards in the next hour. With the name of Dr. Jack Tarvin of MIT.

I made a call to Captain Al Moore, the ordnance specialist at Fort Carson. I detailed my request to him.

His reply was a long whistle. "What are you going to do, Rand, start a private war?"

"No, no." I laughed. "It's all part of those tests we were working on when I asked you for the incendiaries. I wish I could tell you more about—"

"Pray, not one word more!" he broke in. "Spare me any security lectures from the Dragon Smythe who guards the portals of your precious labyrinths. I'll do it; beat me not again."

After our shared laughter he reminded me that he would need a justifying paper for "all those goodies." I promised to get that to him the moment I returned to my office; that was good enough for him. He assured me that everything I'd requested would be delivered that same day.

I hung up the phone and rubbed my hands together. Jesus, it felt good to be doing *something*. And there was plenty more yet to do. I kept the telephone busy most of the morning.

I called Kim at her office, and after the first heated words, which I had come to expect, I explained to her that a close friend and former associate of mine at MIT, Dr. Jack Tarvin, would show up at the project within the next two days.

"Tom Smythe is running him through Security and attending to his clearance. Would you be a doll and look after Tarvin for me?"

"I'd rather look after *you*, Steve Rand!"

"Honey, I'll be back within two or three days at the most," I promised. "And I'm wild to be with you together again."

"You certainly haven't been acting like it." She sniffed.

"Kim, I *know*, but—"

"Where are you anyway, Steve?"

No hedging this time. "Washington, hon. I couldn't tell you before—look, I'll explain it all when I see you. Be a sweetheart, will you, and look after Tarvin for me?"

She promised she would do that.

I looked at my watch. Damn, I'd have to hurry. My plane left in just one hour. The ticket read Salt Lake City, change planes for the flight to Las Vegas, Nevada.

I laughed when I thought of my flying to Las Vegas. I was wrapped up in a gamble wilder than they had ever seen in the gambling capital of the world.

Theatrical makeup supplies are common fare in Las Vegas; it's got more shows and acts than any city in the world. Where there are actors and actresses there's a need for, and a supply of, theatrical materials.

I felt like an ass when I walked through the door of a men's beauty shop. They didn't use that name for it, but the sight of grown men being anointed, fluffed, and dyed had me shifting my feet like some idiotic schoolboy. But it was the only place I knew to which I could go without attracting undue attention for what I wanted. Fortunately, for the right price it was possible to obtain a private room. For an extra fifty dollars André, "the man who could do anything with other men," would forget what I looked like before he went to work on me.

My hair is light brown. When André got through with me my hair was almost black. So were my eyebrows, and so was the moustache I'd grown—under André's sure hands. "One week, ah! It will remain, I assure you. One week without any difficulty whatsoever. I, André, promise this. But of course"—he smiled —"You do not wish to soak your upper lip for too long in hot water, eh?" I assured him I had no intentions of doing any such thing.

André also supplied lightly tinted glasses—flat glass, of course—in horn-rims. When I looked in the mirror, I failed to recognize msyelf. The transformation was startling.

André, who'd been in this business for a long time and expected anything from his clients in Las Vegas, studied me carefully. "It is not enough, you know?"

"What?" I was startled by his words; I'd been engrossed in my mirror reflection of a stranger.

André's hand waved casually. "I am not interested in your

purposes, Mr., ah, Smith"—he smiled—"but what you are doing is not enough. Mannerisms, voice, eh? All these things, too, mark a person. There are little touches, eh?"

I gave in to his knowledge. He worked on the hair again, and I came out from under the dryer with unmistakably wavy hair. I also gained nearly an inch in height from elevated shoes. André suggested a complete change in clothing; he was right. I hated lumpy tweed jackets, but I got one—a size larger than I wear normally. This was necessary because of the corset I wore beneath my shirt—which quite neatly added fifteen pounds to my weight and changed my appearance in a subtle but extraordinarily effective manner.

"Ahh, beautiful! Whoever you are, that is." André winked at me. "I am finished with you," he said after a meticulous inspection of the man he'd created. "But may I suggest one more thing?"

"Please do, André. It's important. Maybe one day I can tell you what this is—"

"Tut tut!" A finger wagged beneath my nose to reproach me. "Say no more. Ah, but what I started to tell you, no? Your voice. It identifies you, it identifies anyone, of course. So I have an advice for you."

He handed me a card. "Go to this drugstore and ask for Mr. Scragg. A friend of mine. Here"—he scribbled on the card— "this will assure him I sent you to him. He will give you the drug I have written here, and—"

"Drug?"

"But of course! Twelve hours after you take this drug, no one will recognize your voice, not even you. You will have," he winked again, "first a runny nose, and then a stuffed nose, oh, it will be terrible, this cold that you have! And no one will be able to recognize your voice. Not even you, perhaps." He laughed.

I hoped it worked as well as he promised. I handed André another fifty as I left.

I caught the first plane out of Pueblo, Colorado, due south of Colorado Springs. There I ran into my first error of omission; fortunately, it didn't present any problems. Although my business card and the initials on my new attaché case indicated I was Jack Tarvin, the driver's license I carried was still that belonging to Steven Rand. It didn't matter. Renting a car in Pueblo was just as safe for Steven Rand as for anyone else. I drove north and registered in the Broadmoor Hotel in Colorado Springs. That evening I dialed Kim.

"Miss Michele? This is Dr. Tarvin. I'm a friend of Steve Rand, and he suggested that I call you as soon as I got in. I'm at the Broodmoor. . . ."

Bless André! Kim sympathized with Dr. Tarvin's "terrible cold." She also promised to meet him the next morning at the main entrance to the "NORAD Auxiliary Data Center," as Project 79 was known to the outside world.

The whole thing went beautifully. There wasn't the slightest indication that Kim found anything unusual in Dr. Jack Tarvin or that she harbored any suspicion he might not be the genuine article. The telephone call to Kim from Steve Rand set up the first phase. That Tom Smythe had the facilities and personnel ready to prepare the security clearance for Dr. Tarvin served to reinforce the position of the MIT visitor as just one more of the many visiting firemen who were cleared for one reason or another into Project 79.

I did my best, and apparently I was successful. To those about me I was the overly preoccupied, slightly exasperating scientist who had a hell of a cold and who was always blowing or drying his nose and who talked as if his voice came from the bottom of a well filled with cotton.

My initial meeting with Tom Smythe went as smoothly as it had done with Kim. We went through the usual banalities; I made pleasant noises about how impressed I was and, between sniffling and rubbing my watery eyes, I also made it clear that I had little time to spare from my work at MIT and that I should be grateful for getting through the preliminaries as quickly as possible. Tom Smythe obliged; he led me through the long corridors while I snuffled alongside him like a walrus, anxious in more ways than Tom ever knew to have my initial encounter with the cybernetics Brain.

In the security office I stared into the optical sensors that produced a record of my retinal pattern. The glasses proved no problem, for the subject was required to remove them before the test was made. My fingerprints were taken, my body mass made a matter of record, and pertinent data—height, weight, color of eyes and hair, complexion, all went into the records.

I'd won the first hand in the poker game.

I knew that, when Smythe handed me my identicard—a duplicate of the one I had always carried as Steven Rand. I had managed to pull the wool over the eyes of the omnipotent computer—first by setting the stage and then by lying through my teeth.

It was all bluff. The first step in this critical maneuver was to feed into 79 the daily newspaper reports that included the story of the airplane crash and the death of one Steven Rand, cybernetics specialist. Tom Smythe followed through with the official data update that Steven Rand of Project 79, reason death, was to be deleted from security and other requirements of the project. The computer correlated and cross-checked such inputs. Then came the key moment.

Computers have total recall, of course, *but only of the data retained by intention.* All sorts of garbage get into the input of a cybernetics system. Incorrect reports, data proved by experiments to be no longer applicable to any science or technology, obsolescence, and so forth. To eliminate the clutter that builds inevitably, and because the data not only no longer are pertinent but misleading, automatic systems are built into the memory mechanisms to delete such superfluous material.

Since Steven Rand no longer existed as a living person, there was no need to retain his active file in the security banks of the cybernetics system. Ergo—79 deleted from its electronic recall the person of Steven Rand.

The retinal pattern, fingerprints, and other information pertaining to Steven Rand were scoured from the records.

When Dr. Jack Tarvin of MIT submitted to retinal pattern tests, fingerprinting, and other security-applicable data, the computer automatically cross-checked its references on file. *The response proved to be negative.*

79 approved the identification for Dr. Jack Tarvin.

And Steven Rand—alias Dr. Jack Tarvin—was provided with a means of penetrating the automatic defense mechanisms of the cybernetics system.

Kim took me through a VIP tour of the facilities that involved the work of the Bionics Division. I—Dr. Tarvin—even met Dr. Selig Albracht and had a brief (if, to me, bizarre) conversation with the famous heuristics scientist.

I made certain the tour would test the security systems of 79. The automatic check mechanism accepted the identicard, and approved identification of the retinal pattern and fingerprints.

I was ready to play the second hand.

That evening I ran into a sticky problem I just couldn't shake. Tom Smythe insisted we have dinner together. He wanted to discuss with me my work at MIT as it applied to Project 79. He also made it clear that Steve Rand had asked him to be certain to look after Tarvin during his visit. I couldn't get out from under.

It went well, all things considered. I remained vague and fell back on my severe cold to beg off early so that I could take some medicine and crawl into bed. Tom Smythe sympathized with me and drove me to the Broadmoor after dinner. He promised to have a car waiting to pick me up at eight o'clock sharp the next morning.

When I left the hotel, the car was there. Dr. Tarvin was certainly getting the VIP treatment. The only unpleasant part of the whole affair was that damnable "cold drug" I'd taken. I felt almost as bad as I sounded. But—I shrugged—it was an easy price to pay for the tremendous success I'd achieved so far.

I walked directly to Smythe's office on arrival at the project center. Tom greeted me warmly, explained he had my itinerary all set for the day. He called his secretary, told her "no calls or visitors for a while," and turned to give me his undivided attention.

Seated behind his desk, Tom Smythe calmly opened his jacket, reached inside. The next moment I stared into the unwavering muzzle of a .38.

"Party time is over. You're not Tarvin. Put your hands on the sides of your chair. Don't even twitch."

I froze.

36

"JACK TARVIN HAS been in Japan for two years. He's still there."

I had never met Tom Smythe on *this* end of his business. The .38 didn't move a hair to either side. With a sabotage attempt still fresh in his mind, with attempted murder something with which he lived every day, with problems multiplying all about him, Tom Smythe was not the man with whom to make unexpected moves. He was as friendly as a cobra, and many times more dangerous.

"The only reason you're not behind bars at this moment," Tom went on in the same steely tone, "is Steve Rand. Now we get down to business. Who are you?"

I started to remove the false glasses. My hand didn't move a fraction of an inch when one word locked my arm right where it was.

"Freeze."

Fear rushed through me. Christ, I'd forgotten. Tom Smythe knew the man before him only as an impostor, a danger to Project 79.

"Tom, I'm Steve."

He didn't say anything.

"I'm Steve Rand," I persisted.

He looked carefully at me. "That's interesting."

"Easy enough to prove," I said. "Compare my fingerprints, do your own retinal check, and—"

"Hold it right there," he broke in. I held it, doing my best to imitate a statue. My nose was running and it began to itch, but I didn't make a move for my handkerchief. Not yet, anyway.

Tom Smythe reached out with his left hand, his eyes and the .38 still locked on me. He picked up his telephone, stabbed the left button on the dial console.

"Get me Wilkins. Priority."

He waited only a few seconds; Wilkins came on the phone immediately.

"Dick; Smythe here. Priority, drop whatever else you're doing. Pull the security file on Steven Rand. Then do the same for the one we ran yesterday on Tarvin. Dr. Jack Tarvin, from MIT. I'll wait here on the phone. Do a comparison check of the thumbprints. Right, I'll hold on."

The seconds dragged and my nose itched and I forced down the urge to sneeze. Perspiration began to drip along my neck and down my ribs. That damned corset and the padding! It felt like an hour, but I know that no more than minutes passed. Dick Wilkins came back on the phone; still with his eyes on my hands, Tom Smythe punched the other end of his telephone call to the small speaker box on his desk. I listened to Wilkins' voice.

"Tom, I've run the check. Something crazy here."

"Go ahead."

"It's impossible. The thumbprints match. But Rand is supposed to be dead and . . . and, well, according to this, they're both, Rand and Tarvin, I mean, they're both the same person."

My muscles relaxed like piano wires being cut in the middle. I closed my eyes and breathed deeply.

"No question?" Smythe talking to Wilkins.

"Absolutely none, Tom. When I got the cross-check I ran the comparators on all prints. There's no question about it; Rand and Tarvin are one and the same."

"Thanks, Dick. Keep it under your hat. No one besides me is to know of this. Understand?"

"Yes, sir."

"And lock those files in our safe. No entry to anyone else but me."

"Right; will do."

Tom Smythe broke the connection.

[288]

I let my breath out in a long sigh as the .38 went back into the shoulder holster. "Christ, can I move now?"

"Welcome home, you blasted idiot."

I sneezed wildly and scrubbed at my itchy nose.

"Where did you get a cold like that? It's a beaut."

"Not a cold," I said, my ears ringing. "Drugs. Gives all the symptoms of a cold. Disguises the voice." *Achoooo!*

Tom looked unhappy. "It works, too. I never had you figured. Got to remember that little trick." He cracked his knuckles and he still had that angry expression on his face. Tom didn't like being swept under the rug by an amateur—and he'd been taken cold. Well, not really— I think he'd already suspected that Tarvin might be a bogus identity. It was Tom's nature to be suspicious, and he would run his own checks as a matter of routine. He'd done just that, and although he hadn't recognized me—André deserved a bonus—he spotted the security breach almost at once.

"All right, Sherlock," he said nastily. "Spill it. I'm all ears."

He leaned forward to stab the control that would record everything I said. "And start at the beginning."

I did.

Three hours later Tom was still firing questions at me in an unending stream. We had received everything. I gained one great sense of comfort from that exhausting session. There was no question but that Tom had avoided the hypnotic control of 79. When a man holds a gun pointed unerringly at your heart and puts away the weapon, he's not out to smear you into a corpse.

I thought we had covered every aspect of the situation. Tom Smythe, however, wasn't satisfied.

"It still doesn't fit together, not completely, anyway," he complained. "I know something's fouled up with 79, but I am not yet ready to agree that an electronic brain is trying to take over the country."

I started a heated protest, but he cut me off swiftly. "I'm looking at this thing from all sides, Steve," he pointed out.

"You're the individual who got into a wild and bitter public fight with Selig Albracht. Remember? That was stupid. It was not the action of a man who's fully in control of what he's doing. And what's more—"

I shot to my feet, anger sweeping through me. "What the hell are you trying to say?" I shouted. "Are you blind? What else do you need for proof? People have shot at me, tried to kill me with cars, and . . ." I ground to a halt, rage making me shake. I fought for control.

"All right," I said, the anger checked. "There's nothing preposterous about Charles Kane trying to kill me. That damned brain can do things hypnotically that the best hypnotists in the business couldn't even begin to approach. And I haven't any doubt but that what took place before is much worse now."

"Spell that out," Tom said.

"Oh, hell, it's easy enough to figure." I was disgusted with the turn of the conversation. "79 has failed to achieve its goal through those people it controls. Careful planning, subterfuge, traps . . . they haven't worked. What's next is inevitable. It will—I'd bet my life it *has*—reprogrammed Kane and the others it controls. These people are in a trap, a psychological cell. Just like any Pavlovian creature, and—"

"Hold it. What do you mean by 'Pavlovian'? What has that got to do with—"

I broke in. "If you can't accomplish your goal, where hypnotic control is involved, anyway," I explained, "you go a different route. You eliminate the matter of planning. You set up posthypnotic controls so that the individual, in a given situation, reacts to that situation. It triggers the actions. It's a response, not a directed movement thought out beforehand. Pavlov's dogs . . . What the hell am I telling you this for? You're the psychological mastermind around here, not me."

I slouched in the chair, suffering a sense of failure.

"You've got a point there," Tom said after several moments. "All right, we'll give it a whirl."

"What do you mean?"

"Never mind," he said. "Do you trust me, Steve?"

"Of—of course I do."

[290]

"Then do exactly as I tell you to. *And nothing else,* do you hear?"

I nodded. What could Tom be up to? I decided to wait it out and see.

He called his secretary. "Get Charles Kane for me. He's working in, umm, let's see; yes, he's in Data Review right now. Tell him to get here on the double."

He switched off and turned back to me. "Put your glasses back on."

I did as he asked. "What are you trying to pull?" I demanded.

"I told you. Trust me." He made a sour face. "And shut up. I want to think."

Several minutes later Charles Kane walked into the office. He glanced at me and turned to Tom Smythe.

Tom studied his face. "Charlie, this is Dr. Jack Tarvin from MIT."

Charlie smiled. "Nice to meet you, sir."

I nodded, afraid to open my mouth.

Tom Smythe opened his desk drawer, glanced down, and turned back to Charles Kane.

"Charlie, Tarvin's an impostor."

I gasped. This was crazy!

Charlie turned again to look at me.

"His real name isn't Tarvin. He's wearing makeup. That man is really Steven Rand!"

Charlie's eyes were wide, his body instantly tense.

"What the hell are you—"

I didn't finish. Tom's voice filled the room.

"Charlie!" he shouted. "Here! Take *this!*"

Smythe reached into the open desk drawer, withdrew an ugly-looking revolver and tossed it to Charlie Kane.

"Steve Rand—that's who it is!"

Charlie's features dissolved into a snarling mask as he grasped the revolver, swinging it toward me.

I came to my feet, sick through and through. "You rotten son of a bitch!" I screamed.

The gun roared.

37

THE SOUND SMASHED against my ears. Stupidly, I tensed for the impact of the bullets. A third shot, a fourth! My ears screamed from the sound. Five! Six!

But I'd felt nothing!

I stared openmouthed at Charlie Kane, the gun smoking in his hand, his face twisted into animal hatred.

He had fired point-blank at me! How could he—it wasn't possible for him to have missed!

The next thing I saw shook me almost as much as the sight of Charlie Kane swinging the gun at me and squeezing the trigger. Shock made me numb; by now I knew I should have been on the floor, a corpse. But I wasn't, and I wasn't prepared for Tom Smythe moving swiftly around his desk, getting between me and Charlie Kane.

Charlie was screaming incoherently. He hurled the gun away, hooking his fingers into claws. The next instant he came at me like a thing berserk.

He didn't make it. Tom Smythe's left fist thundered into his midsection. As Charlie doubled over, the side of Tom's right hand smacked against the exposed neck. Charlie Kane fell like a poled steer.

Tom stood straight, looking me in the eye.

"Congratulations," he said. "Your theory on Pavlovian reactions was right." He gave a short laugh. "Lucky for you that gun had blanks, huh?"

I gaped at him. "All right, watch what you say," he snapped. "People will be pouring through that d—"

He never finished the sentence. Two men burst through the

door, guns drawn. Tom Smythe gestured at the unconscious form of Charles Kane.

"He went off the deep end again," Tom rasped. "Get him into the security ward of the hospital. Maximum cover on him, and I want a man in there with him every second; when he sleeps, eats, and goes to the crapper. And no questions for now."

There's nothing quite like organization. Charlie's unconscious form disappeared before my eyes, whisked from the floor by the two husky agents. The door closed behind them, and I collapsed in my seat, my ears ringing and every nerve in my body twitching wildly.

Tom returned to his chair behind his desk. "Sorry I had to do that to you, Steve," he said quickly. "But if I do what I think I'm going to be doing, I've *got* to have unquestionable reasons and justifications behind me." His face sobered. "You're aware, I hope, that we will be considered in some quarters as treasonous?"

I'd thought about that, all right. I nodded, still not wanting to speak.

While Tom called the security ward of the hospital, I tried to collect my thoughts. He hung up the telephone and looked at me.

"All right, Steve," he said. "What do we do now?"

"I've had something in mind for a few days," I said slowly. "But I think it's wisest not to say anything to you or to anyone else. Not at this point, anyway."

"What if you get clobbered? Ever think of that? What happens to your precious plan then?"

"I've thought of it."

"And?"

"If it happens, you'll be given . . . it will be delivered to you; the means doesn't matter now. You'll be given a complete rundown of what I'm attempting to do."

"That's risky as hell," he said, irritated.

"I know, I know," I gritted. "Don't you think I'm aware of

that? But I've lived with this and I think it's the best way." I shook my head. "You'll just have to go along with me, Tom." His eyes bored into mine. "Does Kim know?"

"Christ, no. I wouldn't dare. She thinks I'm Jack Tarvin."

"Do you think 79 has gotten to her?"

I felt a sickening sensation crawl into my stomach. "I—I honestly don't know, Tom," I admitted. "Yesterday she was absolutely normal. I mean, I couldn't find a thing about her that wasn't Kim. But I don't *know*." I shrugged, helpless.

"That's right," Tom said. "You don't know and you can't afford to take any chances. I'd hate to have you find out you made a mistake—*after* it was too late," he appended.

I nodded.

"Do you realize that if something slips up—with Kim, I mean—and she cottons on to your being Steve Rand, and if she has been put under by 79, that—"

"I *know*," I snapped.

"Don't get touchy with me," he shot back without a pause. "I want to be sure you *do* think of these things. You get dewy-eyed, and you can blow the whole thing."

"I know that too, damn you."

"You might be put into a position where you would find yourself forced to . . ." He paused. "To kill her," he finished.

"Jesus, you twist it after you get it in, don't you?" My voice was a hoarse whisper.

"You could say that," Tom replied with a blank face. "That's my business. You might even have to consider—if the circumstances demanded it—killing *me*."

I didn't want to answer. Why make noble comments about what's so obvious?

Tom was holding a deep think-session with himself. Finally he shook his body, as a dog might shake water from himself. He'd made a decision.

"All right, Steve," he said, "I'll buy *your* way. For now, anyway. What do you want me to do?"

I leaned forward, aware that I'd passed the final hurdle to my plans.

[294]

"Leave everything just the way it is," I said. "Take whatever steps are necessary to give me a free hand. You may have to run interference a couple of times."

He showed his distaste for letting events out of his direct control. "What if you get clobbered *and* I get clobbered? What happens to your house of cards then?"

I looked carefully at him. "I've thought of that, of course," I said. "It's all written out. If I go several days without making —certain—telephone calls, the whole story, from beginning to end, all of it, the works . . . will be mailed to six different places."

Instantly alert: "Any newspapers?"

I nodded. "Yes, Tom," I said with complete honesty. "Four of them. All in the right place to do something about it."

"God damn it, Steve," he said angrily. "That's dynamite! If there's a slipup and this ever gets out—"

"To hell with that," I said, my voice sharp. "It will be a thousand times worse if something happens to you and me and this is buried. Don't you realize that? I had to do it this way. Besides," I said to end the argument, "it's all set up and I will *not* change it at this late stage."

He leaned back in his chair, controlling his anger, knowing he had no choice but to drop the matter. "All right, *all right!* What's your next move?"

"I'm supposed to be given a work tour this afternoon," I said. "Kim has been assigned to me again. It will give me the chance to get around and check into a couple of things without being too obvious about it."

He nodded. "Sounds good."

"I think I've got the weak spot in this whole damn thing figured out pretty well."

If I'm wrong, I said to myself, *this could be the kind of hand where I lose by default.*

"After I finish this afternoon with Kim," I said to Tom Smythe, "I want to grab a bite to eat—"

"We'll eat together in the cafeteria," he interrupted. "Won't hurt at all to have you seen publicly with me some more."

[295]

"Fine. Then I'll want about thirty minutes by myself." I said.

"Where?"

"My office. I've got to be alone, Tom," I stressed.

He nodded. "Consider it done. What else?"

"Can you keep servicing crews on duty tonight? The more people, the better."

He chewed over my request and, finally, nodded slowly. "Can do. I suppose one day you'll explain all this to me?"

I grinned at him. "You'll get a first edition of my memoirs," I promised.

"Got a time schedule worked out?" he asked.

"Yes," I replied. "I'd like to have everything moving at eight tonight. Can you be with me?"

He laughed without humor. "I wouldn't miss this for the world."

38

PRECISELY AT TWENTY-TWO minutes past eight o'clock that night I entered Service Compartment Number 11. SC 11 was one of a series of servicing facilities located throughout the huge complex of Project 79 where technicians could attend to monitoring and systems checking of the intricate equipment that made up the cybernetics organism. Essentially the servicing technician was a cybernetics diagnostician who searched for symptoms of existing or potential difficulties. Each such compartment was linked directly to the master and the slaved subsystems of 79. Here you could read the bio-electronic heartbeat and other "living rhythms" of the cybernetics Brain and its many appendages. If there were a need for direct servicing of the computer systems, the compartment monitors pinpointed the specific location for such work and gave some idea of the equipment and parts that would be needed.

There was also a random pattern of direct visual inspection of the internal systems of the computer. Past experience proved that no matter how exhaustive a planned program of inspection, maintenance, and repairs for the servicing of any complex cybernetics system, you still couldn't do away with a skilled technician eyeballing the mechanisms for which he was responsible. For example, any automatic system will indicate a wire that has snapped or worked itself loose. It won't show what a man can see with a glance—that the wire is loose or frayed or being subjected to pressures that will make it come loose sooner or later. The eyeball inspection adds up to preventive maintenance at its best.

And that held one of the key elements of the plan I'd worked out so carefully. Such inspections were maintained on both the regular schedules of the project *and*—it was an all-important "and"—random scanning of the inner mechanisms of 79. It was through this established procedure that I hoped to gain access —through the security-cleared person of Dr. Jack Tarvin, of course—to the internal cybernetics systems.

In each servicing compartment the maintenance inspector had available a programming keyboard with which he could interrogate the computer as to the status of its systems. It worked easily enough. The inspector sat before the keyboard—it was no more complicated than a typewriter with a number of additional keys for automatic interrogation—and typed out the questions he wished to ask the computer. Most questions were not in the form of direct interrogation; the queries went into the automatic sensing systems of 79 and were simply readouts of pressure, electrical flow, temperature, humidity, and so forth. If there was to be a direct contact with 79, the inspector punched the DCM button for Direct Contact Mode. The answer came back on a teletype system or, if there were no requirement for permanent records, the inspector could read the answer on an electrical-word display, something like a moving signboard. When I came into Compartment SC 11, I punched for DCM.

Tom Smythe stood behind me and to my side, watching as I activated the DCM and began to query 79 as to the status of its bionics subsystems. I didn't take any chances; I stayed in the area where I knew better than anyone else the structure of the computer systems. For ten minutes I followed what would have been the normal, expected routine of any inspector, typing out the questions and studying the answers as they slid past us on the readout display. Everything went as smoothly as it did on any other occasion when such maintenance interrogation was put to 79.

Until I punched out the notification that a random personal inspection would be conducted within the next two-hour period:

INSPECTION RANDOM PATTERN CHECK MECHANICAL PLUS ELECTRONIC SYSTEMS PLUS SUBSYSTEMS. SECURITY ADMISSION SMYTHE NUMBER ZERO ONE NINE SEVEN TWO SIX TARVIN

[298]

NUMBER EIGHT EIGHT FIVE ONE SIX ONE. TIME PRESENT PLUS
MINUTES ONE TWO ZERO. CONFIRM.

The answer should have been before us immediately. 79 requires less than a millionth of one second to receive the message, check its memory cells, and start the reply. This time that
didn't happen. The readout display remained dark.

Behind me, Tom Smythe cursed in a low, unhappy voice.
"That's exactly what I meant when I told you we were having
difficulties with this overgrown mechanical ego," he complained. "I know and you know and that blasted machine
knows the answer should have been immediate, but—"

"Did they run systems operations checks?" I broke in, turning to glance at Tom.

He nodded quickly. "Everything checked out perfectly," he
replied. "Nothing wrong anywhere. No blocks, no stoppages, no
problems in the systems. Nothing. Except that the son of a bitch
won't play."

Silence filled the compartment. I became aware of what was
almost an electrical feeling in the room. I found myself shifting
my feet, uneasy, a prickling sensation starting along the back of
my neck.

Tom watched me carefully. "You feel it also?" he said suddenly. "Like the damned air is ionized or something. We ran
checks on *that* also. Nothing, just like before. But you can feel
it, all right."

He gestured angrily at the computer. "That thing is trying to
make up its mind whether or not to go along with you. You
know that, don't you? It's going to make a decision as to
whether or not you should even be allowed to get inside its systems where—"

"Where it considers itself to be vulnerable," I finished for
him. "Tom, I don't—"

The message light flashed on to cut off my words. We weren't
prepared for the computer's response:

CONFIRMATION DENIED.

"What the hell—" The words burst from me without
thinking.

[299]

Tom leaned back against a tape console, lighting a cigarette. "Cute, isn't it?" He gestured unhappily. "This has happened before, by the way. It flatly refuses entry—even," he added significantly, "to requested maintenance personnel."

"How long has this been going on?" I asked.

"Couple of weeks," he answered.

"But why haven't they done something about this?" I was amazed. How could they let this situation continue?

"We're still trying to figure out how," Tom said. "At the same time we're trying to keep it as quiet as we can. Once the word gets out among the people who work here that our electronic friend has slipped a circuit or something, we'd have a mild panic on our hands." He took a long drag on his cigarette. "If this keeps on like this, well . . ." He shook his head slowly. "It could mean we're going to blow all these years of work and more money than you or I could count in a hundred years."

I didn't like what I was hearing. "Why the hell didn't you tell me all this before right now?" I demanded. "It could have saved a lot of time and trouble, and—"

"Just hang loose," Tom broke in. "It's been unpredictable, no pattern to how 79 is acting. You're a newcomer—as Tarvin, I mean—and I wanted to see what would happen with a new name cleared through Security. Evidently"—he nodded at the computer—"it's making its new habits inclusive to one and all. Another point, Steve," he said, his voice intent on the moment, "I didn't want you forming any opinions before the act." He shrugged. "It will be sort of interesting to see what happens from here on in." He grinned. Despite the problem weighing so heavily on his shoulders, he could still enjoy my own discomfort at the hands of the machine I'd helped give the same intelligence that was now defying me. And that had tried to kill me. I didn't much see the humor in it. But maybe it's better to laugh than to cry.

I turned back to the communicator keyboard.

JUSTIFICATION. I banged out the word.

This time the response was immediate: NUCLEAR REACTOR COMPLEX ENTRY FORBIDDEN.

[300]

"But I hadn't queried for the reactor!" I said, vexed.

Tom didn't say anything. At this point he just watched. I moved again to the keyboard.

JUSTIFICATION. I felt helpless with being forced to communicate in this manner. The reply glowed across the response panel:

FAILURE REACTOR CHAMBER PERSONNEL SECURITY SYSTEM. RADIATION PRIMARILY GAMMA. LEVELS PROHIBITIVE HUMAN SUBJECTS.

I wanted to curse. Tom stared at the letters sliding along the readout. "There hasn't been a thing about any radiation leakage," he said quietly. "The damn thing is lying."

I shook my head. "No, it isn't," I replied. It can't 'lie' as we understand the term. It's beyond the capability . . . the conceptual capability, of the system. It's not lying, Tom," I repeated. "If we check we'll find radiation, all right. Only, it's not an accident. 79 created the problem to justify its refusal to permit entry."

SPECIFY INTENSITY. We waited for the answer. Bang; it was there: just like that.

ROENTGENS ONE ZERO ZERO.

One hundred roentgens per hour . . . That was a rate that could affect seriously anyone exposed to the gamma radiation for more than an hour. 79 knew the level exceeded the permissible safety limits. Between four hundred and six hundred roentgens direct dosage is lethal to most people. And if one hundred rad didn't do the job, then I was quite certain 79 would just increase the intensity. Well, two could play the game.

CONFIRM ADMITTANCE EMERGENCY RADIATION TEAMS. HUMAN PERSONNEL PROTECTED FULLY. CONFIRM.

No luck. The answer stabbed into my eyes.

FORBIDDEN. LEAKAGE SERIOUS. ROENTGEN LEVEL INCREASING EXPOSED AREAS. DANGEROUS HUMAN SUBJECTS.

Here we go again, I thought. My fingers moved in a blur across the keys.

BASIC SECURITY WAIVED. DECISION EMERGENCY, CANCEL BASIC REQUIREMENTS SAFETY. I thought for a moment, but no good. I turned swiftly to Tom. "What's the overriding justification?"

"Code Six Six Able Eight One."

PRIORITY CODE SIX SIX ABLE EIGHT ONE. CONFIRM.

Code Six Six Able Eight One was *the* emergency signal to shunt aside all safety and security requirements for any person authorized to enter the complex. I knew the combination to the final door to get into the reactor complex. But first there was the matter of being provided with "security acceptance" by 79 so that I might first get to that damned door. And 79 just wasn't having any of it. I wasn't surprised when the next response came to life on the readout.

CODE SIX SIX ABLE EIGHT ONE REJECTED. RADIATION LEVELS INCREASING LETHAL INTENSITY. ADMITTANCE FORBIDDEN.

Well, to hell with the damned reactor room, Rand. Try something else! Muttering to myself I banged on the keys—

REPORT INSPECTION STATUS PRIMARY COMPUTATION CENTER.

The lights glowed.

FORBIDDEN. RADIATION LEVELS . . .

I didn't wait to see the rest. I fumed, helpless. Because even with the proper ID security materials and passing the checks of Tarvin, I could never get through to where I wanted. Either to the main power center or to the primary computation center; either one would do for my purposes. But I couldn't get through those laser beams and other defenses. Damn!

I turned to a monitoring panel, twisted open the cover, and stared at the radiation indicators for the reactor complex.

Tom looked over my shoulder, and whistled. "Christ, look at that! It's up to three hundred already."

I nodded.

"I'm going in there, Tom."

"But it's certain death! You know it will raise the intensity of the gamma—"

I cut him off. "No matter. You know that," I said quickly, wanting anything but a discussion of my own courage. I would

[302]

need all I had to get this private mission accomplished as I'd planned.

Once I got past the basic defenses, I could get into the reactor room.

79 wouldn't bother to seal the final entrance door to that room. Because it could immediately raise the level of radiation to a thousand roentgens or more. And that was certain death for a human being. It would be suicide for any man to force his way there.

Suicide.

That was the key.

I turned to Tom. "Listen, no arguments now, for Christ's sake," I pleaded. "I know what I'm doing, Tom. But I need your help."

He started to object, then caught himself, and nodded. "All right, Steve. But if you get killed, I'll never talk to you again."

I was startled to find myself with a smile on my face. "Fair enough," I said. "Now, can you start an attempt by, well, a couple of men will do, to get into the primary computation center?"

He nodded. "Can do."

"Great. Just don't get anyone hurt. All I want is for them to raise enough of a flap for 79 to get its attention diverted."

He looked carefully at me as I started to check the equipment strapped to my belt and work vest beneath my jacket.

"What are you going to do, Steve?"

I looked back at him. My lips felt cold and bloodless from my decision, from the realization of what I was going to try to do.

"I'm going to teach that egotistical son of a bitch how to play poker," I said.

39

WE DISCOVERED—the hard way—that we had created a monster. But all along we believed the aberration was something we could cure. The cure was drastic—surgery with explosives to smash critical elements of the great cybernetics organism. But it was the kind of surgery that would retain the essential elements of 79, permitting us to reprogram the computer with safeguards to prevent the hellish situation into which we had blundered.

If we failed—myself and the small team sent out by Tom Smythe to create a diversion for me—the future boded ill for us. Failure could result in our own destruction. From then on, everything would depend upon the effectiveness of the reports I had secreted with friends, to be mailed to newspapers and certain officials upon my absence to report in to them at scheduled intervals. I was not sanguine about the possibilities of success at such a venture. 79 could cover effectively its own errors. It already held under its direct sway an unknown number of technicians, government officials, scientists, military officers, in God only knew what number. It would be able to carry out a holding struggle while it consolidated its position, while it utilized the skills and the knowledge it accumulated with every passing day.

I had the feeling that if we failed, this very evening, I would have shot the last bolt. To me, what was happening wasn't just critical. It had become literally a matter of life and death. Against the terrible future portended in a world under cybernetics domination, a world of nonwar (which often is vastly different from peace) and human beings transformed into biological ciphers . . . well, there comes a time in every man's life when he knows that against that vast sweep his own life is unimportant.

I had come to that realization. It gave me the courage I needed.

I said we discovered the hard way that we had created a monster. The special group Tom Smythe dispatched to gain entry to the computation center stumbled in grisly fashion against the terrible truth. Because we were unaware of just how far 79 had gone in assembling its select legion of controlled technicians.

79 had gained hypnotic control over a key group of technicians and engineers. These men, unknown to the central directors of the project, had modified the defenses that guarded the approaches to the think center of 79.

Where there should have been a system that warned the men to stand back from the entrance corridors, they walked unknowingly to their deaths. 79 had already begun its own program to seal off from all human beings, except for its controlled ciphers, admission to its vulnerable interior.

Four men went through the security check of fingerprints, retinal patterns, and automatic scanning of their identicards. The system flashed the AUTHORIZED ENTRY signal, and the men took off at a dead run to gain entrance to the computation nerve center. Tom Smythe came behind them, and that saved his life.

There was no warning. In the long final entrance corridor, secure in the knowledge that the computer had provided them authorized access, the four men fell prey to laser beams that crisscrossed the corridor. Just like that. In almost complete silence, the only sound the barely discernible clicking of relays.

Tom heard a gurgling sound. Not a shriek from a throat, but a gurgling sound. Blood spurting from where the lasers severed arms and legs and necks and torsos. Arterial blood gushed through the air to splash against the corridor walls and floors. Four human beings collapsed in bloody chunks and pieces to the floor.

Not until it was over did there come the bone-chilling announcement through the corridor speakers *that this was a warning!*

Tom nearly went out of his head with rage. Four men with whom he had worked for years slashed coldly—no, *indifferently*—from existence struck him with the impact of a physical blow. Tom had lived with danger and with imminent death for so many years that its appearance never caught him off balance. But this was in a way he had never imagined. In that instant Tom's attitude changed from considering 79 a critical problem. With the hot, wet sounds of death in the corridor, 79 became an enemy to be destroyed.

He knew he couldn't reach the main power controls, but there were terminals that crisscrossed the complex. And what we called the think center received its power input from terminals separate from the cables that powered the auxiliary security systems of the project complex.

Tom spun on his heel and rushed to the nearest fire-alarm switch. He smashed the glass with the butt of his revolver, tripped the alarm, and ran for the power-servicing room. He cursed at the delay required by inserting his identicard into a scanning receptacle. Seconds later the heavy security door swung open, and Tom burst inside. Immediately he hauled down the main bus bars to cut off any power that might be controlled by 79. For good measure he whaled away with a fire ax at the main terminal itself.

The fire-alarm signal was the fastest means of getting emergency crews and security guards to where Tom wanted them. Tom fanned them out, shouting orders. Get into the computation center and cut the main power. He told them something about electrical overloads that might cripple the computer. He warned them that the security defenses had gone haywire, to be ready for anything. They reacted as they had been trained—to protect the computer. There wasn't time to spell out the incredible truth that Tom knew. Let the men think they had to prevent damage, that they must do the jobs for which they were always in readiness.

One team got within two doors of the computation center, when three men died. By now they were close enough to the main room to enter the area of another power line of which they knew nothing. How could they? It had been installed only the week before, and no records had been filed of its installation.

The men were midway along the corridor when a tremendous electrical charge surged through the walls and the floor. They died instantly, electrocuted. The men behind them froze in their tracks, only a few feet from that lethal passageway. They were alive, but for the moment they couldn't move.

I didn't know what was happening. Not then, anyway. Because I was even then trying to get into the reactor room—where it was certain death to enter.

I stood outside the last long corridor that would take me directly to the reactor room. Down that corridor three steel doors barred the way. None of them could be opened by key. They required knowledge of the numbers that would open their combination locks. Security changed the numbers every week, and Tom had given me the current number codes.

It took at least three minutes to work the combination. But finally—it seemed like an eternity—the door locks slid free and I pushed the first heavy steel slab away from me. At that moment the alarms clamored throughout the complex.

What had gone wrong? I cursed at the unexpected clanging of the alarm bells. My instinct was to rush ahead into the corridor and get to work opening the final two doors. But reason took over. It was stupid to plunge into what could be a lethal situation when at least I could check on what was happening.

I ran back into the office through which I had just come and jerked a security phone from its wall hook. I punched the triple-three number. Immediately the guard on duty identified himself.

"The fire alarms," I shouted. "Where's the trouble?"

The man was more confused than aware of what was happening. "Sector 24," he blurted. "Don't know what's happening. It's not a fire. Accident. Terrible accident. Oh, Christ—"

"Stop babbling, damn you! What *happened?*"

"I—we're not sure. Couple men were in a corridor when somehow—don't know how it could have happened—the beams, I mean the laser beams, went off without warning!"

That stopped me cold. The guard's voice ran on. "Couple men, don't know how many, killed. Just—" I slammed the phone down. Lasers! And if they had been killed, that meant one of two things. Either the lasers were tripped by 79 deliberately to prevent entrance to the computation center . . . or no one even knew they had been installed. It didn't matter, I thought, running back to the door. Whatever, or just how it had happened, 79 was throwing up its defenses.

I knew long before this moment that I'd better be ready for anything. I knew about several corridors wired with lethal electrical charges if the other defenses didn't hold up. I was wearing rubber gloves and boots over my shoes. They wouldn't mean a thing if I stumbled blindly into a crisscrossing laser pattern, of course, but it was possible that the defense had been rigged *both* with lasers and with a lethal jolt of electricity. I wasn't about to take my chances of escaping one and getting fried by the other.

At the open door, the corridor beckoning beyond, I stopped. Of course! Again I turned and ran back to the office I had just left. I grabbed the nearest swivel chair and wheeled it ahead of me. Just before where the corridor began, I aimed the chair carefully and shoved it with all my strength. The chair banged its way down the corridor, several times scraping along the walls. It was almost to the second door when beams of light harder than steel leaped into existence.

I blinked. The top several inches of the chair were missing.

But it was better than I'd hoped. There had been no crackling roar of electricity. The chair wheels were metal; anything in the floor or the walls would have been triggered. So at least this part of the corridor didn't have the electrical defenses. And I could beat the lasers.

I went down on my belly and started crawling as fast as I could move. The top of the chair had been slashed by the lasers, but there had been nothing beneath that point. So long as I stayed low, I could make it to that second door. Fortunately, the floor was smooth and I made steady progress.

When I reached the door I rested for a moment, trying to calm the shakes that threatened my limbs. I dug into my pockets and came up with my comb. Holding it extended from my fingertips, I moved it carefully through the air, higher and higher. Four inches above the combination lock, the edge of the comb vanished. I leaned back to the floor, cursing at the effect of blinding light on my eyes.

Then I was ready. I dragged myself up to my knees, head low, and began to work the combination.

Another three minutes. I cursed my clumsy position and the rubber gloves and forced myself to move my fingers with deliberate calm on the combination. If I made the slightest error, I would have to start over again. Every minute counted. There was no telling what that damned computer might do in the time it would take me to get to the reactor room.

If you get there . . . I cursed the tendency to allow that inner voice freedom. I concentrated fiercely on the numbers of the combination. Holding my breath, heart pounding, I turned the dial left and right, right and left. There! I twisted the handle and heard the steel bars sliding free.

I shoved the door open. The second passageway extended a hundred feet before me. At its end stood the third and final door. I was almost there!

But first . . . Christ, this was no time to blunder! Again I positioned the chair, aimed carefully, and shoved.

Fifteen feet down the corridor, a powerful electrical charge ripped through it.

I took a deep breath and started out. It was awkward, inching my way along the floor, hunched over, balancing myself like a deformed crab on my feet and my hands. I had to stay below the level where the lasers would slice me into pieces, and I didn't dare to touch either the walls or the floor with anything but the rubber boots or the gloves. Working around the chair required greater balance and agility than I thought I could handle then, but I made it. Barely, because I slipped and fell toward the wall. I stopped myself with extended fingers, froze where I was, breathing deeply, and started out again.

Ahead of me waited the last barrier. My head swam with the effort of my contorted movement. I gritted my teeth and kept on, scrabbling idiot-fashion down the corridor.

Just a few feet more . . . keep going . . . almost there . . .

The door loomed before me. I rested against it with my fingertips, gasping for air. My knees screamed at me from pulled muscles. I did my best to ignore the pain. Still in a squatting position, perspiration running into my eyes, I reached up to start dialing the combination of the lock.

I slipped. I started over again, left, right, right, left, right, dialing the numbers.

Finally I was finished. I sucked in air, waiting for the steel bars to slide free.

The door refused to open.

40

THERE'S A LAW of physics they never teach in the classroom. What can go wrong will go wrong, and I'd run dead against it. But I had come into this long corridor expecting anything. I knew I might have to face the possibility of the standard procedures for opening the heavy steel doors being negated by 79. Now, after getting through the laser beams and electrical defenses of the corridors, I couldn't open the third and final door.

Not with the combination, I can't. But there's always another way. . . . Okay, Rand, now's the time to dig into your bag of tricks.

Bracing myself with one hand against the door, staying in the center of the corridor, I reached with my other hand into my jacket, to the work vest around my body. I removed a package of what looked like wedges of modeling clay. I needed both hands, and I shifted to a squatting position. My knees were being stabbed with knives of pain. But it couldn't be helped. I had to hold out just a bit longer. . . .

I pulled free two strips of heavy tape and pushed the package against the door, checking to see that the wedges were in precisely the required positions. They were a lightweight, malleable plastic explosive, tremendously effective for applying a shaped charge against any surface to which the package was secured. I rubbed the tape as hard as I could to hold the package exactly where I wanted it—dead center of the door. If this didn't work . . . but it *had* to work!

With the package secure, I removed a spool of wire from my inside pocket. At the end of the wire were two small detonators. I jammed these into the plastic explosive and started unwinding wire, working my way back along the corridor in a form of tortuous, squatting duckwalk. The wire extended for two hundred feet, but I had no intention of going back along that entire corridor, working my way around the chair. I knew I could never stay balanced on my legs for that time. I guessed at a distance of thirty feet, and there I stopped.

I turned to put my back to the door. Within the spool was a powerful battery. I balanced myself as best I could, both feet and one hand secure against the corridor floor.

I'm not sure, but I think I said a brief prayer when with my other hand I squeezed the plunger. There wasn't time to think. Instantly, orange light filled the world about me, and something struck my back. Wind roared down the corridor in a blasting pulse.

The next moment I knew that, if nothing else, I'd managed at least to keep my balance. I started turning around, the smell of explosive stinging my nostrils.

The door was still in place. But I didn't try to blast it free. That would never have worked with those powerful steel locking bars. There's always that other way. . . .

The explosion of the shaped charge in dead center of the door had accomplished what I wanted. It had bowed the door, punching a wide and deep depression. In effect, by bending the door, it shortened it at either side. Even as I scrabbled painfully back to the door, I knew I had succeeded. I could see a hairline of light at the left side. The locking bars were free.

I pushed open the door and stumbled into the reactor chamber. Not a moment too soon. My legs buckled beneath me and I collapsed to the floor. But at least here I was safe from the lasers and the electrical energy that could have ended my life.

I knew it was a Pyrrhic victory.

Because the radiation warning lights in the reactor room were flashing wildly. And beneath each light the radiation level in roentgens blazed its terrible warning. The level was already sliding beyond two thousand roentgens per hour.

Six hundred roentgens absorbed within an hour was a lethal dose.

Within fifteen minutes, or less, if the intensity kept rising, I would be a walking corpse.

It didn't matter. I wouldn't need more than five or ten minutes to do what I'd come here for. 79 had failed to keep me from gaining entrance to where it was most vulnerable. I looked about me. At the far wall of the vast, gleaming chamber was the edge of the breeder reactors. To my right, along another massive concrete wall, were the three turbines from which power fed to the computer complex.

Inside my jacket, clipped to the work vest, were a half-dozen charges of plastic explosives. I needed only to get these around the thick cables leading away from the power center to the computer, and I could sever the electrical umbilicals of the cybernetics organism.

An atomic bomb exploding directly outside the mountain within which 79 was secured wouldn't have damaged this chamber. But one man with explosives could plunge 79 into the blackness of eternity—or nonthought or whatever it was that swept over an electronic intelligence. Hell, it didn't matter. Just get those charges in place before it was too late.

I moved as if in a trance. I knew that radiation tore through my body. Every second cells were being destroyed. Every second I was that much closer to death. But I was winning the hand. I was losing my life, but I was winning the hand. The big hand. I thought of Old Mike, and I laughed. The sound came to me as from a great distance.

You're getting hysterical, Steve, old boy.

I knew it and I laughed again, because the plastic explosives were in my hands and I was at the first thick power cable, placing the explosives, tamping them, stabbing in the detonators. Soon, just a few more minutes. Almost done, almost done.

I was at the third cable. There. My head was swimming, and . . . it's a wild feeling to know that you're dying, that you're a corpse that hasn't yet been told it's a corpse.

I think I giggled at that. Because that's how I was winning. 79 didn't have any more defenses aginst me. It had made a disastrous error. In its brilliant-idiotic manner of thinking, it knew that thousands of roentgens were lethal to a human being. Lethal. The end of life. All human beings want to survive. This was suicide. No sane man commits suicide.

I laughed again, stabbing in the final detonators, checking them.

No man commits suicide.

I did.

I was a dead man. I'd lost the hand I was playing when I stumbled into the reactor chambers. Here it was lethal. No admittance. Forbidden. You can't go in there—it's certain death.

But you can be dead fifteen minutes before you die. Sure, sure, you can. That's how radiation kills. Radiation like this, anyway. You're dead, but the body doesn't know it yet. It takes fifteen minutes to break apart and shred and tear slowly at the seams. Dead, dead, *dead!*

God, that's funny! I'm dead and I don't know it. Funny. Big joke.

There, start unreeling the spools. That's it. Keep them unreeling.

Funny. Big joke. Dead and don't know it! God, what a laugh! That's it, keep moving. . . . Get around that concrete wall there. . . . I'd outsmarted that smartass computer, all right.

79, you're a screaming idiot, you know that? You're the world's greatest chess player, all right, you bastard.

But you can't play poker. Funny, funny. Oh, God it was funny.

Stupid bastard. Idiot computer. Didn't know, could never know that I'd throw in the winning hand.

Bet my life. By God, that's what I did! Bet it. One whole life, that's me. I had the winning hand, but I didn't keep it.

I was safe. Then I threw in my cards. Turned them face down. I left the outside and I came in here, inside, where radiation . . . head, spinning. Jesus, I've got to hang on! Hang on . . .

Oh, ha ha ha! Funny! What am I trying to get around that concrete wall for? What for? Stupid. Senseless. No use. Wanna

[314]

protect myself against the blast when I squeeze this little old trigger here. Ha ha. Beautiful little trigger, just squeeze it, and BOOM! everything goes off and slices those cables, and my God it's funny. I'm crying; tears on my cheeks; I can feel them, and what do I want to protect myself against the blast for, because I'm dead already and what was that? Christ, it hurt. My God, I've fallen. . . . I fell down. I can't get up! Where's the trigger, where's the tri— There, in my hand, all the time. That's it. Now. Now do it, Rand, old boy. That's it, just squeeze.

You're a hell of a poker player, old man. Really, you are, a squeeze there, that's it. Great player. Best. Squeeze harder, harder!

Everything was so dark, but I thought about it only for a moment, that's all; no more, only a moment, because the world fell in on me and I knew that when the whole mountain fell down I was smiling.

Tom Smythe stood close to Kim. The hospital room filled with the murmur of the doctors and nurses. Needles pushed into the arms of the unconscious, cruelly white form of Steven Rand. The doctors hovered over the still shape, checked the gleaming bottles suspended above the bed.

Kim wept quietly, leaning against Tom Smythe. She tried to remain silent, not to disturb the struggle being waged in the room.

"Massive transfusions. The new drugs," Tom Smythe said. "Massive injections. Brought them here from the army base. Antiradiation drugs." He stared down at his friend, talking as much to himself as to Kim.

"I had an idea of what he meant, what he was trying to do," he went on in a whisper. "The fool; the crazy wonderful fool. He told me he was going to teach God how to play poker. Mumbled something about throwing in his cards, that he could win by losing.

"When I found out he got into the reactor room and we saw the levels . . . Christ, they were over two thousand! . . . I knew what he'd done. Knew he was successful. What a job he did! Main power went out all over the complex. He'd done it and I knew what had happened. Couple of men got in there, no trouble anymore from the lasers or anything else. Couple of good men. They ran in there and they grabbed him and they ran out with him. They all got a terrible dosage, too, but they're all right. Less than two or three minutes' exposure. They'll make it. They got him out just like that, in nothing flat."

He stared at the still form on the bed, surrounded with the most advanced weapons of medical science.

"Already had a medical team on the way here from Fort Carson," Smythe said, still in that same hoarse whisper. "Only minutes away by helicopter. Radiation alarm; they're set up for that sort of thing. Instant reaction. They got to Steve. Fast, real fast. Ten minutes later he was here, in the hospital. But they had already started injecting him with the drugs right there in the corridor." He glanced at the liquids moving slowly in the gleaming bottles. "Drugs, transfusions. They're doing everything."

He looked across the room. "Everything," he whispered.

Kim moved her lips. She tasted salt from the tears running down her cheeks.

"Will he live, Tom?"

Smythe turned his head to look at her. Their eyes met.

"The doctors say they think they can bring him through," he said slowly. "Be touch and go for a while. But they think he'll make it."

He looked for a long time at Steve Rand. Then, slowly, a smile came to his face.

"You know something, Kim? I think Steve is going to win that last hand, after all."